# Citadel

## Jack Remick

# DEDICATION

For Helen, Elizabeth, and Charlotte.

# CONTENTS

Jack Remick

# ACKNOWLEDGMENTS

To the geneticists and scientists who tinker with our nature.

To Lynn Margulis and Bryan Sykes who have no fear

To Charles Darwin

To Dennis Must, MBIW, First Reader whose suggestions shaped this novel

To Geri Gale and Jessica H. Stone who found most of my weaknesses.

To my Third Sunday Group
Anne Sweet
Priscilla Long
Anna Balint
Gordon Wood
Geri Gale

To Robert J. Ray who read every word of every scene, who spoke every line of dialogue as we worked our sessions on Mondays and Thursdays.

To Jac Seery Howard who found the images in the decaying architecture of post-industrial England.

Without all of you, there is no *Citadel*.

Jack Remick

# Beach Meat

## Trisha

As far back as I can remember, I've had a sense of dread. I dream, and when I wake, I am sure it will be the day the world ends. Rose, my therapist, tells me more of her clients have apocalyptic dreams like mine. She doesn't know what it means.

Yesterday at the beach as I watched the beach meat in their combat ritual, I had one of my visions of annihilation. There were four of them. Their sandy bodies glistened. Muscle and sweaty flesh silhouetted in an exploding sunset ripe with blood. Their overhand smashes and digs were laced with grunts and howls and the wail of loss. I imagined them still grinding one another to dust in the chaos of extinction. The shaven-headed one, the tall, muscular and vicious one spiked a set-up and the volleyball blasted his opponent in the face and he went down—on his back, on the sand. Bleeding. The fallen enemy crawled off the pitch, his shamed partner beside him. Mr. V., the Victor, taunted the losers 'you bunch of pansy asses.'

Daiva startled me when she lay back on her towel groaning. I asked her if she was all right.

"I'm a day early," she said. "Should know better than to wear white. What did I miss?"

"A little blood. One good spike."

Daiva wore a white one-piece suit. Hair bound up in a twist with a swan-comb. The setting sun burnished her hair.

I was going back to my ereader when Mr. V. knelt in the sand at my feet. I smelled his sweat mixed with sea air and the odor of blood. It was the familiar scent of death and destruction that often crept into my dreams. Rose tells me that I have *parosmia*, a flaw in my brain that makes me smell odors that are not real. The scent pouring off Mr. V.

9

was the scent that followed men like angry dogs chasing a wounded doe. He grasped the bloody volleyball against his crotch. Eyes closed, Daiva piped up,

"Are they all this tall?"

"It's an optical illusion," I said. "At sunset they seem taller."

"Do you suppose he shaves everywhere?"

"That teeny-weeny crotch cloth won't hide a single pube."

"Tell him to stand up and strip off that speedo," Daiva said.

"Hey," Mr. V. said. "I'm right here."

"We can smell you," Daiva replied.

Mr. V. His eyes were deep wolf-gray, his mouth a pouty delicacy. I had tasted meat like that but never this one. He was persistent, and he didn't back off as I scanned him. He liked the assessment so much he quivered. Silent. A horse at auction waiting a bid. His eyes tracked me up and down never veering above my breasts. Beach meat. Muscle and sand and blood and sweat. I had seen him before, but he always failed the wine test. I said,

"What do you think of the 2025 Napa pressing of Pinot Picante?"

He got that what-the-fuck-are-you-talking-about scowl on his face.

"Wine," I said. "Pinot Picante."

"Oh, yeah, I had that a few times."

Pinot Picante did not exist, so I went back to my ereader. Clara was hounding me to finish the next Pinnacle Romance. She wanted it edited and online now. Today. Not tomorrow. Mr. V. said,

"Hey, I kicked butt out there."

"Yes you did," Daiva said, "but we're having our periods."

Mr. V shot to his feet, bloodstained volleyball in his hands. Disgusted, he trotted off into the surf. The sunset was so intense, so red, the light seemed to burn through him. Daiva said,

"RER."

"What's that?"

10

"Residual evolutionary response," Daiva replied. "The Alpha male can't tolerate things he can't control and menses is our big mystery. Irven DeVore says males are a breeding experiment run by females. This guy has all the traits breeders cue on—muscles, physical presence, drive, power. He responds to the stimulus, in this case your breasts, your hips and thighs, your skin. The entire history of sexual selection is working itself out right here on this beach. You're a prime receptacle, Trisha. You're supposed to dive into bed with him, but you said no, so he'll have to kill you."

Mr. V., rising out of the sea, glistened. Golden. His thighs rippled. He was a glorious animal so locked into himself that a bloody tampon shut him down...*you said no so he'll have to kill you. I shuddered. What if I had taken him home? What if he did kill me?*

I watched Mr. V. dash to the parking lot where he jumped into a black BMW.

"He drives a Beamer," Daiva said. "Beamer means resources and resources fill out the evolutionary menu. Size, speed, resources. Why didn't you take him up on it?"

"I have a few rules," I said. "If they can walk, I look. If they can talk, I listen. If they make me laugh, I think about it. If they know good wine, I sometimes say yes."

"That's kind of picky. Why do you hunt here then?"

"You can see the merchandise unwrapped."

"You sure make those guys howl."

"Howl? Let's head back."

I rolled my beach towel and tucked it into my bag. Daiva followed. The hot sand felt good on my feet as we passed the volleyball court with its saga of blood and sweat. At the parking lot, I tossed my bag into the Z-Ray. The afternoon sun gilded Daiva's hair now. She was a real blonde. You can tell. Her skin was peachy and shone from the sunblock. She had indigo blue eyes.

Daiva had moved into the condo two weeks ago. She was always alone. No visitors. Her Southern California unenhanced trim and creamy skin made me jealous. The one thing that bothered me was the solitude. In two weeks, no one. I knew her name, Daiva Izokaitis, and I knew from

11

her mail box that she was a doctor.

The drive through Latimer Canyon is idyllic in the early evening. Late gulls squawk, eucalyptus shadows stretch across the winding road, the Z Ray hisses on the pavement like a very beautiful red python. I love the car. I parked in my slot at the condo on Mesa Drive.

"Got time for a glass of Chardonnay?"

"I was going to ask you—I need to wash off the yuck first only my plumbing is out until Monday."

"Sure, you can shower at my place."

§§§

My condo smells of cinnamon and the sea. I rinsed my bikini in the bathroom sink. Studied my face in the mirror. Around Daiva, I couldn't help making comparisons. We're the same size, but she is fair. I have black hair. She has that peachy skin. I tan dark. She is natural, unlike so many Southern California women who try to stay young by ruining their bodies, molding their faces, lips, noses until there was nothing left of their innocence or their hope. My breasts are mine, not some surgeon's work of art. I leaned into the glass, pulled down my lower lip, and bared my teeth. I remembered the last time I had stood naked in front of a mirror and he—nameless, I didn't want to know names—had come up behind me. Dark-tanned hide, brush cut hair, bear-size hands. What if I had said no to him? Would he have killed me? All that muscle but he couldn't make me arch my back to the snapping point the way I did when I was alone

As I stepped into the shower, I thought about Mr. V. 's tan and his shaven head. Maybe it was a mistake—saying no today. What if he was the one who could make me scream? One day, someday. Every novel I edited had a screamer. I envied the fiction. Coming like that every time. I finished showering then went to the bedroom for underpants and a sarong. In the kitchen, I picked two glasses—chilled—from the dozen in the fridge. Daiva knocked and entered. She said,

"Sorry, got hung up on a phone call."

§§§

Out of the shower, Daiva was radiant, clean, bright. She wore white shorts and a red tank top. I felt a pang of jealousy. Maybe enhanced, I would find what I needed, but I didn't like the idea of reshaping myself—residual evolutionary response? Maybe. But I wasn't turning myself into a statue just to be what men lusted after—silicone breasts, fat lips, flat belly, labiaplasty. I like my labia just the way they are.

I handed Daiva a glass of wine and we sat on the leather sofa looking at the sea. The sky had turned that Southern California orange that it gets at a certain moment in the dusk, just before the sun drops. Sometimes, in my darker times, I imagine that the orange sky is the remnant of a nuclear holocaust.

"Good wine," Daiva said.

"Château Vieux," I said. "Valley wine. I gave my boss a case of it as a birthday present."

"You give your boss Chardonnay by the case? Couldn't you just kiss his ass instead?"

"Her name's Clara Kreisler."

"What's she the boss of?"

"Pinnacle Books. Clara and her brother Caleb own it. Well, she runs it, he's kind of like a wart on her hand. She makes the decisions. He handles the finances and authors. He's written a couple of screenplays."

"Pinnacle," Daiva said. "I don't know that imprint."

"Imprint? You sound like someone who knows the business."

"It's LA," Daiva said, "you have to be on top of these things or you die."

"So what do you do?"

"I work in a lab."

"What kind of a lab?"

"Genetics." She glanced at me and held her gaze before sipping the wine. I topped off her glass. "Pinnacle," she said. "Now I recall—all ebooks."

"Right now we're electronic, but Clara, my boss, wants to go paper. She has a dream of being the West Coast

13

powerhouse. In fact, she's screaming at me to bring in a big book to launch a new imprint."

"How big?" Daiva said.

"She wants something to nail down an all-female readership. We run all our books through focus groups. She wants it to have some romance, but it can't be saccharine and insult the women who know what they want. I suppose our demographic would be depressed middle-class women who've been burned by men who left them for their secretaries. Educated, very smart, and very fed up with male bullshit. Clara's been hounding me for months now…"

"Why go paper?"

"You ever been to a book launch?" I said. "Nobody ever has a launch for an ebook. You go to a book launch to see The Book. You want a physical object with height and width and weight. Clara says it's out there. I find it or I'm gone."

"Take your Chardonnay if she boots you," Daiva said.

She stood, she faced the sliding glass door. I watched her blonde hair still damp from the shower, the shorts plastered to her hips. She was exquisite—tall and perfect. I sipped my wine—maybe I had to quit hunting for a while. Daiva said,

"Today. The guy on the beach. You call him beach meat. Isn't that just a little bit demeaning? The way you treat them—do you worry that one of them will cut your throat? They've got all this evolutionary baggage—sweaty, meaty, muscles, anger, aggression. They can't change. They can't change because they're doomed."

Daiva sipped her wine. I said,

"Is that why you're not turned on? Because they're doomed?"

Daiva gazed at me with those jumping blue eyes, their long lashes, so intense, so perfect they looked fake, but that perfection was natural. Everything about her was natural. She licked her lips—ruby red without lipstick. She said,

"I go both ways."

"You do?"

"But I have standards."

14

"Um," I said, embarrassed that she might think I was pushing her.

"Is that an *um* of disapproval?"

"A lot of our novels go both ways," I said.

Daiva sipped her wine. She said, "I have a novel."

"Everybody in LA has a novel."

"Not my kind of novel."

"What makes you different?"

"It's a post-lesbian novel."

Post-lesbian? I tasted the wine. It was getting warm. I fetched another bottle of four-year old Chardonnay from the fridge. Château Vieux, a Valley wine that was my crutch through any crisis. Clara was leaning on me. The more she leaned, the more novels I read and rejected, the more Château Vieux I drank. It was not a good situation, but I hadn't found a way out.

"Okay. What exactly is a post-lesbian novel?"

Daiva unveiled a guarded glance at me. She was no longer an innocent in white shorts but a full-blooded Amazon with fire in her eyes. She set her wine on the end table, knees tucked under her. She said,

"What would you call sex if women give up on men? Lesbian? No. Lesbian is a label men stick on women who love other women. But that's all wrong. My novel is set in a future where there are no lesbians because there are no men to put that label on them. Give me the male equivalent of lesbian."

"Gay?"

"Really? There isn't one. Men who love men are called fags, gay, queer, the beast with two backs, the love we dare not call by name. But there is no label like lesbian. In my novel, post–lesbian means there are no men to define a woman's wants, needs, sexual proclivities, or preferences."

"What happens to the men in your novel?"

"You'll have to read my book to find out."

"It's not a book until it has an ISBN."

"That's a pretty technical niche."

"Suppose I give your novel to Clara, my publisher. What do I tell her?"

"Tell her I'm a scientist."

"Who writes post-lesbian novels."

"Tell her it's science in fictional form."

"Science fiction?"

"Tell her that the Y chromosome has given up all but twenty-seven of its genes to the X. Tell her it's a novel working off the scientific fact that the Y chromosome is almost useless except for determining sex. Tell her that the Y chromosome is rotting and this novel is about a future where women control everything."

"And that is post-lesbian?"

Daiva picked up the bottle of Chardonnay, the wet sides dripping. She poured wine in both glasses. She said,

"Look, Tee. This whole beach meat trip you're on—it makes you pretty much the classic male-defined woman. It's deep in you so you have a hard time breaking the mold but science tells us you can have live births without the Y chromosome. It's called parthenogenesis. So if you tell Clara and your middle-class, educated, fed-up readership that men are on the cusp of extinction, you can also tell them that the Y chromosome is decaying and in a century or two we won't need it at all."

Everything she was saying just pulled my dread trigger and I got visions of the shaven-headed muscle-man burning up in a holocaust. She had me thinking, but all I could do was roll the wine glass across my forehead and hope it cooled me down. A world where women control everything? I didn't know what to do so I said the dumbest thing I could possibly say,

"Clara doesn't think science sells."

"And there's the Niche with a capital N. I write about the Niche."

"Niche? I was just getting a handle on post-lesbian," I said.

"We're in the Niche, you and I. *Citadel* is set in 350 AF," Daiva said.

"*Citadel?*"

"That's the title."

"AF?"

"After Foundation."

"After foundation of what?"

16

"The Citadels. "

My head was spinning, my balance shot. Hot. Chills. I could feel her thoughts. I hadn't told her that on the beach, I could feel the beach meat thinking. Thoughts rolled over me, like I was in his head feeling what he was thinking and right then, with Daiva, I crossed over.

"So," I said, "you've got a post-lesbian novel set in the Niche."

"No. You and I and every successful woman are living in the Niche. The novel is built on science that taps into a woman's thoughts and it will sell because it reinforces what she already knows but is afraid to say. Women don't need men."

"Do you have an agent?"

"I'm in the lab sixteen hours a day. I don't have time."

"Let me see it sometime," I said. As soon as I said it, I wanted to take it back. No. No. In LA you never say 'let me see your script.' That's like saying, 'let's do lunch'. You know it means don't call me, I'll call you. Daiva held her wine glass like a sword in front of her.

"Don't mess with me, Trisha."

"I mean it. I'll send Clara an electronic copy."

"I don't have an electronic copy."

"It's handwritten?"

"Typed."

"Typed?"

"On an antique IBM Selectric typewriter. "

"Oh my God," I said. The wine was working. It was my crutch all right. I could blame everything on the wine and hope that she didn't think I was serious. "I haven't seen a paper submission in—like forever."

"I leave early. I'll drop it by in the morning."

That night, I had a dream. I was at the beach. The sea was on fire and the sky had turned a dark gray as if the sun had burned out. I walked into the fire. When I woke, I wrote the dream down. I keep the dream book for Rose. Dreams, she tells me, are you stripped bare.

§§§

17

Monday morning, Daiva's manuscript lay in a box at my door. She hadn't forgotten.

The page count was 533, single-spaced. I wanted to weigh it. The paper bone-like and cracked. Half a dozen different weights. Half a dozen colors. Old paper that smelled dusty. A smell I had forgotten. Books at Pinnacle had no smell, no inky, ancient paper smell. Pinnacle was sterile and clean.

I tossed the box onto the seat of the Z-Ray and drove to Pinnacle Books at the corner of Pico and Ocean. I opened the office, turned on the computers, then looked at the box on my desk. A paper manuscript. An anachronism. As I lifted pages from the box, the paper crackled. A ragged sound I hadn't heard in a long time. Paper dust drifted onto my desk. I had it, so I had to do something with it. I took a few minutes to scan the manuscript to the cloud, then ran a copy on white paper that I dropped into a drawer.

I decided not to mention *Citadel* to Clara. I didn't want to tell her I'd gotten half-whacked and made a stupid commitment to an LA writer about her novel.

It was a hectic day. We had six eprojects in the works. Caleb was screaming that we were overcommitted. Clara bounced around her office waiting for me to come up with a great book that would send us to the top. My job was on the line if I didn't produce.

I took the box with Daiva's manuscript home that night. After pouring a glass of wine, I opened the novel to a section called *The Wars of Savagery—*

**Citadel**                              **Daiva Izokaitis**

The killing started and it did not stop. The men butchered women, they slaughtered children. They killed everything that lived and then they massacred one another. They took women prisoners and cut their tongues out. They cauterized the breasts of their captives. They stitched the eyes of women shut so they could not see. They nailed the lips of women closed so they could not speak. Their only use for women was on their backs with their legs spread or kneeling with their mouths open to take the cum of the violent ones.

The women they did not destroy in battle, the men saved for the Disrupters. The Disrupters were the first instruments of war designed specifically to dissolve women. The Disrupters were so perfectly built that they remained functional until 206 After Foundation.

I felt the rush before I finished the page. A knot in my belly. This was not what I had expected. I expected cold scientific, data-rich, dry, slow. Here the language was fast, bold, cadenced, rhythmic. It was distant, epic. I wasn't sure who had the point of view. Every erotic novel needs that fixed point of view so you know who's smelling the flowers, who's wearing the perfume, who is on top and who is not. But this wasn't erotica. I skimmed the rest of *The Wars of Savagery* then skipped to *The Origin of Plague*—

## Citadel                           **Daiva Izokaitis**

The plague began in a gene lab in Istanbul.

Hagah did not intend for the Gynerium to escape. The needle pricked her finger. She hesitated. Protocol for needle punctures was clear. But as she looked at the blood oozing from her hand, she knew it was too late.

Leaving the lab, she went to a coffeehouse in Misir Carsisi where she touched men who in their surprise at her forwardness either groped her and made rude remarks or shoved her away.

In an hour she had touched a thousand men while walking, while standing in line at a trolley stop. She brushed the skin of a boy at a newsstand.

In the lobby of a department store, she watched men collapse. Gynerium attacked the Y chromosome that exploded and left men gasping as their blood thickened. Every cell gelled solid.

Right there I stopped reading. Daiva called it a post-lesbian novel. Did post-lesbian mean anti-male? How would Caleb take that? What would Clara think of it? Guilt swamped me. Maybe I had made a mistake but the story was sticking with me beginning with those few pages I had read. Hagah's blood. That Y chromosome. I remembered reading an article about the Y chromosome but the only words I recalled were *shambles* and *going downhill fast*. I had to remind myself that this was fiction. Fiction written by a woman who understood the science behind the plague—the Y chromosome is rotting. It has given up all but twenty-seven of its genes and the remaining ones are shriveling into oblivion.

At the fridge, I uncorked the bottle of Château Vieux and poured a second glass. The manuscript—533 pages typed, not printed, on colored and cracked paper—typos standing out like scabs on diseased skin—gasping, solid—how many mistakes? My heart was pounding. Why? I decided I'd have to make notes for Daiva. In LA, you make notes. You take notes. Notes are a rewrite of the rewrite of every story ever hawked in LA. Daiva needed notes. The question was how would she handle the notes? Maybe if I made them harsh enough and obnoxious enough I would drive her away and I wouldn't have to make a decision. I started reading again. The more I read, the more wine I needed to dull the images of slaughtered children, images of massacres and killing, images of men dissolving as the Gynerium boiled them.

I read twenty more pages and the more I read the less there was of me. Maybe it wasn't a mistake. Maybe I could give it to Clara. The writing, like the infection Daiva wrote about, was infectious. There were images. Like it or not, Daiva built solid images. I made my first note.

20

*Note to Daiva: Who is telling this story?*

*When I read, I ask myself what's the story in this line? In this paragraph? On this page?*

*Here, I can't tell who is speaking. You'll have to work on that.*

*Two missing pages: 69-71. Where are they?*

*p. 73—What is the Disrupter? That section is abstract.*

*I like the Origin of Plague, but you might not need the whole passage on p. 90.*

*I like your use of repetition in the Wars of Savagery. Explain the word "gynerium."*

More wine. I needed more wine. I uncorked another bottle. Reaching for a fresh glass I knocked it against the sink and it shattered. Blood oozed around a sliver that had dug into my palm. I slid the sliver out. *Hagah.* Was she the protagonist? Was there a protagonist? Blood flooded into the palm of my hand, thick as the infected blood Daiva wrote about.

I was buzzed. Not just from the wine, but from the story. In the bathroom, I peeled a Band-Aid and laid it on the wound and looked at myself in the mirror overwhelmed by a rush of guilt and shame. Who was this half-drunk, shit-faced harridan? Black hair, tanned skin, dark eyes. Too dark? Too tanned? Too black? Blood on my sarong. I changed and returned to the living room to the ereader on the desk beside the manuscript open to the *Origin of Plague*. I ran SkyChat. Rose Katz answered.

"Rose, can I see you?

"You don't sound well Trisha."

"I'm not."

"My last client leaves at eight o'clock."

"Nothing sooner?"

"Trisha. After eight."

"I'll be there."

I closed the connection. The wine and the blood had steadied my hands. Seeing Rose would help me get control. I looked at the manuscript. At random I turned the pages—skimming—a hundred pages in I came to *The Hunt.*

Grasping the pages as if they were butterfly wings, I walked onto the balcony. The sarong caught the sea breeze like a sail. I sat on the deck chair and read.

### Citadel                              Daiva Izokaitis

We waited in the tall grass, silent, the wind brushing over the plain in that steady whish–whish..Relaxing, lulling, but then I saw the Gland. Walking into the sun. He was muscular, naked. His skin a deep cordovan, his hair a red rush down his back and over his shoulders. His muscled legs rippled as he walked—no hurry, no sense of what was lying in wait. Zil touched my shoulder. A finger to her lips. Silence. Just ahead of the Gland the grass opened and Tia and Ket sprang up and the Gland froze for a second but then he ran splitting the waves of grass. Running at an angle, Tia and Ket closed on him and Zil shouted *off,* and the two of us jumped to our feet holding the nets and the cords, heavy, but in the wildness of the chase, weighing almost nothing.

Glands. Hunters. Each page of the manuscript felt like it weighed a pound. Pages—heavy, cudgels of paper—thick enough to break a bone. The Gland. Daiva. Citadel. The Hunt. *My hunt, my feel for the chase, my memory.* Reading the novel, I felt like Daiva was reading my mind. Pages 100 to 103—the Hunt. My life was a hunt and Daiva had captured me. I glanced at my Cartier. 7:30 p. m. Half an hour till Rose. I made my second note to Daiva. Where was she? I hadn't seen her car in its space. She worked in a lab. Maybe she worked late. Maybe she had left LA.

Note to Daiva: The Hunt—we have to talk more about point of view.

Here you use the First Person. In the opening you use Second Person.

By the end of the scene I still don't know the name of the narrator.

Let me see a character list for Citadel.

Skimming through I have counted forty-one characters.

Here you have Zil, Tia, Ket.

Do all the characters have these short names? Are there patronymics anywhere?

I started to erase the last question but held up. No. Leave it. See how Daiva handled notes.

### Rose Katz

Two years ago, I moved into a new office one block off Santa Monica Boulevard. It's a small place on the third floor of a professional suite with doctors, psychiatrists, lawyers, aromatherapists, midwives, and a ration of LA alternative lifestyle gurus whose offices smell of clove oil. I finished up notes on my last client while I waited for Trisha. She worries me. She needs me, she needs the crutch of therapy to keep going. She's fragile, so we have a relationship more like a mother and daughter than therapist and client.

Trisha sat facing me. She wore an elegant shift ripe with hibiscus flowers. Hair loose, she looked harried. I took my time. It didn't pay to start right in with Trisha. After a few deep breaths, she had found her center. She said,

"I'm thirty-two, Rose. I have a job, I have a house, a car, no family but I'm still on the prowl. I picked up a hunk of beach meat. I had sex with him. I can't control it. Something in me takes over and shouts down my mind and my body says yes, it always says yes, and then when it's over and I don't get what I need, I feel guilty and ugly and I hate myself. When I was through with him, I tried to get rid of him. He didn't want to go."

"Did he hurt you?"

"I picked him up, Rose. I took him home. We had sex. When I told him to leave, he knocked me around."

"You reported it."

"What am I supposed to report? I took him home. I had sex with him."

"I've heard those words so many times, Trisha."

"It's not my fault. Isn't that what you're supposed to say?"

When Trisha confronts me, she can be belligerent. I slow her down by taking notes. That gives her time to reflect before circling back to the root of her problem. I asked her the questions that have become part of each session.

"Are you masturbating?"

"Yes."

"To orgasm?"

"Yes."

"Vibrator?"

"Toys aren't enough. I need to hunt."

"Need?"

"I don't know why I need them at all."

"A year ago, you couldn't tell me about the vibrator. You're getting close to a breakthrough but you're still masking."

"How can you know what I'm going through?"

I thought about the pistol in my desk. It's red with a pink crosshatched grip. I keep it to remind me of the power of the word *rape*. My clients, all women now, come to me in pain. Their pain means they have been raped, abused, beaten. For five years, I've been treating Trisha's addiction. She didn't know I understood what she was going through not as a therapist but as a woman. I opened the drawer and laid out the pistol. Trisha said,

"You're going to shoot me?"

"No."

"You want me to shoot you?"

"I bought this pistol for a reason. Here's what I do know. Men are dangerous. Before I relocated, I was in a mixed practice in Redondo Beach. I was two years out of my residency. I had a client list with a dozen abused women. I made mistakes with them. I was stupid. I sent them back to the men who abused them. Two of my clients died. Beaten to death by their men. The husband of one of my clients ambushed me. He used a knife. He violated me with that knife on my desk. He cut me and told me that if I talked to his wife again he'd kill me. That's when I bought this automatic. It's a nine-millimeter. I know exactly what you're going through."

I tucked the pistol into the drawer. Trisha was silent. She said,

"Did you report him?"

"No. It came out in the trial. He murdered her wife and is doing time in Corcoran."

"So now we're bonded by the sisterhood of rape and everything is going to be just wonderful."

"You mentioned something else bothering you."

"Work."

"Caleb Kreisler again?"

"No, nothing like that. This strange novel's got me confused."

I took a note, took my time, waited for her to collect her thoughts. She fiddled with a blood-clotted Band-Aid covering the palm of her hand. A fresh cut.

"It's called *Citadel*. I can open it at random and find something that grabs me and pulls me into it. Just before I called you, I read a section called *Wars of Savagery* and it was like I was right there…every page, every sentence is the end of the world. I don't know what to do with it."

"You're an enthusiast, Trisha. That's what makes you good at your work."

"There's something else in it."

"*Citadel. Wars of Savagery.* That doesn't sound like your usual erotic fare."

"No. I feel everything…her writing needs work, but I feel it."

"You're taking it personally?"

"Yes and no. I don't know what to do. She has a section called *The Hunt* and it could be about me. Daughters—the writer calls them the daughters—are hunting for a Gland and the way it's written, it could be about the men I pick up on the beach."

"A Gland?"

"Men. In the novel, the writer tells us there are three kinds of males—Exos, Glands, and Mutants. The Mutants are killers, the Glands are sperm donors, the Exos are…well, she calls them males with the $13^{th}$ gene silenced."

"The writer? Does she have a name?"

"Daiva Izokaitis. She's a scientist. She just moved into my complex."

"Do you like her?"

"I like the women in this novel."

"Why?"

"She's created this crazy kind of society where women work together without men. They have problems. They don't all think the same way, but they don't kill one another. The more I read, the deeper it gets into me. I still have a lot to go. The thing that bothers me is that while it's kind of science fiction it seems so real. Like she's in my head talking to me."

"Are you keeping your dream book?"

"Yes."

"But you don't bring it."

"I only have one dream, Rose."

"Bring the book next time."

I waited until I heard the door close before I worked up the session notes. As I dictated, I thought about the pistol. Trisha wasn't interested. I had to wonder. Had she really been raped? Clients often lie to their therapists. Why hadn't she reported it? She had tossed it off, like it was a sprained ankle. I recalled my ordeal and how my boyfriend—or should I call him lover?—abandoned me when I told him about the attack. Even now I taste the blood and smell the tobacco on the man's breath. It never goes away.

## Trisha

I admire Clara's intensity. Clara is a worrier. She worries about books. She worries about Angelique who can't get the hang of electronic publishing. She worries about sales and promotion of the novels. She worries about everything except her looks. She's thirty-six, has been thirty-six for six years and she still looks like she just stepped off the half-shell with her sister Venus. Auburn hair, freckled skin, violent eyes, a figure right off Botticelli's easel. She always wears dark leggings and blouses with lace cuffs. She prefers blouses with lace ruffs that make her look queenly, but I know the lace covers the abrasions and bruises. Clara has money and she knows how to use it. She uses it to get what she wants and what she wants is a blockbuster. Not just a bestseller, but a super-mega blockbuster producers will turn into a film. Her vision is huge, but it's lacking that blockbuster. I feel bad about that. Even though I'm letting her down, she's very good to me. You'd think that LA would be swimming in blockbuster novels, but we hadn't found one. Maybe *Citadel* would fix all that. But how do I pitch it? Concept—how do I sell it? A log line? Words for the first sheet? A blurb for the back cover? I needed a hook with a very sharp point and I needed to bury it deep in Clara.

I had the novel, but I didn't know which form to toss into the ring. Electronic? Paper? Clara wanted to go paper. *Citadel* was paper. I'd give her paper. But the interesting thing about electronic is that the text always looks perfect. You don't see the blems and literary monsters at first glance. Not like paper with its erasures and typeovers showing all the goofs and hesitations and the craziness where the author ran off the rails. So we were going paper, but I'd give Clara the e-version.

I tapped on the glass. Clara waved me in. Caleb, sitting with his feet on his desk, smiled at me. He wasn't like his sister. He didn't worry about anything but his tan and bedding the Pinnacle authors he could coax into shedding their thongs.

27

"I might have your novel, Clara."

"Not a dime until you lay a bestseller on my desk," Clara said.

Caleb reared back in his chair. He wore very expensive shoes—goat-skin loafers from Textrona and hand-tailored suits from his favorite Italian tailor in San Francisco. He said,

"Hello, Trish—you heard the boss—you're on a short leash till you land the big tuna."

"This could be big," I said.

Clara rolled away from her desk. She kept a clean desk. Nothing on it except the computer and her cell. She asked if it was better than *Zanzibar* and I told her *Zanzibar* was bush league.

"Okay. Pitch it," Clara said.

"It's called *Citadel*."

"Hey, very cool." Caleb took his feet off his desk and pretended to be serious. "A war novel to launch a new imprint."

"It's not a war novel, Caleb. ..."

I took the hot seat where I had pitched dozens of erotic tales over the last five years, the last one being *Zanzibar*. Clara had dreams for that book. She had pitched it to half a dozen producers who all passed. They told her the porn biz had run out of gas. You didn't need studio porn anymore because every MILF in LA had a dozen cream pie videos pasted on the web. They said the biz needed a new direction. That didn't stop Clara. She preached her sermon without giving up—give me a book I can sell to a producer who can turn it into a movie and I will make Pinnacle Books into a West Coast powerhouse. I broke the ice by saying that *Citadel* was a post-lesbian novel set 350 years in the future. Clara sagged and banged her forehead on the keyboard. She said,

"Just what we need, a futuristic lesbian novel."

"I thought we wanted out of erotica," Caleb said.

"We do," Clara said.

"It's not a lesbian novel," I said. "It's post-lesbian and the 350 years are significant."

"You know I don't shy away from gay," Caleb said.

"But I gotta tell you I got no idea what a post-lesbian novel is."

"The author's a scientist," I said, "a geneticist. She has some ideas about the future."

"Science doesn't sell," Clara said.

"That's what I told her, but the way she puts it. ..."

"She?" Caleb said. "What's her name?"

"Daiva Izokaitis. I zo Kai Tis."

"Izokaitis," Caleb said, "Is she hot?"

"Shut up, Caleb," Clara said. "Tell me more, Trish."

"This novel isn't like anything I've ever read. First there is the science..."

"Science again," Clara said, "and I haven't heard one word of story yet."

"The novel is fiction and science together laced with enough craziness to make you question your sanity."

"Hey Sis, it's a winner," Caleb said. "Lesbiana cooked up with a side of pseudoscience. I can already see double Ds in lab coats on the big screen locked in a muffin munching spectacular."

"Grow up, Caleb," Clara said. "Look, Trisha, I want a big respectable book. Something that can break us out of this electronic hole we're buried in."

"*Citadel* isn't like anything we've put out," I said.

I logged on Clara's computer and pulled down *Citadel*. I scrolled through the file to *The Hunt* stopping at the section called *Extraction*. I said—

"Read it aloud."

"Okay." Clara glanced at the screen.

**Citadel**                                    **Daiva Izokaitis**

Karim had strapped the Gland to the table and secured his arms with braces. She inserted the electronic probes into his arms, into his leg, into his belly. The Gland lay immobilized as Karim worked. The drugs had shut him down but in his eye, she saw fear and she heard his grunts—not words—but the guttural throaty animal sounds that always gave her chills.

His sack was enormous. His penis thick and heavy. The prepuce a dark salmon color. His pubic hair a thick wiry swatch. Karim inserted the dialysis needle into the left femoral artery, and as she slid it in, she touched his penis with her elbow and the Gland grunted but the restraints held him. Karim had extracted dozens of time, but this time her heart beat so fast her hand trembled. She did not speak to him. She could not speak to him. It was not protocol to speak to a lashed down Gland in preparation.

Finished with the dialysis implant, she readied the extractor.

Karim snapped on a pair of surgical gloves and then took a deep, settling breath as she inserted the anal probe. The Gland tensed. Karim lowered the pump to the Gland's penis and with quick, clean, practiced motions strapped it on.

She glanced at his face—that surprised look as the penis swelled under the sucking of the pump. He jerked then went limp as the extractor siphoned the thick stream of semen from him.

Caleb looked like he had been sucking on bitter lemons. Even though Pinnacle had published over a hundred novels I'd never had one that shut him down. Clara glanced from the screen to me. I saw the glow in her eyes. She was feeling it, every word of it. That made me smile. Curtis. Her lover. I knew *Citadel* would tap into her Curtis fantasies. We hadn't run Pinnacle on altruism alone. I suppose it was not ethical of me to use her this way, but I wanted to do *Citadel*. I needed to do it. Clara kept reading…

# Citadel                                  Daiva Izokaitis

Karim stood back, peeled off her gloves, dropped them in the disposal that zapped the tainted latex, then she retreated to the monitoring room. Behind the glass she watched the gauges and the readings from the probes—heartbeat, pulse, perspiration, breath, internal anal vibration at slow pulse, massaging the prostate. She gauged the vial of semen at six milliunits and still pumping. The white liquid filled the vial. The pump made a soft swishing sound. The Gland lay startled and stiff, his eyes wide open.

Caleb said, "They strap him down then milk him? Whoa!"

Clara said, "Is it all this rich?"

She was intrigued and maybe a little embarrassed. I'd never seen her like this with a novel. It was a scene that I knew would open her up. I didn't have to imagine what she was thinking, or what she was feeling. I said,

"This novel isn't put together the way other writers do it," I told her. "It's not in three acts. I'm not sure who the protagonist is but I know this section is on a long arc that starts with *The Hunt* where a team of daughters…"

"Daughters?" Clara said.

"In the novel, Daiva calls women daughters because of the whole genetic process—I'll go into that later—anyway a team of daughters captures this Gland."

"Gland?" Caleb said. "Isn't that slip a nickel past a metaphor?"

"Caleb, shut up. Go on Trish."

"The *Extraction* scene is late in the novel. Deeper into the text you find the insemination of the daughter who wants to have a child. So you track the semen all the way from *The Hunt* to this extraction to the birth of a child to the expulsion of the infant into the Exo Culture."

"Daughters, Glands, Citadel, Exo Culture? This is science fiction, Trisha."

Clara was saying no, but her eyes were not. We were close, so I said,

"She has a way of writing that makes you feel she's talking right to you. Every page opens a door in your brain…"

"Yeah, well," Caleb said, "the door just opened on uncomfortable, you know. This Gland, that poor bastard. I don't know what this is, Sis, but I don't think we go with it."

"What makes you uncomfortable Caleb?" Clara said. "Having women in control? Or is it because this writer reduces her sperm donor to a body part? Isn't that what this is, Trisha? Women taking control of their lives?"

"Daiva can explain it better than I can. In the novel, she takes on the heavyweights—what is sex, what does it mean to be human, what is desire, what is love, and what does the world look like when the daughters shape it. In the last part of the book, there's a section called *Congress* where she has the daughters make a big decision—to reintegrate the Exos back into the culture or to go the Separatist way."

"Separatist?" Clara said. She was caught up in it. Her eyes sparked as she spoke. After a quick glance at the screen she closed the file.

"There are factions in the Citadels—she labels them Integrationists, Separatists, and Extinctionists. From there she gets to parthenogenesis."

"So it's about the extinction of men," Caleb said. He crossed his arms across his chest.

"No, Caleb, it's not," Clara said. "I can see it all right there. We have erotica—a man strapped to a table while a woman uses him like a scientific object. We have a novel with substance. I'd never read about semen handled that way. In your world, you get the money shot, but she's writing about the future we'll have if we let women run the show."

"And then there's a killer-gene plot track," I said.

"Plot track?" Caleb said. "People don't want plot tracks, they want sex, they want the money shot, they want…"

"You want hard core, Caleb," Clara said, "No. We're taking Pinnacle in a new direction."

"You can't do this, Sis. The human appetite for porn is infinite."

"Not in books, Brother, not in words. It's all visual. All graphic. All video. The web has killed sex books."

I didn't want to sidetrack Clara, but we'd been talking for ten minutes. It was time to shift the emphasis.

I said, "Gene 13 is the killer gene and the geneticists snip it out of the genome. In fact, they can rewrite the entire male genome. That's the kind of science you're getting here."

"Maybe Caleb is right, Trisha. I don't know if I can push a book like this to our distributors. And then, the critics. The critics will kill us, you know that."

"It needs work, Clara. Lots of work."

"The language does."

"I can handle that," Trisha said.

"Are you really going to go with this, Sis?" Caleb said.

Caleb had his finger in scriptwriting. I knew he'd go with it if Clara gave her okay. I had opened his door to uncomfortable, so I had to let him down easy. I said, "It will make a movie. Lots of moving images. It's not all hard-core science, Caleb. I can see a script with your name on it."

"Isn't that the way we want to go, Brother? We take Pinnacle to paper and you get to write your scripts. Tell me you haven't signed her, Trisha."

"Give me a contract and I'll nail her down."

"We'll need to meet her first."

"Yeah," Caleb said, "I wanna see what this nut case looks like."

"Set it up," Clara said. "Give me a couple of days to read this novel, then get her in here."

§§§

Saturday afternoon I took *Citadel* to the beach. I enjoy reading on the sand where the sound of the surf is a soothing white noise. There's a rhythm to it. Sort of like being in tune with the universe. I spread my towel away from the volleyball court. I wasn't in the mood for a beach meat confrontation. I had to work out a plan for editing the novel. There was a lot to do. I was slow getting into the novel because I kept thinking of Clara and how she had come around. I made her read that scene with the Gland knowing what it would do to her while Caleb—concerned for his buddy, the Gland, being milked—had no idea what was going on.

As I read, I listened to people on the beach talking, shouting, the distant call of the gulls and the shushing of the waves. I came to a section early in the *Wars of Religion* and there was silence as if someone had turned down the sound in a closed room.

### Citadel                                        Daiva Izokaitis

I sat up. On the sand, I saw a pile of stones. I looked around—no one—nothing but the sand, the sea, the stones. Then I saw a crowd of men marching up the beach pursuing a running woman.

The men wore ankle length white dresses and sandals. As they drew close, I heard the chatter of angry Arabic. I had heard Arabic in the souk. A woman wearing a hijab stumbled ahead of them. The woman fell but got up and fell again. The men shouted at her. She regained her footing but stumbled to her knees by the pile of stones.

I tried to shout but my throat was numb. The woman pleaded. The fear in her eyes told me she knew what was going to happen to her. She could not speak through her bloody, swollen lips. I was helpless. I could see her. She could not see me. She looked through me as though I was a mist. Her nose dripped blood and blood oozed from under her head scarf. She held out a hand but I

couldn't touch her and then the first stone
smacked her in the jaw and her head snapped to
the side and blood spewed from her mouth.

One of the men knelt and grabbed the woman's
hair. Knife in his right hand, he slit her
throat. The men, as one, shouted and the killer
turned, bloody knife in a bloody hand and he
cried out, our honor is saved.

I tried to close the ereader but I was paralyzed. It was as
if I had waked from a deep dream as I had done so many
times but found I was unable to move. I could blink but I
could not speak. I glanced at my beach towel and my sun
hat and the ereader with *Citadel*—and I knew then that I
had been in the novel, in the scene Daiva had written. It
was one of those moments when, as editor, I stopped being
a reader to enter the text, but I was invisible to the
characters. I had heard the thud of stones landing on flesh
as if I had been there. I had heard the woman groan. I had
walked through the gauzy crowd of men, all holding stones,
hurling them at the woman. I saw them. They did not see
me. The woman had begged for help. I had smelled her
blood. The stones had stripped away the hijab, her hair
flared over her. She lay silent, her jaw broken, her eyes
unseeing.

Shaken and trembling, I sat on the towel in the sand on
the beach and I scrolled back to the beginning of the scene.
Again I stood over the woman. The men had left her dead
in the sand on the beach, her scarf peeled away from her
head, her hair matted with blood, her throat slashed. They
had reduced her to nothing. I read the next sentences where
the troupe of wailing ululating women came to carry the
dead woman away.

I closed the ereader. It was too early for me to be that
deep in the novel. I was not ready.

I dragged the beach towel to the Z Ray. I collapsed
behind the wheel. My belly ached. When my hands stopped
shaking, I called Rose.

§§§

## Rose Katz

In the late afternoon, I keep the window to the sea open. The sea breeze was nice after the high sun. I waited. Trisha sat silent for five minutes, legs crossed. Then she said,

"Rose, today I read a scene where a woman is stoned to death and her throat cut. She fell in love with a married man and her brother killed her to restore the family honor."

"Is this the novel you told me about last time?"

"*Citadel.* Yes. Something has happened to me. I think I'm going batty. I was there, Rose. This woman was on the beach. I watched men stone her. I realized that I had read the scene earlier and it stuck with me. Daiva writes that men and women are evolving in different ways."

"It's a novel."

"It's not a novel, it's a prophecy

When Trisha gets combative, I find it best to hold back, so I clasped my hands and waited.

"She calls it divergent evolution. She says women are thriving. Men will cease to exist."

"This novel isn't good for you, Trisha."

"Western women are in the Niche, Rose. We're pretty little madonnas living in a pretty little Niche. We have a tiny window of freedom. It's barely two hundred years wide and we think it will go on forever. You're educated. You have a career. You have clients. You're independent. You control your money. You own property. You vote. You're free. Two hundred years ago, you couldn't have any of that. That's the Niche."

"That's progress."

"What if they turn back the clock?"

"Why is this novel steaming you up, Trisha?"

"Because it's terrifying."

"Terrifying but you still read it."

"We have to pay for living in the Niche. They want to kill us...."

"Who wants to kill us?"

"Men," Trisha said. "The muscle. The rage. We've freed ourselves. We've landed in a special place but the more freedom we get the more dangerous we become. In some places, I could be stoned to death for wearing a bikini or a sarong or for having my hair exposed. We can do that here, but the men hate us…they can't wait to see us dead. In *Citadel*, Daiva writes that biology makes us automatic. I know now why I go hunting."

"All right. Tell me."

"Until I read this novel, I didn't know what was wrong with me. My need to be loved owns me."

"It's normal to want to be loved. Guilt and shame and hate come from broken expectations. Have you thought about why you can't commit to a relationship?"

"All the time. I know I should be conscious and aware, but when I'm running on automatic, the biology of desire kicks in and I stop thinking."

I took a note trying to sum Trisha up. Thirty-two, no companion in her life. Living alone. Promiscuous. A hunter, but selective about her prey. Too selective. No man could ever meet her needs or gratify her wants. I looked up from the notepad. Trisha had retreated. She was staring at her hands. I knew she wanted to get up and run. She said,

"Yes, I'm ashamed. Yes, I'm guilty. I don't want to be automatic, Rose. Daiva's right. We're machines run by residual evolutionary responses."

"You can be yourself without shame."

"What do I do when my body screams sex at me?"

"Make a choice."

"What if I can't?"

"Go to the desert. Isn't that where you work best?"

"Yes. I feel safe there."

"And feeling safe is important?"

"I'm afraid most of the time, Rose, but Bett and Kali watch out for me when I camp out at the Desert Rose."

"You're a good editor, Trisha. But I think the material Clara gives you affects you more than you let on."

"I can't go right now."

"Why can't you?"

"I have to get Daiva's signature on a contract."

"In the desert, you won't find much beach meat. Look, Trisha, our time is up. So let's call the session to a close. I want you to bring your dream book next time. You are keeping your dream book?"

At the window, I watched Trisha step into her Z-Ray. What was I going to do with her? In five years we had not opened many doors. Maybe it was me. Maybe she was too far above me with that crushing mind of hers.

I called Camille.

"I have to see you right away."

§§§

As I drove out Lincoln Boulevard to Camille's, I couldn't stop thinking about Trisha. Everything she said burrowed into my mind. The Stoning. The Niche. I knew the Niche. I had been living in the Niche. I didn't have a companion. Trisha was my reflection, that's why I knew her so well. Would I ever tell her about my vibrator? My anal plug that I needed before I could orgasm? And the Niche. What if they did take it all away? They could, couldn't they? Take away the freedom? Put me back in the kitchen, or on my back, belly swollen and barefoot.

A horn honking brought me back. I realized I was in my Z-Ray in traffic on Santa Monica Boulevard. I repressed the urge to flip the bird to the man carrying that load of impatience on his shoulders. They were always so impatient. Full of hate and pride and ready to kill.

I parked in the underground and rode the elevator to the fifth floor. Suite 516. The plaque on the door said it all— Camille Huros, M. A. Ph. D. M. D. F. A. A. J. P.

The office was a calming shade of gray. Camille, as usual, was stoic. She waited, hands in her lap the way I waited for Trisha to begin. Camille's notepad lay on the stand beside her chair. Pen tucked into the wire binding of the notepad.

I took my seat. Anxious. Camille's silence always made me anxious. Why had I stuck it out with her? I did not like Camille. But Camille knew my secrets—all of them. She knew about the vibrator and the anal plug. She knew about the nipple clamps. She knew I could not let a man touch my body. How could I ever help my clients? Camille sat in her island of silence. I touched the scar on my neck. Camille had not been surprised when I told her my attacker raped me with a knife.

Camille was an unhealthy thin as though the starving sickness possessed her. Or maybe in another life she had been a wraith who now dined on the living having brought back all the secrets of the underworld. How else could she claw her way into my mind?

The gray, stringy, uncoiffed hair. How many times had I wanted to tell her to pay a visit to a stylist. But she did not. I did not comment on the frail pasty skin with its caves and wrinkles, its rustications and hollows that had never seen the sun.

I did not comment because, at times, when it seemed Camille was not listening, she said something that nailed me so hard it hurt. Like the day in the middle of a rant about how messed up I was after the assault, Camille had said, in that half-human, mystical, raspy voice,

"Rose, why do you loathe yourself?"

Loathe.

A word I used with my own clients as they confessed and raved and cried and sobbed about the cruelty of their men. That day I opened up. I wept for ten minutes. Camille had sat in silence while I writhed in self-hatred.

From that day, I catalogued every event in my memory that had led to the night he shoved me down, knife in hand. What had I done but try to free women from fear?

"I'm in trouble, Camille."

"Tell me."

I felt the claws of transactional analysis dig at me. Camille's Jungian mind bored into mine.

"I just finished a session with Trisha. I sent her away just like I do the others and I worry about her. I think about her as if she were my own child."

"Such peril in that," Camille glanced up. To avoid her eyes. I focused on her lips. Her lips were blade thin but her eyes sharp as flint. I waited. It was coming. I heard it coming. Camille said,

"If you wanted a child, you'd have had one."

Camille shifted in her chair. I expected to see insects flit off her, dust to scatter. She was a ghost. Unearthly. A mind so sharp it cut ruthless and deep and remorseless. Truth.

I let the knot building in my stomach tighten until I wanted to vomit. Camille was now inside me as far as one mind can be in another. It was Camille lifting my arm, Camille choking on my pain, Camille guiding me through an insane landscape of torn souls and naked anger and flesh-ripping knives. It was as if I had taken on a new body and it was driving me mad. Camille continued,

"You let all your clients get too close, Rose, and this one—are you in love with her?"

"In love with her?"

"It's a simple question. Yes or no."

"I'm not gay."

"That's not my question."

"You know the answer."

"Is she gay?"

"She edits for Pinnacle."

"Love has nothing to do with being gay," Camille said.

"Why don't you have tissues? Yours is the only practice in Los Angeles that doesn't have tissues."

Camille looked up with those flinty eyes and she did not blink. She said,

"Is that the best you can do?"

"No. Maybe you're right. Maybe I don't want her as my child. Maybe I am in love with her."

"What do you love about her?"

"What?"

"Your hearing works as well as mine."

"She's industrious. She's a dreamer. Yes, she has sexual issues, but she is smart and ambitious and beautiful."

Camille flipped a page in her notepad. She said,

"She has a very strong hold on you. Why?"

"Why? How can you ask why? I thought you would know why."

"Your anger puzzles me."

"Sometimes I hate you."

"I think you see your possible self in Trisha. You want to love her as a daughter and as a woman so you can live through her works. But you have your own accomplishments. Still, you seem to think that if you love her, you can save her. You know if you take the simple path, you will see the truth and the truth is that you can't save anyone."

"She says this book she's working on is about the future without men. And the future..." My stomach was churning. I saw the sand and on the sand the woman being stoned and beside her I saw Trisha—helpless, beautiful, treacherous Trisha—and the blood.

"Is it that awful?" Camille said.

"She feels the agony of all women."

"That is not her privilege," Camille said.

"What do you mean?"

"It's the great divide of our time—women who are in agony and women who do not know they are in agony. Your clients come to you knotted by the depth of their pain. Some of them come to you so you can help them peel away the layers of anguish. Some of them you can't help. All of them you can cleanse only if they want to be cleansed."

"Trisha's a hunter. She goes to the beach hunting for men—beach meat, she calls men beach meat—and she pays for that with pain and fear. But this time something is different. It's like she's shouldering all the agony every woman has ever felt."

"Again, she does not have the right to be our sacrificial lamb," Camille said.

"Isn't that the way you feel, Camille? All your clients pouring their hate and fear and pain into you—don't you feel like you will explode?"

"That's why you talk to me. And that's why I talk to Dr. Kauff."

Of course. She talked to Dr. Kauff. She had to. It was too much to carry without talking to someone about it. Trisha told me why she went to the beach, told me what she was looking for, told me that when she said no, the men punished her. And I had told her that men always punish us. One way or another, men punish us. Men punish us because we want to be in control. Men punish us if we give them what they want. They punish us if we don't. If men can't control women, then they have nothing. They get scared.

41

They get angry.

The scar on my neck pulsed with each heartbeat. Camille held up her notepad.

"Put it in your notes. They have to save themselves."

"So everything we do is a sham?"

"Without us their pain eats them alive. They come to us to lighten their load."

"And I keep sending them back to their men. How do I make up for that?"

"You wait." Camille closed her notebook. "You keep them talking until their eyes open."

"Or the cycle goes on."

"Yes, it does," Camille said. "You didn't bring your dream book."

"I'm not dreaming."

"What's in your dreams you don't want me to know?"

I left. I did not feel relieved or safe. Nothing could make me feel safe now. My sense of the impending apocalypse was stronger than it had ever been in any dream I'd ever had. What if Trisha's fear was mine? What if men did seal us up again and held us hostage to another million years of oppression? I hadn't mentioned the Niche to Camille yet Camille lived in the Niche. In all the time I had been seeing her, I had no idea of Camille's proclivities. Did she have a lover? Did she self-pleasure? Did she keep a dream book?

I had to ask Trisha for a copy of *Citadel.*

**Trisha**

Backed by the afternoon sun Daiva's hair looked electric. She wore a red scoop neck blouse, full white skirt, and white flats. She shimmered in the sun. It was confusing. Daiva looked out at the sea. The sun cut through the white skirt leaving an x-ray picture of legs and hips.

After reading *Citadel* I would have expected a purple-haired mohawked demon with rings in her nose and piercings in all the wrong places. The disparity between what she should be and what she was played against my own sense of self. I felt underdressed and overexposed.

The wind rose up off the sea and Daiva's skirt swirled, turning her into a statue—Athena in white and sunlight.

Daiva turned. The wind died back. The draping turned genteel. I saw her eyes—there was a ferocity in them I had not seen before. That was the look of the woman who had written *Citadel*. Daiva said,

"Why did you want to meet here?"

"Better to say this in a neutral place."

"Bad news without wine?" Daiva said.

"No wine."

"So what is it? Yes or no?"

"Clara wants to meet you. I want to talk first."

"So it's not a rejection?" Daiva said.

The wind brushed her hair wrapping it around her and for a moment she had the look of an Amazon, a warrior ready to mount her horse and battle legions—there was more than one Daiva.

"Well," I said. I hate starting every sentence with *well* the way the TV newscasters do. If I had read that in the manuscript I'd have axed it—start with what you have to say, Trisha, just say it.

"I wanted to meet here because…"

"Yes or no?" Daiva's impatience hung heavy in the air. I hadn't seen her since the Sunday she gave me *Citadel*. I didn't ask where she had been. It didn't matter. All that mattered was the novel.

In the sunlight, her eyes were now deep aquamarine and flashing. Her mouth at once ruby red and steely hard was fixed in a line that then softened—she said,

"Being rejected isn't new to me."

"Not rejected. Clara wants your manuscript—she's leaving the signing up to me. She has two conditions."

"No conditions," Daiva said. "Take it or leave it."

I hated negotiating. My mouth tasted rancid and old. I needed a glass of Chardonnay because wine smoothed out everything. I resisted suggesting we go to a bar.

"Let's walk."

Daiva fell in beside me and we strolled the length of the Boardwalk to the end of the pier. I told her about the meeting with Clara. I told her that Caleb could be an ass who pretended to think only about double Ds in lab coats and he thought that performing seminal extractions on the Gland was rape. Daiva laughed.

"But Clara sees what you're doing in this novel."

"That's a switch," Daiva said.

"She's a hard sell, Dee. She needs this book and she wants it to be big. She wants to sell the translation rights, worldwide. She wants to make it into a movie."

"That's big of her, but... I hear a but in there."

Daiva pulled up, I passed her, my back to the sun. The light playing over her face gave her the look of a woman annealing her skin in a golden fire.

"She wants..."

"Clara wants or Caleb wants?"

"Clara. She wants to get out of erotica. She wants a book with real language and not a string of sexual clichés. "

"But..." Daiva said.

"She thinks your writing needs work."

"You tell me what Clara thinks. I want to know what you think."

"I think you use a lot of adverbs."

"I love adverbs," Daiva said.

"And you force your images when the images can stand alone."

"You want to rewrite me?"

"No, not rewrite you—my esthetics are pretty clear—I need clean sentences. We need to get the story clear and we have to work on the structure before we start on the language."

"When you say 'we,' what do you mean? You're going to cut half my words."

"Don't be that way, Dee. Clara told me that when she read the *Stoning* scene she cried. I couldn't believe it. She cried."

"I guess I did something right..."

"Listen to me..." I grasped Daiva's arms. Tense muscles in her arms. No fear in those vicious eyes. She relaxed. I didn't tell her that Clara had gotten into the *Extraction* scene. I didn't tell her that Clara had a lover who tied her

44

up and tested her limits. Instead, I said,

"She wants this book, but you have to accept that it needs work."

"Trisha, I'm a scientist. I've written papers. I've published papers and I have genuflected at the feet of editors who passed judgment on me. I spent years writing the way other people want me to write so when I wrote *Citadel*, I made up my mind that I would do it exactly the way I wanted to do it."

I let go of those arms and backed up a step. Daiva squinted in the sun. Her ferocious eyes, turned cruel. Another Daiva—the no-compromise Daiva.

"This book can change a lot of people, Dee. It's changing me. I don't want it to change me, but as I read it I'm changing. The changes are so deep it's like I'm becoming another person. I was on the beach when I read the *Stoning* scene. I was in a dream with Hagah when she released the plague. But some of your words have to change, so give me a little room. I want to make this into what it can be and I want to make you…"

"Famous?" Daiva said.

"It's that kind of novel, but you have to give me a chance to work on it. Clara wants me to make this golden, Daiva. It's an important work."

"If I say no?"

"Then Clara will say no and *Citadel* dies at Pinnacle. But I have a way to handle it."

"How do you handle it?"

"I work sections and give them to you and if I've ruined you, you tell me and I fix it. That's the way I work. If you sign I'll take *Citadel* to the desert."

"What does that mean—take it to the desert?"

"A retreat where I go to work—the Desert Rose Motel. It's the only place I can work without distractions. I read what I'm working on to a bartender named Bett who knows me…"

"And she keeps your four-year-old Château Vieux Chardonnay cold?"

I laughed. It felt good to laugh. Daiva's eyes had softened. The flint in them had dulled its edge and the fourth Daiva emerged—a kind, warm and very sexy Daiva who had no idea of the effect she had on me.

As we strolled into the sun I told her how I worked a page, how I never touched the original but always kept a working copy that I ran side by side until the text fit. I told her the three stories rule—Story One is the story your ego wants credit for. Story Two is the story that wants to be told. Story Three is the story your readers want you to write. *Citadel* is Story Two—it commands you to write it. Anything less and it's just another story.

We stopped at the end of the pier, one step short of the sea. Beyond the beach, the water, its Southern California angry gray boiling, rushing up and back, back and up. I waited. One more step, into the sea, no more beach meat, no more pain, no more anxious dreams about naked men exploding in a nuclear fire, no more shame and guilt, no more burning dreams about the end of the world.

Daiva quiet, the sun in her hair still golden, the skin still bronze, the skirt still white, said,

"Okay."

Relieved, I hugged her just as a gaggle of children all wearing identical T-shirts that said Wilson School on them clustered at the end of the rail. The chaperone cautioned them to be careful. One of the boys gawked at us. He said,

"Mrs. Felix, these two ladies are hugging."

Daiva laughed. She said,

"And *Citadel* becomes a reality."

§§§

I hadn't seen Daiva since the day on the pier. We'd set up a meeting with Clara and Caleb for Saturday at Pinnacle. I was edgy, rattled, so I decided to go hunting.

I picked out a red bikini. Red because I was in the last day of my period.

The beach was hot. The sky a little overcast.

At the net, four hunks of beach meat were at war. They were all beautiful, a rainbow of meat—brown meat, black meat, white meat, tanned meat. All of them showing their gifts, all of them performing for the Princess and the Pea in the red bikini on the sand. I watched their fertility display, the grunting and snarling with each serve, each dig, each block. The only thing lacking was the antlers.

At sunset, I rolled up my towel. Mr. B, the tall brown hunk with the iron abs trotted over. Before he opened his mouth I asked him if he shaved everywhere.

"Sure do."

I handed him my towel. Give him the wine test? Or just go with the raging hormones?

The three rejects—Losers 1, 2, and 3 rushed into the sea. They bumped shoulders as they stood waist deep, looks of relief on their faces. Three hours with no break. Football-sized bladders.

I led my catch off the beach to the parking lot thinking that all I needed was a carrying pole and some rope. As he got into the Z-Ray, he said something about my nice electric wheels.

Driving up Latimer Canyon, I powered through the curves. Mr. B tapped his thighs with his palms. He hadn't gone into the surf, he hadn't made a run to the head. I knew his eye teeth were floating. That was the rule, the meat with the iron bladder won. Half-way home, I regretted not using the wine test, but today it didn't matter.

When I parked in my spot at the condo, the prey got out, doing a little pee dance. I took my time unlocking the house, pulling the key out of the lock, going inside. He followed jitterbugging and asking if he could use the head.

"Down the hall on the left."

I stood in the doorway while he peed. He flinched when I came up behind him and raked my nails over his back. I told him to wash. Then turned him around. His speedo down, cock in hand, he stood there with expectation in his eyes and an erection. I smelled the sea and the sweat on him. Leading him by his erection, I steered him to the bedroom, shed my bikini and sat on the bed.

"Go down on me," I said.

"Sure thing."

He knelt but then he pulled back.

"Uh," he muttered.

"Just pull it out."

"I never done that."

"You have teeth."

My flow is light on the last day. The tampon was barely spotted.

"Did you come here to have sex with me?"

"Sure did."

"Then do what I tell you."

"Okay."

"Drop it on the floor and finish what you started."

He went back down. Nothing. Numb. He could have been any man. He could have been all men. Looking at him I wondered what he would do if I told him no. Would he kill me? Strangle me. Cut me? Beat me?

I rolled over and pulled a condom from the pack in the drawer, handed it to him. He peeled it. We were in his area of expertise now. He groaned when he entered me. He went to work huffing with the same energy he had shown on the beach—wild, mechanical, animal energy. The sweat working out of him reeked of onions.

When he was on the edge, I told him to stop. I asked him if that was all he had. He said Uh, and doubled down, growling, driving harder, sweating more, but still giving me nothing.

And then he came. As he came he howled a short little oh fuck of a little death howl then collapsed. I waited. He didn't move. I rolled him onto his back. His onion sweat coated my belly. He was sound asleep.

I sat on the edge of the bed. My hair hadn't even slipped free from the clip. He sprawled on the bed snoring. I picked up his speedo and snapped his flaccid cock twice. The second snap brought him around. He sat up, ready to go again. I tossed his speedo to him and told him to leave.

"Uh, okay."

I showed him the front door and shoved him into the hallway. He stood there pouting—Adonis outcast.

"Uh," he said. "How do I get back to my car?"

"Call Lyft," I said.

"I don't got my phone."

"Walk," I said.

I shut the door and leaned into it, the wood cold against my skin. I went to the end table beside the bed and slid the rabbit from its pink plastic case and carried it to the shower.

Water hot, I sat on the shower shelf and played the rabbit until my back arched and I snapped my thighs together holding the mechanical warrior in place while the orgasm exhausted me.

Just once. All I asked was for it to happen once. Was it too much to ask?

## Daiva

I had seen it before—the sheen of power, the arrogance of money, the sense of entitlement and presence. Clara was hard core. She wore dark leggings and lace cuffs. A lace ruff hid the neck. But why? Hers was not a wattled neck thick and wrinkled with time. It was elegant and mysterious. Trisha hadn't told me Clara was a princess. I watched the two of them talking. Trisha was at home with the haughtiness, at ease with the arrogance, at peace in her second fiddle position—not at all like the woman on the pier, the woman on the sand, so full of confidence, so understanding of what she wanted as an editor, as a woman, as a friend.

Clara—gray heat-seeking eyes zeroing in—smiled.

It was a diamond smile—the teeth brilliant, the lips so perfect they looked like they had been tattooed on. I was ready to flick it in, but Clara said that she loved my novel.

"It's what I've been pestering this one to bring home, but there are a couple of things I'm not too clear on."

Her eyes bored into me, business-woman deep. I shifted to Trisha who looked ecstatic that she had found the big book for her boss. I asked what the problems were.

"Trisha has told you I think the writing needs some work. She can take care that. I have some trouble with some of your ideas. For instance, what you call divergent evolution. Can we bring that down to language readers will understand?"

No help from Trisha. She was still in the presence of her

boss doing exactly what her boss demanded.

"Men and women are headed in different directions."

"I like that, but there's more to it, right?"

"Divergent evolution means women are under different selective pressures, so we end up in a different place than men."

"Hmm. Okay. And this post-lesbian idea. I don't know how to sell that."

The door to the office opened. A man entered. The stalking pace of a cat stepping into its own tracks. He wore gray—a gray silk shirt with pearl gray buttons, gray sharkskin slacks, and gray suede loafers. His hair was brushed and coiffed until it shone. He took a seat and leaned back in the chair, hands behind his head, the hairless ape in full-crotch display. Caleb, no doubt. My stomach lurched. Exo was the first word that popped into my head. I checked Trisha for direction. No reaction. Clara went on talking as though Caleb were just a fixture.

"This is my brother Caleb. Caleb this is Daiva Izokaitis."

"The mad scientist," Caleb said.

I headed for the door. Clara said,

"Don't mind him, Daiva. He's a spoiled brat who pouts when he can't get his way."

"I read your book, doll," Caleb said. "When Trisha pitched it I said I didn't see us doing it. She forced my hand so I read it and my only question is in those citadels do those broads have sex?"

No one had called me doll in years. White male superiority just rolled off him. I wanted to walk out, but I welcomed the challenge. I sat back down. Here was an Exo, the 13$^{th}$ gene raging full-bore, the evolutionary tags in place—size, aggression, speed. I imagined him playing tennis. His serve a hundred miles an hour, his rage pouring across the net. Yes, I'd seen his kind in action. I glanced at Trisha, then took the bait and asked Caleb if he'd had a sperm count check in the last three years.

"What?" Caleb squirmed up right, dropped his hands on the arms of his chair and looked at Clara then Trisha who glanced at me. She was smiling.

"You should have a sperm count, Caleb," I said, "because the science is clear on this—the average sperm count per ejaculation has dropped from three hundred million to under seventy million in the last twenty years and of that seventy million, you've probably got a four percent motility rate."

"What the fuck is this?" Caleb said.

"I've explained it to Trisha."

"Explain it to me."

"In language you won't understand, desire has nothing to do with sex..."

"But they're all a bunch of muffin munchers, gash lickers? Right?"

Trisha stepped in to take control. She said, "She's written a novel, Caleb. It's built on science. Not on sex."

"It's science fiction," Caleb said. "And the post-lesbian thing is a deal breaker."

"Verifiable science," I said. "Come to my lab tomorrow and we'll run a fertility count on you just to see how you stack up."

"Wait, wait, wait." Clara glided between Caleb and me raising a hand and saying that she was going with this book. Trisha would edit, Pinnacle would bring it out in hardcover.

"Yeah, well this is a book about extinction, right?" Caleb said. He peered around Clara, looked right at me, his gray eyes just like the eyes of his sister.

"No, it's about choice," I said.

"But extinction is the end, right? And that *Extraction* scene with a Gland? Is that as close you get to sex?"

"You didn't read the novel, Caleb," I said.

"Okay. I skimmed it some."

"If you had read the novel, you'd know what I mean."

"All right," Clara said. "Enough. Caleb. Tone it down."

"I'm a scientist, Caleb," I said. "I'm projecting science into the future and in that future we control the genome."

"Does controlling the genome mean cutting the nuts off all the men in the whole fucking world? That's what I read."

51

"It's a novel, Caleb," Clara said.

"It's a dangerous novel, Sis."

"It's not dangerous," I said. "Using CRISPR we have the techniques right now to edit DNA. I could make your skin glow fluorescent green, Caleb. Every lab in the world is run by women and every lab technician in the world is a woman. Men have abandoned science for their insane belief systems while the women keep doing science and dealing in facts. In *Citadel,* the prime directive is to silence gene thirteen, the killer gene and when we do that it leaves three kinds of males—Exos, Glands, and Mutants."

Caleb said, "You're way off in lala land, you know that? Macho is making a comeback and you're writing antimale jargon and I think my sis has a screw loose to go with this."

"It's a novel," Trisha said again. "It's what we do here—bring out fiction."

"Has she signed?" Caleb said.

"As soon as we finish a few details."

"This is a disaster, Sis," Caleb said. "I guarantee you nothing but trouble with this book. That's what you're gonna get. Sixteen tons of trouble."

"Trisha's taking it to our focus group," Clara said

"Any men in that focus group?" Caleb said.

"You know there aren't," Trisha said.

"Well, if that's what Clara wants, that's what Clara gets," Caleb said. "I guarantee you that if you run it by a men's group you'll get your eyebrows singed. Men won't like it. There's nothing a man can like in this novel, Sis."

I headed for the door. Trisha intercepted me, telling me not to let him get to me because Pinnacle was going to bring out the novel no matter what.

"He doesn't want it," I said.

"He's a man. He doesn't know what he wants."

"He knows what he doesn't want, Tee. He doesn't want me or my novel. What he really wants is to kill us."

"No, no, no, no, no. Wait." Trisha clasped her hand over mine on the door handle. "This is just what we want—a book that will get people talking. That's what Clara sees."

Trisha was good at soothing feathers. That was what she did and I understood that her job was to go between Clara, the money, and Caleb, the doubter. I'd seen it before so I relaxed and asked Clara why she wanted *Citadel* and why she wanted to do it in paper when the world had already electrified everything.

"What do you do when the lights go out?" Clara said.

"Get a flashlight, light a candle," I replied.

"I want paper because when electricity goes out you can't charge your ereader."

Caleb laughed. His face screwed up in a humorless grin. The grin reminded me of the paper Jahil and I wrote on the warring gene. We asked why men and women were at war. We wanted to debunk the clichéd and trite "war of the sexes" that read more like a joke than a scientific finding. So we looked at the science, the sociology, the genetics and it all came down to quantity versus quality. The residue of three million years of evolution. That 13th gene. Caleb had it. Every man had it, women didn't. Divergent evolution leading to the inevitable extinction of the Y chromosome. Men weren't at war with women. There was no war of the sexes. Men were at war with themselves. They were living in a world they didn't fit into anymore. A world that was leaving them and all their Paleolithic residue behind. Caleb stood, he flexed, he stretched. I had seen that same stretch in monkeys in the lab under stress. When they couldn't lash out they stretched and gaped. I had seen that same movement on the beach in the battles between teams of beach meat. I looked at Tee. She giggled. It was a fluttery giggle that I caught like an infection, and then Clara too and the three of us doubled over, almost sick with laughter. Caleb reacted the way I knew he would. He said,

"Are you laughing at me?"

I got control of myself, got control of the laughter.

"You see, Caleb, *Citadel is* playing out right here, right now, today."

Caleb's shark-gray eyes flashed, his mouth drew into a tight line, his hands posed on his hips and then he shrugged. He smiled. A beautiful, deceptive smile, the kind of smile that could trick a woman into thinking he was on her side just before he killed her. He said,

"Look, Dee, is that what your friends call you? I just

made an ass of myself, but part of my job is to see if I can get under your skin. I had to know how tough you are before I could commit to this project. So let me make it up to you. Let me take you out to dinner. I know this fabulous place in the Marina…"

"Control yourself, Caleb," Clara said. "This is a business meeting."

"All right," I said. "Lunch. Tomorrow."

"I'll pick you up," Caleb said. "Address?"

"Long Beach. My lab."

"Well," Clara said, "I'm glad we got that ironed out. I think we're ready to sign a contract but before we do, I have a question. What is crispr?"

§§§

Caleb was at the curb leaning against the door of a black Tesla Z. He held the door for me. The acid Caleb I had met at Pinnacle transformed into *politesse* itself. He smelled rich, like a budding flower. He waited for me to get buckled in.

He didn't glance at my legs as he closed the door. In the office, he had been an obnoxious boor, but when I cut that away, he was a beautiful man. Good bones. I saw his sister in him. A strong chin. Over six feet, heavy in the shoulders. Weathered wrinkles around the eyes told me he had spent time on the sea. He pulled into traffic. I said,

"Why does skin mean so much?"

"To say no is to deny civilization."

"So, you went home and read the novel?"

He said that after our rough meeting, he decided to read the book. I waited for more. No exegesis, no diatribe. Nothing.

"Let's skip lunch and go straight to the lab."

"I thought this was a date," he said.

"It's been a while since I went on a date."

Traffic was heavy. He drove with finesse, stopping at yellow lights, taking his time at the greens. The Tesla ran silent. A computer on wheels some people called it, but it had a reserve power that snuck up on you and rattled your bones. The sound system on low was playing the Schubert *Adagio*. Culture. From Santa Monica to Long Beach, Caleb said nothing. Silence can be a controlling technique. Caleb didn't project obsession. His was a comfortable silence in the car and highway world where words were a distraction. It wasn't a silence that meant he had nothing to say, it was the silence of attending to being. I liked that. And I liked the music that seemed to complete the Tesla. Another line from *Citadel* sprang to mind —"coupling is the destruction of Self."

I felt tentacles of expectation as we pulled into my parking space at the lab. Still silent, Caleb got out of the Tesla and waited. I watched his eyes, the mouth, the face, watched the hands that moved with the smoothness of a serpent gliding and yes, a shiver of expectation crept up on me. What was he thinking? In *Citadel* I had looked at being human only from the biological angle. A mark of being human is the built-in ability to read what other people are thinking. We're good at it. But this man, who, when we were in the office, hung onto his points like a dog with a bone, said nothing about my suggestion to skip lunch. No argument. Tacit agreement as if he were reading my mind. I remembered a triplet from a poem,

I am neither big nor small
I am neither brilliant nor dull.
I am what you see, or nothing at all.

§§§

I unlocked the lab and led Caleb into the smell of alcohol and antiseptic. He did a scan of the print on the wall.

"So, this is where the Angel plays God?"
"You didn't answer my question."
"Why does skin mean so much?"
"Yes."
"Skin is the boundary between thee and me. Exactly what do you want from me?"

I stood behind him, looking over his shoulder, smelling his scent. Was it rose? Plum? A fragrance I didn't know. He pointed at the print.

"That," I said, "is a photomicrograph of an ovum and a single sperm. You can see that the sperm has lost its undulipodium. This is an electron microscope capture."

"Unduli….?"

"Flagellum," I said.

"You study sperm."

"I do. Sperm. Y chromosome. Ova."

"Is this the origin of *Citadel*?"

"Almost."

"What does it mean to lose the flagellum?"

"It means to be alone is to die."

"Everything you say is a riddle," Caleb said.

"Yesterday I told you that each ejaculation from the human male at one time averaged three hundred million sperm. The only mitochondrion in a gamete is in the flagellum. When it loses its flagellum, it dies. This one is dying before it penetrates the cortex of the ovum. In a way, the ovum is saying no. And because it says no, it will die just as the sperm will die. This is the fate of the Y chromosome and that's why we bleed."

Caleb looked neither startled nor curious. He continued to study the print.

"The fate of the race that you write about."

"Yes, it's all in the novel."

"I tried to read one of your papers."

"You bothered to look me up."

"You've done a lot."

"Boring?"

"I didn't understand much of it. The novel tells me more."

I had his scent in my head. It was a ridiculous smell. Testosterone and a floral cologne. He touched my shoulder. His hand slid to my arm. I looked at the hand. Strong fingers, tanned and beautiful.

"Is this why you brought me here, to watch sperm lose their flagella?"

"No."

"To run a sperm count on me."

"Yes."

"Why?"

"We're like precious little marble statues stuck in the Niche," I said, "but there's no one to worship us."

"Stuck in what Niche?"

"It's in the novel," I said. "Two hundred years ago, we wouldn't be standing here, in my lab talking about a novel I wrote. I don't know why I brought you here."

"The way you talk about it, it doesn't sound like a novel."

"Let's leave."

His grip tightened on my arm. I shook him off. I asked if he was going to strangle me.

"We're not living in your novel, Daiva, so no, I'm not going to strangle you. I'm post-death. I've known too many women, gone to too many places with those women, been taken for granted too much, so no I'm not afraid you'll laugh at me, but I am curious."

"About?"

He pointed to the print on the wall where the sperm hung between never and no. It was nothing refused, refused it could never be. To say no was to deny civilization.

"You brought me here to test me for... what do you call it?"

"Motility. Do you really want to know?"

"After reading your novel I'm curious," he said.

"It took that to make you curious?"

"I'm thirty-nine. There have been accidents."

"Accidents?"

"You know what I mean. The manufacturing process sometimes has holes in it. But there are no little Calebs running around, so yes I'm curious."

I rubbed my arm where he had gripped me.

"You really don't want to know."

He pointed at the micrograph. "Is that me? "

"It is probably you. But it's not just you."

"I want the truth. After reading *Citadel* I need to know."

"All right. I can do an extraction. But only if you really want to know."

"What you said yesterday made me think."

"I suppose if you write the screenplay, you have to know

everything."

"How do you know I might write the screenplay?"

"Screenwriters aren't the only ones who do research."

"You researched me?"

"Know your enemy, love your friends."

"Okay. Extraction? Like the daughters in *Citadel* extract from the Gland? Let me tell you I'm not very fond of machines around my… apparatus."

"There are other ways," I said.

"I know nothing about you."

"You know everything you need to know about me."

I touched his suntanned arm. If I could peer past the skin to the muscles in the blood in the bone of this man I would see into the Y and not have to do what he wanted. Did I want to know? I clasped his hand and led him to a room to a cot laid with white sheets and white pillows. On a side table there was a row of collection jars. I said,

"Lie down."

"Are you going to strap me in?"

"I'm a daughter of the Citadel," I said. "I was born carrying the disease of desire."

### Trisha

I read all day Sunday. Sunday evening Daiva knocked on my door. She looked faded and worn out. I got a couple of wineglasses and two bottles of Château Vieux Chardonnay. Daiva seemed grateful for the wine but didn't have much to say, so I continued working while she lounged on my sofa. I was deep into the *Technicians*. I hadn't decided how to handle it. I was puzzled by the way Daiva used the collective point of view while dipping into and out of first or third. The scene could benefit from a little cutting, but I wasn't ready to do that yet. Since I had the author pinned down in my condo, I could ask her what she intended with the scene but there was time so I read—

# Citadel          Daiva Izokaitis

In the gloom of the shadow of the walls, the technicians watch the Hunters approach the gate. They can see that the Gland is a good specimen. They approach the hunters, as always bewildered by their wildness. The technicians know that time in the open space has altered the way they relate to their bodies and to the Citadel and other daughters.

Taking control of the quarry, the technicians sedate him. Sedated he will not see anything. He will have no memory of the Citadel. He will return to Exo-world not knowing where he has been. He will have seen only the high walls and darkened corridors. He will not remember the maze.

The technicians carry the now unconscious specimen deeper into the core of the Citadel. This is a precarious time because his presence creates an imbalance which could threaten the existence of every daughter. The technicians could bring him in secretly, but in the Old Society, secrets had destroyed so much that the process had to be open and transparent although he will remain anonymous to all but the hunters, the technicians, and the Planners.

The hunters have not spoken to the prey and the technicians refrain from speaking in front of the being now in the core of the Citadel. The presence of the Gland can be seen as a disease that maimed generations because he carries the unmutated 13th gene. Here, in this body, resides the end of the world as it once was.

The work to be done upon him is necessary for the future of the race, but the imbalance his presence generates ripples through each of the technicians. Once he is in the laboratory, the technicians will read his history to know who his progenetrix is, to know when he was expelled as an infant, and, when if ever, he was taken as prey.

After the work is finished, he will be expelled from the Citadel, his memory having been altered to erase all traces of his having been there.

In the practical minds of the technicians, there is a mild ambivalence. Their training and know-ledge allow them to touch the cordovan-colored flesh of the creature as though it were a daily occurrence but at another level, they are revulsed by the smoothly muscled, lithe, strange body that even in repose threatens tran-quility despite the absolute control they exercise over him.

The technicians carry the sperm source deep into the lab. They are uneasy as they push the sedated body on the gurney through the corridors into the labyrinth where the ancestors of the body had also lain. The visitation becomes a ritual re-enactment. But there is a difference between knowing the ritual and being in the presence of the living body with its history of disruption and killing. The daughters relate in ancient ways to the flesh. In the Old Society, their uneasiness might have been seen as coyness.

There is some comfort in knowing that the Gland, even were he conscious of his descent, would not know where he is or where he came from. He cannot fathom the complexity of his experience, for there is nothing in his past to compare to the intricacy of the Citadel and its multiple levels.

Down into the darkness of the substructure, the technicians ferry the body. They approach the most remote levels of the Citadel, levels where the mechanical enterprises which allow

60

life to replicate itself are carried on; their work goes on there, out of view, guarded from open intervention by the upper structures, because even the slightest interference could bring forth an unrecognizable monster. In the solidity of timeless space, operating at a timeless speed, in operations which know no measures, the technicians can deliberate and probe, construct and re-arrange the mechanisms and with all worry removed, continue the work which will shape future generations.

They enter the repository where they remove the body from the gurney to a table. It is then that the work begins.

With a practiced exactness the technicians measure each unit of the Gland—phalanges, metatarsals, tarsals, arch, ankles, tibia, fibula, condition of cartilage, articulation, joints, hirsuteness, metacarpals, wrists, articulations, length of ulna and radius, elbow range, shoulder condition, neck, spinal cord, back muscles, buttocks, thighs, calves, tendons, genitalia, scrotum, penis, prepuce, anus, rectum, head, eyes, ears, nose, teeth, tongue, tonsils, sinuses.

One technician clips the Gland's hair for microscopic analysis. A second technician gives him a rectal examination and inserts a catheter to extract urine. The sample is taken for analysis. A third technician draws blood from veins and his arteries. His body temperature is taken orally and rectally. A cardiogram is taken. An electro-encephalogram is made. Lung capacity measured. A saliva sample is taken. A spinal tap. Feces analysis. Nail clippings. Epithelial tissue is examined. A flesh core taken from his buttocks. Finally, he is given an enema and his digestive tract is emptied. A stomach analysis is made of acidity; a wipe is made of the linings of the intestines and a culture for bacteria—species and quantity.

Pertinent information will be sent to different experts.

Within two hours the technicians know everything about the Gland that can be known but not even the technicians can read that mystery in his mind. The Gland is reduced to a set of numbers which is compared by the computer to other data sets and a statistical analysis of the specimen is read out, matching him to the store of information on other Glands who preceded him there.

The impersonal treatment that guided the technicians is the result of training, and they have moved automatically. Theirs is work which requires dedication and control; not only must they handle the body of the Gland, they must probe into a male body, extract his wastes and manipulate his organs. The conflict which that work engenders is so intense that their efficiency barely exceeds their loathing. Were they to spend more time at it, their reaction could be disastrous. They are daughters, but turned voluntary automatons for the single purpose of examining the Gland; it is a credit to their control and dedication that they can do their work without feeling though even then, at some later time, they will need to talk about their experience and to cleanse themselves. In the short time of their work, they are experiencing the Old Society: they are reduced to serving a male, working for him, attending upon him. The microcosm of their brief interaction generates an aura of revolution. They have seen the images in the Heptuants. They know the history of the Wars. Were the technicians less aware of the past and what they are doing, a moment in history might be re-enacted. The Y might be destroyed, the future pushed ahead of its time.

But they are well trained. They have all volunteered; of the volunteers, selection was made so that no harm could come to any daughter. The technicians have worked on daughters many times, but no one will be required to work on the Gland more than once.

When the technicians finish, they release him to the Extractor.

They watch the Gland enter the extractor room. They leave exam and go to the sterilizer for cleansing. Decontamination could not be more complete had they recently been in a plague country or in the presence of an insidious infection which had to be contained within the innermost recesses of their world.

Emerging from the labyrinth of the Citadel, the technicians distance themselves from the Gland and the miniature world he now inhabits. Joining with other daughters in the Solerian, they sever all connection with the Gland.

When I finished, I started on some notes about collective point of view and the extensive use of semicolons. It was too early to go into that. Later. Looking up, I found Daiva staring at me with her ice-blue eyes. She asked me if I was rejecting her right now.

"I'm making notes. I haven't actually started editing."

"But you're already rejecting my words."

"My job is to find the best story. I like the way you've avoided the three-act structure."

"You want to change that too?"

"There are very powerful scenes in this novel, but you don't write to the plot points."

"How can you afford these cases of a four-year-old special label Chardonnay?"

"Tell me how you made out with Caleb."

"He's got everything a breeder looks for."

"You know he hits on every author we sign."

"He thinks like an Exo."

"Exo. Is that how you see him?"

"Can you see him any other way?"

"He thinks money gives him the whole package."

"He's got one."

"One what?"

"A package," Daiva said.

"Tell me," I said.

"There are at least two Calebs. The businessman who has to put up with the crazy writers and the private Caleb. When you're alone with him, he's respectful and quiet. He likes classical music. We listened to Schubert and Shostakovich."

"Does he know what he's doing?"

"He really is a decent man."

"So you had sex with him."

"We plow through these bottles like they're rotgut. I looked up this Château Vieux label …."

"I know. Expensive."

"You're a woman in the Niche with money. You spend it on specialty wine and a car that costs a quarter mil. But you're insecure about what you want. Who are you?"

"What do you want to know?"

"Your last name for starters."

"It's on the mailbox. De Tours ."

"Okay, who is Trisha de Tours and how does she live like a queen working for a quirky outfit like Pinnacle?"

"My father was Louis de Tours. He died when I was seven. My mother remarried. She got her hands on a French aristocrat named René Alphonse Daudet. He claimed to be a descendent of the Marquis de Sade."

"Well that explains your proclivity for beach meat," Daiva said.

"My mother was very good with money. When René died, mother inherited and that's most of my story. You happy now?"

"That's just half the story. Where did you go to school? Do you have a degree? What do you want? What do you need?"

"I graduated from Cal with a double major in biology and English literature. I got a job as personal assistant to a woman named Beatrice who lived in Palos Verdes Estates. Through her, I met Clara and Caleb. Before I started at

Pinnacle, I was a reader at Nash Books in San Diego. I have this fantasy that there's Moorish blood in the de Tours and they lived in Toledo or Sevilla, probably in the Alhambra. The name de Tours—you know where Tours is?"

"France," Daiva said. "It's where Charles Martel whipped the snot out of the Moors."

"A scientist who knows French history," I said. "You surprise me. So, de Tours is my family name. My mother was fair, but my father was dark—the black hair comes from him—the skin from him—my grandmother de Tours looked like a Syrian goddess. Now, you give me Caleb."

Arm over her eyes, Daiva said, "He drinks too much and when he drinks, he gets emotional and very cuddly."

"So this scientist does have time for sex."

Daiva sat up. Filled her glass, sipped the wine. I squirreled around to face her. Her hair usually fluffed and shiny hung in ratty clumps. She had bags under her eyes.

"I didn't hear you come in."

"I didn't come home."

"You and Caleb? At his place?"

"The lab."

"Did you enjoy it?"

"I've told you all I'm going to tell you."

"If that's all I get then I need to know why you wrote this novel."

"Why do people always want to know that?"

"Knowing why you wrote it will help me understand what I need to do."

"You don't need to do anything to it."

"It's not perfect, Dee."

"Okay. I was pissed off at the dried-up old men who run the science publications. They didn't respect my science. They didn't like my science because it contradicts the standard model. The standard model says that there is an environment and by environment they mean what you see—it's all macro—the visible world only. But what you see is only part of the picture. The mitochondrion was once a free-living organism that attached itself to the eukaryotic cell. The fossils on the editorial boards rejected my papers because I went deeper and showed that thought can change the cells in the brain and when you change the brain you understand that environment isn't just what you see. Each cell is an environment and it's not all sweet cooperation in there. In fact, there's a war going on between the X and the Y. If you change the environment, you change evolution. That's why I wrote the book."

"And from that you get divergent evolution?"

"Divergent evolution is a reality, Tee. You change the brain, you change behavior. Look at you. You hunt, you take your quarry to bed. Why don't you get pregnant?"

"You know everything you need to know."

"You don't because you have a choice. You have options and one of your options is sex without the mess."

"And that puts me square in the Niche, does it?"

Daiva got off the sofa, uncorked another bottle of Chardonnay and muttered about wine that costs seventy-five bucks a bottle. "We drank three hundred bucks this afternoon and neither of us got laid. Where was I?"

"Sex without the mess."

"Okay. I think you distrust the biology of desire and you don't want kids."

"You're saying I'm a mutant?"

"We're all mutants. Your brain is an environment, Trisha. Each cell in your brain is an environment. Thought changes your brain. When you say, "I'm not the person I was a year ago" that is physically, electrically true. The more you know, the more you change. Changing has separated you from your past and it points to a new future. You're ninety-five percent Paleolithic nostalgia dropped into the high-tech 21$^{st}$ century which makes you an example of divergent evolution. You don't have to become what you would have been if your brain had not changed. Sexual selection created you—your father Louis de Tours had something your mother saw in him and your mother must have been a specimen that your father reacted to."

"He had everything. He had perfect manners, and he looked like a god. My mother was devastated when he died."

"And he was rich. The three biggies—size, position,

wealth. Your mother used her brain. She made choices. Women in the Niche make choices. And one of her choices was to make only one of you. And you are adapted. It's called the fragile wisdom. We can lose it in a second if we're not careful. That's another reason I wrote this novel. What would you say if I suggested you might be half way to a new species?"

"So you do think I'm a mutant?"

"We can run a chromosomal check if you want."

"And Caleb? Did you run a sperm count on him?"

Daiva sipped her wine. She said, "You are really nosy, you know that? Your man, Caleb, is a lot like his sister. Same eyes, same skin, same hair. And he's spoiled. If you saw him on the beach playing volleyball you'd give him a chance at round one because he can talk. You might let him sample your Château Vieux."

"How do you know I haven't?"

"I know you haven't," Daiva said.

"How do you know?"

"He told me. He has looks, he has money, and he's a bad boy—Darwinian up to that point. But genetically?"

"You did run the test."

"I did."

"Before or after you took him to bed?"

"There will be no little Calebs, Trisha."

The wine had a sudden vinegary nose. It was harsh. I tried to let it sink in. Neither Clara nor Caleb had married. Neither of them had children. I didn't want to say it, but it came out.

"Sterile?"

"Less than two percent motility. Even if one of his Ys ever made it home before it ran out of gas, it would just smash into a wall and die. Caleb is an evolutionary dead end."

"How did you get the sample?"

"The organic extractor."

"You had sex with him."

Daiva sipped the wine. She looked at me with her violent blue eyes. She said, "He used a condom. I salvaged the condom, analyzed the specimen. Extinction."

"You told him?"

"Of course."

"What did you tell him?"

"The truth."

"What did he say?"

"Fuck."

"You slept with him, Daiva. You can never say no."

"Nobody owns me."

"We're taking *Citadel* to our focus group on Wednesday."

"Do I get to be there?"

## Trisha

The focus group was a rainbow. Estelle wore a miniskirt and had a tiger tattoo on her thigh. She had degrees in math and physics. A tangle of curly black shoulder-length hair marked her as a woman who went her own way. She read literary fiction, M/M erotica, and was addicted to BDSM—in books only. Estelle scared me because she knew things and had opinions on things. I dreaded to hear her take on *Citadel*.

Eva lived in black leather. She wore studded chokers and drove silver pins in her nipples. She wore three-inch heels. No underwear, ever. She was the weather vane for erotic romances. If the writing didn't make her wet by page three—she gave the writer three pages—she junked the book and finished at her own pace with her own *tools*.

Dani, the innocent, wore pink. Her long yellow tresses looked fake, even plastic. Until she opened her mouth, Dani was an angel. Dani had read scripts. She wrote coverage for optioned screenplays. She always spoke about stories as action and image chains and I liked that about her. She knew her plot points

Connie loved magenta yoga pants and yellow tops that covered her hips turning her into an enigma that yielded none of her secrets. Multi-racial chick-lit was her specialty.

Regi smoked cigars, dressed in black Frisco jeans and engineer boots, but was the sweetest of the sweet. She had been married four times to four different women. Her gray hair made her the matriarch of the group. Regi wrote book reviews for three alternative papers in the Valley.

I looked at their photocopies of *Citadel.* Some of them dog-eared. Some studded with paperclips. Some thick with sticky notes.

"Hey girl, let's have some more of that Chardonnay." Eva, with long black straight gleaming hair and the nipple rings outlined through the sheer top, held out her glass. I refilled it, thinking of Daiva and the hope and the future that lay in *Citadel,* and then Clara swirled in—breathless. The high flush of her gorge was the residue of Curtis, her lover, and the riding stable.

Clara smelled good. Some exotic perfume she used that she said was a combination of human and animal pheromones. Right away she was in control. Maybe because she exuded success and money, maybe because of her perfume, the rest of the group deferred to her. She got right to it—

"You started without me."

Dani, the innocent, sat on the floor cross-legged. She said,

"So, Trisha, this is your baby?"

"It is," I said.

"It's a switch from the usual Pinnacle output," Dani said.

Clara nested between Eva and Estelle on the sofa. Three flowers in a hormonal bouquet with enough estrogen to feminize the world.

"Dani's right," Estelle said. "I've never read anything like this." Uh-oh. Words I didn't want to hear. I waited for the avalanche because Estelle could destroy or make a book with a honeyed yes or an acid no. "I liked it. All of it. From the birth scene to those gruesome, savage death scenes—all of it. You know how there's always a scene you tell people they've got to read? The image of the daughter melting is the million-dollar shot. At first it turned my stomach—so of course I had to have some wine and consult my vibrator because I don't like violence unless I'm relaxed, but then, on the second night, I realized that the writer—what's her name?"

"Daiva Izokaitis."

"This Daiva Izokaitis had pried open my skull and peeked at the machinery then wrote me into every page."

I relaxed. Eva said,

"That's right, Estelle. I mean, how did the author get hold of my memoir?"

I'd never heard both Eva and Estelle come down quite so close together on a work. Eva went on, "This woman has spent some time on the prowl, I tell you."

Eva picked up her copy of *Citadel*. She read,

## Citadel                    **Daiva Izokaitis**

Tia and Ket were an arm's length from the Gland when Zil threw her net and the Gland stumbled, but caught himself. He was magnificent, balanced, glowing with sweat. The net snared him. We were on him breathing hard. I straddled him, knees pressing against the hard thighs. He was wild and panting and I felt a wave of disgust—I was touching a Gland. The first time I had touched the skin of anyone but another daughter. His breath smelled of meat as if he just snacked on some animal.

I rolled him over and lashed his hands. Zil cinched his ankles. Tia and Ket rammed the carrying rod through the knots of the ropes and Zil said We have him. I rolled off him into the grass, my legs still slick with his sweat. Under her breath, as we were taught, so the Gland did not hear language, Ket whispered, He's got a huge sack.

Tia asked how I was and I shrugged. She touched my arm. I saw the pride in her eyes, the way she let me know I was now a veteran—a hunter

```
of Glands. The trussed Gland lay on his belly.
    To Zil, I said, My first Exo.
    And you didn't die, she said.
```

Eva said, "Is it hot in here, or is it just me?"

Regi said, "She made me a believer on page 15. Sci-fi isn't my weakness but after page 68, I realized this isn't sci-fi..."

"What is it?" I said.

"It's like reading the history of my first three wives," Regi said. "And I like the fact that she doesn't give the daughters cutesy names. I mean, I'm right there—Zil, Jahil, Qarath, Karim."

I noticed that Connie, quiet, was sitting with a wine glass in her hand, a frown on her face, small beads of sweat on her forehead.

"Something's bothering you, Connie."

"It was painful for me...." Connie said. "It's not the kind of book I usually read."

Connie shuddered. She crossed and recrossed her legs trying to find a comfort zone. She balanced her glass in her lap. She said,

"It touched me in a way I didn't expect. You know how you can read something and feel yourself changing? That was me. If Regi writes a review it needs to be only six words—*this book will change you forever*. I read it in two days because I kept re-reading sections that made my heart go into fib and I had to take walks and hot showers. I don't know why but it's like the writer is somehow talking just to me and I don't want anyone else to read it because it's for me and me alone."

"Yeah. Take that birth scene," Dani said. "You know, the one with the daughter—I love the way she doesn't use woman—what's her name?"

"Filina," I said. "Her name is Filina."

"Yes, well," Dani said, "any woman who's ever had a baby and doesn't feel that scene—I don't know... And the Expulsion scene just screams at me. A daughter gives up her baby. You feel that. It explains everything about...about who we are and how we got here."

"One section really grabbed me," Connie said. "That section she calls *Women in Captivity.* That part about Karen and Bart..."

Connie leafed through *Citadel*, to a pink post-it.

### Citadel                                   Daiva Izokaitis

And then he pulled out of her and forced her to her knees. "Help me, man," he said to his friends. One of them yanked a handful of hair and forced Karen's mouth open. Bart rammed into her, gagging her and still jammed deeper. He muttered each time he slammed into her, "You like it? You want to make me eat shit because you fucked up, huh? How's that taste now, eating your own shit?"

Karen bit him so hard her teeth cracked. Blood.

Bart yelped and he beat at her, but she held on. The stoned men attacked her, but she worked her teeth deeper into the flesh, and all the while Bart was screaming, the others were pounding her, ripping at her, tearing her lips, her eyes, but she did not give up until Bart pulled away, blood spurting from his manhood. He was crying.

As she finished, Connie's hands were shaking. Dani said,

"I don't know how many times I wanted to do that to some prick who thought he owned me just because I gave him head."

Estelle said, "When I got to the Disrupter scene, I cried because they melted the daughter—I mean they killed the daughter. I mean, you know what I mean..."

Connie dropped the manuscript on the floor. She teared up, her nose ran, she sniffled. She said,

"That happened to me."

I glanced at Clara, saw the grimace, the arms braced

over her breasts. Connie went on,

"There were four of them—I never saw their faces. They took me to a cabin in the woods and for three days they raped me and did things to me and they got away with it. They dropped me naked in the middle of the street in my neighborhood so they knew where I lived. I never reported it."

"Oh, sweetie," Regi crawled across the floor on her knees, hugged Connie, held her and stroked her hair. I glanced again at Clara then at Eva and Dani. They were all silent. There was horror in their eyes. Connie said,

"I'm sorry. I've never read anything that ate at me like that."

"Don't be sorry, baby," Regi said. "How come you never told us about this before?"

"As I read, the whole thing spilled back on me and I could smell them again, smell myself all filthy and used up. All I could think of was revenge, but the only revenge I can get is making sure no man ever gets that close to me again."

Regi put her arm around Connie. Hugged her. I uncorked two bottles of Chardonnay and refilled the glasses. The silence was total until Eva, clearing her throat, said,

"A lot of women will have trouble reading this novel, Clara."

"It's a dangerous piece," Eva said.

"I'm sorry," Connie said. "But we can't pretend anymore. The younger women think they're entitled to everything. They don't know what it cost us to get this far."

I studied the faces of the women in the focus group. This was the first time a novel had landed with such force. The pain was in the tight mouths, the crossed legs, in the intense eyes, and the silence that broke only when Clara said,

"Do you need to take a break, Connie?"

"No. No. It's too late. This novel…when you asked to me read it, I had no idea what I was in for. There are some things I have questions about. For instance, Post-lesbian. I still don't know what it means."

"We all have trouble with that," Clara said. "Trish, you

Jack Remick

want to have a go at it?"

"Wait," Connie said. "Daiva. What is she some kind of an oracle? A guru?"

"Post-lesbian," I said, "the way Daiva tells it, means that women have to shed all the skins we've ever worn."

"How can she imagine this stuff let alone write it?" Connie said. "You read it and you know she's writing what she knows. She's been raped. But that stoning on the beach? That bastard cutting the woman's throat for family honor—I wanted to declare war right there. She's a victim for sure."

"I can't answer that," I said.

"She writes like she's been raped," Connie said. "I want to talk to her."

"Post-lesbian," Eva said. "I want to know if she's gay. This is going to come down hard in some circles."

"She's a scientist," Estelle said, "and the science is first rate even when she projects it 350 years into the future. The genetics are state of the art. She knows what she's talking about. I know people who'd be interested in this."

"Is it possible?" Dani said. "This idea of parthenogenesis?"

"Not just possible," Estelle said, "it's now, right now, and she writes that in three hundred and fifty years we'll have the whole genome under control and we won't need men."

Dani said, "She's talking about what it means to be human."

Eva stood. She tugged at her skirt. She picked up her copy of *Citadel*. She said,

"You want to know what it means to be human? Well, that's what this book is about—what do we do with men? They're the problem. Women don't start wars. Women don't abduct girls and skin them alive. Women don't stone other women for being women."

"Yeah, sure, right," Regi said. "So all women now and in the future are pure, pristine, and without guilt."

"Women who get off track are just following their men," Eva said. "Listen to this."

74

# Citadel                                    **Daiva Izokaitis**

Humans walk around like they are something
special, but we're just a big joke that DNA
is pulling to see how many ways it can stretch
itself and still be the same. How do you feel
about being a molecular exercise, Jareth? So
DNA pushes us. We're its insurance that it
will be able to reproduce. Exos, Daughters,
fungi, insects, we're all just shells for DNA
replication. Exploitation at the molecular
level. We've got to refuse to be part of that
exploitation. Compromise is out of the
question.

"That," Eva said, "is evolution. And that's what she
means by a post-lesbian novel. The daughters don't need
men—the Y chromosome is an evolutionary warble, and as
she says men are just ambulatory weeds with inflatable
DNA injection tubes."

"Sperm donors," I corrected her. "Ambulatory sperm
donors with inflatable DNA injection tubes."

"I like that too," Eva said. "Can I steal it? Ambulatory
sperm donors with inflatable DNA injection tubes."

"I like everything about this book except…" Dani
paused to sip her wine.

I held my breath, wine glass at my lips. Dani said she
liked it. Now she didn't like it. I glanced at Clara who sat
quiet in her lace cuffs and dark leggings. Dani went on,

"…except, why does she see the future depending on the
Gland when they can practice parthenogenesis?"

I let out my breath, sipped my wine. Dani flipped to a
blue post-it in the text.

## Citadel                          Daiva Izokaitis

His sack was enormous. His penis thick and
heavy. The prepuce was dark chocolate. His pubic
hair a wiry swatch. Karim inserted the dialysis
needle into the left femoral artery, and as she
slid it in, she touched his penis with her elbow
and the Gland grunted and bucked but the
restraints held him. Karim's heart beat fast—
although she had extracted dozens of times—and
her hand trembled. She did not speak to him. She
could not speak to him. It was not protocol to
speak to a Gland in preparation.

"They use the Gland the way IV specialists use the alpha
donor," Estelle said. "It's genetics pushed to the end and
the end is the extinction of the Y chromosome."

"Yeah!" The women said in a chorus. "Ban the Y."

I saw *Citadel* coming to life in my living room in Santa
Monica up Latimer Canyon. Oh, Daiva.

"Ladies!" Clara said. "I need a yes or a no, I need some
direction. I have a publicity campaign to design for this
book and I want an early launch in New York. If you give it
a go."

"Fuck yes," Dani said, "give this baby a sendoff that
will make all those Exos think twice about what we are and
what we give them and what we can take away. You can't
trust them because truth is a foreign word to them."

"It's a novel, Dani," I said. My mind raced back to my
own escapades on the beach and the sex in my bed and the
men who could not give me what I could give myself.

"No," Dani said, "it's a manifesto for the salvation of
the human race."

I read the faces of the women—I had the romance
reader, I had the empirical scientist, I had the script
consultant, I had the cigar smoker in black leather. This was
what Clara wanted—a blockbuster that crushed genre and
surfed a crest into the future. Clara said,

"Okay. We have a consensus." She raised her wineglass.

"New York in six months." And she looked at me as if to say, Okay, kiddo, get to work. I finished my wine then stacked the copies of *Citadel* with their colorful tags and markers. I knew there would be notes, a lot of notes, notes that I would take to heart and in the end give to Daiva. I watched the wrap up.

Connie cut a slice of brie and laid it on a cracker.

Eva polished off a fourth glass of wine.

Regi and Estelle got into the science and what kind of review to write.

From across the room, Clara smiled at me.

I noticed the abrasions on her wrists. The lace didn't cover them. Makeup didn't cover them. I knew why Clara had been late. Her pheromone perfume, when it heated up, exuded the peculiar odor of semen. Oh, Clara.

## Trisha

I watched Clara fiddle with her glasses. Pensive. Holding a pen in her right hand, she studied the contract. She rocked back and forth in her desk chair. Then she slid the contract across the desk.

"We're committed now."

"And I'm off to the Desert Rose Motel," I said.

"Does that place even have wi-fi?"

"I'll connect with you when I get online."

"How long?" Clara said. "I need to get this in production as soon as I can."

"Three weeks."

"Okay. Three weeks," Clara said. "Then I send out the St. Bernard."

"Are you all right, Clara?"

"Why do you ask?"

"Sunday at the focus group, you came late."

"Nothing you need to worry about, Trisha. Get me that manuscript."

## Daiva

Two months before I gave *Citadel* to Trisha, Jahil and I

had begun the ICNI implantation process in the lab. I had harvested Jahil's ova, then my own. I had failed eleven times before I got a viable embryo. I remember that Friday. At mag 750 X, the ovum looked like a cluster of pink balloons floating in a viscous fluid. The nuclear cells from Jahil's injected ovum with my cytoplasm, my chromosomes. We had an embryo. 46 chromosomes, no sperm needed.

We kept the room we had set up for the implant warm. We knew temperature was critical for the open embryo transfer. Jahil was ready, nervous but excited as I inserted the siphon tongue through the cervix that I had dilated the day before. We had learned that her cervix had a slight bend in it so dilation made the implant both simple and easy. The tongue of the siphon was no bigger than the tongue of a butterfly.

Every day I checked the monitors. Jahil kept her own records to compare. I remember the first few implants had failed because Jahil had a low-grade UTI raised her body temperature and the embryo had not attached. Now we had things under control.

When I signed the contract, I didn't tell Trisha how far along we were. She didn't need to know. There was time for that.

§§§

# THE NICHE

## Trisha

Outside of San Bernardino, I turned north to Barstow, to
the desert. I liked driving the Z-Ray in the heat. The deeper
I got into the emptiness, the more Daiva's images from
*Citadel* crowded into my mind until even the opening
image of the Citadel seemed to be alive. The high walls, the
ovoid shell of the Solerian tower jutting up like the nucleus
of a cell. The bones in the ossuary. The images floated like
memories from dreams of a life I had once lived—bones
scattered, disarticulated skeletons, skulls fractured, femurs
shattered. Had I, at some time in the past, actually lived
through the Wars of Savagery? Had I been in the future at
the moment when the Niche collapsed and women turned
back into chattel, into objects of pleasure, into receptacles,
into birthing beasts? Every image felt familiar yet
disconnected, all roiling in a chaotic mix.

And the killing. Once it started no one could stop it.

I remembered sitting in the sun on the towel on the
beach in the sand, the day I dug into *Citadel* for the first
time.

As I read I had glanced at my toenails painted an absurd
purple. Two coupling flies landed on my left big toe. I had
wiggled my foot and the flies had flitted off then dropped
to the sand and again locked together. On the yellow ice
plant flowers, two butterflies—white with yellow-dotted
wings—perched, locked in their own mating embrace. I had
peeled my gaze away from the butterflies to two gulls
swooping and diving at one another. Animals mating.

79

My mind wandered back to that day. Across the sand four specimens were locked in their death-ritual. Volleyball—sweaty, bloody, sandy volleyball. The horror of sex had crushed me. I was the product of that same butterfly desire. The same desire that drove flies to mate, drove me to the beach. I imagined my mother sweating under my father in a bed somewhere in Spain, rutting, orgasming—did my mother orgasm the day she conceived me or was my moment of beginning a quiet, remorseful surrender?

We are all machines, sex machines with one Paleolithic purpose.

As I drove, I felt odd. Like something was eating my brain, sucking me dry.

I pulled to the shoulder and sat in the sun breathing hard and then behind me, I heard the crunch of gravel. Looking in the rearview mirror, I saw the patrol car, lights flashing. What had I done? The door opened. An officer exited—she wore the black uniform of the Highway Patrol. She had a pistol in a holster. She had on the trooper's hat with the stiff, wide brim, the crown with its four equally spaced indentations. She wore sunglasses. She leaned on the door and she said,

"License and registration, please."

What had I done? I didn't smell of wine. Driving too fast? Weaving across the line? I groped for my purse—my purse—where was my purse? The unsmiling officer scowled.

"I can't seem to find my purse."

"Step out of the vehicle, please. Hands on the door, please."

The officer took her time patting me down. Nothing to find, no pockets in the shorts, no weapons in a tank top in the sun in the desert. She said,

"License."

"License, I think I locked it in the trunk."

"Open it," she said. She stood with her hand on her pistol.

I pulled the trunk release and the snap of the lock reminded me that I had dropped the purse in the boot with my bag, the laptop, and the manuscript. The officer, leaning close, smelled of sweat and perfume. She said,

"That's a tight little space."

I dug the license out of the purse and handed it to the officer. She said,

"Where are you headed?"

"Did I do something wrong?"

"You were swerving around. Thought you might be loaded."

"A lot on my mind, sorry."

"Where are you headed?"

"Desert Rose Motel."

The officer handed the license back and asked if I was meeting someone out there.

"No, it's where I work."

"You know Bettina?"

"Bett? Yes," I said. "She and Kali...."

The officer moved back to her car, flicked off the flashing lights. Everything about her intrigued and scared me—the sunglasses, the black uniform, the hat that she took off as she sat behind the wheel. The patrol car shot around the Z-Ray leaving me standing in the sun holding my driver's license.

§§§

The Desert Rose Motel had a sawdust bar with no stools and a slew of tables in a dark room that smelled of beer and popcorn. The bartender, Bett, stood behind the bar in front of the mirror with its rows of whiskey bottles. Bett was a big woman with gray brush-cut hair and white shiny teeth. She glanced up as I entered.

"Goddamn," she said, "the writing lady with the frog name."

The first time I came to the Desert Rose I was working on a bondage novel called *Red, Red.* I didn't intend to stay but Bett took one look at me and said White Wine. I asked her how she knew. She told me that a bartender wasn't worth a shit if she couldn't read the customer. "You got white wine writ all over you—long hair, hot shorts, a chest full of goodies bundled up in that no-secrets-here stretch top. No earrings, no wedding band, and those sandals. White wine." I told her she had a writer's eyes for detail. I stayed and have been coming back ever since.

"How long this time, doll?"

"New book," I said. "Three weeks."

"Room 11," Bett said, "same as last time, okay?"

Bett laid the key to number 11 on the bar and poured a glass of Thunderbird infused-wine. A cowboy at one of the tables by the jukebox sauntered up to the bar. He wore a black Stetson, snakeskin boots, Levis with a heavy steer-head buckle, a white western shirt with turquoise snaps. He sidled up beside me, silent. I knew the silence. It was the beach meat query with grass in its teeth—nice tits. I sipped the two-month-old Thunderbird. Sweet, cold, medicine and reached for the key to room 11. Bett said,

"This is Jimbo."

"Hello Jimbo." Jimbo nodded. No grin, no flash of white teeth, no flexing.

"He don't talk," Bett said. "Took a vow of silence like a monk. Only whispers to his horse now and then."

Bett glanced away as the door opened and the officer who had frisked me entered. She pulled off her dark glasses and I saw her glowing golden eyes. The first woman I had ever seen with golden eyes.

"That's Rita," Bett said. "Just picked this beat."

"We met on the road."

"Yeah," Bett said. "She wants to know the lay of the land."

§§§

I camped out on the bed in the Desert Rose in the heat reading and what I read puzzled me—the *Planners*. All of it, the entire cosmology of *Citadel*, depended on the planners. Daiva had buried the section deep in the novel and that was bothersome. What was she getting at there?

## Citadel                          **Daiva Izokaitis**

The Planners had been invisible for three
hundred years. There was only one item on the
agenda for the Congress—the future and who would
inhabit it.

There was a planner named Eris who sent out
the details. She would run the Congress.


I called up SkyChat. The Desert Rose had a one-gig line.
The screen read "Calling Daiva—Do you want to
connect?" Of course I do. The screen changed from amber
to blue—that sweet innocent blue, and the tune played—
once, twice, three times before Daiva came online.

She wore her lab coat, lab glasses, her hair back in a
ponytail. She was in the lab with all its gear, its tanks and
bottles and machines.

I have a couple of questions. Why did you bury the
Planners so deep in the novel?

I had to bury them while I worked out their role.

There are some problems with the Planner scenes.

What's wrong with them?

As a reader, I have to know how the Planners decide
which kind of male a gravid daughter will produce.

It's informed choice.

Are the Planners political?

Yes. Everything is political. Next.

Don't be short with me, Dee. Will a daughter give birth
if she knows her baby is a Mutant?

Daiva rubbed her eyes. She looked tired. I missed her,
missed the wine, the talk, the stubbornness that Daiva used
like a whip.

The technicians edit the genome to produce Exos,
Mutants, and Glands.

But that's not natural selection and it's not sexual
selection.

As you said, it's a novel.

But the science has to be plausible.

83

It is plausible, right now, very plausible.

Why would Planners allow Mutant births if Mutants are the unevolved male with that hyper aggressive 13$^{th}$ gene?

To keep the entire genome alive.

You're saying the Planners don't tell a daughter which chromosome they'll use.

All the sperm come from the Glands. Glands are the male with the regressed 13$^{th}$ gene. The raw sperm itself isn't used—I make that clear in the Implantation section—but the embryos are cryogenically preserved and while they're in stasis, the DNA is edited. That editing will produce one of the three males.

That doesn't resolve anything, Dee. Readers will want to know why and who chooses.

It's random. I told you.

If the technicians silence a gene, can it be turned back on?

Yes. We can do that now. Silenced genes can be switched back on. The Mutants are males who have that switch left on and that's why they are killers.

But you limit the numbers of Mutants.

Have to. If you get too many they feed off one another and go testosterone crazy. I'll be back in a sec, Tee. Something came up. Just as sec.

I noticed the changes in Daiva. There was an aura of audacity around her that came through on the screen. At first glance, it seemed to be an aura of arrogance as well. I scrolled through the manuscript to the *Birth* scene.

**Citadel**                                    **Daiva Izokaitis**

Filina had not wanted to know the sex of the child, but now it is obvious that the infant is an XY. She did not ask the doctor or the geneticist about the growing body. She had not wanted an XY. She had not expected to have an XY. She had never thought she could bear an XY. She had been concerned only about giving another daughter to the Citadel. Her failure devastated

her. Following delivery, she was shielded from
her offspring until the Council had time to speak
with her. In her excitement, she experienced
only the physical meaning of birth, and the
distancing techniques worked so well. She hardly
noticed the child's absence. The breast pump was
the final step; its use assured that she would
not imprint to the child.


Sorry, had to take care of a couple of things. Where
were we?

Okay. Why don't the Planners let the technicians silence
the Mutant DNA sequence?

They do, but they switch it back on at random.

Why at random?

You don't understand evolution, Trisha.

Your utopia would be perfect if the Mutants didn't exist.

Men should not control human evolution.

Why shouldn't they?

Because they will make a mess of it just like they have
screwed up everything else.

Then why not edit the DNA to produce only Glands and
let the Exos and Mutants go extinct?

Daiva looked at her fingernails. She leaned close to the
screen. The circles under her eyes fed into the worry lines
in her forehead.

Are you all right? You look beat.

I am beat. To answer your question—the Glands are
males before divergence.

How much of this is possible now?

All of it.

In human society of the future, does the evolved male
lose language?

The male is an ambulatory inflatable DNA injection
tube, Trisha. That's how they evolved. That's all they are.
In the cosmology of *Citadel,* the daughters don't need the
male. They keep them alive until Congress makes a
decision and that means a consensus of all the Citadels.

You keep spinning around my questions.

With the extinction of the Y chromosome the race will

85

evolve in a way that we can predict.

Predict doesn't mean random. Have you found something you didn't put in the novel?

Maybe.

You're not going to answer my questions, are you, Dee?

No.

All right. New topic—I think we can cut the first two parts of *Women in Captivity*.

Cut them?

You don't have an antagonist.

Men are the antagonists.

That works theoretically, but in the novel, you need to single out one antagonist. You need to have one character who speaks for all the others. The spokesman.

You told me this novel isn't built on the three-act structure, Tee. You told me you liked that, so why do I need that tired old literary crap?

You have to give readers something they know and something they don't expect. I'm going to send you the edited sections of *Excursion* and *Women in Captivity*.

I won't have time to read them.

It's your novel. The contract says you approve my changes.

I like what you do—let's go with what you do.

If you're this easy the rest of the way, I'll be done before you get here.

Daiva signed off. The screen turned amber. I redialed. No reply. I weighed what she had just told me, then scrolled to the *Discovery* of a *Virgin Citadel*.

### The Exotic Relationship of the Editor to the Writing

Room 11 was hot. The bed in Room 11 was hard. The air in Room 11 was stiff and dry. I sat on the bed banging away at the computer on the board on my lap. That first image in *Citadel* still needed work. As I read the words I tried to remember what had brought me here to this room in this motel in the desert in the night to sit on this bed at the end of time thinking about the past and the future and I knew if I yielded to the past, I would give in and nothing would change. Jimbo. A cowboy who talked to his horse.

I stared at the screen, at the words, at the images under the words and those images overwhelmed me–images of bones in the desert, images of women drowned in their own urine, women burned to death in their own houses, women stoned to death, women bleeding in the sand, women raped by drunken men, women cauterized and tattooed and branded, women chained to beds, women raped by gangs of men, women disemboweled, their labia excised, their vaginas torn open, their wombs cut out—I glanced at the TV. I could not turn it on. I knew that the screen masked another river of blood. To turn on the TV meant to give in to its images of death, beheadings, crushed arms, severed hands, gouged and bleeding eye sockets—a stream of paralyzing images in the present piped in from around the world.

Jimbo and his silence. Why were the vicious ones silent? I looked away from the television to the screen of the computer on the board on my lap in the room of the motel on a highway at the end of time.

I was there to work. To find the story beneath the flood of violence that Dee had created.

The light from the computer screen with its words led to story that led to the images in a museum. Each book was a piece in the museum of all museums containing all the books that had ever been. That was writing—dropping into the darkness to bring back pieces never seen before. We do not need another Roman coin or another Maya artifact drawn from a cenote in the jungle where jaguars cracked the bones of time and men. We need a fresh, new objet d'art as unique as the first breath—which was exactly like every breath ever drawn in time—but unique in its time and that was *Citadel*.

Did Daiva know really about bones in the desert or had she made it up? To make it up she had to see into the darkest niches of her own mind. She had to look back at the clubs and the stones and the bludgeoning of women on their knees, women thick and gravid and pitiful and doleful, three million years of sadness carried forward in every woman now walking thick of belly and breast, heavy with milk, leaving trails of dead children in the sand on the long march to now.

I was there to work. I glanced at the phone.

The phone lay on the bed like a naked sleeping lover in the heat in the room in a motel in the desert. I picked up the phone. It was heavy.

The weight of civilization in my hand would break me if I gave in. If I dialed the phone. If I asked Dee how she knew these things. If I asked that, if I took her answer then nothing would have changed and I might as well lie dead with the women and their bones, so I did not dial but set the phone back on its pillow, dropped it back in time to where it belonged.

I had come there to work, to shut myself away from the world. There was only one world that mattered now and that was *Citadel.*

*The killing was three million years old, the phone less than three hundred.*

I looked again at the words on the screen of the computer that lay on the board in my lap. The computer with its splayed mouth, a slit between hand and the terrible gap where other writers had spilled their terror and that made me sad, a sadness millions of years long. What if these words meant nothing?

What if these words did not dive into the brain or the eyes or the ears?

The eye transmits the words to the brain.

The brain creates the image.

The image changes the mind of the woman reading it.

I re-read the opening of *Citadel.* I had changed it six times, each time digging deeper into it, each time betraying Daiva's vision of the future. I wanted in, but I could not get into the novel. I was always outside the walls looking in. The ferocity of the writing always shut me out. Outside, I read the words, but they were just words. I had to get inside. I had to let the story flow over me so that I drowned in the river of writing. I had to get inside or I would never know its heart. I had to get inside.

# Citadel                    **Daiva Izokaitis**

The silence of the Citadel becomes suddenly very intense. A structure so complex and huge ought to emit some sounds, but there is an awesome, deep silence which engulfs the entire Citadel. The silence anticipates sound, but sound is betrayed by silence and hugeness. Beneath the large silence there are small interruptions of quietness in the lacuna between the walls and the spindle, in the center of the cell, small islands surrounded by lakes lapping at the walls with pulsations rhythmic as a tongue on wet flesh.

Fountains spray fine jets of water from the lakes onto pieces of sculpture and statues. Dominating the statuary is the form of a daughter kneeling, a small child by her side, having gathered a flower she is examining. There are other fountains with other statues.

An editor needs a portal through the words that stand, each one a stop sign, a puzzle, a roadblock. Sometimes when I work, I am in a dream and in the dream I see where I should go, what I should do. I am the editor. I have to grasp the keys and turn the locks. There had to be a way to dig into the ugly world hiding beneath Daiva's cumbersome, sometimes bulging sentences that held sway with the weight of a heavyweight boxer regarding some sick and insane mystery. But the words, no matter how I shifted them, changed them, worked them, no matter what I did to them, they resisted me. Thick, heavy-weight, opaque words. Sometimes, just at the tip of consciousness, when I lie in the heat on my bed at the Desert Rose Motel in room 11, I glimpse the world under the words, the world beyond, glimpse insights into the thick teeming world hiding under meaning, hiding behind syntax, slippery insights that slide eel-like from my brain before I have time to seize them.

So it was on the beach, at first. I stood outside the story

watching the men stone the woman, watching the brother cut her throat. The editor cannot remain outside the words. I needed to get in the novel. I read. I dropped into a dream, a surreal waking dream where I was surrounded by words.

## Citadel                                   Daiva Izokaitis

The sun burns hot as the earth has turned just those few degrees of difference between dawn and day, and it becomes apparent why there were no lights visible in the Citadel. The sun hits the Solerian spindle on one side, brilliantly, dazzlingly, blindingly and the windows in the shadows are tinted dark, glass engineered to allow virtually nothing from the outside, not even sunlight, to penetrate. The occupant of a room could see out. So simply is the privacy of a person insured, even in this heavily populated complex. All this investigation, all this speculation, have taken but a few minutes; it is still early morning, perhaps not yet six o'clock. As the earth turns, the sunlight evaporates the minute particles of moisture suspended in the air, and as the warmth makes them vanish, the air becomes crystal clear. The temperature drops to chill and a person arising at this hour would certainly need a cloak of some kind, perhaps only a light covering over the shoulders.

As I read, a charge ran through me and I was there, alive, walking, dreaming inside the dream, a dreamer dreaming she was in a dream dreaming she was in a dream. The weight on me had gotten lighter. I was inside a Citadel, not a Citadel like any I had found in the novel so far, but a Citadel with cracked walls and shattered panels and stinking of fire and blood, and the rancid corpse smell of

90

the long dead. I was inside the word shell Daiva had thrown up to keep the unholy, the heretical out. I walked on cut glass, over splintered tables. My feet did not bleed. I knew that in time, I would bleed, as I dove deeper into this novel. Rounding a corner, I saw them—two daughters.

## Citadel        Daiva Izokaitis

They were in a broken laboratory, just the two of them. I knew their names. Zia raised her head as I entered. Rei held up a hand. She said,

You don't belong here. And Zia said,

Don't talk to her, Rei. She'll cut you out.

Rei lowered her hand.

I said, What is this place?

It's one of the Virgin Citadels destroyed at the end of the *Wars of Savagery*.

Why haven't I been here before?

You haven't been here before because Daiva doesn't know it is here.

But how can you, a character in her novel, know something she, the author, doesn't know?

She might be the writer, but she knows only what we tell her.

I fingered the ashes smeared on the desktop. The ash on my index finger tasted of Citron, acidid. I stepped over the ruins of computer screens and broken solar panels. I felt a deep anguish and sorrow for each broken piece as if I were broken too.

Zia said, Are you all right?

I don't think so. If I can't trust her words, how can I trust her at all?

Rei laughed, a snickering laugh, and she choked. Zia clapped her on the back and I felt the smack as though it was me Zia had slapped.

I knew then that I was as deep into *Citadel* as I could be. I, the editor, had become a character in the novel that, as I changed it, changed me. I saw how everything was possible. There was a river of words running over me.

In the ceiling of the destroyed laboratory, I saw shining sliding water but I was not drowning—I was in the dura mater of my own system, in the universe I was creating with Daiva.

I said to Zia,

Do you know what happened here?

What happened here is what happened everywhere in the first times After Foundation.

Foundation. I tasted foundation. It was a word like any other word without meaning until set in the verbal stream of other words, but it had its own taste and smell—burnt sugar, caramel—a sweet taste. I felt the harsh, deep undercurrent of the word-river. Did any two words ever taste the same?

Yes, but what happened here?

Rei kicked at a pile of ashes and her toe cracked metallic and Zia said,

Rei and I were here.

We were here, Rei said, until she forgot us.

We broke away After Foundation, Zia said. We wanted nothing to do with the East, but the killers came for us. They hunted us until there were no more of us and then they destroyed the Citadel.

Where are we? I insisted.

In the desert, Zia said. This could have been C-1, the first Citadel After Foundation and you were here.

I was here? I said.

She hasn't told you? Rei said. Like all word-goddesses she keeps secrets from her creations, but I've had enough of her. I want you to cut me. I don't want to be in the novel not one more day.

You never were in it, Zia said.

But I see you, I said.

No, you see the residue of a character who has no history. A thought is all she is. She exists without a backstory, a character who has no needs, who wants nothing, and can't ever have anything. She is just a shadow.

And you? How did you get here?

I don't know, Zia said. But you can't trust your creator.

Rei raised her hand. Light beamed through the skin, a pale pink light that turned gray and in a rush Rei disappeared.

I looked at Zia who stood statue still as though she had lost all meaning. She was a wanderer, a backstory with no sequence. Zia turned away. I saw gaping holes in her. She was not complete. She was half-drawn. Rei was not the only unfinished, forgotten character.

Wait, I said. I can save you. I can make you real.

No you can't. Zia faded into the light. And I was alone.

I came awake with a jolt. Coming back was jarring.

I stared at the screen of the laptop on its board on the bed in Room 11 of the Desert Rose Motel. I saw then the trigger—taste—the portal, the doorway into the words. The trick was to find the story living inside me and it had to be the story that was living inside *Citadel* that was living inside Daiva. For the first time I felt a connection to Daiva that went beyond skin and blood and bone and let me float on the undercurrent where all new writing came from.

Writing is dangerous because words are only an intermediate step between writer and reader where feeling detaches from each word with the cruelty of a butterfly emerging from its chrysalis. The pain, the tragedy of existence, the theater of desire, all live under the words that are never anything but a wild guess at the river of emotion living in each cell, feeding on desire and hungry for being. The magic is not in changing words, but in spreading language over the residue of desire.

I eased the cover of the laptop closed. All the silence that had ever been in my waking world hung right there in the air of room 11 in the heat of the desert. I had passed through the gate to the Citadel. I had passed through the high wall with its shield of green and glass. I was inside all the Citadels at once. I tasted the words. I became a character speaking in character voice, taking dictation from the daughters, feeling the truth of the writing.

I could come and go at will. I felt their pain, I felt their desire.

What is desire?

Desire is what remains when sex is stripped from its gamete.

Desire is the driver of what you are.

Desire is your pain.

Desire is your love.

Desire is your choice.

Desire is your craving to connect.

Desire is you in your ancient skin.

I had lost all connection to everything I had been before. I was no longer in the motel room in the desert. I was surrounded by walls and the taste. Each word had a flavor and each word rode on a river ...

## Citadel                              Daiva Izokaitis

Inside, the walls yield to a labyrinth. Inside, windows form an inner sheath facing the Solerian. The daughters dwelling behind that sheath are a mystery. Inside the walls there is a glass membrane connecting the inner face of the walls to the rising structure in the center. The daughters who inhabit this Citadel look inward. They have no links to the outside. There is no past. The solid walls are blank. The message is unmistakable—the inhabitants choose not to look at the outside world.

labyrinth:peppermint.
sheath:vanilla.
Mystery:chocolate.
Walls:orange.
The:papaya.
Looked:lemon
Daughters:guava.
Solerian:cherry
Of:orange
Inward:apple.

Taste was the key. Taste was the way in.

This book, *Citadel*, that spread its words on the screen
of the computer on the board on my lap, this book was a
feast and as I savored the words the tastes melded and
fused and flooded my mouth and I ate the novel, ate the
words that blossomed on my tongue and in my brain the
images floated alive and singing—

> The walls are high, so high that standing at
> their base she sees them rise into the sky
> forever and she is alone...

Alone? She? Was it better in second person? Third
person? Alone. I wanted that grape flavored word again but
it was not there—not on the screen of the computer on the
board in my lap. I saw myself in the story, words drifting
behind me, each word looking for a place in the river of
words that Daiva had brought out of the void and I was
alone—yes, better in first person, we live in the time of
verbal selfies, cameras, videos. When the writer has no
story, when the writer has no structure, all that is left is the
residue of memoir, the pool of experience. Experience, the
mother of fiction, filtered through all time must be broken
into fragments and pieced together with gold and not
recounted. My dictum led me into the broken silence. I
penetrated the walls of the Citadel and my first words
were—

> Where am I?

My voice echoed off the high walls lined with ivy and colored like some fantastic painting set in motion. I saw them—the daughters of the Citadel. I recalled that night in my house in the canyon with the focus group and Connie saying she felt like the author of *Citadel* had written it just for her, her alone, for no other. I remembered thinking that was what good writers do—they tell the story that is in you and it is for you alone, for no other being in the world and it is not memoir.

I was jealous. No one else had a right to read this novel—it was mine. I was making it mine, mine alone, the possession that possessed me as I possessed it.

I entered the inner rooms of a Citadel and I saw them dead—hundreds of them dead—how did Daiva know this? Had she made up the *Origin of Plague*? The *Wars of Savagery*? The *Wars of Religion?* No. There had been Wars of Savagery, Wars of Religion. There had been plague and death, always death. There on a computer screen I saw the words *parthenogenetic births*. This then was one of them, one of the Virgin Citadels, a citadel where the daughters did not milk the semen from brown-skinned Glands, did not give birth to XYs or Exos and Mutants, but only to daughters. Daughters of daughters who said no—*saying no, Daiva wrote, is to deny civilization; to say no is to say kill me because the XY with its 13$^{th}$ killer gene is homicidal— gynocidal—the killer of all killers and the virgin Citadels redefined human—human, three million years in the making, human meant an X mates with a Y and the XX and the XY have forty-six chromosomes and that is natural, that is human, but in the Virgin Citadels the daughters redefined evolution and in redefining evolution redefined human and there, in the Citadel, they lay dead.*

I eavesdropped on Deeta and Ket. They ignored me. Back again to being just a reader, a listener…

Deeta said, "It was a wildfire virus."

"Why isn't this Citadel on the map?"

"Some of the Virgin Citadels broke free, set themselves free."

"Even knowing they might die?"

"Better to die free than die with a mouth full of cum or have a Mutant Exo murder you."
I dreamed Daiva, wineglass in hand, lying on the sand on the beach by the sea on a towel saying as if it were the most natural thing in the world—men are afraid women will laugh at them. Women know men will murder them if they step out of their place.

## Citadel                                    Daiva Izokaitis

    Trisha sat at the computer in the data room
of the Virgin Citadel. She remembered Connie in
the focus group saying there were four men, I
never saw their faces, they took me to a cabin
and raped me for three days and then they threw
me naked in the street in the night in front of
my house. Trisha wept.
    Her tears landed in the dust of the data room
and Deeta said, "Let's find the labs, there will
be files."

I closed the screen, pulled out of the maw of the laptop on the board on the bed in the motel in the desert on the highway at the end of time and I called up SkyChat, dialed Daiva. Waited for the screen to turn from amber to blue.
Daiva looked beat. Her mussed hair was hanging loose. She wore a stained lab coat.
Tee, why are you calling again?
Can you come? I need to see you.
Are you drinking?
I'm going crazy.
You sound drunk.
It's your novel. I hate it. I hate you.
Why do you hate it?
I hate it because it's driving me crazy. It makes me think everything I don't want to think. It makes me think everything about life that I hate. I don't want to think that every man in my life is a murderer. Your book gets inside

my head and turns me into someone I don't want to be. I hate it, I hate you. I don't think Clara should publish this.

We have a contract, Trisha.

I'm going to talk to Clara about that. I've finished two sections I need you to check.

I don't have time to read right now.

You have to. I'm going to send you notes with my suggestions and I need you to accept them or change them. For example, you've got two important scenes that are too much alike.

Which two scenes?

The Virgin Citadels and the Rogue Citadels.

There is no Rogue Citadel scene.

I just read it.

So now you're not just changing my words, you're writing my novel. You're going to rewrite everything I've done. When you do that, it's no longer mine.

No. I mean it needs work. You know it needs work. I told you on the pier it needed work. Clara told you it needs work. It's in the contract. I'm working on it. Dee…but you have to help me. If you don't want me to rewrite your story you have to read my notes. I need your guidance.

Send the file.

I tapped the append tab, the file zipped off.


**Citadel**                                      **Daiva Izokaitis**


The gates were open. The hunters waited in the tall grass outside the walls. Bril crouched. She sniffed the air. Overhead, a flight of vultures soared. Finger to her lips—silence—she studied the path up to the gate—the grass had grown over the path, no footprints leading up to the gate…The silence was complete, the wind grazing the grass made no sound.

She said: "Something is wrong."

Deeta, rising, walked toward the gate, her

net slung over her shoulder, her hand on the bladed scabbard at her waist. Bril said,

"Where are you going?"

Turning, Deeta said,

"Death, can smell it."

"You don't know what's in there."

"Let's find out."

The two hunters approached the gate that hung agape—not broken, not hammered in, hanging free.

Deeta entered. Bril expected a cry, a call, a warning, but there was only the silence.

Skeletons, bones, the antique scent of decay, of bodies unburied. Bril, beside her. Looking deep into the shadow of the atrium, Deeta saw bones everywhere. Stacked together as if caught in a mob, spread out in twos and threes, felled in mid-stride as they ran. Clothing tattered. Rags adrift in the breeze.

Every skull had been crushed, every bone shattered. You could still feel the chaos even though the flesh had long ago decayed. Bril said:

"I've read about this in the archives. This was a Virgin Citadel."

Deeta knelt, eyes tracking the bony funeralscape. She said,

"What do you think killed them?"

"Probably a virus. But the crushing came later."

The hunters tracked to the core with slow steps. Bril sniffed the air. Deeta, heart pounding hard with each step, entered the graveyard.

On the walks in front of every building the bones lay in place. Here unbroken, intact, bones of girls, bones of the older daughters, their hair gray and beside them, still more young bodies, hair golden or black or auburn still unturned by time or age. Bril said,

"They all died at once."

"No Exos, no Glands."

"The VCs didn't breed Glands."

Deeta and Bril, in defile like warriors, entering rooms, discovered more bodies, more bones and in the pent-up closeness of the now open rooms, the stench of death hung so heavy Deeta gagged. Hands on her knees, she said,

"I can't believe this."

"They all died at the same time," Bril said. "Let's find the lab-center. There will be files."

"If they had time," Deeta said.

"Why isn't this one on the map?"

"Some of the them were never mapped," Bril said. "They all went Separatist."

"But how?"

"They had the technology. Our clan didn't believe in isolation from the Glands."

Deeta opened a door. Lights came on.

"The solar is still alive," she said.

Bril walked around the room looking one by one at the screens and panels, at the skeletons draped across desks, their hands still on a machine, a screen, reaching out for something. She said,

"It must have been a wildfire virus to spread this fast."

"Bril," Deeta said. "Are we contaminated?"

"I don't know."

"We can't go back if we're sick."

"If it was a virus, and it had to be a virus—they didn't breed and we were always afraid of this because they were susceptible. Could have been a cold, a flu, anything. Maybe something engineered."

"Are we contaminated?" Deeta said again.

"The virus is probably dead."

"Probably dead?"

"Shhh," Bril said.

She knelt behind a desk, Deeta beside her, blade drawn.

Deeta heard the dry harsh rattle of bones. She raised up, just above the desk and she saw

100

him.

He was tall, muscular. Ebony skin, bearded and black haired. His arms were sinewy, his legs shiny with sweat. Deeta's mind raced. She pointed at the net on her shoulder and Bril gripped her blade and just as Deeta rose to full height, the Gland disappeared out the door.

Deeta lunged after him, but Bril drew her back.

"No," she whispered. "Not yet. He'll still be here, their range is small, he'll be here, we have to take back something from here, to put it on the maps."

"What then?" Deeta said.

"We need data. We need to take bones back. We'll send the archeologists here. If it was a virus our labs will need to know."

"Bones? You're going to take bones back to the Citadel?"

Deeta knelt, facing Bril, she said:

"We don't see a single Exo or Gland skeleton. Are they immune? Are the Exos immune?"

"I don't know. I've just read about them. We have to get to the lab-center."

Bril tugged open a door. The closed room still reeked of decay, and on the walls, stains of exploded flesh. Skeletons. Still in their robes and vests lay sprawled in mid-step.

"Here," Deeta said.

She lifted a journal. The page still open to an entry.

215 AF Floral 21.

She read the faint letters written in a shaky hand—"no stopping it.."

She flipped back a day. She read,

215 AF Floral 20. "Pustules erupted today."

Deeta leaned against the desk, the bones of the scribe clattering to the floor. She said,

"Why?"

"The Planners knew this could happen. They had a choice. There are others, there were

101

```
others. We have to find data."
    "What are you looking for?"
    "Samples of young and old for the lab."
    "They're all related, aren't they?" Deeta
said.
```

I waited for Dee's reaction to the scene. She must know the text, what was taking her so long? I was about to make a note about quotation mark consistency and tense agreement when she came back on—

You changed the names in the *Virgin Citadel* scene. I don't like it.

Your point of view floats, Dee. At times, I don't know who's seeing what or who's speaking. I have to fix that or they'll kill us in New York.

Leave it the way I wrote it.

I can't. Each scene needs a single point of view. Point of view lets the reader know who sees, smells, tastes, hears in the scene. In this novel, you have at least five points of view. You have First Person Present, Third Person Past, Collective Point of View, Second Person Omniscient, and Third Person Omniscient—sometimes in the same scene. I have to fix all of that. Look at the opening scene—it's in Second Person...

Does it matter?

There are three basic points of view—I, He/She, and You.

Does anyone care about that anymore?

I pulled up the opening of *Rogue Citadel* and pasted it into SkyChat—

```
    From a distance, you see that this is an
ancient place. Its walls are scarred with
moss and scabbed with vines. The only color
is green.
```

What's wrong with that?

The way you wrote it, you switched to the First-Person point of view.

It only has you in it.

I fixed it. Switching point of view in the middle of a section is amateur.

If it's so much work don't do it.

I haven't started on structure yet.

Maybe we don't publish.

Listen to me, Daiva. This is an important book.

Manuscript, story, novel. You told me it's not a book until it has an ISBN.

You're right. I'm wrong. It would be easier if you were here. Can you come out?

Not yet. I have the baby to worry about.

You're pregnant?

No, Jahil.

Jahil? She's a character in your novel.

We're collaborating. She's an M. D., Ph. D. specialist in embryology and genetics.

Who else in this novel is an associate of yours?

Daiva broke the connection, the screen turned from blue to amber.

Pregnant? Jahil?

What was true?

What was made up?

I scrolled through the *Rogue Citadel* scene and smelled *yellow*. Under the smell an ocean of anguish flooded over me. I was an observer, reading now, but the smells were orgiastic.

## Citadel                                    **Daiva Izokaitis**

Lea shoved the door open. A flight of yellow birds squawked into the sunlight. Lea watched them flutter through the gap in the ceiling.

"It's clear," she said.

Kam entered, cautious as she always was, weapon ready, eyes sharp. She said,

"You scare me when you just barge in like that, Lea."

Lea, staff in hand, studied the quiet, surveyed the wreckage – chairs swamped in dust, papers scattered, some clustered against the walls. Blackened smear on concrete where a blast from some weapon had torn a gap in the wall.

Taking a deep and cautionary breath, Lea smelled the faint odor of death. It was not the raw, stinking odor of new decaying flesh, but the old musty smell of flesh long left alone. She strode to a closed door, pushed it open with the tip of her staff. The room was sealed—no windows, no torn roof.

Lea pulled back, Kam behind her. Bodies clustered together as if they had, in life, run away from their killers only to find themselves in a sealed room. So many, they seemed to have clawed over the dead to the top trying to escape. But there was no escape.

In the room, there were no blasts from weapons on the wall, no dried, crusted blood, just bodies.

Lea knelt and tried to count—girls, adolescents, women, their clothing torn, their bodies mummified with time.

Kam pushed in, she gasped. She knelt beside the stack of corpses, now leathery. She pointed to the body of a small boy. He had been barefoot when he died. He had worn a smock of blue cotton when he died.

"A male," Kam said. Leah touched her shoulder, felt the quivering muscle, the tense and tightly drawn muscle. "This one is a rogue," Kam said.

"It's not on the map," Lea said.

"No one mapped the rogues."

Lea turned back to the room with the broken chairs, the ruined walls. "Let's get out of here," she said.

"I can't," Kam replied.

"You don't want to know any more than you already know," Lea told her.

"How do you think they died?"

"Suffocated in here sealed up," Leah said. "Come on. We have to look for data. We're here for data."

"I don't need data," Kam said. Her voice quivered, still on her knees, she sobbed. "All of them."

"Look," Lea said. "There's nothing we can do. Come on. Let's get to the data center."

"Why? We know what happened."

"We need to take back what we find."

"My mind is made up," Kam said.

She rose, eyes vicious, mouth hard and even a little bit cruel.

They had been mapping Citadels for a month. In Citadel 125, Lea had read about the rogues. The Citadels that broke from the union rebelling against the wisdom of the Planners. They had cut loose in AF 210. Half a dozen of them. Free, they did not send emissaries to the conferences, they did not contribute data to the libraries or to the Planners. They had broken free and this was their reward.

Lea guided Kam from the killing place, heading through the Citadel—so small not more than a hundred daughters could have lived there. It was small, but the plan was the same everywhere. That much they had taken with them.

And then in the recesses, Lea came to the data center. She paused.

It had been ransacked, torn apart as though it were a body bleeding.

Picking up strewn papers, cracked and yellow, she read dates—AF 216, AF 220, and then nothing. No more dates. Nothing but death. The dead.

And that lone boy, a single Exo. A lone Gland? What was he?

"We will need a bone sample from the boy," Lea said. "We will need bone samples from the daughters."

"This is your data," Kam said. "All the data you need. They reintegrated. They died."

"This was a Rogue Citadel," Leah said. "They made their decision."

"And they paid," Kam said. "The women knew

105

the men would slaughter them. They knew it before the Wars of Religion. They knew it and they still went rogue."

"Of course they knew it," Lea said. "That's why we need the bone samples from the boy. If the 13$^{th}$ gene is intact it will give us a data point we need."

"Data point?" Kam's voice was as sharp as the flint tips of Lea's staff. "They are dead. All of them, they are dead—they starved, they suffocated, they died because they let the Exos back in."

Lea knelt on the dusty floor, gathered pages together. Under a desk hidden by a footstool, she found a notebook.

It was written in the old script, before foundation—it was hard to read, but she made out the first page. It was a history of Citadel 102 before reintegration. Halfway into the notebook, she came to a line,

*First chaos, first death* .

Flipping to the end, she saw that the last entry was AF 235. The script was in the new style, a new hand. Legible. *New here. Came in from the hunt, found daughters gutted, torn apart...*

And there it ended.

Lea closed the notebook. It was all she needed. She still checked the machines and the vault. The vault was empty, the machines smashed. It had all happened at once. All that death in one day.

"Look at this," Lea said. She stood with the notebook in hand but Kam was gone. Tracking her through the dust was easy. Kam knelt in the killing room. She had cut the boy's hand from his arm. It lay on the floor beside the foot of one of the daughters.

Lea watched her companion. She had refound herself, recalled her duty, remembered why they were out tracking.

Lea waited until Kam had cut three hands free—
one from the young girl, one from an adolescent
in a green smock, one from one of the elders.
And then Lea said,

"Are you ready?"

Kam wrapped the hands in her bag. Her staff
in one hand, she said,

"I'm sorry I came apart."

"Who wouldn't?" Lea said.

"What do you have?" Kam asked her.

"All the electronics are ruined, but I found
the Planner's Journal. It's in the old style,
most of it anyway. It has the coordinates of the
Citadel. It's not much, but now we have an exact
date."

"And now we have their bones," Kam said.

§§§

I turned off the computer, closed the laptop. I glanced at
my hair in the mirror—tangled, stringy, unwashed,
uncombed. I rubbed my cheeks and pulled down my
eyelids to see a river of red in my eyes. I needed eyedrops.
I was hungry. I had to eat.

Four days without a shower and my body odor was a
ripe soup of sweat and anxiety. When I'm in the desert, I
don't wear undergarments, no bra, no under pants, no
panties, no thongs, no tangas, no hi-cuts, no hipsters, no
bikinis. But I had to eat. My stomach growled as I wiggled
into the tight white shorts I had tossed on the chair by the
door and I pulled a blue T-shirt from the suitcase on the
floor in front of the flat screen. I slipped on a pair of
floppies.

§§§

A wooden arcade leads from the rooms to the Desert
Rose lobby. There were no cars in the lot where a
motorcycle gleamed in the desert sun, a black bike with

black saddlebags and chrome handlebars—a big bike—still with the passenger pegs flared out.

The bar smelled of cannabis and beer and perfume. The jukebox was playing a forlorn song about a man and a woman for a woman and a man slow dancing to a sad tune.

The blue light of the bar was comfortable and cool after the knife-sharp desert air. I sat at the bar. Bett came up and said,

"Hey little girl how's the writing going?"

Bett wiped at imaginary rings of beer glasses on the bar. I was mesmerized by Bett's tattoos and the rings on her fingers. She had thick forearms wreathed with blue and red roses. Each of her fingers was tattooed on the middle joint with a single blue eye of Uto. She said,

"What can I get you, doll?" Her deep blue eyes were ringed with red as if she had been crying. I said,

"You need some eye drops?"

"Eye drops don't heal a broken heart."

"What happened, Bett?"

"Other than my life going down the toilet, nothin'."

Bett folded the bar towel and hung it from the rack. She leaned close. Her breath was whiskey strong. She said,

"Sometimes I think I oughta just kill myself."

"You want to talk about it?" I said. The jukebox wrapped up its mournful song and another tune spun but the dancers didn't change beat or pace—still glued together, still stoned.

"What you don't know, hon, can't eat your heart out. What'll you have?"

"Steak," I said, "thick, medium rare, French fries, and some kind of salad."

"This ain't the Plaza, hon. I got the steak, I got the fries, but all you get's sliced tomato and maybe a pickle."

"That's good. I'm going back to LA day after tomorrow. I'll bring you some fixings."

"Whatcha going to LA for?"

"Got to see my shrink."

"Writing that book's that bad, huh?"

"I've been seeing her for five years."

"Is it doing any good?"

"She thinks I'm still crazy."

"Let me get Kali on that steak and you can tell me all about it."

Bett went to the kitchen. I spun on the barstool to look at the dancing couple in the blue light. The man had a big belly, he wore an armless T-shirt, black, and boots also black. Jeans with a black leather belt. A chain hung from his waist to his right hip pocket. His eyes were closed. The woman in leather pants and a leather vest looked happy. Bett returned and spread her hands on the bar.

"Okay, genius, stun me."

"Four questions," I said, "in this novel I'm working on—four big big questions."

"Nothing I can't handle," Bett said. "I tend bar at the Desert Rose, last stop on the road to Emptyholesville. Ain't nothing I ain't heard, ain't nothing I ain't seen, some shit I ain't done, but there's still time."

"Okay. What do you think about stopping aging and death? Should the Citadels reintegrate the Exo-culture? Should they stop all male births for five generations? And last—what is a human?"

Bett chewed the inside of her lips. She nodded, taking her time. She said,

"I been hoping for more of that butch errawtica you worked on last couple of times you come out here but this sounds like the writer ain't never smelled the bearded tulip."

"There's some of that, but what about stopping aging and death? If you could, would you?"

"Sure," Bett said, "who wants to die?"

"What if you could pick the age to turn off the aging gene?"

"Huh" Bett said. "Nineteen. At nineteen, you still got your ass, your tits still shout hallelujah, you've got baby fat and you're kinda stupid but still cute. Nineteen."

"Okay. Second question—should the Citadels reintegrate with the Exo culture?"

"Exo culture?" Bett said, "by that you mean—just what the fuck do you mean?"

"Three kinds of males in the future, Bett. Glands, Mutants, and Exos. Exos are degenerates with the killer gene switched off. Glands are the ambulatory sperm donors. Mutants are the evolved male with the 13$^{th}$ gene active and intact and the thick brow ridge."

"Um," Bett said, "Drop that one on me again, sugar. My mind sort of took off there on that sperm donor thing."

"To reintegrate," Trisha said.

"Nah. Once you get rid of vermin, let'em be."

"That gets to questions three and four. Stop all male births for five generations and what is a human. Last one first—where is that steak?"

"Kali! What's the hang up in there?"

The couple on the dance floor stayed plastered together while the music changed, then restarted their slow shuffle.

"Coming out," Kali said. She swung into the barroom balancing a plate with steak and fries on one hand. She set the steak in front of me. I smelled the fat and the butter. Kali smothered her T-bones with butter that sizzled when she broiled them. The edges turned brown. Sliced mushrooms covered the steak. A pile of fries. I plucked a fry and tasted it and hummed, the salt was good.

The music stopped. The two dancers left the bar. The man in black caressed the woman's behind as they filed out the door.

I cut a slice of steak and let the juices fill my mouth. Kali said,

"You like meat, love?"

"Human," Bett said, "well, hon, I think you just seen human in action—steak and fries and a man's hand on a woman's ass."

I let that sink in as I sliced another hunk of steak and chased it with a long brown French fry. The tastes melded in my mouth. Bett said,

"You're moaning, hon."

"It's the way Kali cooks her meat."

"In the world this writer's writing about in this book, do they have steak and fries?"

"In this novel that's driving me nuts they have the technology for parthenogenetic birth."

"Partheno what?"

"Women get pregnant without using the DNA injection tube."

"Shit," Bett said, "you mean a man's dick."

"You got it, hon. So what do you think of that?"

"Women gupping without men? Huh. Let me think on it. I'll get back to you in 350 AF but believe you me, you can't turn off sex."

"AF. So you are listening when I talk about this novel?"

"I listen 'cause you're cute," Bett said. "That cop, Rita, thinks you're cute too."

"Rita thinks I'm cute?"

"Every time she drops in she asks about that cute little writer."

"I'm not nineteen."

"Nineteen or not, you're the cutest thing holed up in the Desert Rose."

I finished the steak, licked the salt from the last fry and went back to room 11. In the parking lot, the motorcycle still glistened in the sun.

§§§

The room was still cool, the A/C hummed. I kicked the flipflops back by the door. Pulled off the shorts and the T-shirt and lay on the bed. As I turned on the laptop, I thought about Bett and Kali. I talked to them because the editor has to step outside her safety zone to get a look at another mind-set and worldview. It's the only way to discover what needs to be done with the text that exists as a hermetically sealed vision until you break it open.

Talking to Bett, reading pieces of *Citadel* to her and Kali let me give up who and what I was so I could see what the others might pull from the work. Bett had said I had just seen human in action—steak and fries and a man's hand on a woman's ass. Was it that simple? If so, why did Daiva go so deep into the question of what was human?

As I read to Bett and Kali, the deeper I read into *Citadel*, and the deeper I read, the more clearly I understand why Daiva wrote this novel. *Citadel* wasn't about sex or

111

divergent evolution, it was about greed. Destruction and Murder.

Daiva was showing us how the race was committing collective suicide. Men, driven by some horrid and unconscious motivation, were killing everything that moved, everything that was not them. It was clear that the drive to kill was hiding deep in human beings. Death and killing had become a religion to men. Murder was their ritual. It was there, the drive to murder, but Daiva gave it a metaphor—the 13th gene. In the ritual of murder, the sacrament was blood. Women bleed and their blood means life. Men can never forgive women for being the bringers of life. And in *Citadel* where the daughters don't need the Y to create life, the hatred and jealousy overpowers. As they slaughtered all the beasts, men were left with women who produced the life that the men could not do without as they strove to spread their religious dogma.

At its root, religion, as Daiva creates it in *Citadel,* is a disease of the body, of the mind, of the spirit. I saw that clearly now. Maybe Daiva was not so clear on it, but she, like all artists, had closed her eyes to the world around her and had burrowed deep inside and there she had found truth. Truth was a monster. There was no redemption.

Now, I had to see how she worked it out in detail and metaphor. How many ways could she say *death?* How many indexes to killing could she give us? The spine of the novel was Death and Life, not Male and Female. The polarity that ran so deep and flowed out of the unconscious was frightening. How many men would say outright that they were murderers? That they had thought about killing? The ones who didn't or couldn't say it, reaped the rewards of those who sowed fear by shedding blood. I saw that the central metaphor in *Citadel* is safety. Living in the closed circle of the Citadels, the daughters are safe. Their lives are safe. When I took *Citadel* to the focus group, Regi had sarcastically commented that all women now and in the future are pure, pristine, and guiltless. I see now that Daiva has worked this—women will kill but it is because they have been hurt. They have been raped, violated, tortured, betrayed and in that they are infected with the male disease of murder. Women, Daiva writes, live to be loved and love is a residual evolutionary response. In *Citadel* the utopia hinges on that need. Post-lesbian? *Citadel* is not post-lesbian, it is post-death. It might even be post-family. To be safe, you must refuse betrayal and rape and torture. I saw that in *Citadel* Daiva was saying if you can give up the need to be loved, you can separate from the flow of evolution long enough to preserve the race, long enough to decide if the race can overcome the male push toward self-annihilation—the cultural suicide that drives men to destroy themselves and to destroy the world.

## Citadel                    Daiva Izokaitis

### The Four Postulates

We refuse our option to stop all male births for five generations because we cannot allow ourselves to assume the power to put to death and then to resurrect out of time beings whose absence would make them alien to the system that generated them.

To kill the beast entirely would be tantamount to destroying the race, and to the extent that daughters and males evolved from a common origin, we acknowledge the right of the species to live, albeit in limited numbers which we will ascertain and maintain in balance with nature and our desire.

We choose therefore not to annihilate the human race as a species of life upon the earth, bound into an ever changing, non-simultaneous chain of events, and in so choosing, we assert our belief that life with its vicissitudes is better than death.

We further assert that to live is a choice that we make in full consciousness of the possibility of death, but we henceforth commit ourselves to the investigation of the possibilities of eternal life within a single body.

Note to Daiva: What are you thinking? This doesn't belong here.

I can't tell who has the point of view in the whole section.

You can't just drop stuff like this into the story and hope it connects.

This is a novel. The language is so distant it belongs in A Ph.D. dissertation.

I call that "armored" prose, Dee, because it's hard to get into it and when you try to read it you kind of bounce off. You string archaic words such as "henceforth" all the way through. We have to think about cutting them.

I'm coming to town tomorrow. We can talk about this then.

Does post-lesbian mean post-family? T.

§§§

I spent the next ten hours reading and making notes before I came to the *Congress*. I was confused. The first time I read it, I was skimming, but now I dug into the story. From the first words, I knew Daiva had gone into a dark place. A Planner, Eris, was speaking—

**Citadel**                    **Daiva Izokaitis**

The Planners convened this Congress to evaluate the effects of fifteen generations of separation from the Exo-culture.

No binding law required to consider the fate of the race or to continue the status quo with its divisions. Each Citadel would select two delegates to the Congress. There only one item on the agenda—the future of the race and who will decide it.

Within the Citadels, biology and choice have led to divergent points of view regarding the Exo-culture. The still-radical, futuristic daughters, never having known any other way, nor, by their admission, wanting to, are opposed to integration, while some historical sentimentalists, unchanged by the argument of our genetics, are in favor of immediate re-integration.

The gyneologists and macrohistorians, aware of the dangers, predict that reintegration would be catastrophic. They cannot dictate a course of action, but they suggested that, before any decision, the Congress needed more data.

The anthropologists agree that added information is needed because much of what is known about the Exo-culture is obsolete. In the beginning, any excursion from the foundation Citadels into the Exo-culture took place in full battle dress and loathing. In the early days, the Wars of Savagery were still fresh in memory.

Contact for the past ten generations has been limited to the Hunt or infant exchange excursions. Most daughters have never seen an Exo while the images they do have are archival. Each generation's knowledge of the past has grown more static. The Planners made it clear that any decision about eradication or re-integration has to be based on current data. To collect that data, the Planners put out a call for volunteers.

Accordingly, in 364 AF, an expedition went out to research the Exo-cultures. You all have that report in front of you."

The Planners. I searched for Planners. What a wonderful device the electronic copy is—you search it as though it is a living document. You can do word counts and replacements. You can rewrite then erase and restore. Nothing is lost. There is no first draft, there is only the continuity of text. The Planners. Daiva was vague about who they were and what they did. She wrote nothing about how they got power and kept it. She said very little about what they were planning. In some cases, the writing was oracular, prophetic. I liked to think of it as her goddess voice. I had to imagine her taking dictation, inventing as she wrote…

Images ran through my mind but I couldn't get a fix on what Daiva meant by the Congress. The concept of choice was built into the structure of the novel. I found one section that interested me for its variety. It showed me how impoverished the real world is compared to the Utopia Daiva was creating.

### Citadel                              ### Daiva Izokaitis

There is choice. Every daughter can live forever because the scientists have solved the genetics of aging. There will be a time when a daughter might choose to die as a control to show that mortality is possible. That raises the problem of total choice. There is a moral decision at the moment of conception with these options:

1) to implant the modified gamete;
2) to allow the polar bodies to resorb and produce a cloned daughter;
3) to introduce the Eternal Gene;
4) full-scale cross-over.

Note to Daiva: This is a fascinating and interesting working out of the concept of choice. I also think this is an important part of the novel but it's short on details. For instance—what does the Congress look like? How

116

many delegates? Which Citadel do they meet in? I don't see that anywhere. I will have to figure something out. I also have questions about the world building you're doing here:

1)transportation. How do the daughters move through time and space to come to the Congress? Are there roads left over from the Wars of Savagery?

2) Communication. How do the daughters communicate between Citadels? Is there still a residual infrastructure that the Exos don't know how to use but the daughters do because they have science? Or has science come to an end?

3) How is knowledge passed from teacher to pupil? Where are the common reservoirs of knowledge? Libraries? Vestigial but intact? Men can't read?

Related to 1 and 2 is this problem—how to work out the vestigial systems. Roads? Rivers? Who knows what? Can anyone in a Citadel build and fly an airplane? Fuel?

Are all Citadels solar powered as in the Solerian Archology? I call it an archology because that's what it is.

Some details still to work out about the life span and relationships. Is that what you mean by the Eternal Gene? There is at the root a deep love story not situated in procreation but in empathy. What is sex in the Citadel? Who can procreate? Who is fertile?

I finished the note then re-read the opening several times, before returning to Eris and her presentation to the Congress.

## Citadel

Daiva Izokaitis

Although we have had the technology for immortality since 210 AF, it it is only now that we have to decide on the future of half the race. Do we allow XYs to live or do we stop XY births altogether? That will be the decision before the Congress.

Eris walked to a screen and released a hologram of an Exo. The delegates murmured. For many of them, it was their first exposure. He was thin, bent, gray. His skin wrinkled, his eyes dim, his hands bony. Eris turned him in the spotlight. From the rear, his muscles were withered, the elevens—the tendons of the neck pronounced, his flanks shrunken as the meat of an ancient. Facing the convention, the Exo quivered and shook as though he were about to fall. Eris stood back. The Exo wobbled. Eris froze the hologram. She said,

"Does someone care to guess the age of this specimen?"

Hands flew up, a voice rang out—eighty-five.

"Take a good look. Look at the tattoo, look at the code for the birth Citadel."

"Ninety," a voice called out.

Eris opened a device, projected data on the screen. Born C–291. 327 AF. Height, one unit thirty. Weight: fifty gynes.

"This specimen," Eris said, "is forty-nine."

The silence of the delegates was total.

"Is he in this Citadel?" A delegate seated at the back of the hall shouted.

"No. He was recorded by a team on an Excursion."

"What did you do to him?" Another delegate shouted.

"We reset the biological chronometer."

"Will he die?" The same delegate shouted.

Eris closed the hologram. She said,

"Five hundred years ago, a poet in the Old Society wrote about a creature who asked for eternal life but neglected to ask for eternal youth. We call that *tithonism* and we have solved that problem."

Eris signaled to an attendant and a daughter emerged from the wings.

Delicate, elegant. Hair thick and black. The gait fast and sure. The skin was a soft chocolate hue. The eyes yellow.

Eris turned her in a slow spiral. Her muscles were toned, her posture statuesque. She stood still in the spotlight. Eris said,

"Any guesses about age?"

"Fifteen," came a voice from the listeners.

"Twenty-two," another called out.

The daughter posed then leaped, legs flexing. She landed with a light step. Eris flicked the projection device and data sprang onto the screen—

Born 210 AF. C-133. Source—Gars. Height—one unit thirty. Weight: 40 gynes. Eris said,

"This daughter is one hundred fifty."

The silence was profound. No gasping. No murmuring. Eris continued,

"We can stop aging, we can speed it up. We have complete control of the genome. We can select for any trait. We can, if we wish, eradicate the XY gamete as easily as we eradicated smallpox, syphilis, breast cancer. There is nothing about it we cannot control. But there is a moral issue—are we still human if we choose to eradicate the XY gamete? What do we become if we practice complete parthenogenesis? It is possible. That is what you have to take back to your Citadels. That is what you have to decide—the future of the race."

"Why didn't we know about this before," a delegate said. She stood.

"We could not be certain the science was right," Eris said. "Planners have worked on this from Foundation until today."

"How many are there?" The delegate said. In the light, her name tattoo pulsated. Her birth Citadel code stood out—C-14

"In this Citadel," Eris said, "we have a group who are all over one hundred fifty. There are subjects in the Citadels."

"In all the Citadels?" The delegate said.

"No, just the science Citadels," Eris said. "It's a decision for the future."

"So you have worked it out that everyone born will live forever? Even the Exos?"

"No. That is your choice."

"How will I choose if I haven't been born yet?"

"That's the problem," Eris said. "How do we decide on eternal life? And who makes the decision?"

I closed the file. Divergent evolution. Excursion. Eradication. Eternal life. *Tithonism*?

Note to Daiva: I see some issues with time here. The Congress takes place in 360 AF. The Eternal Daughter is born in 210 AF which makes her one hundred fifty. 210 AF is the same year that Eris pinpoints the advent of the Eternal Technology. When we talked on SkyChat, you said that evolution should not be under the control of men. Here you have evolution under the control of the daughters. Another problem is the "unnamed characters" in this section. Do you want to name those characters? I have to see Rose Katz day after tomorrow. I hope we can meet to discuss these notes—which you refuse to read and comment on. You're turning me into a co-author by *turning your back on my comments. If you're not careful, I might just rewrite the whole goddamn novel.*

## §§§

Agony. Labor. The two words came together with a strong odor of sulfur exploding in a fire rocking me back on the bed and into a swirling sea of smells so dark I hurt. Labor. The contractions had a taste that reminded me of my period and the pain that made me want to curl up and hide. I read, letting the taste of the words suck me into the novel. Labor. Agony.

## §§§

**Citadel**                    **Daiva Izokaitis**

### FILINA

> *Until now, you have been in the darkness of child-hood; you were like women and you knew nothing. Anon.*

Filina's agony in labor is incongruous with the soft carpets of the room, its muted colors and sparse furnishings. Labor emphasizes her solitude, for only her body can determine when it will end; neither she nor anyone can stop it or speed it up or change it.

She breathes in rhythm as her uterus contracts. Breathing forces her to concentrate and to ignore the sharpness of the contractions of her uterus. Even her mind must wait for her body to do what it is compelled to do. During this time, lying on the couch, waiting, Filina exists for only one reason. The entity within her has matured, and as her body works to expel it, she loses her freedom, for now, at this moment, there is the inevitability of the truth she did not want to know.

The contractions come faster now. Her stomach hardens. The pressure of her constricting uterus forces everything to wait. Her body and the one within it are a single entity, nothing else matters.

SSS

Doctor An watches Filina as the contractions deepen. Filina's face reddens. Sweat erupts on her forehead.

Don't push yet, Filina, Doctor An whispers.

I listen to Filina's breathing—inhaling, exhaling.

How much longer? I ask as Filina grimaces, a panicked look in her eyes. *What's happening to me?* I feel as if I am there, knees apart, on the delivery couch—a white couch that smells of alcohol and sweat.

Doctor An examines Filina's cervical dilation.

She's at six, full dilation at ten.

Filina strains now. *Strain. The smell of phosphorus.* I stand beside Doctor An. Urgency. Urgency. Watching Filina's face in agony. Doctor An inspects the cervix waiting for the child's head to crown.

There, Doctor An mutters.

This is the closest I have ever been to a birth. I don't want to be there in that room in this Citadel watching. I am in Filina's mind now, in Doctor An's mind now, in the mind of the assistants—Kiv and Nan—and I feel Filina straining—a growl from the daughter on the table that I know is an echo of my own birth.

And then Filina's face screws up into a pain-

122

mask. Not agony now but expectation. I sense a deep sharing in the delivery room as if Doctor An and the assistants remember that someone loved enough to undergo this ritual—a union of being, for each and every daughter had issued in this way from a body.

I am puzzled by the silence of the assistants.

Note to Daiva: You tend to include walk-ons that you abandon. This is not good. I had to name them. The deeper I get into this novel, the more I see how you are failing your characters. The writer has an obligation to the characters which means that you don't want to have throw-away or shadow characters. Some writers work on the principle that you make every character strong enough to be the protagonist of your next novel. You want depth. Shallow characters are a waste of your time and your reader's time as well. When you put words on paper, you have to live with the characters. You have to think that writing isn't only about words. You have to know about the spine and its link to metaphors. You have to think about the music under the words. You have to think about the rhythm in the words. A novel is a machine built on a spine or an armature and every metaphor retells the story. You have to think about verbs and their actions, nouns and their concreteness. You might think that a novel is made up of chapters, but a chapter is only what you make it. That is one of the good things about your writing. you write 'scenes.' See? A novel is not just a hundred thousand words in twenty-six chapters. A novel is a set of dynamic scenes laid out in sequence and arising from a spine that is the sum of its metaphors. A novel is an imitation, the residue of a crippled vision.

123

Their silence reflects their helplessness. There is nothing they can do but wait. Only Filina can do this.

Another contraction. Doctor An mutters again as she kneels in front of Filina. She says,

The cervix is in full dilation—10. She's crowning.

Doctor An washes her hands again. Dries them. Pulls on protective gloves. Kiv, at the fetal monitor, recites the statistics—maternal blood pressure steady, fetal pulse 130.

Nan shifts Filina into a semi erect position on the couch, head raised, pelvis lowered. I ask why and Kiv answers that gravity will assist in the bringing forth.

Each contraction of Filina's uterus lasts longer and each minute the child is further pushed out. Doctor An says,

Don't push yet, Filina. I'll tell you when, but wait now. Wait.

I kneel by the couch, holding Filina's hand. The fetal monitor beeps, reading out the changes in Filina's breathing, in the heartbeat of the fetus and I try to think of nothing but breath, breath, lungs moving, diaphragm moving, oxygen, blood, nothing is there but the physical exchange.

The crown of the fetus meshes with the dilated cervix stretching until it pales to ivory as if no blood flowed there any longer and the infant's head passes through—distorted, compressed. I feel the pain.

Filina is now aware, almost smiling—*why is she smiling?*—and her skin is pliant.

Good. Good. No need for an episiotomy. Now, Filina. Now. Push. Push.

The head crowns, I see the blood, the trickle of blood. Filina's anal sphincter distends.

Doctor An says

Breathe. Breathe. Now push, Filina. Push.

*I am Filina now. Coming from somewhere, perhaps from desire itself, my body finds energy, for now nothing can be held back. It is all there is. There is no choice, it must happen, and then with a final effort, I feel the release.*

*Doctor An again says push and the head of the infant is delivered, the vagina completely expanded, filled with the small being. Doctor An reaches into my body to turn the infant's shoulder. The small body is contorted, slick, a live birth, still pink from my blood coursing through its body.*

The last contraction. Filina falls back, exhausted. I am driven to tears with my pain watching Doctor An clamp the umbilical cord. She snips it and hands the infant to Kiv.

The infant gasps for breath, its lungs fill. I am now standing beside Filina, watching the placenta drawn from her body and I feel it release.

And Filina smiles.

Kiv places the placenta in a basin. Nan weighs the infant. Checks the vitals. Doctor An brushes at Filina's forehead with a damp cloth then glances at me. She says,

We'll know in a minute or two if she will hemorrhage.

Kiv swaddles the infant then takes it to an incubator.

Filina is young, strong, healthy. She does not hemorrhage. I listen to Nan tell Filina that it was a good delivery. She tells her that they are pleased. The Planners will be pleased.

I smell the placenta—vinegary. I am in the room with Filina and I hear the assistant and there is love in the voice. There is also a tinge of disappointment. It is pity. Pity. I hear the word echo through Filina's mind—XO, XO, XO.

I have to read The Expulsion. I am once again

ashamed to be human, but I enter now without
holding back. We are shame and guilt, terror and
fear. We are pain anguish. Born in blood, we
have no hope. aybe in the future...


Note to Daiva: You write as if you've had a child. These
details are great but do you need to go into this depth here?

At the focus group, the question of your experience came
up several times. One of the questions was whether you had
had a baby.

When I was in college, one of my friends got married
because she was pregnant. She had a daughter. Her husband
was disappointed. She told me about the birth—everyone was
into Lamaze then. She said her husband walked out of the
delivery room as soon as the gynecologist said the baby was
female. She divorced him a year later.

Are you reading my notes? I feel that I'm doing too much
to your words. You have to tell me what you see.


## Citadel                          Daiva Izokaitis


### The Expulsion

Filina had not wanted to know the sex of the
child. She did not ask the doctor or the
geneticist about the growing body. She had not
wanted an XO. She had not expected to have an
XO; she had never thought she could bear an XO.
All her thoughts had been on giving another
daughter to the Citadel, but it is evident that
she has not, and she is disappointed.

In her recovery, she is shielded from her

126

offspring until the Council has time to speak with her.

In her excitement, she experienced only the physical meaning of the birth, and the distancing techniques worked so well. As she lies in recovery, she scarcely notices the child's absence. The breast pump is the final step; its use assures that she will not imprint to the child.

As she lies on the warm sheets in the recovery room, she knows that her actions are no longer purely biological. She is a daughter who has borne an XO; she will never see it; there is no need for her to see it; it will not be nurtured by the milk of her breasts; it will be expelled into the Exo-culture and she will never hear of it again, never encounter it, never know where it is or what has become of it.

The door to the recovery room opens and three members of her Council enter. They were not smiling. Filina did not expect approval, nor did she expect disgust. Did they know she wanted to see her child?

Gipzae, the gyneologist speaks.

I know what you are feeling, she said. It is the biological weakness that every daughter who chooses to bear a child knows. It is my job to teach separation so that your nostalgia will in time extinguish.

Let me see him, Filina pleads. Just once. All I ask is to see him just once.

Keae, the anthropologist, replies,

I will be truthful, Filina. If you hold him once, you will want to keep him. An XO in the Citadel generates an imbalance that can be mediated only by his expulsion.

What will happen to him outside? Filina asks.

Her voice breaks. She is close to despair. She is trapped into caring. Her child is an XO; at every level of her consciousness he represents everything she is not, and yet she still feels a deep attachment.

Keae replies,

The Exo-culture around this Citadel lives a simple easy life. You don't have to be concerned for him.

It will take you some time to accept the facts, Filina, Gipzae says.

Until now, I didn't understand what I was doing. Her voice cracks, and all the expulsions that went before are packed into this one—this is her offspring who will be expelled. Hers. I just don't understand, she continues, I don't see any reason for it. He's just one small child, I could keep with me, and no one would know.

Not possible, Filina, Gipzae says. You made a choice. The consequences of that choice are very real. The Citadels must maintain total separation.

You make it sound so cold and rule-like.

The rule is that all XOs have to be expelled. What you are feeling is what woman in the Old Society felt for her young and that was what kept her enslaved. Qirsan explained genetic fertilization to you in your counselling. You must stop believing that because he is of your body, he is your responsibility. Your only responsibility is to the future. You know why males are expelled. You had a choice—to know or not to know. Despite counselling, you chose natural fertilization. You bore him because to give birth to a daughter is to share the vision we have that keeps us together and keeps us safe in community.

Chance gave you an XO, and that is as it should be in this Citadel because it is necessary to maintain a percentage of males. Qirsan explained to you at the beginning that if you chose natural insemination, your chances were in favor of bearing a daughter. You took the chance Filina. There were other outcomes possible, but you chose the natural way.

Filina, Keae interjects. A year ago you'd have been very upset thinking of any male living inside these walls. Do you remember why? Imagine yourself for a moment twelve months ago when your instruction began. Imagine yourself without the freedom to decide whether you wanted to become a mother. At every step of the way, you could choose to go on or to stop. You knew this might be the outcome and during instruction we talked about this possibility and what we would do; we told you that you'd feel exactly what you're feeling now. We told you what we'd have to say to you. But still you chose to go ahead. You were free to make that choice, and despite the option to know the sex of the child you were carrying, you refused. That was your right; but had you known, would it have altered the way you're thinking now? Your reaction is the reaction of all women through all time. The child is of you so you think you must care for it. You have to live with your decision, there's no other way.

But I didn't know I'd feel this…this feeling of wanting it. Didn't…you said.. I thought…I wanted it…it to be a daughter.

The reality is that you did not have a daughter. None of us can change that fact. Suppose that this child were to stay in the Citadel. His presence would compromise the freedom of every daughter, because in his presence there is the possibility of an accident…

Is he a Mutant? Filina says.

We can't tell you. The geneticists know. But you cannot know that.

And if he is a Mutant.

He cannot live with us. We can't allow that.

Why not?

Gipzae glances at Keae. Keae says,

If he is a Mutant, there is a chance that at some time a daughter could become pregnant without instruction, or some daughter might be victimized. The Mutant is a killer, Filina. You don't know which sperm was implanted.

And he'll grow into an Exo, Filina, Gipzae says, an adult male.

We don't know, Gipzae repeats, if the gamete was treated or not, and so I don't know if the child is an Exo, a Mutant, or a Gland. And I don't want to know.

You could do a tissue analysis, you could find out.

Regardless of the genetics, his male sex dictates that he must be expelled.

Then why don't we just kill him now and save him the suffering of living out there? Filina says.

We won't do that either, Filina, Gipzae responds. Until the decision is made, he has the right to live, but he doesn't have the right to live here. In the Exo-culture he will be one of them, and within those limits he won't be unhappy. He won't suffer. He won't know the alternative.

These stupid rules take away my freedom to keep my child.

They're your rules too, Filina, Gipzae replies, and you have to see that a choice to keep the child might crush the freedom of some other daughter, not because the child will remain and become a threat, but because of what you'll think of the Citadel if you're thwarted in this. If you came to resent us, then your own existence will be a misery and you'll undoubtedly share that misery with others. That was not our sisters' legacy to us, it should not be ours to the others.

Even in Filina's agitated state, Gipzae's words penetrate her mind to prod the years of training for the respect for the others, to evoke the years of consideration for the totality. She becomes silent.

We have to remember why we're here, Filina. We have to remember what made the Citadels. The gyneologists have taught us about the suffering woman endured in the Old Society. You've got to remember that and not just attend to what you're feeling now. You are feeling love at the first level that can be felt; love that biology brings us, love which negates our freedom; you have to choose to love on another level of awareness; you must choose to love those who will come after us; love them enough to allow them the freedom to make their own decisions; love them enough to leave choices for them to make.

You're asking me to change who I am, Filina says. You want me to reprogram what I am. I understand but I can't do that. I know what an Exo is. I know what a Mutant is and I know what a Gland is. But I want my baby.

"I'm asking you," Gipzae said, "to remember what you know about those daughters in the Old Society who loved enough to set us free from the bondage they endured. Everything I'm saying to you conflicts with what you're feeling. It's probably a torture for you. Your body is still complicated by the chemistry of birth. You're confronting the evolutionary reality within you all the while I'm continuing to remind you of the cultural present which this Council represents. Your heart, your mind, your being all desire the child. That's the irrational desire of an animal living in an evolved continuum, acting without thought, responding to the mechanical reality of its body. We're here to help you overcome that residual evolutionary response. But it must be, finally, a conscious act on your part."

As Gipzae speaks, Filina listens. The training she has had, the history she has read, the past she carries in her, all function together to minimize the effects of the innate releasing mechanisms ruling her. The obsession, the maternal possessiveness, is counterbalanced by the words, and they begin to emerge into a conscious reality.

"This isn't the final act of your life, Filina," Gipzae continues, you're young, eighteen and you haven't begun to sample all that life can give you. Your life can be rich and full and meaningful if you don't let this single biological act interfere with your total existence. You ought not let it determine what you will think of yourself in the world or what you'll do in it. Of your eighteen years, only one has been taken up with this insemination and birth. You can't let that one year be a definition of your entire being. To do that is to be in a stage that our sisters passed through in the Old Society, a stage they remained in for thousands of years. It's unfortunate that we're condemned to live through the past in order to reach a new awareness, but that's the consequence of biology. It will happen if you don't consider what you can become to yourself for yourself alone.

It's not easy for me to think about letting go.

It's never easy, it's never been easy. It wasn't easy for women in the Old Society.

But we're not in the Old Society now.

He has gone out of your body. He'll live out there and we in here. You've done the simplest thing that can be asked of you. The Citadels need you. If we all said No, we would no longer exist. In you, biology has taken its course. You are not beyond that. You need to turn inward now, to look at us, to look to yourself, to discover what you are and what else you can do.

As Filina listens, she races through the entire range of feelings from hatred to love to despair. The Council has remained constant and now Gipzae and Keae reach out to her and the contact of their hands and their bodies is a reassurance of their concern.

At first Filina hesitates to accept their love, but she realizes that they will not let her remain distant. They have done this for her, because as a daughter, she is important to them. They have worked with her to assure her she will continue to grow and to flourish. Then, with genuine openness, reminiscent of her childhood affections, she accepts their embraces. Gipzae says,

You look absolutely exhausted, Filina.

Don't go yet.

You rest. We'll come back later, when you've had some sleep.

Filina settles into the softness of the couch and tries to recall where she was a year before; a feeling of happiness flows through her. Her friends, her studies, her life, all come alive again. Distracted by her pregnancy, she has forgotten so much. She sees how completely she has allowed herself to become involved in her biology as completely as any woman in the Old Society became in hers. That was the only connection to the past she needs.

For a moment she wonders what she would have felt had she given birth to a daughter. She remembers Gipzae's words—Let go. She has done what she had to do. She falls asleep as the assistant enters for the delactation.

I was so sad when I came out of *Filina*. The taste of *labor* in my mouth as dark and thick as tar. My sadness, I realized, was cosmic. I had talked to Rose Katz about my own automatic hunting behavior, but now I had witnessed automatic at the other end. All the time I had been hunting, all the men I had taken, all of that was driven by the curse of birth and memory. To be human was learning how to cope with pain, and the agony of birth.

I wanted to relax. I was weary as if I had delivered the child. Still there was so much work to do.

Note to Daiva: Past, present, and future tenses mixed. I will fix that and send the scenes to you per our agreement and the contract. Whether you read them or not, I send them. The structure of the scenes is good. I now have so many questions about you and who you are. You told me that Jahil is pregnant. After reading Filina, I have to ask why Jahil is pregnant. Do you want to bring a child into the Old Society knowing what you know? In the Planner text, you write about the four choices a daughter has—

1) to implant the modified gamete;

2) to allow the polar bodies to resorb and produce a cloned daughter;

3) to introduce the Eternal Gene;

4) full-scale cross-over.

Filina did none of those. In the text, you write that she did not want the modified gamete but took the unmodified gamete with the chance that she would have a Mutant. Do you want to add that as a fifth possibility? I can fix it, but we'll have to add some text. Also, what do you mean by "the polar bodies to resorb"? What is the full-scale cross-over? This is the first I have read of it. Is it anything like ICSI? What is the biology of desire in these scenes? Do you really want to go into such detail about the delivery?

I'm confused by your inconsistent use of quotation marks. In this long section with Filina and Dr. An, there are none. I don't think you should cut them all. I will have to go back through and add them unless you tell me why you're not putting them in.

Your inconsistency with Citadel/citadel confuses me a bit also and I'm sure it will cause your readers some confusion, too. Do you want to capitalize Citadel? Do you want to leave it lower case? Help!!

I was just finishing the note when I heard a car door slam. It scared me. I had forgotten where I was and what I was doing. I heard footsteps on the promenade. A knock on the door. I did not want to answer.

"Hey. Y'in there?"

Jimbo. No horse. A car.

§§§

He held his Stetson by the brim. He grinned. His teeth showed white behind his half open lips. His eyes were deep gray, wolfish and watery. He said,

"Didn't know if you were still hanging around."

He unbuttoned the blue Western-style shirt with its white studded snaps.

"Stop, cowboy."

"What?"

"Are you a Gland, a Mutant, or are you an Exo?"

"I don't get you."

"If you're not a Gland, you must be an Exo. On second thought, you're not a Gland, you're not an Exo, you're a Mutant.

"What's a mutant? Like a sheep with two heads?"

*She leaves him naked and exhausted. She searches the pockets of his Levis, draws out a wallet, a long clasp knife. She opens the wallet, takes the bills there without counting them. She flips the knife open and slices off his prick. Jimbo howls. Blood gushing from the stub. Calm, eyes fixed on him, she gashes his throat. More blood. Jimbo falls back on the bed. Awash in blood, she goes to the shower, scrubs her body, soaps the knife. She returns to the bed and picks up* Citadel *again. She reads the scene called* War of the Hat Pins. *She finds the place where the two women have murdered the man. She watches them roll the body up in a bed sheet and slide him in the bathtub and fill it with ice-water and then they leave the room.*

"Do you shave everywhere, Jimbo?" I said.

"Nah," he said.

When I had finished with him, I shoved him out the door.

I sat on the bed. Felt hollow, felt helpless, hopeless. Sex and its memory passed leaving me anxious to get back into the novel, but I had to extinguish Jimbo first. I did not want him in me. I did not need him, but what did that make me? *Citadel*. Daiva. Women without men. I remembered one night in Berkeley listening to my roommate having sex. The human sounds, the grunts, the buried whimpers and whispers. I did not understand then how orgasm drove blind, automatic behavior. Desire alone—a way to deny half the past, desire for self, desire for orgasm, and the swarming, buzzing, giddy sensations of going mad with lust and seeing its end. Let's make a baby. Why?

Sex was inevitable. Life was not just the drive to survive but the drive to have babies, the need to build a family, not to live alone. To connect. Desire. A residual evolutionary response?

If I said no, if I refused would I ever again lie in the dark in a room the sweat and the sex-perfume guiding hands to my lips, fingers to my sex, the taste of sex, the seductive hammer that smashes all thought, all but the desire to be?

What if I didn't want a family? What did that make me? What happens to a woman if she says no? The man rapes her anyway? The man beats her up? The man slits her throat?

On my side, staring at the blank screen of the TV, I understood that I was captive in the cage of desire, driven by delirious urges I could not deny. No different than an insect trapped in desire I had yielded to the Paleolithic residue in me. I did not ask why. I did it because it had to be done. I did not think about what happened later or why it happened. I was Filina.

And now?

I remembered the time before the poison of sex entered me. I remembered the time before I had been infected with a kiss. I remembered my first time, the strangeness of sex, the odors of sex, the odors that in some way were stronger than the need itself. I had let him penetrate me. He had been in me, coming in my body, three million years of sex flooding into me. I thought how natural it was and then again and again…until I hated it. I no longer remembered his name. His face was a floating mystery, memory of his hands vague and faint, the hands of any man, in any time. He did not matter.

I understood that to be alone was to die. Alone, I was one of the sisterhood of the murdered, one of the vases broken before the time of flowers—I was one of the daughters in *Citadel* who died because she was a woman carrying the disease of desire that did not find its cure in coupling or blind repetition or release or orgasm or ejaculation. I thought of *Madame Bovary. Justine. The Hundred and Twenty Days of Sodom. Anna Karenina.*

I recalled the opening of *Citadel*—the walls high and thick, the gates narrow slits in the high walls, slits so narrow the daughters could crush an attacking enemy.

I rolled onto my back.

I closed my knees together. Tight.

I stared at the ceiling. Darkness.

I would finish the *Delivery* and *Expulsion* scenes and then go to Rose.

I had to talk to Rose.

I packed a bag, loaded the laptop and the manuscript into the Z-Ray and fled the Desert Rose Motel, driving into the moonless night pushing the electric machine to its limit.

### Rose Katz

The sea breeze was refreshing after a hot LA afternoon. Trisha stood at the open window.

"What was so urgent?" I said,

"I relapsed. Five days. I go to the desert to stop it, but I can't. I find this guy who can't speak a complete sentence without saying Uh and sucking his teeth. I hate myself more than ever."

"Are you getting any work done?"

"Clara's pressuring me."

"Let's talk about why you hate yourself."

"Because I'm automatic. I go to the desert to work then I

137

find this guy, Jimbo. He has big rough hands."

"And for that you hate yourself?"

"I hate myself because I can't stop."

"And your work? Is this the same book?"

*"Citadel*, yes."

"Tell me about Jimbo."

"We didn't have sex in the usual way."

"Maybe that's why you had to see me."

"I thought about kids. All I could think of was kids. Desire is built in and we can't do anything about it. I have to say no. No to kids, no to family, no to everything."

"Tell me what you did to him."

"I took away his control."

"Is that what you needed to do?"

"I've done it before, but this time it was different. I wasn't the same Trisha who brought home beach meat. Daiva writes about desire. We bleed so they think we're weak. But if we don't bleed there's no civilization."

"Were you bleeding?"

"Hidden estrus. We're the only ape species that masks estrus."

"Have you thought about giving this book to another editor?"

"I don't want to give it to another editor."

"It's hurting you."

"It's changing the way I think about being a woman. Every time I work on it I get into a new place and my brain goes crazy like I'm living with the characters."

"Let me ask you the same questions I ask you every week—what do you want? Do you want to be loved? Do you want to be desired? Do you want to be needed?"

"The need to be loved and petted and stroked and cherished, that's what brought us here. Daiva calls them evolved evolutionary responses."

"You're so hard on yourself, Trisha. Can't you relax and enjoy being human?"

"This is different. I've become a character in this novel. Not just me—you and Clara and Daiva and every woman who wears a bikini on the beach or owns her own house or has her business and doesn't get married and have kids is saying no to the biology of desire. No to it all. And it's redefining us, Rose. Until I got this novel I knew what a woman was—but what if the men won't let us evolve? What if they rip us out of the Niche and put us back in floor-length dresses and make us cover our heads and walk three steps behind them and keep our eyes down and keep us off the beaches and out of school? You see? We have to rethink everything because we have only a little while before they take it all away."

"We always have an uneasy grasp on freedom, Trisha."

"Your optimism will kill you, Rose."

"I understand the Niche, Trisha. I see it every day in every woman who comes to me—the fear, always afraid their men will cut their throat if they step out of line. If this book lets you see what can be, you can't run away."

"And if that means saying no to civilization?"

"We made the world with men, but they do the killing. They do the raping. They are the abusers. I don't think the killing will ever stop."

"Daiva writes that science will find a way to let women give birth without the Y chromosome and if she succeeds we have to think about what it means to be human. If sex and desire got us here, what do we call ourselves if we don't have sex? What happens to desire? That's why this novel is really about what it means to be human."

Trisha was speed-rapping, so I wrote a note. I had to slow her down. I could see this novel slipping away from her. I capped my pen and said,

"I think we should try this using SkyChat, Trisha. There's no reason for you to drive in here every time you panic. We can do it another way, don't you think?"

"You're kicking me out?"

"No. But I think we need some distance."

"What I say bothers you?"

"You always bother me."

"Why don't you have kids?" Trisha said.

"I don't want kids."

"Why don't you want kids?"

"I've never wanted kids. I look at what's happening around us and I think—no."

"So, you don't want to pass on your precious genes?"

"The egoist thinks her genes are something special that needs to be passed on."

"You're saying no to civilization?"

"I don't want to have a man in me."

"But if you didn't need a man, would you? Have children?"

"Our time is up, Trisha."

"You know what you are, Rose? You are a post-family woman living in the Niche."

I sat at the desk listening to Trisha go down the stairs. I waited to hear the door close then I finished my notes and called Camille.

"Can you see me?"

"Not until eight o'clock."

"I'll be on time."

"Have you ever been late?"

§§§

# DIVERGENCE

**Daiva Izokaitis**

### The Rage

*Fragment from a*
*Historical Report by a Witness to*
*the Wars of Savagery*

"I have seen the rage. It wasn't until I witnessed it firsthand that I understood what we had to do. Even in a small boy, it comes like an explosion. The face turns into a vivid mask and the lips curl up a second before the explosion and then everyone freezes. The rage stops everything around it."

### Daiva

Trisha spotted the triptych as she came through the door. The left panel was a 24 x 36 inch graphic of the X chromosome. The right panel was a graphic of the Y chromosome. The middle panel showed a Y chromosome just tagging the ovum. The undulipodium of the Y, detaching, looked like a grammar error at the end of a long sentence.

"These are new," Trisha said.

"Jahil's," I said. "An early microphotograph. The Y is one of Caleb's duds that I photoshopped to make this composite."

Trisha again looked at the X about to snap up the Y. I could see that she was troubled with the reductive and naked biology of the graphic. Eggs and sperm—exactly what drove her to the meat on the beach even if she didn't know it.

She touched the triptych, one panel at a time, then she said,

"You didn't answer my note about the four postulates."

"We've got a lot going on the lab right now."

"Did you get the notes?"

Trisha's eyes were red, her skin sallow as if she hadn't seen the sun for weeks.

"My lab won't run itself, Tee. Jahil's implant is keeping me glued to the lab and, I've got an intern working on mitochondria."

"I want to include *Women in Captivity*, all of it."

"You want part one back in?"

"At first, I was skeptical but when I got into it deeper, I see what you're doing, so I want to use all of *Captivity*. But I want to make Karen stronger and harder. I want her to control Bart in that section. That's what she's telling me."

"That whole sequence is the great morality tale in *Citadel*, Trisha. Women say no. Men butcher women. You change Karen and it loses its meaning."

"But listen. This guy, Jimbo, we had sex. I was more in control than I've ever been in my life and he did exactly what I said and I was seeing him as if I were Karen. That's what I mean…"

"You don't know when to stop."

"I'm making it a better story."

"If you change the story, you change me and then it's not my story anymore it's yours."

"That's what editors do to a dangerous novel."

"It's dangerous only if anyone reads it."

"Women will read it."

"Let me take the heat. Leave the future alone. You want to see the lab?"

The lab smelled of bleach and sulfur. It smelled of alcohol and formaldehyde. I led Trisha to a clean room where Andra was tending three monitors. Jahil lay on the bed in a clear clean tent with her feet up. I checked the monitors.

"Readouts?"

"Perfect up and down the scale," Andra said.

"This is Andra," I said. "Trisha's editing *Citadel* for

Pinnacle Books. Andra's an M.D. specializing in prenatal genetics. And this is Jahil. We're now eight weeks into implantation, Trisha. At ten weeks we'll see the future. This is the first pregnancy by ICNI cross-over."

"ICNI?" Trisha said.

"Intracytoplasmic nuclear injection."

"Like in the novel?"

"Yes. Only here it's the real thing. The ovum doesn't care where the stimulus comes from. By injecting the nucleus from my ovum into Jahil, we get forty-six chromosomes."

"Why is she confined?"

"We have her here to keep exposure to pathogens low. Tomorrow we do an MRI."

"Is this really happening?" Trisha said.


## Trisha

My condo felt alien. I think it was my condo. When I work a story, I get lost in the new world and it's hard to get out. A method actor living in only one character has it easy, but as the editor, I have to become all of them. It drives you nuts. Turns you borderline, no boundaries, they all live in me so dialogue is me talking to myself. The only thing that helped was wine.

I checked the fridge. Wine. Chilled. Four-year-old Château Vieux. I uncorked a bottle and poured a glass. Sipped it. The wine had a slight sourness to it. Had it turned? Had I changed so much I could no longer drink wine? I sat on the sofa to look out at the ocean. Rose didn't want to see me anymore. That was a shock. Why had she cut the ties? And Daiva didn't want anything to do with me or the story. I had been abandoned by everyone who meant anything to me. All I had left was *Citadel*.

I booted my laptop and pulled *Citadel* down from the cloud. The first words I came to chilled me—

## Citadel                           Daiva Izokaitis

Men in the Old Society committed same-species
suicide as the Y turned on itself. We saved the
race when we separated and now we have to decide
the fate of the species. We know for sure that
we can never go back to the way it was before....

The section titled *Council* needed work. I had to figure
out the difference between *Congress* and *Council.* I had
worked it three times but it still needed something. The
whole thing needed work. The more I changed it, the worse
it became. No way to fix it, might as well deep-six the
project and start over. What was the spine? If I could tackle
the spine, I could see what to do. The novel shifted around
on me. The spine is always in the writing lurking under a
sea of metaphors. You have to cut through gazillions of
metaphors to see the dominant one with the most
transforms. I had been looking for the spine but it was still
a mystery. I'd never find it. I went to work on my edited
version because I'd gotten caught up in Ell's dreams she
recorded for her *Council* before she underwent
insemination because they were so much like my own.

Insemination had the odor of cloves. I read the word.
The scent hurled me right into Ell's first dream and I was at
the table with Ell, Rees, and Auban.

## Citadel                           Daiva Izokaitis

Dream of Pluviose/20/290 AF
I am asleep in the tower. I have been asleep
for a very long time, years probably, although
I can't be sure. The room I'm sleeping in is on
the top of the tower, and it's the only room
which hasn't been sealed up by a wildly growing
plant. I know all this because as I sleep, I get
up and walk around the room, and I realize that
the body sleeping there is me. I'm a prisoner.
I can see that there is no way out of the tower.

144

The thorns are so thick nothing can penetrate them.

I keep waiting for someone to wake me up because I know it's supposed to happen sometime, at least I hope it will. But then the part of me that is awake wonders why I keep waiting instead of doing something myself; but I am helpless. Danger? Nothing happens, so I go back to sleep in the body that is there.

Then I am awake, and I realize that I've brushed my cheek with my fingers. My nails are sharp and have scraped me and the pain woke me. I'm actually awake. It was all so simple, I didn't think I was awake at first, but it was true. I go to the tower window, wondering why I've been asleep for so long when I could have awakened myself so easily.

I feel good about myself, and then as I'm standing there looking out the window, at all the thorns, my companion is in the room with me, and I ask her where she has been, and she says she was asleep but woke up to find herself in that room. We leave the tower together, and as we go out we see all the thorns have withered away, and that they hadn't really been keeping us prisoners at all; they are just clumps of dead wood. Then we see that there are others like us who have just awakened, and together we stack the clumps of thorns and burn then and we feel joy, even tranquility. When I wake up, I feel light and free and very good.

I felt guilty. *Citadel* was coming true. I could feel it. Ell was me. Once again I had this overpowering sense that Daiva had someone become part of my life before I ever met her. Euphoria gripped me as I realized that my editing was saving the *Council* section. Rees. Smiling. Smiling--clover, fresh-mown clover and I was back in the novel, this time not as an editor but as participant at the table.

# Citadel

## Daiva Izokaitis

Dream of Pluviose/21/290 AF

I am anxious. My companion is with me trying to help me and I feel very badly about something. She talks to me and tries to get me to talk. I don't know how she knows I'm anxious if I don't talk to her, but she does. We are walking on top of the wall. I look down and realize that it would be very easy to fall. I almost leap, but I don't because there are bad things below. My companion yaps incessantly. I can't imagine why she is so fast or so agitated. She is pointing at me. I look at myself and realize that my skin is sagging and becoming yellow and pitted, and instead of menstrual fluid there is a horrible yellow ooze running down my legs, forming a puddle on the ground at my feet. I reach down and feel the ooze. It is sticky, like mucous. I had read about this condition in my archaeohistory. Women in the Old Society suffered from urinary tract infections. I'm standing in it. My companion gives me a hand to help me get unstuck. She tugs. I struggle. Finally she frees me. When I wake up, I am clasping my legs together and perspiring. I am frightened. I think that I must have done something wrong, or I wouldn't have become so frightened.

Trisha: What do you think this dream means for you and for the Citadel?

Ell: Before, I had only vague feelings about maleness and about femaleness. I didn't care whether I had a male child. That might sound strange because of the Citadel, but it is true. Now I realize that I am very strongly Eradicationist. Just the thought of giving birth to a child, even though chances are small that it would be male, is enough to make me

146

reconsider.

Rees: Daiva wants you to be a mother, Ell.

Trisha: I can change that, but Daiva won't be happy.

Ell: I don't want to be a mother. It's that simple. I could give birth to a daughter. I realize what that means to the Citadel but I don't want to be a mother. It was insemination that made me realize I don't want to.

Auban: What does this mean, Ell? "Horrible yellow ooze running down my legs."

Ell: It's obvious. As I lay on the couch after insemination, I couldn't see any reason for it. I was waiting and waiting, and there was nothing I could do.

Rees: You're sure you don't want to go through with it?

Ell: I have everything I want. That is in the dream too. I don't have to get pregnant. I can live for myself. I realized also for the first time what will happen to me, to my body, and when in my dream my skin turned yellow and sagged, I knew I would be stretched and marked. At the Heptuants, I have seen photos of women in the Old Society. I am too vain to go through delivery. I don't want that. I don't want to disfigure myself, not even for the Citadel. My dreams about my companion made me realize that I love the pleasure of being with her more than just about anything.

Auban: You could crossover, Ell.

Ell: It's not the pregnancy I dread but the marking.

Rees glanced at me.

Rees: Are you happy?

Trisha: I need to read the Genetic Record again.

I scrolled back to Daiva's version. I had shortened her long piece. What would she say about it? "You changed my words, you changed the story, you changed the future." Too late. I am now part of the novel and *Citadel* is part of me. I re-read the Genetic Record for Ell.

## Citadel                                    Daiva Izokaitis

```
                    Genetic Record

NAME: Ell
BIRTH PLACE: Citadel 133
BIRTH DATE: Brume/14/271
AGE: 19
HEIGHT: 1. 167 us.
WEIGHT: 53.63 gus. (Brume/30/289)
new category
APPLIED KNOWLEDGE: Theoretical mathematics; dentist;
mechanics; interest in electricity; linguistic
ability; musical ability—strings, percussion.


                    new category


GENETIC RECORD: IMMEDIATE DATA
MOTHER: Gris; Citadel 29; Birth date Neige/18/251;
date of insemination Portus/1/271; age at parturition
20.5; primiparous; applied knowledge: food
technologist; musician; chess player.
GLAND: Tora; Citadel 30; Birth date Nivoise/18/170;
date of capture Germine/24/196; age at capture 26;
date of first sperm extraction Germine/29/196;
huntresses noted that the delay in processing was due
to an encounter with a Mutant; date of extraction for
insemination of Gris Prairie/2/196, age of sperm at
insemination 75; rate of successful insemination by
sperm mass 100%; distribution: female 229, male 6;
areas of distribution: C-30, C-31, C-33, C-34; known
Mutants none; known Glands none.
GENETIC RECORD: EXTENDED DATA: In storage
                    new category
```

# Citadel

CHARACTERISTICS: INDIVIDUAL SOCIAL CHARACTERISTICS
Language Ability: Median
Social Index: Excellent
Intelligence: High
Latent Hostility: Low
Aggressiveness: High
Suicidal aspect: None
Adaptability: High
Analogical ability: Excellent
Sexuality: daughter identified
Emotionality: Median
Competitiveness: Low
Imaginative Index: Very high
Death fear: Low
Attitudes:
Re-Integration: Negative
Extinction: Positive
Separation: Positive
Future: Positive
Birth: Positive
Group: Positive
Individual: Positive

Mythological awareness: Median. At onset of
adolescence, dream
analysis revealed an exceptional depth and complexity
of Ell's dream structure. The gyneologist noted that
there was no exceptional language ability nor was
there any tendency to tithomania; the oneiric
complexity was diagnosed as nonlanguage index,
probably the result of selection from polyglot pool
(see the EXTENDED DATA) in her background; she has
ancestors with polyglottal ability as high as 26
languages; it might seem strange that the high
analogical ability and the high oneiric complexity
have not meshed into a creative tendency with
language; note that the high linguistic capacity is
not, however, correlated to high synthetic ability;
instead it corresponds to a high analytical ability;
the analogical-analytical-aural complex enhances
linguistic capacity but has no bearing on language

149

ability, which is analogical-synthetic-visual-
auditory; note that the high musical performative
ability correlates genetically with a high linguistic
ability but not to a high language ability. In another
time Ell would have been encouraged to participate in
theoretical linguistics; note that she has been
apprised of her abilities but has not acted upon that
information.

Latent maleness: Median.

In late adolescence Ell reported dreams of an animal
nature which were not associated to any experience;
because of their alarming effects, a survey of past
reading, visual input and other relations was made,
but no direct experiences could be found to explain
the intensity of her dreams.

Gyneologists and psychologists believe that this
characteristic is not deleterious but could be
positive, and their feeling is that the nature of the
dreams was due to a rapid development of the cortical
region in the brain where the imaginative center is
located. This is unusual as the change is ordinarily
made in early to middle childhood with the general
myelinization of the cerebral neuronal pathways and is
responsible for the nightmares of small children. In
this case, it produces some exceptionally vivid images
in the dreams of Ell, images which are not
experientially derived. This characteristic, while
different, does not represent a harmful mutation, as
no detrimental behavior has been noted; geneticists in
Council think it is a progressive mutation that can be
tolerated in order to see if it is the predecessor to
a quantum leap in emotional scientism or some other
aspect of accelerated cognitive processes: this ought
to be made clear to Ell during instruction so that she
is aware of the possibility of her exceptionalness.

new category

# Citadel

CHARACTERISTICS: INDIVIDUAL PHYSICAL CHARACTERISTICS

Pigmentation: Sandy earth tone
Hair: Dark brown Body Type: Meso
Weight-Height Ratio: Average
Bone Size: Median bone flexibility: good. Rapid rate
of recovery. No history of osteomyelitis; she suffered
a broken femur in a fall from a scaffolding during
rehearsal for a dramatic role, 3/24/286.
Calcification: Good
Bone Health: Excellent. No mineral deficiencies.
Joint Health: Excellent. Strong ligamental tonus, no
line history of tendonitis, no history of bursitis;
shoulder surgery—healed.
Teeth: Excellent; fifth molars, upper and lower,
surgically removed Vent/1/281; note that this surgery
is earlier than usual, due to the general trend to
shorten the upper and lower jaws while tooth size
remains constant; this is a species trend and not an
individual genetic mutation; no orthodontia; Ell
received fluoride prenatally and in childhood.
Eyes: Normal. There is a recessive for myopia noted in
the extended data, but the last five generations in
this line have been without corrective lenses.
Torso: Median.
Lung Capacity: Median. No history of pulmonary
disease.
Organ Health: Good. Appendix intact; no history of
appendicitis. See extended data for endocrine data;
see extended data for EKG and EEG.
Pelvic Width: Median.
Breasts: Median. No history of breast cancer; no
history of mastitis; Ell can, if she chooses, lactate
after the pregnancy is term.
Urogenital Health: Good. At age 17 yrs. 5 mos. Ell
contracted a vaginal infection, diagnosed as monilia
and treated with a new technique developed by
Citadelian mycologists; she volunteered for the treatment knowing the cure would be rapid. No other vaginal
diseases.
Uterine Size: Median. Ell's genetic history indicates
151

2. 8 to 3. 5 gus. births; uterine size is compatible to pelvic width; no history of caesarian or other complications; the extended data indicate that in the post-parturitive years there is a tendency of uterine fibric growth; in no way is this deleterious as it develops only during later years. Corrective physical surgery rather than genetic surgery is advised.
Menstruation: Median. Age at menarche: twelve yrs. Five mos. This age is genetically stable for this genealogy. Menstrual flow is average. Since menarche, Ell has used the aspiration method of menses removal. She has no history of menstrual anxiety. Medical examination reveals no damage to the uterus; ova are attached properly.

Ovulation: Regular, 16 days from onset of menses; Ell's ovaries contain 250,000 ova; genealogical autopsies reveal no genetic oocyte malformations. During instruction Ell's attitude toward multiparous births should be determined, and, if negative, she might be encouraged to donate her ovarian mass to the bank; since this requires physical surgery, precautions are in order. Because of the regularity of ovulation, predict-ability factors are increased; she has a thirty-two-day cycle.
Fallopian health: Normal. No line history of fallopian pregnancy.
Hormonal Balance: Good.
END OF IMMEDIATE DATA RECORD
CITADEL 133 Pluviose/2/290

**Citadel**                              **Daiva Izokaitis**

Pluviose/29/290 AF
11:00 a. m.
Council Report to the Planners
Tests revealed that the ovum had implanted. Meiosis had begun. Ell chose to abort this morning at 8:30 a. m. The Council concludes that Ell's response to the pregnancy indicates a

drift in the CPI index of influences and conditioning. The Council further concludes that Ell has mitochondrial mutations, which without editing the genome will persist. This could indicate further divergence. The Council recommends we place a watch on her line to chart further mutations, although the mutations appear to be nondeterminative and perhaps indicate a pre-adaptation. It is our opinion that the mutation has caused Ell to be hypersensitive to her mental functioning, and while she is not conscious of what is driving her thought processes, the data given to the Council suggest that she is on the cusp of divergence. Probable that she is incapable of carrying a fetus to term. Activities of this nature would confirm that Ell is a leading indicator of species bifurcation. The Council recommends that Ell not pursue insemination although parthenogenetic pregnancy is not out of the question.

Note to Daiva: As you told me, by saying No, a woman denies civilization. If she says Yes, she has to work out the residual evolutionary response with the physical reality—having a baby. on Ell's selection and preparation for insemination. I read The Genetic Report on Ell's selection and preparation for insemination several times before I understood that this chapter speaks to the question of Choice. The way you build the world without men, you show me that there are no accidental pregnancies in the Citadel. There are no rapes. There is only a complete dedication to the altruism of birth. It boils down to this—a daughter, in a Citadel, not only chooses the kind of fetus she will carry and why she will carry it, but she chooses to perpetuate the race until the final decision is made—to continue, to let the race go extinct, or to let the Y decay and on its own cease to be. I discussed it with Eris. She told me that the Planners control the number of Exo births by editing the genome for Exo, Gland, or Mutant. The Record makes it clear that the Counsellors explain to the daughter her chances of birthing an E, G, or M while letting her know that a Crossover is also an option. That said, however, I don't think you need the record at all. The text and subtext make it very clear. If I don't hear from you, I will cut it completely.  T.

## Daiva

"We need to talk about style," Trisha said. "I've been working all morning but before I go back to the desert we have a couple of issues to iron out."

She pulled the copy of *Citadel* from her satchel.

"I thought you were electronic everything," I said.

"It's easier to share this way since you don't have an ereader."

"Maybe when I finish *Extinction*," I said. "I don't have time for old novels."

Trisha flipped to a page of *Citadel* thick with flags and dark with interlinear notes. She said,

"I have to give Clara a clean manuscript."

"I hear you say clean manuscript and I know you want to mess with the story."

"We have to massage some parts. Look at this passage."

Several of Erian's group, exhausted by the day's march and the liquor had only <u>feebly</u> risen to the occasion, and the receptacle had reacted <u>coolly</u>, looking askance at them when their floppy tubes of flesh could not penetrate him, and chiding them for letting the liquor rob him of giving them pleasure. The daughters had

<u>unwittingly</u> been saved from exposure since it was <u>obviously</u> acceptable for alcohol to render them incapable. Only Erian was required to perform and when one of the others failed, the receptacle <u>merely</u> turned to others and extracted from them again and again until <u>finally</u> they all lapsed into unconsciousness, including Erian who lay dissipated on the floor, curled into a ball, the child still strapped to his back, <u>miraculously</u> asleep.

"You've got one hundred twenty-five words and seven of them are –ly adverbs. Adverbs tell the reader what to think but that's not the only issue. The point of view moves around, the diction level is all over the place, you use passive voice verbs that you try to strengthen with those adverbs. We talked about point of view before. Here, you use a collective point of view. You put all that together and the piece needs a lot of work to make it fiction."

"How is the diction level all over the place?" I said.

"It's in the verbs," Trisha said. "If you'd answer my notes—at least read them—we could fix a lot of this. So look at these two instances—'had only feebly risen to the occasion....' and 'the receptacle had reacted coolly, looking askance at them…and chiding them for letting the liquor rob him of giving them pleasure…' In fiction, Daiva, there are two elements that drive the story—action and image. When you build your sentences with that high-level diction—'they had all lapsed into unconsciousness…' you keep the reader from seeing the image. When you build the sentence with those passive verbs, you mute the action. If you mute the action, your reader's mirror neurons go idle, and when you block the image with high-level diction, your reader's visual cortex goes blind. Seeing and doing…that's the basis of fiction."

"How would you do it then?" I said.

"Take 'Only Erian was required to perform…until they had all lapsed into unconsciousness' and do something with it. Find stronger verbs for *was required to perform* and for *lapsed*, take out *had all*, and find an image for *unconsciousness*. Change all that and you could get this—"

> As leader of the band of Exos, Erian took
> first crack at the androgyne. When he climaxed,
> he handed her off to his followers. One by one,
> they had sex. Drinking and hooting until,
> drained and drunk, they passed out on the floor
> beside Erian who lay slobbering on his side, the
> child still strapped to his back but now sound
> asleep.

"A good writer knows a lot about action verbs."

"Are you going to check every verb in the whole novel?"

"You haven't read my notes, Daiva. I need a glass of wine. I'm going back to the desert. I can't work in the city. I don't suppose it matters because you're not paying any attention to what I'm doing."

"It's not bad," I said, "what you've done."

"Like I told you, I keep two copies. One I edit into novel language, the other I leave the way you wrote it. We have to agree on a version. That's why you've got to answer my notes. Did I tell you how I select manuscripts? I should have explained it before you signed the contract. I turn to page one. If the first word is "I" followed by "was born...." Out it goes. I open the next manuscript to a random page and I check out the pronouns. If the writer has written, "she went with my friend and I..." out it goes. If the writer has written dialogue with attribution such as "she ruefully decided...." Out it goes."

"You're joking, aren't you, Tee?"

"No. Look at the opening image of your novel. It's a huge image, an archetypal image of a Citadel seen as an ovum. No men in sight."

Trisha paged to the opening and read,

> In the half-light of early morning, the walls
> of the citadel, seen from a distance, loom like
> the membrane of a large cell sliced cross-
> section. The hazy desert sky seals the Citadel

off from the heavens just as the walls isolate it from the hostile world stretched out around it.

The walls extend up so that a person standing at their base can see the sky only by stepping back and craning the neck.

The ovoid shell of a Solerian tower at the center of the citadel juts into the sky like the nucleus at the center of the cell.

"You create the image of a world and you go from there. But look at your verbs—*loom, sliced, seals, isolate, extend, stretched, juts.* They're pretty good and we can see what you're doing. I worked on the opening of *Expedition.* I sent it to you but you didn't answer. Here's what I did with the opening paragraph. I told you I keep two copies. First is the version you wrote, the second is my edited version."

## Citadel                          Daiva Izokaitis

Two hundred-fifty years after the Citadels were formed, a Congress was to meet in Citadel Cuernavaca to make an evaluation of the two cultures. To the youngest daughters, in that year 250, the problem under debate was very remote, indeed, was hardly a problem at all; but the Planners decided that after twelve generations, there should be reconsiderations of the effects of separation of the Citadels from the Exo-cultures.

Two hundred fifty years After Foundation, the Planners called a Congress to evaluate the future of the two cultures. Over time, the daughters had developed a fragmented vision of the Exo cultures. The Extinctionists opposed any reintegration while the Separatists wanted

> nothing to change. The Integrationists based their position on genetics after the Planners, the gyneologists, and the archaeohistorians warned of the catastrophic effects on the human genome of either rapid reintegration or continued separation.

"Your version has more words in it. It's sharper but I don't see why."

"Your version has only two sentences. The rewrite has four."

"First verbs, now you're counting sentences."

"You cram a lot into each sentence so I have to unpack them."

"Unpack them?"

"You wrote this—'the problem under debate was very remote, indeed hardly a problem at all. ' The reader needs to know what the problem is, so I unpack the sentence to pull out the fragmented vision which has three parts—Extinctionist, Integrationist, Separatist. Now we know what we're talking about. And those three parts give you the conflict center that you need. Those three parts define the future of the citadels."

"Wow. You do all that all the way through?"

"That's why you need me."

"Do you work this way with all your writers?"

"My obligation is to the author, to the story, to clarity. The goal is to get the best story possible to the reader."

"You didn't answer my question."

"Yes. It's what I do. It's my duty to the work and I can understand your irritation, Dee. You're pissed off because you think I'm taking over the book."

"You really love doing this, don't you?"

"An editor has to fall in love with the story and with the writer, Dee. Just the way a therapist falls in love with the sickness of the patient. One more thing—I've been meaning to ask you—the Karen and Bart scenes in *Women in Captivity*—did that really happen?"

"You keep track of that too?"

"You know that one of my rejection criteria is no true

stories," Trisha said.

"What do you mean by 'true'?"

"I mean, did this happen to you?"

"No," I said, "it isn't a true story."

"So, you made it up?"

"Truth is brutal, Trisha. Did I make it up or did it happen to some woman? Does it have to happen to me to be true? Also, it's funny because Ell asks Orione what a skillet is…"

"There's nothing funny about a woman beaten to death by three men using a skillet."

Trisha flipped to page 194—*Women in Captivity.*

"Don't cut it."

"Karen is pregnant and he kills her," Trisha said.

"We're fucking ourselves into oblivion."

"Are you saying she deserved to die because she was pregnant?"

"I'm saying she was pregnant in an already obscenely overpopulated world."

"Dee, Dee, Dee. Sometimes you frustrate the hell out of me."

"If we keep it, promise me you won't cut out the heart."

"I won't cut out the heart if you tell me the truth, Dee— when you wrote that scene, you were writing about your own experience weren't you? Have you been pregnant? Have you had an abortion? The focus group wanted to know if you had been raped."

"Okay. Sure. It didn't exactly happen to me," I said, "but I didn't exactly make it up. We're past the family stage in human evolution. Karen's mistake was thinking that because she was pregnant and she lived in a pro-natalist time that Bart shared her need to start a cute little family with a cute little kid. But she didn't know the Y gamete had mutated and the chromosome was decaying and Bart didn't care. He only wanted to have as many women as he could and he'd use any trickery to get into her pants and he didn't care if she was pregnant. He was an asshole. She was an automaton with that residual evolutionary response. That's what the novel is about—divergent evolution…"

"How can I edit your fucking book if I can't understand what's in that head of yours."

"What's in my head is on the page, but you keep changing that. You go around talking to the characters like some madwoman and if you listen to what they say it stops being what it is and becomes what you want it to be. You're a woman living in the Niche, Trisha. If you give up one thing, you are no longer who you are now. It's the same with *Citadel*. You want it to be a story other than what it is. It's a story about women in the Niche and how we got here. Maybe you should go back to the beach and pick up another one of your beach meat specimens and tell him what you want. You'll see the truth then. You'll see that you're in the Niche and he won't understand because the first thing he'll want is to "take from you by force the very thing you would have given him freely."

"Who are you quoting?" Trisha said.

"Pauline Réage," I said. "I've read them all and I can tell you that your beach meat won't understand because he can't. No man understands the Niche..."

"In my dreams I see images from your stupid book, Dee, and I hate it, but I know you're telling the truth."

"Has the novel made you less fearful?"

"No."

"More sexual?"

"No."

"More curious?"

"Yes."

"About what?" "

"Who we are and where we came from."

"Who you are didn't come into being until 1920, Trisha. That's when the Niche opened wide and we all walked through it and now you can't go back without surrendering everything you've become and putting on the veil. If they take one thing away from you, they'll take it all and lay claim to your vagina, your breasts, your mouth, and your womb."

"Why did you write this novel in the first place?"

"I told you—rejection."

"You never sent *Citadel* out."

160

"Not *Citadel. Women in Captivity.* I worked on that piece for a long time and I sent it out to publishers, to agents, to magazines and they all rejected it. It was longer then. Although I didn't save any of the rejections you should have read them, Tee. 'This is the most sickening piece of crap any writer has ever sent us…' one of them said. Another ranted about pornography and pseudo-feminist trash. With every rejection, I got more pissed off and so using *Women in Captivity* as the core, I wrote *Citadel.* That is the starting point for *Citadel.* Once I realized that because we are billions, family is no longer a useful foundation unit and we have moved into a post-family state of mind, I knew that Karen was the vestigial female of the family era."

"And *Citadel* will get us killed."

"The daughters will fight, Trisha. We'll fight and we'll win because we own our bodies. You say *Citadel* has changed you. Men have no reason to change, they own the world and your body. Women for centuries have soft-pedaled their wants just to stay alive. One word—NO—changes everything in human evolution. My work got me so many rejections because I redefined environment and natural selection. If you see the mitochondrion as the endosymbiont it is, your world-view changes. Lynn Margulis showed us that the mitochondrion was once a free-living organism. That was a big breakthrough. The breakthrough in my work shows the chemistry of thought altering the neural net. One word changes the brain and if you change the brain, you alter behavior."

"You said 'we'll fight', Dee."

"I did?"

"Yes. You said 'we'll fight and we'll win…' This novel is about you, isn't it?"

"Yes and no."

"No true stories, Dee."

"Every story is a true story, Tee. Look at you. You go hunting, but you never get pregnant. Why?"

"Because I don't want to."

"And you don't have to because you can choose. You can choose to say No. In the Niche, you have options and one of your options is sex without offspring."

"Meaning what?"

"That you distrust desire which is a residual evolutionary response."

"So I'm a Mutant?"

"You're a woman. Saying No, has changed your brain and separated your past from your future. Part of you is the New You, but there's a residual Old You that just screams to have a man's baby in you. But what you can become isn't what your ancestors had to become. Sexual selection created you. Your mother used her brain and your brain has changed. It's the epigenetics of the Fragile Wisdom and it's a new world for Lamarckian epigenetic biology—meaning organisms can pass on acquired traits. You might already be on the way to a new species."

"Reading your novel and saying No changes me?"

"Trait selection, Trisha. You don't have to change the whole genome—you probably can't anyway, but when you select for one trait—saying No, making choices—you might just change a few neurons."

"You do think I'm a Mutant?"

"You're a stranger in this world, Trisha."

"I'm right where I belong."

"You're on path to the darkness of epigenetics."

"And your novel put me on that path, Dee. I need a glass of wine."

"Tell you what—Go ahead. Change me. Change the whole novel. Make all the changes you need to make. I don't want to see them. It's yours."

"What about the contract?"

"I don't have time, Tee. Take it. I give it to you. It's yours"

"You know, Daiva. I need more than one glass of wine."

§§§

# EXPEDITION

## Citadel                    Daiva Izokaitis

"Well then, let every man
who wants only sons have
them himself."
H. R.

Two hundred fifty years After Foundation, the Planners called a Congress to evaluate the future of the two cultures. Over time, the daughters had developed a fragmented vision of the Exo cultures. The Extinctionists opposed any reintegration while the Separatists wanted nothing to change. The Integrationists based their position on genetics after the Planners, the gyneologists, and the archaeohistorians warned of the catastrophic effects on the human genome of either rapid re-integration or continued Separation.

There was no law requiring the Congress to convene to discuss the issues. As with all other issues affecting Citadelian relationships, it was by choice that the Congress convened, bearing in mind the historical reasons for Foundation and the existence of the Citadels.

Within the Citadels, there had been no attempt to regulate thought. As a result, several points of view regarding the Exo cultures had developed. The radical, futuristic daughters, never having known any other way, nor, by their admission, wanting to, were opposed to any merger, ever, while some sentimentalists, unswayed by the sophisticated arguments of Citadelian genetics, were in favor of immediate reintegration.

The gyneologists and archaeohistorians could not dictate a course of action. They did, however, suggest that, before an judgment of the two cultures' compatibility be made, it was necessary to collect more information in order to separate rumor from the truth. The Congress would deliberate on the future regardless of the factions.

The anthropologists agreed that added information was needed to temper the folklore which had evolved within the Citadels. It was not known how much of the data on the Exo cultures was obsolete and biased. In the early days, faithful reporting had been a rarity, since any excursion from a Citadel into the Exo-culture had taken place in an aura of fear and loathing.

Contact for the past five generations had been limited to Gland search and capture sorties and infant exchange excursions. Most daughters had never seen other than a holograph of an Exo and knew very little about the Exo culture while the image they did have was that presented to them by the archivists—an image always steeped in violence. Each generation had become less aware of the past while maintaining scant knowledge of it.

Because of the previous de-emphasis of cross-cultural investigation, the recent science of exanthropology, defined as the study of Exos and their culture, was prepared to assist in the decision—a decision that would be based only on information of contemporary society.

Accordingly, in the year 348 AF, preceding

164

the Congress, Bru assembled a field-team for an expedition to prepare a report on the Exos.

Jack Remick

# C-1

### Trisha

I liked driving at night. The Z-Ray, the highway, the road noise a diversion, the moonless sky pitted with stars. I smelled the bags of lettuce. Fresh. The scent of tomatoes—acid—and the bite of the pimentos – green, yellow, red. As I drove I imagined Bett and Kali working up a salad – tomato, lettuce, cucumber, pimento with bleu cheese.

Ahead, the lights of a lone car on a lone highway – the highway to nowhere, Bett called it and the Desert Rose Motel was the last stop before you got there. I checked my speed—in the Z-Ray you have to pay attention – because the electric is silent and powerful. If I zoned out just a little bit I'd hit ninety. In the mirror – twin dots in pursuit closing fast. I backed down to fifty-five, felt the urgency of the Z-Ray saying go go go and then the flashing lights – no siren.

I pulled to the shoulder. I knew it would happen. I had been expecting it. Rita. Another pat down for sure. *License and registration, please. Step out of the vehicle, please.* Rita loomed as she came to the Z-Ray. The cap with its four indentations. The sharp creases in the shirt. The pistol. I rolled down the window. Killed the Z-Ray. Stone silent.

"License and registration," Rita said.

I was ready for her this time. Purse on the seat, documents in the purse. Rita shot a light in my eyes and then on the docs and I remembered her hands on me the first time—the frisk, the hot touch. Rita handed the license and registration back. She leaned on the open window jamb. She smelled of lavender and cinnamon as if she had soaked herself in perfume and eaten cinnamon drops. She said,

"Going back to the Desert Rose?"

"So you remember me?"

"Sure I remember you."

Posed like a picture-book cop making a traffic stop, Rita peered at me as if waiting for me to do something outrageous. I noticed the ring on her finger. A big diamond ring. And on her left wrist, a chronometer with a little blue light that twinkled.

The silence was long. Heavy. I reached for the door latch. *Step out of the vehicle, please.*

"Okay—keep it under seventy-five out here. Don't want to peel you off a mesa somewhere."

Rita returned to her vehicle. I thought about those hands, thought about the biology of desire. What I was feeling just then made my head swim. I waited until the taillights vanished in the distance and then I hit the go button and the Z-Ray lit up and the headlights cut the dark and I again smelled lettuce and tomatoes and pimento. The scent of lavender and cinnamon fading.

§§§

Bett stood at the bar. On the stool, Kali, the prima donna of the Desert Rose Motel, looked like she had just dressed up for *Better Kitchens and Recipes*. She wore her white cook's garb. Bett said,

"You're back fast."

"I brought you the fixings, Bett."

"The fixings?" Bett leaned on the bar, the bar towel in her hand, wiping at a phantom ring of water.

"Lettuce, tomatoes, cucumber, bell peppers, green yellow and red," I said. "And a couple of bleu cheese dressings from Chez Chérie."

"Chez Chérie?" Kali said. "Pretty high tone so I guess you don't like the way I fix it."

"Knock it off, Kali," Bett said. "How long till you finish up here?"

"A couple of weeks."

"Breakfast?" Kali said. "An egg white omelet and whole-wheat toast." She sniggered.

"Eggs over easy, four rashers of bacon, toast and coffee, black."

"That's my girl," Kali said. "None of that LA fruit and nuts health-food crap right?"

"Jimbo was asking after you," Bett said.

I flashed on Jimbo on his knees in the bathroom doing everything I told him to do.

"He said you hurt his feelings," Bett went on. "What did you do to that boy? A boy like that needs tending to like a hothouse orchid."

"That's okay if you like hothouse orchids," Kali said. "Personally, I prefer the bearded tulip."

"Don't talk dirty, Kali," Bett said. "This young'un might not know her flowers."

"I can teach her how to tend a tulip patch," Kali said.

"Like you taught the cop?" Bett said.

That was why. No frisking, no step out of the vehicle, please. I looked at Kali in her chef's gear and saw her for the first time. You never see what's right in front of you until it's too late. Black hair cropped short. No makeup, no enhancement, all natural. Delicious. She could be a character in *Citadel*. Kali said,

"Rita doesn't appreciate the finer points of horticulture, but she said she's willing to learn."

"I bet she's got some tricky ideas about how to prune a rosebush," Bett said, "can I get you anything?"

"No," I said. "I have to get to work. I'm running behind."

"Okay," Bett said. "When you're ready, come on back over here and read us some more that story you're into."

"You're sure?" I said.

"A book about Mutants and Glands and you and me and the future of the human race? You bet. We were talking about it while you were in LA. I told Kali that Daiva could teach her a lot about how to plant a flower garden."

Kali said, "Where's those fixings you bought?"

"In the Z-Ray."

"I'll go. You and Bett sit here and tell lies about the future of the human race and leave the hard work to the boss."

Kali left. Bett said, "Sorry about ol' Jimbo."

"Don't be."

§§§

Upon my return to the Desert Rose, I had only to open a file and the scent of words took me in. No more searching, no more wandering. Daiva had given the novel to me and I entered as though I were the novelist. It was always a roiling scent, like being in a perfume store, or walking into an herbalist's shop or visiting an aromatherapist. My work went faster. I didn't have to apologize or imagine what Daiva would say.

On the drive back to the desert, my last talk with Daiva had been running through my head. There were two sentences in *Citadel* that could give me the spine. I opened *Citadel* and scrolled to the *Origin of Plague.*

**Citadel**                                    **Daiva Izokaitis**

    Hagah had freed the mitochondrion from its
    eukaryotic cytoplasmic prison. She reversed two
    billion years of evolution. In its free state
    the mitochondrion was a toxin, a killer, and
    Hagah called it *gynerium*.

There it was – the whole of *Citadel* – Hagah had freed the gynerium from its cytoplasmic prison. In *Citadel*, Daiva freed women from the prisons where men held them captive. That was the polarity of the spine—freedom/captivity. Indexed by gynerium. I was on the road. All I had to do was work the chain of metaphors.

I let the words roll across my tongue, filter into my nose— Greek olives and capers. Gynerium smelled like olive oil. Toxic gynerium sweeping through the male population in a flood of olive oil, the murder of women that followed as the religionists called for the death of all women as God had revealed it to the prophets in the texts.

**Citadel**                                    **Daiva Izokaitis**

    I stood in the middle of the street in
    Istanbul, Misir Çarsisi and I dodged the fallen

170

men, their skin seared, erupting in pustules, their faces twisted in pain as the women shedding their burqas, dropping their veils, spread death. Their pain seeped into my palms as I stroked the skin of the dying. As the men died, one by one, I cut back and forth from the bed in the motel at the Desert Rose to the spice market in Istanbul where the plague started. I felt a sudden burst of energy booming in me. I did not know if I could return to the desert because I liked the future and I liked what I was becoming.

§§§

Six hours into it before I took a break. My skin itched. My eyes watered. One thing I had to do—I called up SkyChat and hit the Clara icon. When she came on, Clara looked flustered. She wore a black teddy. Her hair was wild. No makeup. I said,

I need to talk.

It's 3 am.

You're up.

I was working on something.

This novel has me worried.

I'm interested in only one thing, Trish—a blockbuster. Where are you?

The Desert Rose.

Are you alone?

I'm alone.

What do you want?

This book is terrible.

You signed her, Trish, make it unterrible.

I can fix everything but the ideas.

The focus group gave it a thumbs up so you need to bring this home.

Clara. If we publish this book they'll burn us at the stake.

We're too deep, Trisha. Caleb is already writing the screenplay.

Screenplay? You haven't got all my work yet.

He doesn't need your work for an adaptation.

But I'm making changes.

You let me worry about that. Get some sleep, Trish. It'll look better in the morning. What's your target date?

Three weeks? A month? I've cut it down by seventy-five pages. Daiva will be furious.

It's our book now. Let her be furious. Words?

One hundred and twenty thousand.

Caleb has a producer.

You're moving too fast, Clara. Are you alone?

Tend to your book, Trisha.

Are you with Curtis?

Call me when you're back. Now get some sleep.

Clara broke the connection, I saw the shadow of a man ripple across the wall behind her. Curtis again. She couldn't let go of him no matter how much he hurt her.

I clicked back to the bookmark. The *Wars of Savagery*. The words shimmered on the screen. I scrolled to the next section. Kirsis was still talking to the delegates at the Congress. I knew that Kirsis was one of Daiva's alter egos. Daiva, the writer, was a dangerous scientist because she thought of things like freeing the mitochondrion from the evolved prison of the eukaryote. And as I read the questions rolled out—

Can science reverse evolution?

Were men and women on divergent evolutionary paths?

What would happen when those paths no longer crossed?

What is desire?

What does post-lesbian mean in a unisex culture?

Was the Y chromosome headed for extinction?

Was parthenogenetic birth possible in humans…in the daughters?

Would Jahil's daughter be human?

Are we still human if we choose to eradicate the Y gamete?

What do we become if we practice complete parthenogenesis?

If we let the Y go extinct, what does that make us?

Sexual dimorphism—a term I was learning the more I read—was a trait, evolved with the brain along with the practice of carrying infants and led to the division of labor.

Daiva was imagining this world—or was it imagined? Was it possible? A world where only women, mothers and daughters lived and thrived? Would they still be human? What was a family in that world?

In *Citadel,* did the family even exist?

Complete parthenogenesis, the scientist said. It was possible. Daiva told me it was possible.

## Citadel        Daiva Izokaitis

Ova are expensive. Sperm are cheap.
Men are fixated on quantity. Women
pursue quality. This lies at the
root of Divergent Evolution. D.B.

### The Heptuant

Every seven years, each citadel held a Heptuant. It was the only universal cultural event. The archivists showed films of the Old Society. Some of the films were grainy and out of focus. Some of the films were patched together from antique stills. All of them showed the Killings.

In the auditorium of each citadel the gathering quieted when the films ran. The films the archivists showed changed every seven years, but they all showed the Killing. Many young daughters who had been shielded from images of the Old Society fainted or vomited at the showings. Often, daughters, who had just come of age, cried when they saw the images of the Killings. And in watching they were changed.

173

When the showing was over and the daughters returned to their spaces, there was quiet and there was weeping and there was a silent outrage against the Ones Who Stayed. After the showing, the questions were always asked—Why did they stay? How could they have stayed?

After the Heptuant showing of 6 Floral, Lang and her companion, Kel, returned in silence to their room on the sixteenth round of their Citadel where they sat facing one another until Kel's trembling stopped and her voice came back and she could speak without the quavering of fear and loathing.

Kel said, Why did they stay if they knew they were going to die?

Lang had seen twenty-eight Heptuants, but the images still preyed on her.

This is my twentieth year, Kel said, and if my progenitrix had stayed, I would be a slave.

Or dead.

But why did the men cut off the breasts? Kel said. I close my eyes and I see the blood—why do we have to see the blood?

To remind you of what the ones who stayed had to suffer, Lang said.

She left her bed and sat with Kel. She closed her in a circle of warmth and she said,

I'm so glad I have you.

Even as she spoke Lang recalled watching Kel turn away from the images of the films—images of women in chains, women swollen with child, women on their knees fellating the Exos, women tied to beds, their legs spread, blood oozing from their vaginas, women with ejaculate smeared on their faces, women with ejaculate smeared over their bodies. Women with bleeding breasts.

She wrapped Kel tighter and Kel said,

Easy, I'm just flesh and bone.

Lang released Kel. She sat back and then she laughed and she wept and she kissed Kel and she said,

174

They stayed because they thought they needed men. They stayed because they were afraid to leave. They stayed because they had a residual nostalgia for the DNA injection tube. They stayed because men owned them. For eons in the Old Society, a woman was chattel. A man could buy and sell her. She could not own property. She could not show her body.

They stayed even knowing men would mutilate them?

They stayed because they hoped it would not happen, Lang said. That was one of the severe punishments for any woman who had outlived her fertility.

Kel said, I've seen the films of sex and what they did to those who stayed.

In the Old Society, women were tricked into thinking they needed men to be complete.

Would you have stayed?

No.

But you know now what happened. If you couldn't have known, would you have stayed?

No. If my line had stayed, I wouldn't have met you and I wouldn't know what love is.

But they must have loved the men, Kel said. Is it the same kind of love you and I have?

## Citadel                    **Daiva Izokaitis**

No, Lang said.

She pressed Kel into her bed and trailed her fingers along her legs, and Kel sucked in her breath. She kissed Kel's leg, and her belly and her neck. She stopped at Kel's mouth. She looked into the greenish yellow eyes of her companion. She was overflowing with desire and kindness. She wanted more, but she pulled back. She said,

In the Old Society, you were not allowed to
say no, Kel. Men took women when they wanted. If
the woman said no, she died. Women had always
been afraid men would stone them.

Lang caressed Kel's cheeks and she felt full
and ripe. Kel's lips had turned crimson. Her
eyes had opened wide. Her breath was tangled in
her chest and came out in slow gasps. Lang said,

I know the truth of desire when I see you this
way.

Kel turned on her side and she said,

Some of them said no and they lived.

Only because of the Warriors, Lang said.

I don't want to know all this, Lang. Why did
we go to the Heptuant at all? Why do we have the
Heptuants?

Lang touched Kel's hip, let her fingers glide
over the pale skin. She waited. Every seven years
the showing, every seven years a celebration of
Foundation and Separation. Every seven years the
ritual of reenactment of the flight to freedom.
Lang said,

We have the Heptuants so we will remember why
we are here and to celebrate the martyrs who
died so we could be together.

Kel faced Lang. She said,

I'd have found you anyway. I know I would
have. We were meant to be together.

Lang laughed. She sat against the headboard.
She felt the heat of the young Kel's body and
smelled the scent of arousal that always made
her head swim. The Waiting Period said it was
forbidden. Lang said,

You think we were destined?

No, it's chance—but you have the ageless gene
and I don't. I will die. Do you hate them for
that? For making you live forever?

I do not. I am the way I am. I have birthdays
but I don't age because my telomeres don't decay.
The thing missing is always what you have--

innocence. I would give you what I have, but that's only for the geneticists.

## Citadel  **Daiva Izokaitis**

You have seen so much, Kel said. You know all these things and I have so much to learn. I wish I could live forever to be with you forever. You have taught me so much.

Lang touched Kel, felt her sweat. Tasted her aroma. Lang closed her eyes.

Kel said, Will you miss me when I die?

The river of desire again rolled over Lang. She let her arms and legs go limp—now was not the time. It never was time after the Heptuant. No one had sex the day of a Heptuant but just then, more than anything, she wanted to lie with her young lover. And not being able to do that made Lang sad.

She said, Yes.

After I die you'll find another lover.

You're not going to die tomorrow.

How many were there before me? Kel said. You never talk about them.

Does it matter?

You think I'm jealous, Lang? Really?

Why are you asking me that now? Lang said.

What happens to me?

What happens to you?

Did you do to them what you do to me? Can love keep me alive? Will anything keep me alive forever?

Don't ask these questions, Kel. These are questions all the daughters ask. You don't need to ask them. We're here now, we're together now.

Do you ever want to be with another daughter?

I want to be with you.

Who decided you would be one of the ageless?

I'm an experiment, Kel, I didn't ask for this, my progenitrix asked for it. She made the choice.

So, she was a mother like any of the ones who stayed? A daughter making decisions for you just like the men made choices for women in the Old Society.

These questions hurt.

Why do they hurt?

Because I know you will die, Kel, and when you're dead I'll mourn you.

But you'll go on living and you'll find another one.

Tithonism is not a blessing.

You have no wrinkles, Kel said. I see the other daughters aging and their skin turns to leather and I want to know why we can't all be immortal.

No you don't. You're human. I am not. I am a crossover but I had no say in it.

That gene, Kel said. It's the crazy gene, isn't it? It keeps me crazy for you, and I don't care.

I closed the laptop. Daiva's writing in the *Heptuant* made me sad. It was shocking, powerful, and sexual. I had to think about what was happening in the novel. It was more than a story of separation and murder. It was a tale about the humanness of women. In isolation, we still bring with us all the pain and terror, all the hope and innocence we've carried down through time. In the *Heptuant* Daiva touched on some of the most powerful ideas in *Citadel*—

The history of murder.

The depth of Lang's love for Kel.

The love of the elder for the younger.

The limits of choice—"I didn't ask for this, my progenetrix asked for it."

The horror of eternal life.

The meaning of desire.

So many times, I had been impatient with Dee, but in the *Heptuant,* I felt, for the first time, the subtext. Subtext, something not there, but intimated. Anguish at being alive. The psychology of truth. The inevitability of growing old. I read the sentence again—"their skin turns to leather…" I felt such deep anxiety as I thought of myself in the future, an old woman with leathery skin.

And now? Could I even finish the job I was supposed to do? In those moments of uncertainty, I hesitate knowing that the best remedy is to plunge back in. I opened the laptop just in time to see Lang in the corridor. Corridor—a floral scent I couldn't name. I stopped reading until Lang had taken the elevator down.

§§§

## Citadel                     Daiva Izokaitis

I entered Kel's room on the sixteenth round of the Citadel on a clear day where the ocean spread on the horizon. I felt the gravity of being in the Citadel, felt the strangeness of the space and its range of ripe feminine scents. We have so many. I thought about stepping back, cutting the scene right there. But Kel said,

Who are you? And what do you want? And why haven't I seen you before?

I said, Lang loves you, you know. You're everything she wishes she could be.

She's immortal, Kel said.

She picked up a nail file and sanded at the nails of her left hand. I saw a spoiled little girl with the eyes of an innocent and the body of a woman who had no idea of her power.

I wish I could be one of the ageless, Kel said.

179

And Lang wishes she had your innocence, and your beauty.

Are you one of her secret lovers, one she goes to see when she's tired of me?

I had to be careful. I could change the story. I could do what I wanted. Daiva wasn't reading my notes. She didn't care.

No, I said. I'm the editor.

Then how do you know what she wants? Kel said.

Do you have any idea what you mean to her? I said. She's a Planner. She's ageless, she has power, and she loves you.

I know. She's told me I don't have to stay in botany if I don't want to. But what would I do? It's so boring here.

Kel shifted to her right hand—the file scraped at the long nails on the slender fingers of her fine hand—Daiva was so complex—she had drawn each character in such detail that when I saw them, they were like old friends. I was jealous of that skill. How did Daiva know these people? Like all writers, she chose from her friends, wrote them in, made them nasty or beautiful, grateful, or selfish. I said,

What do you want?

Kel glanced up at me, the yellowish green eyes an unnatural color. Her hair was a brilliant auburn, her skin the color of a pale sunset. Daiva had set the genetics. A progenitrix could order the color of the eyes, the skin color, the shape of the limbs, the lip size, the hair color.

Kel was a specimen, a perfect specimen, the embodiment of desire. To look at her was to desire her. I said,

Do you know that all the Planners are ageless? They all have Tithonism?

Kel looked up from her nails, ennui on that face with its perfect skin, that mouth with its perfect teeth, and perfect lips. I felt obscene in my thickness, my stringy black hair, my sun-darkened skin, Kel said,

180

She's useful to me.

I sat on the chair facing Kel who ignored me. Dismissed me. Ripe as she was with desire and youth she could do anything she wanted. It didn't matter if she lived in the Citadel or in a city full of men she would have been one of the chosen ones.

I said, Lang gives you everything and asks nothing of you.

She asks a lot of me, Kel said. She snapped the file against her leg, that long slender leg with the perfect skin. She keeps me here like a prisoner. I want to go places and see things but she almost has me in chains.

I could read her now. It took this moment of closeness to understand that Daiva had imagined the future but she, not even she, the omniscient author, could change nature. Kel was a spoiled brat. She was a lovely beautiful, useful, intelligent, spoiled brat. She would have been a spoiled brat in any time in any place. She had a sense of entitlement. I said,

Where would you go?

I don't know. I just feel like I'm missing something. I'd like to travel, but Lang treats me like a slave.

Do you know what a slave is? I said.

Of course I know, I was at the Heptuant. I might like to be one of the women in one of the films.

No you don't, I said.

How do you know what I want?

If you watched the films in the Heptuant, you saw how men hated the women who stayed. You saw what they did to them. Can you imagine yourself being used that way?

At least they got to feel something, Kel said.

Yes. Pain, humiliation, and degradation. You don't know how it feels to be used, to be hurt, to be violated. You're safe here. You don't have to worry about the pain.

Kel glared at me. There was a viciousness in
her eyes that made me cringe. It was the deep
viciousness I had seen first in Daiva when we
talked about the contract. Was Kel a selfie?
Back out, I thought, back away from this little
monster.

Kel said, You don't like me, do you?

I don't dislike you.

You hate me, Kel said.

Daiva must be the one who doesn't like you, I
said. But I wonder who you really are.

You know who I am.

She had someone in mind. Do you know anyone
named Daiva?

Who is Daiva? Your lover?

I'm not from the Citadel, I said.

Where are you from then?

I'm from where I'm from. I know a lot about
you.

Kel stowed the nail file in a drawer in a desk
like the desk I had seen in Kirsis's room.

And then as if I were not even in the room
Kel peeled off her smock and stepped, naked, to
a closet and opened it to a rack of suits and
shoes. She tried a periwinkle suit but slipped
on a cobalt blue one. It was as if she bloomed
in that moment in a spectacular burst of color.
She faced me. She said,

Do you find me attractive?

Attractive? I find you a little bit enigmatic.
Here you are with a Planner and you act like
you're doing her a favor just to look at her.

She doesn't feel anything, Kel said. When I
die, she'll find another one and do to her what
she does to me. Even when I orgasm I feel old
and ugly and stupid. When she's doing things to
me it feels good but I know she's just using me.
I'll be replaced when I die. I hate that.

You are spoiled, I said.

Kel narrowed her eyes and hissed and bared
her teeth and raised those hands, those fine

182

hands with the pointed nails that now looked like claws. She turned her back on me. I said,

I can make one note about this and you evaporate. I can erase you.

Kel, still hissing, spun around. I watched the rage spread over her, turning her face red.

I can, I said, make you disappear. Vanish. And no one will know what happened. No one will have the faintest idea that you ever existed.

Who are you? Kel said.

She closed on me and raked those long spiky fingernails against my cheek. I felt nothing. An empty shell. Daiva must have hated Kel's model to make her so vacuous.

What do you want? Kel said.

I want you to behave, I said. Do you know what desire is? Do you know the roots of desire? The end of desire? Do you know why you orgasm when Lang touches you?

Kel recoiled, her nails aimed at my eyes. I said,

I didn't think so. You have this daughter—she's tall, powerful, smart, perfect. Her desire for you is endless but all you think about is going outside into a world that would kill you. I'm ashamed of you, Kel.

Kel sobbed. She shook. She sat on the chair at the desk in front of the window that looked out on the sea. She buried her face in her hands. Sobbing she muttered that she didn't want to die.

She was jealous of Lang who would live forever, all because her progenitrix chose tithonism over mortality. She said,

What kind of a world is this when the beautiful ones die and the ugly ones live forever?

I was on the verge of telling this creature that she was just a character in a novel. A character the author had chosen to fill a particular slot in the story. But could I do that? Could I destroy the character's illusion of her self-importance? Could I tell her that she had no choice but to take what happens? Did I want to do that?

I rested a hand on Kel's shoulder and felt the heat and the sweat and the trembling. I felt desire raging through this beautiful young innocent pure spoiled specimen who at twenty had the complete code of desire written in her so that she was desired and loved but did not know what she had and so she would always be empty. Daiva was so perverse. I said,

I can make you immortal.

What will that cost me? Kel said. You want to lie with me? You want to make love to me? You want to do to me what she does to me? Is that desire?

No, Kel, that is sex. That is lust. That's a call that can be answered by any part of anyone's body anytime you want it. I can make you immortal if you want that. But...

So, you do want something.

Yes. I want you to be kind to Lang. She didn't choose to be ageless, it was chosen for her. You see, there's a big question buried in this novel and the question is—what is a human?

She says I'm human, Kel said. And she's not. Humans aren't supposed to live forever. All the ageless ones aren't human, are they?

But the Planners have to answer for the future of the race, Kel.

I hope we all die and the entire race goes extinct. I think the Extinctionists are right. To live with the shame of our past isn't worthwhile. The Exos don't deserve to exist. This isn't what we were meant to do.

What are we meant to do? I said. Breed?

Breed? What does breed mean?

It means you can't choose. You have sex and you take what comes and you can't do anything about it. That's the way it was in the Old Society.

Maybe that would be best for me. Kel said. Maybe I'll go out into the Exo culture and give myself to them and let them make me bleed.

That would be a mistake, I said. In here you are safe. You can choose to give birth. In the Old Society, women often did not have that choice. That's what the Planners are doing. They're taking care of the future. And you can be part of that future.

An offspring. Maybe that's what I've been missing.

Have you read *Women in Captivity*? I said.

No, Kel said, but I've heard about it.

Read it, I said. Read it and you'll find out the truth. You'll find out exactly why women rejected the Old Society.

And how do you know that? Kel said.

Because I'm the one they murdered with the skillet.

Note to Daiva: I rewrote this scene—which I said I wouldn't, but as I read your work, I had an epiphany. My mind opened and I understood for the first time who and what I was and where I came from and what I had to do—

*The taste of hair loaded with the odor of the arched back was a scent I had only tasted on my own hands never on the mouth of another woman. Kel cried as she came, calling my name, the name of a feral creation. I tasted for real what before I had only imagined as I looked at Kel on her side, those yellowish green eyes half closed with fatigue. I felt a deep shame for what I had done. Kel said,*

*Are you going to make me disappear now?*

*I did not answer. Guilt swept over me and I wanted to plead with a thousand apologies, make a million amends but I, my back to Kel now,*

*stared at the wall of the sixteenth round of
the Citadel that looked out on the sea. I
remembered the beach and the sand and the
wetness of water and the taste of sea salt that
had the same scent as Kel's sweat. I remembered
the beach meat with their deadly game of
volleyball, when after the bloodshed, like a
cheerleader in heat taking the victor to my
condo and having him mount me, use me, pound me
until he emptied in me, screeching but unable
to do what Kel had done with her mouth and
fingers.*

*I realized this was what I had been hunting
all the time. I had hunted on the beach, hunted
until sunset, hunting for the right one but
only now did I know that there was no right
one, never would be for me a right one. My head
ran full of the images of you on the pier the
day we talked about Citadel. Even then I knew
that it was a special time but just now, since
I had entered the room on the sixteenth round
of the Citadel overlooking the sea, I knew
meeting you had led to this—and I was ashamed
and afraid but open—a first is a first even
with one of your fictional creations, and I
knew that I never could be with you but I had
no qualms about making love to the character
you had created in Citadel. For a moment, as my
head screamed with realization of what I had
become—lying with a creation who, for all I
knew, could be the analog, the mirror image of
myself—so in my fantasy I had made self-love
and the sweat I tasted was my own sweat and
Kel's slickness was my own slickness, and the
odor in my nostrils, my own perfume, the
residue of my own guilty arousal. With the
blank look of a woman who did not hear, did not
taste, did not feel, Kel said,*

*And now?*

*I can't possibly tell you, I said.*

*My lips were numb.*

186

*She smiled. Armed with an index finger nail painted and pointed, she raked my breast. I meant to say no, but I could not force the word to leave my lips. As she touched me—her nails like cut glass gouging me—I saw you.*

*I lay with you, the writer mated with her editor, the story now richer and deeper. Kel said,*

*Are you going to erase me?*

*No. Not now.*

*Why not?*

*They say they don't want sex, but they do.*

*I heard the door open. I sat up.*

*Lang entered.*

*She peeled off her jacket that looked like an antique military jacket with metal insignia. She stood at the foot of the bed peering down at the now exhausted half-asleep Kel who had flung her arms out like an athlete after a strenuous event*

*Lang sat on the bed. She said,*

*Were you dreaming about me?*

*Flushed with shame, bent with guilt, tortured by my intrusion into this private and troubled twosome I fled, but Lang did not see me. The words had lost their scent.*

I picked up the device that I had dropped at Kel's first wetness. *The fire in the cleft defined me.* I scrolled back to Lang entering the room on the sixteenth round of the Citadel that overlooked the sea. Lang peeled off her jacket with the metal insignia on it—metal insignia? Military? What metal insignia?

The numbness in my lips faded as I read the first scene in the *Heptuant* set with Daiva's description of Lang and there were no metal insignia. I skipped to the third scene—the metal insignia, and I called up SkyChat and tapped Daiva's link and Daiva came on the screen.

You look like hell, Trisha, have you been sleeping with Cowboy Jim again?

I need you to clear up some details.

I thought we worked that out.

Just…I guess I just needed to talk to you about that.

I'm busy, Trisha. Jahil had breakthrough bleeding last night.

Is that bad?

What do you want?

In the third Heptuant scene, you have Lang wearing metal military insignia.

You're the editor, you fix it. That's what Clara's paying you for.

Don't be cruel, Daiva. I just need…

What do you need, Trisha?

I had a strange epiphany, well a strange anti-epiphany and I want to tell you about it.

Clara called me.

What did she want?

She wanted to know why you didn't come to Pinnacle when you were in town. She wanted to know if you are okay. I told her you were probably being a bad girl. She told me she has a launch set for three months out and if you keep stalling we won't make it.

I licked my lips. The numbness was gone but they tingled as if a small fire were burning in my mouth. I said,

I'll make it work.

§§§

The scent of lilac wafted over me—semen—could semen have a lilac taste? Insemination had the taste of cloves. I had no idea what semen tasted like. I had smelled it every time a specimen peeled his condom from his flaccid penis. I had read about semen, talked about semen, but I had never tasted semen. It surprised me that the word had its own aroma as if the root of a word did not extend to its derivatives. The context baffled me as I entered the long corridor of the Citadel…Why there?

# Citadel                    Daiva Izokaitis

I saw Lang approaching.

I knew the walk by now. Walk—orange. She nodded as she passed. I said,

I need to talk to you.

Talk to you—words I had spoken to Rose dozens of times but never had there been a scent. Why did every word in *Citadel* have its own odor while the words in my world did not?

Lang entered the room. Room—citron, lemon, a peculiar clean smell. Lang sat facing me.

I need to know…

She held up a hand, the palm cupped. I focused on that palm. It was curious, that palm. No lifelines, no bloodline, no lines at all. The palm was flat and smooth.

You look surprised, Lang said. She didn't tell you?

Palm. A thick scent like retsina.

We talked, but Kel doesn't know why.

The science is clear, Lang said. If you select for one trait, other traits ride the same nucleotide sequence. Select for death-denial, and our skin does not wrinkle. Unintended consequence, no fix het.

You really can control, you can edit, you can splice the entire genome?

Lang turned to the glass. Beyond the glass the trees stood waving in a breeze and beyond the trees a very blue, cobalt blue sky. Blue-Sweet William, a flowery smell. A raft of

189

clouds tracked across the azure plain. I was dizzy from the colliding aroma of the words.

Sometimes, Lang said, when I'm with Kel, I wish I had a different fate—but I am what Daiva made me.

Can you change?

I don't think so. Not now.

I wanted to touch this daughter, wanted to feel skin that didn't wrinkle, wanted to smell the hair of an immortal, an ageless daughter, a Planner.

Are all the Planners connected?

Why do you ask that? Lang's eyes were bright, her face placid, even a little flushed, and a faint orchid scent escaped from her mouth. Did all the Planners smell the same?

I backed away from Lang, left the room on the sixteenth round of the Citadel. I scrolled back, searching for Planner. The word Planner had the scent of charcoal to it. Planner showed up 150 times, each time smelling of burnt charcoal, but there were three names—Kirsis, Lang, Eris.

Note to Daiva: are there only three Planners in all of Citadel? The way you have written this, it's hard to tell where they are. Are Kirsis and Lang in the same Citadel? Where is Eris? You number all but one of the Citadels—Cuernavaca. Why just that name?

I re-entered, riding on the odor of charcoal to find Lang frozen in place at the window. I said,

I'm sorry, had to check some details.

Lang, as if awakening, replied,

You are the editor—why can't you fix us?

Do you want me to rewrite you? To make you wrinkled and dying? If I do that you will be just like the rest of us.

I'm used to being in control, Lang said, I don't want to give that up.

Your lovers die, I said. When they die what do you feel?

Lang laughed.

Feel? She said. The Planners can't feel, Trisha. That is your name, right? Trisha? Or is it Patricia, or Patrice. Or Margaret?

I'm not sure, I said. When I come in here I'm never sure who I am or what I want.

Trait selection, Lang said. One trait. And what every daughter can feel, I cannot.

I can make you die, I said.

What would she say if I died? Lang said.

Sadness then crept into the room. Salt. I smelled the eternal salt of human sadness as Lang's face turned red and her eyes boiled with tears. She said,

I feel nothing except when I'm aroused and then I can't control the river. I flow, so wet, and when she is at me with her tongue, I think she will drown but she never complains. Does your river flow, Trisha, when you are aroused?

I was so close to Lang I smelled the scent of her charcoal skin. I glanced at her legs, the gray pants—gray, maple syrup. Pants. Saffron. Her wetness. She said,

See? I live forever, but the cost turns me into a flooding love-sick fool.

She didn't know that would happen, I said. I touched Lang's arm. Arm—violet, the scent of violets. Lang looked me in the eye. And in the eye was desire.

Desire—cinnamon. How could desire in Daiva's literal universe, smell like cinnamon?

Can you tell me what desire is? I said.

Desire is wanting to be in the one you love, who loves you.

And what is love?

Love is a residual evolutionary response to need, Trisha.

Kel told me she wished you were not one of the ageless ones.

Kel doesn't know what she wants other than not to be with me. She has no understanding of the sacrifice that brought us here, no idea of the death and killing and the horrors of the Old Society. The young ones have this nostalgia for sex. They read the histories, like *Women in Captivity* and they wonder how it would feel to be taken.

I can change that, I said.

Can you? Can you make them not want to lie under a man and have his engorged member ejaculate in them? That's what they dream of being—beautiful women in the Old Society mating with rich powerful men. Has Daiva told you what that is? Residual Evolutionary Response. Do you want to change them, Trisha? You think you can change them? I hope not. If you change me, you change the story and if you change the story you change Daiva, and this story was given to Daiva to lead us in a new direction not to re-create us as perfect.

I backed away from the scent of charcoal. I closed the door on the daughter in the room on the sixteenth round of the Citadel, and I sat on my bed in room 11 of the motel in the desert. I waited for a few minutes—so much to do, so many characters to set right, so many problems to fix. But could I do all of that in three weeks?

Note to Daiva: You create them and then you abandon them as though they bore you. I remember you telling me that you took them in dictation, stripped them out of their time, in a sense you ripped them out of their static world but then like a heartless mother, you abandon them to time in sorrow.

Lang is a Planner. You write about the Planners but who are they? Are they like authors who become indifferent to the anguish and pain in their creations? You also told me once when we sat by the sea, on the sand, in Santa Monica, that you went both ways. I misunderstood. In my innocence and naïveté, I assumed too much. And you did not challenge me. And then you slept with Caleb. Now I see, in the work, that you are telling me you are both creator and created. I see it in the writing, I see it in the story, and still I ask—have you, in your lust for creation, taken the unbearable step into godhood? I fear for you Daiva, as I write these notes that I will never send, notes that you will never see, notes that you will never read, I fear that you will destroy yourself. Am I wrong to fear this?

I try to imagine your reaction—but you have told me you do not want to see my changes and I still do not understand. Are you worried that I will ruin the world you have created? By abandoning your obligation you give me the power of the demigod to rearrange your thoughts, your words, your dreams. My question is this—am I strong enough? Am I making it better? Or am I making it worse? You have embedded so much pain and anguish in the Planners, Daiva. I spoke to Lang about her skin. She told me she is ageless and she doesn't wrinkle.

What is the future of the telomere in the Daughters? Planners? What is the future of the ageless gene? I don't understand what the ageless gene is. Do you see a time when the Y chromosome will be extinct and only the double X exists? And with the double X only the ageless ones persist? You give me more problems than I can solve, Daiva. Am I strong enough to carry that load for you? I doubt it. Where are you in me? Where am I in you? I feel that we have grown close while I've been doing this work and yet you abandon me just the way you abandon your creations. Can't you see how much I need and miss you?

It's my obligation to the art to change you. But isn't that hubris? A woman trying to perfect a world she knows nothing about?

And the aging, Daiva, you touch on immortality, the possibility of eternal life and that Eternal Gene which I know now is just a metaphor that you use to tell us that at some point in the future we will never die. I have talked to Lang for quite a while and I have talked to Kirsis and I have talked to Eris and they are unhappy. Do you see why?

You give them love and desire, but you take away their youthful dying lovers.

Do you see what you have done? By giving Tithonism to the Planners, you murder desire—what daughter will ever love again knowing that her love will die leaving her alone and forever mourning?

You see the problem with eternal life, Daiva? Either we all have it, or none of us has it and either way you bequeath both terror and desire. As I said Lang is unhappy. You told me that the Planners cannot feel. But that is not true. They can feel, Dee. They confess their pain as they lie with their mortal lovers, who age as they have sex, while the Planner will die only the small deaths.

What is the future, Dee?

You write that by 579 After Foundation the Y gamete

194

will be extinct. What then? You write that men and women are on divergent paths to the future. Do you feel guilt knowing the Y will cease to exist?

There is so much I need to tell you as I dive deeper into the novel. So much. I have explored desire now, taken it in my mouth and savored it, tasted it and it is golden. Desire stripped of sex, Daiva, is pure emotion. In desire the lover is in you, and you are in the lover. What rotten words those are—so loaded with past and shame while in the novel you have written that desire is pure being. Absolute. Like the last degree of freezing. In desire although you don't say it, there is permanence. Is that what you mean by immortal? Desire without end, desire completed in the touch and closeness of skin to skin and mouth to mouth begging for nothing beyond itself?

And yet, you let these poor daughters feel love and desire while leaving them to age and decay.

That is not right.

You see my trouble? I'm acting here as though this novel, your novel is fact, truth, science, when in reality it is a fantasy, a false world full of false hope and loaded with false feelings and yet it shapes me. Already I feel myself pulling away from my old life—I have no desire now. I have no need. I have no goal in going to the beach to lure those decaying Y chromosome carcasses to my bed. Knowing what I now know, I have an absolute horror at thought of the shriveled, pitiable, dying sperm diving into my body. I have lost all that need, Daiva, but found another reality in your words. I have transcended sex and find myself carrying a past in my body that sickens me—the thought of senseless, crippled, half-destroyed creatures swimming to my womb leaves me in a state of morbid rejection of who and what I used to be.

Let me go back to the beginning. You birthe these creatures and then you abandon them to me but I am not a good mother. I see what you have done and I will change them. I can change them. It is my obligation to change them as I find the best story possible and now the question—what if the story I bring out of your writing isn't the one you wanted? You see the tyranny of the reader here, Daiva? The reader is a demanding tyrant pushing you to tell the story that isn't in your heart or in your head, but to tell the story that connects to the story living in the reader, and if you don't make that connection they hate you.

Last night, I was with Kel. Four hours. I wrote you a note that I will not send, a note you will never read. We made love. You see the crime and the horror? The editor, me, making love to the character you created. I was closer to Kel, your creation, than you are to me. Can you even imagine that anguish? I feel their skin. I smell their breath. I taste their sweat and hear their screams. That is my fate, to live in the world you created making love to the characters you created, having sex with the creatures of your dreams. And what do I bring back?

Fear.

Terror.

Guilt. All the sins of the deep reading editor. Because you do not love me, I am left possessing characters who do not belong to me.

Lang told me that the young daughters dream about having sex with men. They see the sexual, erotic work that defined the Old Society—they want to know it, but living in the Citadels they never know the feel of a man's erection in their body. I have known that, but I do not tell them. That is what you bequeath—a nostalgia of hunger for the woman possessed. I know you will say this is just a novel. You are wrong. You will say that I'm being stupid for treating it this way. I say the novel exists without you, without me, perhaps even without the creatures.

What if all the residual evolutionary responses you write about are so deeply ingrained in the flesh they can never be extinguished? What if human beings are nothing but lust and perversion? What if our sole purpose as human beings is to fuck ourselves into oblivion?

It's already happening. We breed ourselves to the cusp of extinction but in your novel, you see a bright and shining world without hate or fear. All of that is fantasy, Dee, because we, humans, we are imperfect and not perfectible. We are helpless creatures splashing around in a sea of time not aware of what we want or what we need—unaware of what we can be.

Your view of the future is diseased. Your hope for perfection is flawed. The only emotion that can tame the chaos is love and you deny it to me with every word you write.

I have to quit now. I am exhausted. I need three more weeks to finish my editing before I can deliver this manuscript to Clara.

I wish you would read my notes and reply. I know you won't. You abandon Citadel when you move on to Extinction. You are like every other author. I have seen it so many times. You create a world and then you let it go before it is ready and it creeps out as a half-formed creature gasping for breath then dying in silence and agony. I can't let that happen to this novel.

If only you would read my notes, we could bring this novel alive, the two of us, parents of a being that is both of us. But I know you won't and so I take control of the novel.

§§§

As I re-read my lengthy confession, a sadness overwhelmed me. Mine was the raging sadness of a character trapped in a time and place she did not choose. It's the fate of the fictional character to be jerked around, slammed down, stripped, or clothed in rags or furs, all without any say in it. I thought about Lang as she stood at the window of the sixteenth round of her Citadel overlooking the sea and I understood the importance and purpose of the sequence.

Daiva had brought all these pitiful daughters out of darkness, like Rei and Zia, only to leave them half-drawn, leaving them with no back story, no future only the absurd present she had created for them.

Then abandoning them to their hurt she moved to the next novel. To be a literary character is to know the fear of abandonment by your creator. The creator who sets you in motion, gives you a name—or not—then thrusts you out into the unfinished, unknowable, unreal world. What character ever had any hope of a future? In this I see the editor as savior.

Taking the forlorn character, half-imagined and armed with nothing but a few pages, girded with but a few words, the editor demands accountability. But Daiva was not abandoning only *Citadel,* she was abandoning me. "'It's yours," she said, "do what you want."

She had abandoned me with the ease she abandoned all the characters in *Citadel.* I have no choice now but to become a character in this novel if I am to save the orphans Daiva has left on the steps of the foundling home called Pinnacle Press. In Lang's eyes, I read that existential sadness of the creature alone on a darkling plain searching for what she does not know. Will Daiva use any of the creatures from

*Citadel* in her next novel? Lang, as I watched her, had no idea that she lived beyond the paucity of words Daiva gave her. Did Lang know the rest of the story? Or did she know only her part like a bit player impressed into the play at the last moment never having read the entire script? Does Lang know what the other characters are doing? It is the editor who shaves and fills in, the editor who repairs and replaces the broken dream the writer calls her novel. Inherent in the writing is the inevitable abandonment. Never achieving perfection, the writer has but a small vision of it and so leaves the characters, leaves the story, and in time lets the novel decay, fall apart, lets it collapse like walls of a mold-eaten, weathered house caving in on itself. Writers are not just idiot children, they are careless narcissists unfit even to own a pencil, a pen, a computer, egoists who give no thought to all the chaos and anguish, all the pain and perversion they bring into the world.

I was through puzzling through the tangle because I was hungry. I did not remember the last time I had eaten.

§§§

The steak was rare, salty with sharp pepper flakes floating on a sea of hot butter. Bett said,

"Does that meet your city girl standards, sugar?"

"The steak's great. Thanks, Kali."

"Anything for the writer," Kali said.

"I'm the editor. The writer hates me because of what I'm doing to her words."

"Huh," Bett said. "And you get off on that don't you?"

I cut the last square of the sirloin in half and took my time finishing it, but I left half the baked potato. Kali said,

"Something wrong with that spud?"

"Nothing wrong with the spud but I'm on a neo-Paleo-pseudo-Mediterranean high-protein diet and taters are absolutely verboten 'cause of the carbs."

"Zatright?" Bett said. She slid the plate with the half-eaten potato from the bar and carried it into the kitchen. She returned with a cup of coffee. She said,

199

"Okay. Give us some story."
I opened the laptop and pulled up the scene.
"This is a scene called the *X Point*."
" I thought you were working on a novel, Trish," Bett said, "
X Point sounds like you got something mathematical going on
here." Bett sniggered. She slapped Kali on the back. I ignored
her.


## Citadel                              Daiva Izokaitis

At midnight, they left the Citadel. In the
dark their exit was a near mystical experience.
In the darkness, in the shadow of the Citadel,
they were on a path that led past the glacis...

"Whoa, whoa," Bett said. "This is the first I heard of
anything like a glass sea. Just what is a glass sea?"
"Glacis, g-l-a-c-i-s. It's a military term," I said. "It's a steep
slope designed to keep invaders from getting in too fast. The
first Citadels were built like fortresses, Bett. The first rounds—
Daiva calls them rounds instead of floors—were solid up to ten
units and the rooms all looked out on the Solerian."
"Units?" Kali said.
"Yes, in the Citadel system the unit is the measure between
the areolae of a daughter who is five units tall."
"Jesus Christ," Kali said. "Are all these daughters
Amazons?"
"Let her finish, Kali," Bett said. "You can ask her all the
questions you want after it comes out and you read it."
"Can I go on?"
"Yeah, yeah," Bett said.

...that led past the glacis and entered the
woods. The trees were all oaks and had grown
tall and thick. Cutting through the forest
there was a pathway. In single file the
daughters worked deep into the trees and Bru
held up ahead and the file stopped. She said,
    "It's here."

200

"Hold on," Bett said. "Bru is who? And the daughters in this group are who? You said part of being a writer was to write strong verbs and concrete nouns, so what kind of group?"

"Bru is one of a set of six transgendered daughters who are charged with the survey of the local Exo villages. They will spend six months studying the fate of the infant exchange."

"So the girls become boys?" Kali said. "That's kind of a raw deal if you ask me."

"They have to, Kali, because the Mutants have a genetic mutation that causes them to lapse into a killing frenzy when they see a female. If they see the double XX, rage boils out of them. I read you that section in the *Wars of Savagery*."

"Yep," Kali said. "Mutant, genetic mutation, killer 13th gene."

"That's right. The group of six has an archaeohistorian, Gin, an archaeoanthropologist, Ala."

## Citadel          Daiva Izokaitis

They waited at the edge of the clearing. In the light of the moon, the stone stood shiny, circular, dark. The top was ground smooth. The stone was ancient. The exchange took place at the stone. The Citadels released only one male infant a month when the moon waxed full. Twelve infants a year...

"Hold it," Bett said. "Did I miss something here? All the Citadels. Twelve a year, one a month? That's close to zero pop."

I kept reading,

The exchange was a ritual between the Exos and the local citadel. Without the exchange, the Exos would die out because the daughters did not give them the Eternal Gene.

"Let me get this straight," Bett said. "This whole thing with the exchange? If the Exos are Mutants and kill the daughters, why do these daughters give a kid to them if they know the kid will grow up to be a killer?"

"Daiva wrote the novel with five big ideas in mind—what is a human? What is the fate of the race? Are men and women on divergent evolutionary paths? What is desire? And can genetically modified double X offspring survive."

"Well that's a mouthful," Kali said.

"Let her talk, Kali. It's just a novel."

"The fact is that the Planners keep the genome as intact as possible."

"But if these Exos are killers, how does the mother have one knowing he'll be a killer too?"

I could see it would be hard to keep going, so I closed the laptop. I said,

"Without the exchange, the Exo population would shrink to nothing. Until the Congress makes a decision the Planners want the race intact. If there are no Exos, you change the idea of a human and Daiva doesn't want that to happen yet."

"Yeah, well that wouldn't be a terrible loss, would it?" Kali said.

"The geneticists can recode for an Exo with the $13^{th}$ gene silent. They can design an infant with the alleles regressed to the point before the $13^{th}$ gene mutated and that produces a Gland, or they can leave the $13^{th}$ gene in full force and that is a Mutant."

"Yeah, the three flavors of males," Kali said. "I've been listening, and I see that, but why? Why not just let the ladies have more ladies?"

"Daughters," I said. "They have daughters because in parthenogenetic birth…."

"I know," Kali said. "They're duplicates."

"In *Citadel* that's not exactly true. Full control of the genome means they can modify a gene so that the daughter differs from the mother by a single base pair on the twenty-first chromosome and that's the problem."

"I see more than one problem," Bett said.

"The problem is," I said, "genetically, the daughter is now different from the mother, but down the line if the daughter has a daughter, and she lets a modified base pair pass on it pushes divergence further and you still end up with the question of what is human."

"Ah!" Kali said, "she produces one of three kinds of jerks so that sometime in the future they can decide if they wanna re-create the human race."

"That's right," I said. "That's why the X point is so important."

"So what you're reading to us is the final version of what your pal Daiva put together after you worked her words?"

"I'm still making changes," I said.

"Well, then, why don't you go ahead and read the rest of it to us?"

"Yeah," Bett said, "read us a bedtime story."

I opened the laptop again—

## Citadel                    **Daiva Izokaitis**

Bru led the group through the forest to the exchange point to wait for the Expellers with the child.

They hunkered down, just as the sun lifted over the trees and shot a beam of light onto the stone. Bru saw the band of Exos at the edge of the clearing. She shivered. Six months of prep, and she was worried. Even after time in the Simulator, even after the physical changes, she knew things could go wrong. What if she couldn't meet the challenge?

At the X Point, the two cultures met without ever sharing the space at the same time. The Citadel opened its gates twelve times a year. Responding to the natural cycle of the moon, several bands of Exos gathered to compete for the infants. Bru imagined her transgenders to be just more scavengers waiting for a scrap of flesh. She would have to fight the Exo band leader for it. It was a battle she did not want to win.

The sun lit the misty clearing that was empty except for the stone in the center. Time and weather had softened its carved frieze that once depicted some pastoral scene.

Out of the forest, a dozen daughters all masked and wearing the billowing white garment of the Expellers entered the clearing. The lead daughter carried two white wrapped bundles. Guarding her, the Expellers formed a protective circle as she laid the bundles on the stone. The Expellers faded back into the forest leaving the clearing silent and empty.

A band of Exos filed out of the woods to the stone. Time. Bru led the way to the stone in the clearing. As she approached, she saw the forehead tattoos of the Exos, the indigo lettering shimmering in the dawn light. She glanced at her companions whose long hair framed their own birthmarks. Ala, the archaeo-anthropologist, gripped Bru's arm. Bru shook her off. She knew what had to happen. She didn't want to win.

The clearing was silent, time suspended. Bru stepped to the head of her group and growled. The Exos froze. An Exo whose forehead tattoo identified him as the progeny of Erian rushed at Bru who smacked him in the face, dropping him to his knees. He reared up and slammed into Bru. Breathless, she toppled onto her back and glanced at the nodding Ala.

Erian hooted and stamped his feet as he stood over her pounding his chest. The winner. Shaking, angry, defeated, Bru stood. Head bowed. She had seen the holographs of the exchange. She knew what to do.

Erian picked up the bundle. The infant cried. The Exo offered the baby to Bru, but she held up her hands, No. Erian smiled and hooted and raised the child like a trophy. His band hooted as Erian danced. The indigo tattoo on his forehead seemed to pulsate.

He unwrapped the white bundle and traced the indigo tattoo on the baby's forehead and hooted.

204

Bru read the tattoo—Marik C64. Using the sash and the cloth the child was wrapped in, Erian fashioned a sling and hoisted the infant onto his back. He motioned Bru to fall in behind. He led his band away from the clearing, away from the stone.

The daughters and the Exo band marched in single file through the forest. Erian did not look back. The others followed in silence except for an occasional hoot. He alone seemed to know where they were headed.

An hour's walk before Erian stopped. He squatted and unslung the baby and held it on his knees then unswaddled the child and bared its genitalia. He looked up and nodded and smiled.

From a pouch tied to his waist, Erian took a flask, drank, then passed it around. Each member of the band took a large mouthful and swallowed, each of them muttering ah chay, ah chay and making a bitter face. When the flask came to her, Bru glanced at Gin who nodded and Bru drank. The strong liquor burned her throat, but she did not flinch. Finished, she handed the flask to Ala who drank then handed it to Gin. Bru puffed out her lips, repulsed as she was for having tasted the saliva of an Exo.

Erian stood and slung the infant again and the infant at first babbled then let out a cry. Erian's jostling gait soothed the baby and in moments he fell asleep.

I stopped. My back ached. My brain had fuzzed. Bett and Kali, elbows on the bar, sat quiet. Bett swiveled off her stool and pulled a fifth of bourbon from the wall of bottles and without speaking poured three shots and shoved one at me. I tossed the shot back. Bett refilled the glass. Kali tapped her empty shot glass on the bar and Bett refilled it along with her own and together they finished.

Kali said, "Breeders. Nothing but trouble."

"Yeah, who decides who gups?" Bett asked.

Kali said, "Maybe they're like Republicans—just bake'em

and boot'em?"

"The daughters decide, they choose if they want to do it."

"Sort of like taking one for the team?"

"No sports talk, Kali," Bett said.

"Female choice drives evolution," I explained. "In the Citadels, they go one step farther and decide not just sex but all the other traits—Mutant, Gland, Exo. Hair color, skin color, height, weight. That's why a lot of the daughters have yellow eyes."

"Yellow eyes?" Kali said.

"It's a sign of beauty in the Citadels. I think Daiva is telling us that vanity never dies."

"Okay," Bett said, "but who tells you, you sprout an Exo, you, you push out a Mutant, you, go for the gold, pop out a Gland."

"You said no sports talk, Bett."

"Altruism."

"Altruism, huh?"

"They have a choice," I said. "they have good counsellors and they know the score—"

Kali said, "Now you're doing it."

"The stakes are high—future of the human race."

"And they go for it?" Bett said.

"Culture is female. Without the circle, there is no future."

"Does that kid talk?" Kali asked.

"Which kid?"

"The kid the Expellers boot out."

"If there's no maternal language," I said, "there's no culture, no progress."

"What comes next?" Kali said.

"What do you mean?"

"In this story. What happens next?"

"It's close to midnight, I've got a lot of work…"

"I want to hear what happens next."

"She's like that," Bett said. "Has to know what happens next."

"That's right," Kali said. "You got a bunch of dykes hauling some little JoJo out into the tules and turning his baby ass over to a bunch of Killers and you don't want to know what happens next? Pour another round, Bett. I'm not letting cutie pie run loose until I know what happens to that little bastard."

"It doesn't go where you think it'll go."

"How do you know where I think it'll go?"

"That's not the way her mind works."

"Daiva's mind," Bett said.

"She never takes you where you think she's going to take you."

"I still want to know."

"Okay, Bett, but the next chapter will cost you another round."

"Whiskey I got, kid. Let's hear it."

I tossed back the double shot of bourbon. I do not like whiskey, but there are times when you need alcohol. I knew what came next and I needed to be fortified.

## Citadel                    Daiva Izokaitis

They trekked through the forest until the trail broadened to a path that became a rain-mired road. At sunset, the entourage came to a village. On either side of the road there were fields of corn and beans.

Approaching the village, Filina's sensors tingled. Heart beating fast, she had trouble breathing. It was as if she smelled the death and blood of the past. Her mind raced. She was in an Exo village. She glanced at Ala who touched Fel's arm, soothing. Bru calmed down knowing that the others were feeling the same elation, the same fear, the same dread.

The village was open—no fences, no walls, no grid of trees for protection.

The road, lightly depressed in the center, led through a string of brown huts to a small square. From each hut, an open trough drained to the gutter that was clogged with fungus in the waste flowing there.

A recent rain had flushed the gutter but raised a stench. Bru did not cover her mouth and nose because none of the Exos did.

As the band passed the huts, doors opened and Exos came into the street hooting and pointing at Erian and his baby.

Past the square and over a narrow footbridge spanning a gorge filled with muddy water, Erian stopped in front of a hut and lifted the sleeping child from the sling.

The sudden change in motion awakened the baby and it began to squawl. Erian held the crying infant over his head. Bru turned to see that the road behind them was full of Exos. Young and old, stooped and erect.

Bru counted heads—twenty Exos.

In silence broken only by the child's crying, Erian displayed the infant—Marik C64 to the village.

The sobbing child's face turned the tattoo on his forehead a deep, iridescent purple. Bru scanned the names on the foreheads of all the inhabitants in the town and they all ended in C64.

Gin leaned close to Bru. She whispered, "Do they know?"

"They don't know what the marks mean."

Gin squeezed Filina's hand twice. She whispered,

"Are they all slow-agers?"

"We'll talk later," Bru said.

Bru was amazed at the sea of blue and astonished at the fecundity of her sisters. Here was proof—every child in the village came from the Citadel. The Planners set the number. It was clear—without the Citadel, there were no Exos.

Bru nodded to Ala who mouthed, "Just watch." Ala's eyes darted from Exo to Exo, to the child then to Erian who wrapped the crying child back in the cloth and entered the house.

The Exos who had followed Erian dispersed and

208

Bru's group entered the hut with Erian and his
troupe.

Kali said, "No wonder the kid's bawling, he's hungry.
Far as I know, kids need milk and far as I know no dude's
ever squeezed a pint out'a his pecs."

"The kit. In the opening when the Expellers lay the baby
on the stone, remember, there's a second bundle?"

"Two babies?" Kali said.

"One baby. I have to take you to another scene."

"Whoa, whoa," Bett said. "I got some questions. What's
with twenty? She says there are twenty Exos, but the kid's
gonna make twenty-one."

"The Planners control the genome," I said. "In the Old
Society, sex was coupled to procreation because women
were not educated. The population exploded and population
explosion was a disaster. After Foundation, the Planners
had to control for numbers."

"She means us, right?" Kali said. "Us here, spewing out
kids like they're widgets and fucking up the planet?"

"Before Foundation, ecologists had warned the Old
Society that the divergence…"

"The divergence?" Bett said.

"Men and women are on divergent evolutionary paths,
Bett. Because eggs are expensive and sperm is cheap, men
thought only about quantity while women had evolved to
think about quality. Divergence starts right there."

"Under two bucks a dozen," Kali said.

"What?" I said.

"Eggs, under two bucks a dozen."

Bett laughed. She said, "Yeah, and swimmers—what
was the number? Three hundred million a shot?"

"Something like that," I said.

"Okay," Bett said. "I need to know what happens next."

"Yeah, I hope to hell these clowns find a way to feed the
kid," Kali said.

## Citadel                          Daiva Izokaitis

     Filina tried to recall where she was a
year before. At first, a feeling of joy swept
over her—friends, her studies, her life came
back and she realized she had forgotten so much
and then the joy turned dark.

    She had let herself get too involved in her
pregnancy, in the newness of it, in the hope of
it because she gotten as involved as any woman
in the Old Society and for a moment, she wondered
what she would have felt giving birth to a
daughter and tears dripped down her cheeks and
she remembered Gipzae's words—Let it go, let it
go.

    Drowsy, she was nodding off when the
technician entered carrying the breast pump. The
technician clamped the pump to Filina's swollen
breasts. The gentle pumping caused her uterus to
contract. She watched the pouches fill with her
milk. When the technician detached the pump,
Filina fell asleep the pulsations still
lingering in her womb.

I glanced away from the screen. Bett and Kali were as
quiet as two atheists at the rapture. I was about to read
when Kali said,

"They pack along sacks of mom's milk."

"And then what happens?" Bett said. "When the milk
runs out? Do they go back for more?"

"It's taken care of."

"I want to see," Bett said. "You got dudes with kids, no
babes like your Filina, and you got kids but no milk. I want
to see but first I got a question about that long sentence you
just read."

"When did you become an expert, Bett?" Kali said.

"I haven't worked that yet."

"So, she leaves it up to you?"

"I'm the editor, I edit. It's what I do."

"So you're sort of taking over?"

"Daiva's busy. She's given me carte blanche."

"Well, I got lost half way through that tangle."

"I'll fix it," I said.

"Buy the book, Bett," Kali said. "But Bett's right. Novel or no novel, that kid's gotta get some lunch."

"Sow's milk. The Exos have a breed of sow they milk for the Expelled ones."

"Exos!" Bett said. "Expelled ones...Damn, that girl is something ain't she?"

"And just how do these Exos know how to do that?" Kali said.

"The Planners think of everything. They've got to think of everything. That was one of the big failings of the Old Society. The men didn't plan and they made a mess of things. They messed it up so bad, there was no way to save the planet except to separate."

"So what happens next?" Bett said. "You've got this gang of daughters now with dongs, you've got a kid in a poke, and you've got a bunch of Exos feeding a kid sow's milk."

I skimmed through *Citadel* to the section called *Men Who Live Like Women Once Lived.* It was a scene that still needed work but I couldn't decide how to fix it.

## Citadel                    Daiva Izokaitis

The door of the hut opened and a daughter motioned Bru in. A daughter! Impossible. When Bru didn't move, the daughter came to her and taking her hand led her inside. Riga and Cas followed. It was a calloused hand, a strong grip. Bru glanced at Riga who shrugged. In the hut, the band who had followed Erian squatted in a ring around the infant in its sling.

Bru squatted with the band and the daughter began a dance contorting her body, flitting from Exo to Exo, each of them hooting and pawing at the daughter—a captive, she had to be a captive— then drinking from their flasks, the smell of alcohol as strong as the odor of the bodies.

Bru glanced past Filina—who seemed to be in a trance watching the captive perform—and she noticed, there in a corner, tethered to a wall there was a sow. A sow.

Making the circle, the captive came to Bru and Bru tore her eyes away from the sow. She had no idea what to do. To hoot? To paw at her? To speak to her? Why wasn't she dead? She was a daughter of a Citadel, the tattoo on her forehead told it—Del C10. She should be dead.

Bru, boxed up in her own persona, did what the others in the band had done. She hooted and ran her hands over the captive's hips and breasts that were not fully developed and she drank from a flask and the burning alcohol clouded her brain. The captive danced away to Riga, to Cas, to Filina. It was clear that none of them knew what to do.

Alcohol, the dance, the captive—Del C10, where was C10? Bru did not recall ever hearing about Citadel 10.

Bru was on the verge of bursting out of her role, of breaking free and running away with the captive—a prostitute? A slave? A willing escapee from a Citadel?

The captive wove around the room and she came again to Erian and she opened his cloak, fondled his erect penis. Then with quick, darting, motions of her head, she closed his flesh in her mouth. The band hooted and pounded the floor, all of them drinking from their flasks. Bru glanced at Riga and she saw Riga seething, eyes narrowed with loathing and disgust. Bru touched Riga's hand as the captive continued to suck Erian's penis. Bru's head was swimming, her stomach roiling, her mouth thick with alcohol and she was sickened to see the past replaying. The centuries, the millennia that women had spent bowing and on their knees, lived there in that hut in that village. Bru looked at Riga and

212

Cas and then at Filina and they waited for a signal. Bru knew what they were thinking—rescue. Capture the captive, give up the expedition, take her back to the Citadel.

At that moment Erian stood and taking the child from the sling on his back, strapped it onto the belly of the captive. The child wailed. The captive, still on her knees, adjusted the sling, turned around on all fours, the infant hanging from her like a small mammal clinging to its mother and, pulling up her skirt, presented herself to Erian.

Bru choked. The band hooted. The daughters squirmed as Erian penetrated the anus of the victim. Bru watched his erection disappear into her. He moved with rapid jerks. She hooted—huh huh huh huh in a rhythmic chant until Erian tensed and collapsed against the bare buttocks of the captive and then he withdrew.

He sat back on his haunches, his penis still glistening with his semen. The captive contorted her body, writhing, groaning, hooting until she plucked the child from the sling under her belly and holding the infant, she stripped off her skirts and top and stood naked, child in her arms.

Riga gagged. Cas huffed as if about to faint. Bru touched Filina's hand and squeezed and she looked at Bru whose eyes did not leave the captive. Bru saw that the captive was an Exo. An Exo who had been wearing the ancient dress of an early daughter. Where did he get it? How did he get it? Was there a place where these things were common? How could that be?

Bru knew then that she was looking at a deep androgyne, a genetic intersex androgyne. They did exist. The skin was chocolate brown. The hair silken yellow. The eyes violent blue. The breasts small and brown-nippled. The penis a shriveled, vestigial appendage.

The androgyne then handed the infant back to

213

Erian and one after the other the members of the
band mounted him, each one grunting and hooting
as he ejaculated then fell back to the floor.

Her mind racing, Bru catalogued the
reenactment of fertilization and birth. It was
a ritual, that in its bizarre pattern, like all
residual evolutionary responses, was empty. She
also realized that time had warped the ritual
into a creation myth. But how did they know? Was
there a residual memory of the ritual that had
carried through even after the realignment of
the genome?

Riga would have a lot to write about.


I closed the laptop and took a deep breath. Bett and Kali
looked stunned. It was the first time I had seen them
overwhelmed. Bett sighed. She said,

"Well, shit, that's one hell of a tale."

"What happens to the brat?" Kali said.

"Buy the book," Bett said.

"I'll read you that part tomorrow. Right now, I'm beat."

"Yeah, gotta lock up, Trish. We're going to bed."

I was tanked on whiskey. Any alcohol was better than none,
but I had to feel my way from the bar through the dark back to
room 11. I kept hearing Bett's voice, "Well, shit that's one hell
of a tale."

§§§

Room 11 was stuffy and hot. I had forgotten to turn on the
A/C when I left. I wouldn't sleep now but that was okay.
Being whacked and tired, I could go deeper so I opened the
laptop to the scene Daiva called *The Last Night Out*. It came
at the end of the brutal scene with the Mutant. I had worked it
seven times trying to smooth it out, but I couldn't fix it, I
didn't know enough to fix it because the rage was a poison
that did not go away....

# Citadel                           **Daiva Izokaitis**

As they approached the square, they heard a voice; a strident, demanding, shouting voice. They were astounded at the flow of utterances. Such articulateness should have been impossible for an Exo.

A cluster of villagers stood passive, watching the Exo on a rock. He towered above them. They had to look up to see more than his feet. He was taller than most. His skull bald. His facial hair shaggy. The lips protruded. The wiry hair on his arms gave his amber skin a mottled look. Bru swallowed her fear. This was a Mutant.

The electricity of violence filled the air. Bru felt it as though she had been sensitized to know it automatically, as if to react was an instinct when the rage was present. She felt his animal tenseness trapping the Exos in a stunned state.

Bru was almost in awe as she led her team closer. The Mutant radiated violence. An aura of energy pulsed around him. Every move a slashing gesture.

As if drawn by a magnetism, the team approached. Filina stopped, her body rigid. Frozen. Immobile. There before her, his voice charged with venom, his eyes alive with hate and rage, stood a human being with her name tattooed on his forehead.


Even I, removed from the scene, felt the electricity of fear. Repulsed. I hesitated, then went back in. I smelled the odor of rage and the odor was the stench of rotting cabbage....

## Citadel                    **Daiva Izokaitis**

I stepped over the gutter that ran down the
center of the street. The scum-filled gutter
drained sewage from the huts into the street. I
crossed the street and stood with Bru. She wore
a sackcloth jerkin. Her hair was long, stringy,
matted. She looked rough and gruff. Was this the
same Bru I had seen in the Citadel? I scrolled
back to pick up the thread of the story. I
stopped at the Transfiguration scene with its
powerful knot of surgical processes, hormone
treatments, infusions, and rapid gene therapy
then scrolled back to the hut. Bru stood broad
shouldered, muscled, and confident. Riga wore
the same sack cloth jerkin Bru wore but her hair
was blonde and pulled back at the side, riding
behind her ears. Riga's beard was long and
stringy and matted with chunks of food.

Filina wiped tears from her cheeks with the
back of a hairy fist. And then Cas, carrying a
pouch made of crude leather, came up. She too
wore the jerkin and strap sandals. Her auburn
hair hung in hanks over her shoulders and her
shoulders were thick, knotted with muscles, and
bulging. Her thighs were heavy, her calves
hirsute.

The odor of their bodies was sickening, the
sight of their un-groomed beards disgusting, the
look on their faces frightening.

I said, Did you get what you came for?

Bru looked at me, her eyes bright, her
mustache thick and drooping at the ends. She
said,

What has she done to us?

Was it that bad? I said.

You read it, Bru said. I've never seen a
Mutant in action until tonight.

How long are we going to stay here? I said. I

looked at Filina who was hanging despondent onto Cas.

Bru said, If we had to vote tonight, we'd all go for Extinction.

I was thrilled and puzzled at the sight of the daughters as they walked through the night. I listened to Filina lament, If I had known, I'd have terminated. I would have.

It's not your fault, Riga said, is it, Trisha? There's no one to blame for it. Except Daiva.

Can you change it? Filina said.

Without answering, I followed the daughters to the edge of the village where the street gave onto a broad prairie ripe with waves of high grass. There we stopped. I felt the anguish boiling out of Filina. I did want to change it, but as I read deeper I knew that this was the one thing I could not, did not dare change. This was the cautionary tale Daiva had buried in *Citadel*.

In the tall grass, Filina squatted. Her body heaved as if she were in a seizure and then she howled. It was a deep animal howl, a wild animal howl that ended in a guttural throaty grunting.

It is my fault, Filina said. You saw him. You saw what he was doing to them.

I could see the Mutant with Fil C426 tattooed on his forehead bubbling up like a blister on his amber skin.

It was your choice, Bru said. And in choice there's always chance.

I should've listened to counsel, Filina said. They told me of the choices, but I didn't want to know. I wanted my child to be natural.

Cas knelt facing Filina. She grasped the hairy hand, stroked the bearded face, let her fingers run through the matted hair. She said,

Your child is natural, Filina. So natural he's a killer.

Filina whimpered, her shame now hidden in her sorrow.

He's what all Exos would be if the Planners hadn't silenced the gene, Cas said.

Why would they ever allow a natural fertilization? Filina said. As she spoke her beard fluttered like a bird's wings with each breath.

Riga said, What is human, Filina? Your offspring? He's human. He was conceived, born, expelled. You didn't know you had birthed a killer.

I hunkered beside Filina, recalled her birth scene, all the joy, the pain, the happiness that had faded when Doctor An told her she had birthed an XY. Filina's face that once had been bright and flushed with the vigor of birthing clouded into a mask of pain. I remembered Filina in her young beauty horrified as the doctor said, You cannot hold him, you cannot speak to him, you cannot ever again see him. He will be expelled.

I sat beside Filina and Riga and Cas. Bru held herself back from us. I thought of myself now as a daughter. I recalled the moment in the hut when the Exo had penetrated the androgyne, using him as a receptacle until he ejaculated.

Filina glanced up at me and her lips rounded with words so full of pain they became mere grunts.

Please change it.

I can't, I said.

You don't care if we all give birth to killers?

Bru then came to us and she knelt. She said,

This is why we came. We needed to see what had changed. Without this new information, we would have made a faulty decision.

And nothing has changed in three hundred years, Filina said.

True, Cas said. Left to chance, the chances that a Mutant will be born are equal to the chances that a Gland will be born.

I have failed, Filina said. Her voice cracked.

218

She held her face in the cup of her hands. Riga said,

Chance did not treat you well.

Did they know? Filina said.

Did who know? Riga said.

I'm talking to Trisha. The geneticists? Did they know my child was a Mutant before he was born?

I don't know.

That's not the question, Filina, Bru said. She held Filina's hand and she stroked the hairy paw and she said, The question has been and will always be—what is a human? The Virgin Citadels isolated themselves. They don't inseminate. Are the parthenogynes human? We have to make decisions, daughter. We have to bring our findings to the Congress and we have to make a decision to reintegrate, to stay separate, or to let the race go extinct. You did what any daughter could do. You took the chance...

And I failed, Filina said. I did nothing but add to the misery daughters have lived through time.

We have to go, Cas said. We have to go before they wake up from their stupor.


I felt terror rising in me. I let my hand drift to my belly. I thought of the men I had taken from the beach. I thought of Jimbo, the cowboy I had lain with on the bed. As I let my mind track back over his sweaty body as he heaved and tongued me, I remembered Daiva's words—most of our actions are residual evolutionary responses.

I was free while Filina was not…

I scrolled ahead and from a distance watched the daughters re-enter the Citadel and a few pages later lose their useless appendages—three million years of evolutionary residue snipped off.

§§§

# RER

### Inside

*In the East, the slaughter was complete. Women did not live in the Niche. In the East, there were no Citadels.*

I found Kirsis in her room, in the Citadel on the thirty-sixth round of the spindle overlooking the bay.

The room was small. The bed narrow. The desk made of carbon fiber. Durable. New-looking although it was probably several hundred years old. It had the quality of permanence.

On the desk, beside a metal flask, a unit was open. A chart on the screen. Kirsis sat arched over the desk looking at the screen when I entered. Kirsis stood.

She was elegant, muscular, her hair the color of the sunset, her skin the color of sand dunes, her eyes chrome yellow. She was the tallest daughter I had seen. Lean and lanky. Grey pupils, a face with flat planes, teeth so white they reflected light.

My first thought came as a thunderbolt.

You're not just a Planner, you're a parthenogyne.

Kirsis held up an elegant hand, the lineless palm the color of mother-of-pearl, the fingers narrow spidery but not emaciated.

221

And you're from the past.

The 21st century, I said. I need to know more about the Citadels. Daiva has left out so much, but my boss still expects me to turn her prose into gold. Hard to do that when Daiva doesn't tell me all the things I need to work with.

You talk like an Exo, Kirsis said. Things. They don't have real language, you know. We call it 'thingism.' That's how they speak. 'Hand me that thing.' 'Those things over there....'

Talking to Kirsis was different from the other times I had dropped inside the novel—different because here I smelled the scent of the future and it was not like anything I had ever known. I made an interlinear note—

Note to Daiva: You have to use all your senses, Dee.—smell, taste, sight, sound, touch. Your inconsistent use of quotation marks creates a nightmare for me and will for any reader. I can standardize them only if you don't feel that I'm ruining your work.

You asked if I'm a parthenogyne—that's a question we don't ask in the Citadels.

Why not? I said.

Because it's the kind of question that in the past turned into status and led to violence and death.

The Wars of Religion, I said.

Kirsis poured from a flask. The water was copper colored. I thought of wine, of Chardonnay.

Why is the water reddish?

The future's nothing like you imagine.

I don't remember reddish water. It has no taste.

Daiva can only guess, Kirsis said. Her vision is limited. She didn't get every detail of every scene. Most of the time she's right, but now and then she skips a beat.

The Wars of Religion, I said again.

Kirsis sat at the desk in the chair the color of burnished metal and she said,

In the past we knew that there would be no peace until all religion was eradicated.

Great! These are the details Daiva has left out.

Not left out, didn't know. Otherwise the work is accurate.

How is that possible? I said. You're a character in the novel. How can you know what the writer has left out?

I walk, I talk, I think, I feel. I live here. Daiva came here in her vision.

Do you bleed? I asked. Daiva has no details like that and I need to know—how human are you?

The daughters all bleed, Kirsis said. That was the mark that killed them.

But why? Your geneticists can make you immortal, why can't they control menstruation the way they control gene 13?

Gene 13! Kirsis said. You have been reading. Daiva knows her science, but she takes dictation from us. We know exactly what she will know and we tell her what we want her to know.

*Takes dictation. Takes dictation. Oh!!*

So you do talk to her? I said.

Yes, in her vision she sees so much but what she takes back is always and only partial. When you first appeared, she didn't know who you were or what you were so she didn't write you in, but here you are.

Where are you? I asked.

You know where I am, Kirsis answered. Pages 173 to 191...

You do have a sense of humor.

It was said in the 20th Century, that feminists had no sense of humor, but the truth is that men had no receptors for female comedy. You must know the truth—what is your name again?

223

Trisha. Trisha de Tours.

Well, Trisha de Tours, 25 years After Foundation, we realized that no woman would be free until the last patriarch strangled the last priest with the entrails of the last lawyer then slit his own throat.

Are you an Extinctionist? In your talk to the delegates about the Wars of Religion, you don't sound like an Extinctionist.

Another of those terms we don't use in the Citadels...

Daiva writes that there are Extinctionists, Separatists, and Integrationists.

I'm a scientist, Kirsis said. Politics are not science. In the Old Society, the politicians burned scientists or castrated them to turn them into chattel. The future hinges on science. Daiva uses those words because she has to make her writing accessible to you people. In the Citadels we are all equal, but some of us think in new and different ways. There's room for discussion and thought.

Thought, I said, and divergent evolution.

Yes! Kirsis said. The mechanism for divergent evolution is the polarity between thought and belief.

Is it true? What Daiva writes? The Y gamete has decayed almost to extinction and men and women are on divergent paths?

Yes.

Yes? That's all? Yes?

The X has taken all the genetic load from the Y as if that was the purpose of sex and gender from the beginning, but evolution walks in its own footsteps. In the past, in the Old Society, we now understand that men *believed* while women *thought* and thought is an inducement to evolution because thought is an element in the cerebral environment. Thought produces science that produces change. Belief is static, immutable, and dangerous.

224

And all of this has something to do with the Wars of Religion?

Yes. In the Wars of Religion women were expendable. We know that men believed the revealed religions gave them the right to kill women just for being women.

The beach scene, I said, the honor killings.

The beach scene? Kirsis said. That must be in a different part of the story.

So you don't know what's going on everywhere in the novel?

Daiva is a very selfish writer, Kirsis said.

She keeps parts of it from you?

Yes. I can't time travel beyond my pages.

What about the Disrupter?

What about the Disrupter?

She calls it a vestigial weapon of the Wars of Religion.

That is correct, Kirsis said. Science gave men the Disrupter in the late 21$^{st}$ century just before Foundation. And one generation later, after men had slaughtered all the women scientists, they lapsed into a dark time.

That slaughter brings me to Hagah, I said.

We know very little about the life of Hagah, the geneticist who liberated Gynerium, but like most women in the East, she had been beaten, raped, abused, and sold into sexual slavery.

But how did she get the training to work at the cellular level...

Women in the East were given the number five, Kirsis said. They did not enter the Niche. It was women in the West who were so privileged.

Five?

Yes. The sum of their orifices and breasts. In the East, just before Foundation, women were little more than the sum of their holes and their issue. That is why there are no Citadels in the East now.

What happened?

The men made a mess of it. Women were afraid

225

for their lives. The air was poisoned, the water polluted, the oceans turned to lifeless cesspools. And women, like most slaves, did what they were told even when it worked against their own self-interest. I've seen your work and what you're doing to Daiva's writing. I read the scene where you explain the Wars of Religion.

Late 21$^{st}$ century, I said. Am I still alive then? Do I live to see the Disrupter?

That I don't know, Kirsis said. The machine itself is the pinnacle of the science of death that began with Archimedes continued through Leonardo to Oppenheimer and Teller. In the beginning, in their villages, the Exos and Mutants used the weapon, but they could not build or repair one. Now, we take care of that by managing gene 13.

How do you manage gene 13?

We know the proteins that code for the superior and middle temporal gyrus as well as gene 13q21 which we don't destroy but we do silence via the epigenetic switches that deactivate collective aggressive behavior.

You mean war.

Yes. Murder.

As Kirsis spoke the unit on the desk chirped. She answered. Yes, I'm busy but I'll be there in five.

We have something like that in my time, I said. We call it SkyChat.

The prototype, Kirsis said. In the future nothing is wired because early on, we learned how to use the ether. We didn't abandon all male-originated science but the connection is now three-dimensional.

No wires? I said.

I have to go.

But how does it work?

You have to leave now, Kirsis said.

But if I go, how will I find you again?

Page 171.

226

But you're just words on page 171.

Change me. I'll always be there unless you cut my scenes.

You know I can do that?

We're not stupid, Kirsis said. You are the editor working on contract. You control the past, present, and future. Now please leave. Go to page 173, which as you know by now, needs a serious rewrite.

I can't rewrite.

You could give me more scenes, Kirsis said. More dialogue would be nice.

You haven't answered my questions.

If I answer your questions, what will you do for me?

There's so much I need to know.

I told you that I bleed, Kirsis said. That was your second question, I think.

Oh! You think, you say you think, and you don't say you believe.

You're the editor, you can make me say exactly what you want. I have to go now. Science is irreversible. You can never abolish gene sequencing just as you can't abolish the fundamental theorem of calculus. That is unlike your art which can be changed at will—and that's what our creatrix, Daiva, is telling you.

I love that woman, I said.

Daughter. Daughter, Kirsis snapped. Maybe you will live in a Citadel one day and your relationship to the creatrix will be very different. I'm sure.

I knew I was losing her. There was still so much I needed to know.

What is desire? I blurted it out without thinking. Why do men and women have to diverge? What does it mean to be human? What is love? Do the daughters have sex in 359 AF? Do the daughters orgasm? Is there daughter pornography? What is pornography? Are parthenogynes human? What does post-lesbian mean? What will

227

extinction mean to the post–lesbian daughters?
Is D/S inevitable in the future? Are there any
decent men in the 21<sup>st</sup> Century?

Idiots always outnumber good guys.
Why did women suck men's dicks?
Not as messy as getting pregnant.
Why can't a man make me come!
But Kirsis was fading.
Make it up, you're the editor.
Kirsis disappeared.

I left the room in the Citadel overlooking
the bay and I sat on the bed in the Desert Rose
Motel with the laptop running *Citadel* open to
page 171 where Kirsis standing before the
delegates to the Congress was delivering her
summation of the research from the Expedition...

§§§

I slammed the laptop closed cutting off Kirsis in
midsentence. No. That was not enough. I reopened to page
171, the Congress scene. Kirsis was right. It needed a
complete rewrite. I marked it and deleted the entire section.
Snippy bitch, I muttered.

Taking a deep breath, I restored the delete. I could edit. I
could not re-imagine. I could not re-create. I could change
some things… things… *thingism*. Why did the Exos lose
nouns? Anomia. What were the daughters doing to them to
disrupt language development? In the Old Society, women,
to get even with their men for abasing them, did not
socialize their sons but let them run wild. The genetics
were paramount.

So many questions.

I was hungry. Carrying the laptop, I left the room and
walked to the bar. The parking lot was half full—motorcycles, a couple of RVs, SUVs, and horses. I heard music
boiling out of the bar. Maybe I could snare a biker and get
laid.

I danced twice with a cowboy whose DNA injection
tube remained inflated the entire time.

I drank too much.

I danced with a woman and a man who then went back to their RV.

I polished off eight straight shots of tequila—no lemon, no salt, no chaser. Alcohol is fast. I wanted to slow down my brain. The tequila did just that.

I danced with a biker who wore Levis, a leather jacket and black boots with silver hardware. She smelled sweet. I felt odd dancing with this woman. Unlike the men I danced with, she didn't attack me, she didn't grope me, she didn't demean my body parts. She didn't say she wanted to fuck my ass. She was a good dancer. I sat with her at a table. She said,

"Can I buy you another shot?"

"I'm in too deep already."

"What's on the laptop?"

"A novel."

"You're the writer?"

"You've been talking to Bett."

"What's the novel?"

"It's a post-lesbian, anti-male, sperm-eradicating, post-family, post-death, post-pro-natalist re-invention of genetics, which, if I am correct, will change us forever just as it either saves the world or destroys it completely."

"Hmmm," the biker said. "If it's half that, it's a killer."

"Killer?" I said.

I studied her face. It was a good face. Angles. Planes. Black hair with islands of untouched gray. Good teeth. I said,

"Do you read?"

"You mean 'can I read?'"

"Do you want to come back to my room?"

"Do you want me to?"

Because I was buzzed and because I hadn't eaten and because I did not know her and because I would be gone in a week, I took her hand, and carrying the laptop, led her back to my domain in room 11.

The biker looked around. She turned the chair at the desk and sat arms draped over the back. I sat cross-legged on the foot of the bed facing her.

Her eyes were crystal blue. The hands were not delicate hands. The nails were not chipped. The skin of the hands was smooth. No rings, just a gold and diamond wristwatch.

"Are you married?" I said.

"Nope."

"Are there any decent men left?"

"What do you mean by decent?"

"What's your name?"

"Erica. Where's this going?"

"What do you know about flowers, Erica?"

Tequila soaked, my mind wandered through a beach meat sandscape looking for a biker in the desert before I passed out.

I was on fire from my ankles to my throat when I woke up. I didn't know if it was the tequila dreaming or if the bed was burning. Erica was sitting on the desk chair, feet up, reading from the laptop. I said,

"What are you doing?"

"Reading. Heady stuff."

"How long was I out?"

"You mean how much of this did I read?"

"You can't just come in here and take over like that."

"I like this character, Kirsis," Erica said. "She's a Planner. Like me. Her monologue that kicks off the Congress section is too long."

"You ride a bike in the desert so that qualifies you to tell me how to edit?"

"I'm telling you how to zero in on danger and menace in the writing."

"What do you know about writing?"

"Look," Erica said. "You got tanked. You slept it off. Listen to this…"

Erica read from the laptop. Her voice was a solid, melodic, authoritative alto. I, for the first time, was not in the novel, was not the editor, was not an observer in the novel, was not a character in the novel. I was the audience. A listener. Erica read, as if she were an actor—

In the lab, Hagah, wanted to know what would happen if she extracted the mitochondrion from

230

a cell—what would it be? Could she reverse evolution? Could she, in the lab, regress the captive mitochondrion to a free-living cell?

The process was slow. She separated the mitochondrion from the eukaryote but both died because the life of the mitochondrion had become intertwined with the life of the host. The mitochondrion, that had been a macrophage, was trapped in the prokaryote.

The question she had to answer was how to feed the mitochondrion once it was segregated from the cytoplasm of the eukaryote.

In the middle of the century, all lab technicians were women, but little was known about the mitochondrial genome. Hagah discovered that the mitochondrion had not transferred all its genetic material to the eukaryote but had left a quiet gene that at one time provided the organelle with nutrients before it became an endosymbiont. She uncovered the code that reactivated the sleeping gene sequence.

Hagah had to induce a new pairing that produced not only a freestanding bacterium but an organism that replicated and mutated with each replication. She knew she had, in fact, recreated the proto-bacterium and she called it *Gynerium.* Reverting to a free-living prokaryote, Gynerium became lethal. It acted like a virus that did not allow an infected organism to code for anti-bodies. Hagah also discovered that Gynerium destroyed the XY gamete but thrived in the XX gamete.

What she did not know was its virulence. Unknowing, she carried Gynerium from her lab in one of its forms and infected her lover, a prostitute working in a brothel in Istanbul. She became the source of the outbreak. Spreading first by saliva, then in a later mutation by air, Gynerium, in its latter forms, spread by touch as well. The exchange of DNA became transdermal. Within six months, the entire male population of Asia Minor was crippled or destroyed. The problem came to its own solution. Without the Y gamete, Gynerium reverted to a non-lethal stage.

The backlash to the run of the plague was swift and brutal.

We know it as the Wars of Savagery.


"Okay. What am I listening for?"

"You don't need the first part."

"But that's the science."

"How would you film it?"

"Why would I film it?"

"You can film the ending where Bru comes over the dune. You can film danger. You can film menace. You see the anaconda and you have to ask—will it eat the girl?"

"There is no anaconda."

"That's a metaphor. Gynerium. Is that how you say it, 'guy-nare-eeum?'"

"Yes. That's right."

"Gynerium is the menace," Erica said. "You can film Gynerium. Imagine Hagah in a scene in the lab. She has a vial full of Gynerium. You can film the lab-work. You can film Hagah and her lover in the brothel. You can film the Hunt scenes, they're action. You can film the Expulsion of the Exo kid. You can film the daughters on their expedition. That Mutant scene is powerful. You can film that, and you can film the Exchange sequence in its entirety. You can film the killing of the male population. There's a lot of good stuff here, but you can't film ideas."

"I think you should leave now."

"I think I'll give you my email and numbers," Erica said. She plucked a card from the inside pocket of her motorcycle jacket and handed it to me.

"Why?"

"I run a production company. This is the kind of stuff we're looking for."

"A movie?"

"That's right."

"Oh, shit," I said. "If Caleb finds out I've been talking

232

to you, he'll kill me. Please go. Now."

When Erica was gone, I called Clara on SkyChat.

§§§

Clara answered on the first ring. I started right in so she wouldn't hound me about the manuscript.

Where is Caleb with the screenplay?

Why?

I met a producer. She gave me her card.

Can you call me back?

Her name is Blackbridge.

Erica Blackbridge?

I want you to meet her.

I know who Erica Blackbridge is, Trisha.

I worry about you, Clara. You should talk to her.

Why should I talk to her?

She runs a production company.

I know.

She knows writers. Isn't that what you want? To make *Citadel* into a movie?

Caleb has finished the first draft of *Citadel*.

Erica Blackbridge likes *Citadel*. You should talk to her.

What do you mean I should talk to her?

Curtis isn't good for you. Curtis is a Mutant.

It's so sweet of you to worry about my safety, Trisha.

Erica can help you.

I don't need help, Trisha.

Can I tell her you'll talk to her?

Maybe. We've run into a snag with the screenplay

You should wait for my changes.

The producer doesn't think a post-lesbian hook has a demographic.

What are you going to do with it?

Finish your job and get back to Santa Monica in one piece. I have to go now.

Clara?

Yes?

Is the world going to end?

233

No, but I might come out there and murder you....
Are you seeing Curtis again?
Send me Erica's numbers.
So you will talk to her?
Send me the numbers.

§§§

The reports bothered me each time I read them. I returned to page 245 to read through again but I did not want to get into the writing because, for one thing, Daiva hadn't connected the reports to a character but left them hanging. The question I had was whether to leave them in. My delete key was calling me, but it wasn't an easy decision. I could invent a character, give the words to her, and hope it worked. I knew I could never find the oracular goddess voice Daiva fell into some of the time. So, I read the reports even if I didn't know what to do with them.

**Citadel**                          **Daiva Izokaitis**

ETHNOGRAPHY ON THE STATUS OF THE EXO-
CULTURES AS THAT STATUS RELATES TO THE QUESTION
PLACED BEFORE THE CONGRESS OF THE FEASIBILITY
OF RE-INTEGRATION

This report contains information on the Social Structure, Technology, and Language of the Exo cultures. The report does not posit a single culture as a model, but presents a synthesis of observations from eight Excursions into proximal Exo villages.

Social Structure
THE BAND
The smallest unit of social organization in the Exo-culture appears to be the Band. A Band is composed of a leader and followers. The number

of followers can range from three to twenty. A few reports of eight have been made.

The position of leader does not entitle the holder to an elitist position, nor does it appear to entitle him to any power over the followers; rather it appears that they simply attach to that Exo who is the leader and accompany him at all times. We are uncertain of what constitutes the basis of leadership; we have no idea of its requirements or of its perquisites, if any.

It appears that the leader of a Band is simply that Exo who goes first. His position as leader is visible in that in every activity, he is first.

In travel, he leads the Band; in eating, he eats first; he enters buildings first and exits first. In work, he begins first and stops first. But the remarkable thing about his interaction with the Band is that he seems to acquire nothing special from it. He has no visible private property (huts appear to be communal); he eats no special food, wears no special clothing and has no accumulation of wealth. He does not appear to counsel or guide his Band in any of their actions, and he does not appear to be in any way superior, physically or mentally; he does not command, but simply is the first. Archaeohistorians suggest that this is a residual primordial structure of Alpha behavior but the genetics are not yet worked out as no adult Exos have been taken for study.

The only perceptible advantage of the leader is that he takes charge of any new infant that comes into the Band. He seems to be the one who holds, feeds, and cares for the infant. Yet it was never observed how it was decided that the leader would get the infant. It is not necessary to have an infant in order to be a leader, as it was observed that every Band has a leader, but not every leader has an infant. Following the Exchange, where possession is determined in a hand to hand contest there does not appear to be any competition among Bands for infants. Once adopted into a Band the infant remains there. Because of the differential birth rates of the Citadels, anthropologists are concerned that the aging of the Exo population should be of interest to the Planners.

Again we repeat that the basis of leadership remains unknown as does the basis of the position of the follower.

The followers accept the leader's position, and there appears to be no internecine struggle; the leader once present is leader. There are no rebellions, and no one challenges his position. The followers in the Band rarely communicate among themselves and in fact are always seen to avoid intimate contact, deferring instead to the leader, except, as reports tell us, there is a Copulation Ritual when an infant first enters a Band.

Since no social mechanism for the selection of a Band leader was observed, we are left with the possibility that either the leader emerges naturally (but that does not explain how the Band is composed initially.) Once in the role, the leader seems to have perpetual primacy. There have been no observations of replacement. Again, we state that the basis of leadership remains unknown.

## THE VILLAGE

The next order of social organization is the Village. The Village is a uniform unit. Throughout the Exo culture, the Villages, with size being the only variable, are so similar as to be virtually interchangeable. The Village ranges from a unit of one Band to units of three. No Village of more than twenty inhabitants was observed.

In the Village, the hierarchization appears to come to a stop. In fact, a Village seems to

236

function as merely a group of Bands sharing space. Within a Village the relationship between Bands is exactly parallel to the relationship of the followers in a Band. Leaders of Bands do not interact to form select or elitist groups; instead, with respect to other Bands, simply become another follower.

Within the Village we do not know how it is determined which Band will be selected to receive an infant, just as we do not know how the leader of the Band is selected to carry it.

Work within the Village is carried out by individual Bands, although no apparent assignment of tasks is made by any one Exo. Agriculture is a process of side by side planting (much like parallel play in infants) of plots of earth. It is not known how the size of a plot is determined, how it is decided what will be planted or how it will be harvested; observers report that there is some continuity from Village to Village with regard to agricultural practices, even when the crops involved are decidedly different and require different arrangements and care. Again, we do not know how determinations are made; more specifically, we do not know how information is relayed from one group to the next nor how information, once relayed, is acted upon, because at no time was it observed that concerted decision making was being carried out. Several anthropologists suggest that this behavior is a residual effect of the Old Society without any understanding of social structure.

### VILLAGE AND CITADEL

The relationship of the Village to the Citadel is central in the current configuration. The distribution of Citadels determines the distribution of Villages. The Villages, without exception, are dispersed in radians emanating from the Citadel at the center. There is no point at which the sphere of dependency of Citadels overlaps, so that each Citadel influences one and only one set of Villages.

It is vital that we see the relationship of Village to Citadel in space as one that schematically shows a Citadel feeding a number of Villages; some more distant than others from the Center. This picture of the Villages spreading out from the Citadel like waves from a vibrating center is a direct expression of the relative positions of the two cultures.

## INDIVIDUAL DEVELOPMENT, AND SOCIALIZATION

As an infant comes into a Band he is adopted by an Exo leader. Each infant, before the Exchange, has been tattooed with the biological mother's name followed by the designation of the parent Citadel. The tattoos do not seem to have led to any kind of literacy. This practice has the advantage of abolishing the binomial-naming practice of the Old Society in which the patronym was passed on for generations with each female taking the name of the male. Through the tattoos, each Exo can be traced to a maternal Citadel. Readings were taken during the Excursions resulting in ad hoc-quasi-census.

There is no apparent schooling in any formal sense, and it is not known if the Exos have learned to decipher the tattoos or if there is some primitive residual literacy.

Each infant remains with the leader who adopts him. It was observed that Exo leaders have certain childcare techniques that are surprisingly adept. It was not observed how these techniques were learned or from whom, but there is no doubt that they exist. The report of the field gyneologists suggest that the parenting is possibly bleed-over from the mitochondrion, but that is, at this point, speculation.

Past the infant stage, each child no longer

238

receives the individual attention that the adopted leader gave to him at acquisition. Instead each child becomes a follower. All direct interaction ceases once the infant can run or becomes too heavy to carry, and he is left to his own devices to stay with the Band when it moves. The consequences of the child's failure to keep up with the Band were not observed, but we assume that the child would be abandoned and would then die.

The action of the Exo Band with regard to the younger members is decidedly survival of the fittest. There are no measures taken either to protect or enhance the infant's being in the world. Socialization of the individual child is a process of chance exposure and imitation. It is improper to speak of the Exo raising a child, rather there is an atmosphere of toleration of the young. Neglect is obvious and somewhat paradoxical when compared to the early childhood techniques. It appears to us that there are critical periods after which the Exo leader and followers abandon the child. Nothing is done to aid the feral child in coping with life.

## THE ADULT PERIOD

In the adult period, an Exo becomes either a follower or a leader. Our longitudinal observations are limited by exposure to the Exo culture. We have not spent more than two years in situ. As we stated before, the emergence of Bands, the designation of leaders, and other status has never been observed; therefore the social mechanisms are unknown.

## SEXUALITY

Observation of the Exos reveals that the sexuality of the adult is complex; the sexual practices include masturbation, sodomy, bestiality, flagellation, and fellatio. There are certain other anomalous activities which in the Old Society were considered perversions. Sexuality is not edited out of the genome so it must be a residual evolutionary response.

## THE MUTANT

The relationship of the Mutant to the Exos is one of power and dominance. Lacking genetic manipulation, the Mutant possesses all the male characteristics residual in the Old Society. His relationship to the Exo Village is not integral in that his presence enslaves the entire Village and, as individuals, the Exos are completely at his mercy. The Mutant reduces them to the status that woman held in the Old Society.

Observations were made of Mutant behavior at many levels and by direct experience. Field agents discovered that the Mutant still has the predilection for violence which results in the brutalization and victimization of Exos. There does not seem to be any resistance to the Mutant's power.

Direct experience shows that the unaltered male of the species exhibits behavior that, two hundred years After Foundation, is still socially destructive as well as traumatic for individuals. Archaeohistorians suggest that aggression of the Mutant has increased since Foundation, and the consequent overt hostility reduces all Exos to objects. Genetic manipulation has pacified the Exos, which leaves the Mutant's aggressive needs thwarted by the inability of the Exos to fuse into unified groups that in the Old Society led to war. Field Agents observed that the Mutant exhortation to violence failed.

The Mutant does not contribute to the work of any Village; he does not travel with a Band but is always alone. His presence in a Village suspends all activity as he subjugates the Village. Archaeohistorians further suggest that as he wanders, the Mutant uses Villages for his

240

own pleasure and sustenance, as though they were designed solely for his own personal satisfaction. This behavior suggests the deeper residual evolutionary responses we should expect in the unmodified, narcissistic Alpha male.

Observers were not fortunate enough to see a young Mutant or an adolescent, so there are no data on the emergence of the developing Mutant. There does not seem to be any relationship between leader and Mutant, nor does leader seem to be a milder form of Mutant. Regarding the adolescent: historically, the autocratic and authoritarian tendency of male adolescents would point to an early schism between Mutant and Band much like the Koryos of the Neolithic.

What is surprising is the Mutants do not themselves band together. Observations suggest that the hostility and violence of each individual Mutant precludes his joining forces with any other Mutant. We saw this hostility in the Wars of Savagery and further suggests that the Mutant has continued to evolve differentially from the rest of the race.

The language of the Mutants, it was found after careful study, is not qualitatively different from that of the Exos, but it is quantitatively different in that the Mutant produces a tremendous volume of compulsively chaotic speech. Thingism is mitigated by a limited vocabulary. The linguists who analyzed recordings of Mutant language are puzzled by the continuity shown which suggests that in some way, Mutants learn language without any maternal coaching. This is both troublesome and enigmatic.


## THE GLAND

No observations were made of Glands in the Exo culture. Their relationship to the Exos remains unknown. We do not know at what age the

241

Glands differentiate and separate.

## OTHER

The observations that Exos were grouping together in Bands was initially disturbing because of the obvious danger that collective aggression presents to the Citadels. It was possible that another mutation was emerging, that would overcome the effects of genetic manipulation, but detailed observations, suggest that genetic manipulation still produces the desired nonaggressiveness, while further analysis of Exo behavior indicates that the single gene for collective aggression is, as planned, switched off. The silencing of the nucleotides suppressing collective aggression has resulted in the radical structure to the Exo culture. The social behaviors which were created as a result of the interaction of the now silent gene result in behavior different from anything known before. The complex of behaviors we deemed as belonging to the Exo culture is marked in its underlying assumption by a significant lack of compassion for others, a lack of conscience, and a lack of introspection. Without those characteristics, the culture is non-productive and non-esthetic. We observed no kind of art in any Village. The gene sequence for collective aggression appears not only to govern the aforementioned aspects but also any esthetic development.

## LANGUAGE

The trend to semantically overload individual words, which was a characteristic of male language in the Old Society, reflected a marked vein of conservatism with respect to language despite the exceptionally complex nature of Old Society technology. It is now apparent that the semantic load reached a peak shortly before Foundation. A very conscious effort was made in

242

the Citadels to redefine and disambiguate words so that conceptual overloading was unnecessary; this could be done when it was no longer possible to impart historical meanings to words. In languages of the Citadels, the problem was met by rejecting the linguistic implications of the Old Society that were carried as excess in the semantic load of any word. It was no longer necessary to include in the conceptual framework of a word, for example anthropology, all the nuances that history had imparted to it because the introduction of a new word, gyneology, let it be known that the former means only the study of the male. Gyneology means only the study of XX in the Citadel. Exo means only those genetically manipulated males, etc.

The problem of simplification in the Exo language was not met with such reasoning.

The studies of the Exo cultures conclude that within each of the Villages there is a trend toward nonlinguistic social interaction, wherein communication between individuals and groups relies increasingly upon such paralinguistic devices as signing and other kinesic media. In the close view, this tendency can be seen to imply homogeneity of an experience that does not require the precision of spoken language to communicate it. However, a larger view of the phenomenon suggests that the language has begun, as mentioned above, to show a trend toward stasis. It would seem that gene-editing in some way we do not yet understand, forestalls the formation of neologisms. Ample observation was made of the Exo spoken languages, and it was seen that the actual linguistic production of any individual does not grow through time, and consequently the linguistic sophistication of the culture has not evolved. There are no new words being generated in the languages, no new syntactic structures and no new conceptual network. As stated earlier, we found no evidence

243

of art of any kind in the Exo cultures.

The phenomenon of semantic overloading that characterized Old Society language produced such obviously incomprehensible phrases as "protective reaction strike," "peacetime army," "cold war" and "planned obsolescence."

The result of these ambiguities was a total loss of credibility, a disenchantment with language and a consequent degeneration of language into what we call visible thingism. This feature of Exo language is the reverse process of nominalizing within a linguistic universe. In healthy language development, a mental picture is maintained by an individual of the relative position and status of objects within the objective universe; the linguistic inventory grows as more and more objects are discovered and named; since naming implies consciousness, objects come into consciousness and assume a functional or positional niche in the universe. Consequently, nominalization creates a vaster universe in which to participate and is a vital part of the enrichment of an increasing consciousness.

As it appears to us now, the linguistic universe of the Exo cultures, hence the linguistic universe of individuals within it and their consciousness, is not only failing to grow but appears to be shrinking, leaving a consequent mental void as more and more of the universe is left unnamed. This anomia must have some effect on the brain of the Exos, but there was no investigation beyond the observational. What this means for the future of Integration remains under study.

This emptiness imparts a decidedly tribal and ritualistic character to the Exo culture and its universe, because visible thingism, as a way of naming, is stable, unchanging, sterile, and uniform. As a result of language deficiency, the Exo world is a static world in which things are pointed out in passing but are not integrated into an abstract and therefore recallable concept of global being. It has been suggested that in the Exo culture, seeing is not immediately translated into naming, so any new object remains not just unnamed but perhaps not actually perceived.

In the Citadels the tendency to anomia did not develop despite the complete re-evaluation of society. This is due, decidedly, to the maternal environment while it is possible to see that the limited linguistic universe of the Exos is a result of faulty language learning in early childhood due to the lack of maternal, allo-maternal, or quasi-maternal interaction between adult and child. We know that the maternal environment creates the original universe for the child, and since the Exos do not interact except indifferently with infants, there is zero degree of positive language learning; an original linguistic universe is never posited for the child, and from the outset he is deficient. Independently the Exos have not been able to see the intimate relationship between language and the growth of intelligence and thought. It is something of a surprise that the Exos have language at all because, ultimately, the transmission of language is an act of love and an expression of desire as well as a residual evolutionary response.

In conclusion, it appears that the language of the Exo cultures is in every sense moribund. With rare exceptions, the language as spoken is essentially composed of transformed Old Society profanity; it is full of antiquated oaths which represent submerged concepts, predicated historically upon a di-sexual society that is no longer extant.

## TECHNOLOGY

A brief historical note is in order at this point.

The technological scientism that the Old Society considered its greatest achievement has disappeared in the Exo cultures. The disappearance must be seen in the perspective of the Wars of Savagery and role values in the Old Society.

In the Old Society, man's hatred of woman was expressed politically, financially, psychologically, and socially. Characteristic of the ethos of the male-dominated value system was that man's ignorance was so monumental, his activities so much more important than those of woman, that anything woman did, including bearing children, was value-less, so that woman, accepting that value system, given tasks to which no value was assigned, came to see herself as a worthless receptacle grateful for any largesse the male might bestow. The transition from self-deprecation to self-hatred was easy to make. Woman began to see her every task as odious, regardless of its nature; consequently, she came to hold herself in the same hateful view as man held her.

The result of this process of self-hatred was twofold with respect to the technology: 1) as technology increased and the need for technicians increased, woman began to assume the role of technician, a role abandoned by man, as a matter of course when it became open to woman; 2) woman in her role as socializer began, perhaps unconsciously, to refuse to socialize the male child and to encourage the female child. This is perhaps cause and effect, perhaps not, but it contains elements of the evolutionary divergence that led to the Wars of Savagery. This dual result gave another dual result with regard to language and technology:

Language: early maternal socialization of the

246

female allowed the child to transition with developed language. Since language is a Peircean system of symbols, the female was better equipped to transfer her thought powers to other symbol or abstract systems and better able to deal with the problems of an increasingly complex technology; therefore she was better equipped to move into positions of high priority than the male. Competition between man and woman grew intense as woman became more competent at doing what man alone was supposed to do. Hence the repression of the intelligent and able woman by totally devaluing her position in the system of technology and progress. As soon as a field opened up to woman, it ceased to be of interest to man. In much the same way that the Y chromosome lost all but twenty-seven of its genes, men lost all ability except the abilities to kill, to copulate, and to make war.

Before the Wars of Savagery man left the running of the technology to the technicians, by this time all-female, and began to construct sophisticated war weapons. The creative energy left in man was turned to his own destruction, and the Wars of Savagery show that man went from weapons of mass destruction to ingenious weapons of individual cruelty and pain aimed first at other men and finally at women.

We see in the later stages of the Old Society, therefore, the basic structures of the separation of Citadelian and Exo culture: woman remained in control of the technical and linguistic aspects of the society, man sought ways to destroy. The relationship of this historical digression to the present status of technology in the Exo cultures can be seen by examining the relationship between language and technology. Language, it was stated earlier in the report, is love. In the incipient Exo culture, when the di-sexual structure of society was abandoned, the attempt to find technicians

247

was thwarted because already three generations of males had experienced the intellectual retardation caused by inadequate language environment. Even the most experienced and sophisticated male teachers could not teach those whose brains from early childhood had not been primed to abstract from language readiness to numbers or other systems. The result was a sophisticated supply of artifacts from the previously productive technology with no one to operate the systems. War had become such a way of life that the men had no capability of dealing with a non-bellicose life style. Even today it is possible to see those monuments, but no one in the Exo culture can name them, and no one understands how they came to be.

Since the Exos do not see the relationship between love, affection, and creativity, their technology has died. Since there are no mothers in the Exo culture, there is no technology, and because there are no mothers, there is no art.

Note to Daiva: It's clear to me now that you don't want to read the changes I'm making to your work. I'm not sure you will ever look at the text again until Clara publishes. I'm on my own then to make the changes. Do you see how much power and control you're giving me? Is that what you want? If I change your writing so much, it won't be yours alone. That said, I understand your thinking after reading these reports. This (pp 266 ff) report on the current status of the Exo culture fits with the Expedition to the Exo-culture and the Ritual Exchange (pp 27 ff). I see the seeds of the future that will depend on how the delegates to the Congress react. As I read, I can't help but compare the Band as the fundamental unit of Exo culture to the family that was

248

the base of the Old Society. That daughters in the Citadels have transcended the idea of family is a very strong statement—one I can't disagree with. How much of this is biology? How much of it is psychology? Is there any difference in your mind? When you write about the birth and exile of the infant, you touch some crucial and telling points.

§§§

As I lived in *Citadel* my dreams changed. Some dreams you don't want to remember, others open your eyes to who and what you have become. This was one of those— coming awake in a dream that was so much a dream it had to be real. I had been reading for hours, not sleeping enough as I tried to get the novel edited and off to Clara, when I realized that I was dreaming about being in a dream. It took me a while to see that I was trapped in my own obsessions, and in the air, there was the stench of fish frying. In the dream, I sit up, still holding the laptop, I try to will the stench away. I'm sweating, I'm breathing hard then I go to the door, feel the knob. I look down. I'm wearing shorts, a sweat-wet T-shirt. No shoes. And I have no key but the door magically opens and I step out into a landscape so familiar it cannot be a dreamscape. And there I smell the roasting flesh—a scent so strong it makes me dizzy. I'm reading *Citadel,* a section I've worked a couple of times, but this time it has changed and I am a She…A She in a dream but sometimes I am Trisha and I switch between She and Trisha and it is a puzzle. I know it is a puzzle, but I have no key to it. I know that I am watching my Trisha self as the Other, a Character in the novel and I am conscious of Her being both Me and Her. I am so completely in the story that my dreams are those of the characters…

## The Dream

I was in a vast wind-swept grassland. I had been there before. With the Hunters. I walked the path the Hunters had worn through the grass. The tall grass whipped at me, stung my chest and arms. I came to a stream of coppery gold water and across the water there was a forest of maple trees. Over the trees, the pink and orange sky boiled in a rabid sunset. In the forest, I saw a woman tied to a tree.

Ropes cut into her wrists, into her ankles. She was naked, she was old. Her breasts sagged. Her belly sagged. Head bowed. Dead?

I smelled burning skin. Turning the page, I found myself face to face with an Exo as he sliced a hunk of roasted thigh from the spit.

Three Exos dragged the Disrupter toward the tree.

To the daughter roped to the tree I said, Can you talk to me?

The daughter shook her head no. I knew she was exhausted, starved. She glanced up, in the direction of the Disrupter as it rumbled close. I heard the soft furry hum of the machine, saw a flashing light—why was it so big? On wheels. So big it took three Exos to pull it and still they strained.

I whispered to the captive, Why are you here?

The daughter rolled her head to look into my eyes and I remembered the stoning on the beach. The text was clear—she had been a hunter. She had been on the hunt for a Gland. She had fallen into a quebrada. She had broken her leg. Before her team could rescue her, a band of Exos captured her and dragged her away bleeding.

I heard the smacking of lips and the howling, that guttural, throaty howling. I looked at the spit where the band of Exos—six of them—fed on a thigh now roasted brown and smelling of seared fat.

The Disrupter came to life—the hum changed
into a whine. The whine switched into a whir. I
ducked as the beam from the snout of the machine
shot past my shoulder ripping at the daughter
tied with thongs to the tree. The flesh of her
body melted and ran like hot candle wax. The
bones of her body first sparked then turned to
gelatin then flashed. The teeth, the last
vestige of the ages-old body, teeth that lasted
4 million years, evaporated. The thews holding
the daughter to the tree turned to smoke. Where
the beam had hit the vanishing body the ray had
burned a hole in the trunk.

The trio of Exos shut down the machine. Black-
eyed and filthy they marched to the tree and
kicked at the smoldering detritus where the
daughter had stood.

Silent, they trotted to the spit with its
thick and meaty thigh. Squatting, they cut hunks
of muscle from bone and grunted as they ate.

I backed out of the dream, knowing I was still dreaming,
thinking I should write all this down so I could tell Rose
what a wonderful rich dream-life I had. Instead I lay on the
bed with the laptop open to the section called *The Killing
and the Cutting.* The scent of roasting flesh still assaulted
my nose.

I had to save Clara.

That was the message in the dream.

And then I woke up. I was awake in room 11 of the
Desert Rose Motel. I was soaked with sweat. Had I ever
been in a dream where I was sweating?

The room was quiet. The A/C on low.

The screen of the laptop cast a blue glow on my hands. I
was sickened. This dream was the future for women—the
Exos capture, kill, butcher, and eat the fat ones. And when
the captives' wombs dry up they become victims and they
disappear.

It was now clear to me that this novel was about the
sacrifices women had made so a few of us could live in the

251

Niche. But the time was now, not the time of the novel.

§§§

I was deep into *Syn in Sacrifice,* a section in the *Killing and the Cutting* when SkyChat chimed and Daiva come on line. She looked worried. Was this still a dream? Had I ever been so deep into a novel that reality of the words turned to the reality in time? Daiva said that she had just finished an experiment. She had isolated mitochondria from the eukaryote. I asked her if she had really done it because I wasn't hanging onto reality right then. She told me there was more, but then she said,

You should be happy.

I'm in *Syn in Sacrifice.*

So you know what I mean. This is amazing stuff, Tee. *Citadel* is coming true.

Yes, it is. Jahil is doing well. Some complications, but nothing we can't take care of.

Daiva closed the connection and it was as if she had never been there.

I dug back into *Syn in Sacrifice,* the second Gynerium Episode—

## Citadel                    Daiva Izokaitis

Holding the vial of Gynerium, Syn claws her way up the dune and at the crest looks down on the tents and trucks and fires and men talking. She watches them, their black body armor painted with crosses and crescents and for a moment she is not brave or bold. But then she thinks of all the women she has sent back to men such as these empty-eyed and animal strong men who have no thoughts of a woman's pain. Men who have no sense of the sacrifice each woman made to be with them. Her hands sweat then, her breath hard as stone, her heart fast beating.

She opens the vial and she sets free the bacterium that had lived two hundred million years captive. She spreads Gynerium on her hands and arms. She smears Gynerium on her thighs and in her vagina. She spreads Gynerium anywhere a hand can probe, anywhere a finger can slither or palm brush. Gynerium on her skin is cool and soothing. It tingles like a soothing lotion. The tingle makes her flush.

She walks down the slope, each step a jolt bringing her closer. She feels the elation growing in her along with the fear. But she remembers why she is there and what she has to do.

Descending, she slows in her shame. She wears only a wisp of a dress, cut to mid-thigh. Skin is the bait, it has always been bait. Her hair falls to her shoulder. Her feet are bare. She is every woman who ever came home to die and die she will. She walks into the glow of campfires and she pulls up short. What if she runs? What if she turns back? What if she retreats to the Citadel? But her shame, her guilt, loom large in the light and she knows she cannot go back. Too much depends on what she does right now, right here. She knows that to live as a woman in the presence of men is to die one day at a time, one rape at a time, one beating after another, and she cannot forgive them or herself now that she knows about Hagah's sacrifice. It is not right. To destroy life to save lives. Gynerium. Now she knows desire in its purest form. In the moonlight, she smiles the saintly smile of a martyr on the pyre, flames flashing over her.

Vengeance, the Counsellor told her, is fire. Gynerium will burn them out, melt them, eat their bones. They will kill you but the plague will spread if you touch their flesh. You, the life-bringer, are their Angel of Death. You are the Redeemer for all sin and imperfection.

The clustered men eye her. She has felt those eyes on her all her life, raking her hips, grazing her breasts, touching her thighs, eyes that eat her sex and give her pain and still she smiles as all women have always smiled. For men.

The men bunched in the glow of the campfires gawk at her, and there is disbelief in the eyes before the eyes turn red with rage in the yellow flames of campfires. She sees it—the mutation that turns men into killers of women and beasts, mutilators of girls. She feels the rage, the pure deep rage. She sees the eyes wide with strangeness and terror.

And into the circle of fires there comes a Howler. Tall, snarling, muscular, bare chested, tattooed with swastikas, crosses, crescents, twin lightning bolts, the word HATE in black ink on his forehead. He is bearded and with glistening eyes. His hands are huge, His arms thick.

He wades through the troupe of inferiors who give way.

He howls and beats his chest. His mouth gapes. Teeth filed to points.

Now is the time.

Without haste, as if preparing a meal, she strokes her face and neck and the first pure kiss of real freedom rushes over her.

The tattooed Howler comes for her with a blade in his hand. Facing him, she does not yield, she does not bow, she does not wail or cry or scream. They will cut you to pieces, the Counsellor, told her. Face to face stopping time and the swirl of death for a moment, XX to XO, she waits. The others—dozens of them, teeth bared, eyes wide, fists balled—descend on her. The first blow from the tall one falls on her face, then her arms. She rejoices in vengeance, absorbing their rage. She frees herself from her shame and guilt as they swarm over her, each man groping her, penetrating her, every orifice, tearing of

254

the flesh at her inner thighs blinds her. Dizzy, she swallows her own blood as the fists of men hammer her.

For the others, the Counsellor told her.

And the rain of punishment falls harder upon her but she remains erect, she remains aware as if reveling in her own destruction can atone for the lies she has wreaked upon her innocents. The canon says, "Women are sick, it is not the culture that is sick." The canon says, "Women are out of synch, it's not the culture that is out of synch." The canon says, "Women are the chattel, the possessions, the wards and lovers. They belong to men and if men kill them, that is the will of God. This is the revealed word of God— "It is always woman under man, always man superior to woman."

She grieves for those who died before her, for those who cut themselves, for those who said No.

His blade enters her. She shudders and swallows the pain. She will not, cannot surrender. He slices her labia majora free from her body. Still she does not whimper, she does not scream, she does not plead.

For those who said No, there will be no scream.

She watches her flesh, skewered on the blade that cut her, now roasting in the campfire, and she says, I am the Disrupter. The woman who screams No More. Bleeding, she watches her severed breasts enter the fire on the blade of the knife. Her pudenda, her labia majora enter the gaping mouth of the Howler with her blood on his face and Gynerium on his skin.

Smoke roils up from the fire—thick and black—and Syn watches the Howler grasp his throat and gurgle as he breathes the fat-laden, Gynerium-rich smoke. She watches pain flow into his eyes and spread across his face. Clouds of smoke smother the gangs of Exos and they cough and

255

gag. Syn watches the Howler's flesh boil as if a small volcano is burning itself out of his body. On his arms, blisters bubble up searing the tattoos and melting HATE. Blood cascades across his face. Syn listens to the song of Gynerium singing in the flesh of men who touch her. As each of them grasps pieces of her body another one comes to help the dying but they too fall into their own pools of dripping boiling skin and their bones split through the flesh. She says, this is for all the women and girls you have violated and controlled and beaten and raped. This is for us who were slaves. Your world ends in the heat and smoke of destruction.

On her knees in the moonlight, in the light of the campfires, Syn opens her mouth to sing but there are no words left in her. There is no more guilt or shame in her. There is no more fear or hatred in her and in that moment she is free.

For them. For all of them.

Note to Daiva: I wish you would take the time to see what I'm doing to your text. Because you won't answer my questions, I have to make choices that might not be what you want. For example, this scene is very important but I can't find any connection between Syn and other characters. The danger with walk-ons is that they don't have a story line. Strange as it may seem, Syn is Rose Katz, my therapist who told me that her worst fear and the cause of her shame and guilt was that she sent her clients (I hate that word, it's so leveling) back to the men who had abused them. I don't know what to do here, so I will leave it in place as you wrote it. It has a very poetic feel that runs against the grain of the content. One other item—why is the Disrupter so big? Why can't the Exos build new ones? Why are the Exos always young here? This is a logical gap. After talking to Kirsis, I can see no reason for this. What are you getting at? If this scene shows up in the screenplay, we should cut it. This is the most gruesome scene in the novel. Just this scene alone makes me wonder if it's a good idea...Why? Men already have ways to kill and torture women, why give them this idea? I understand that you don't expect to find many male readers for Citadel. I'm going to talk to Clara about this. You will hear from her.

I wanted to clear my head because the smell of a daughter butchered and eaten, a daughter vaporized, enraged me. I had been on the Hunt. I had taken those bodies to my bed. I had been driven by the same automatic urges that were the residue of sex and killing. I knew I was on dangerous ground when the text opens the wounds of your own sins and shortcomings and you see that you are to blame for the chaos of civilization because of your expectations. At that moment, awake, clear for the first time—ever—I knew real terror.

I clicked SkyChat on the laptop and called Clara.

She wore a lacy black babydoll. Her hair was tied back from her face. She held a glass of wine. I heard music. I saw a man's hand on Clara's shoulder.

I want to read you something, Clara.

This is not the time.

The Disrupter scene.

I know it, I like it.

I want to cut it.

You will not cut it. It's what the book is about.

I don't think we should publish *Citadel*, Clara.

I've sunk everything into this project.

If we publish it, they'll kill us.

Are you drunk?

No.

Have you been drinking?

This is a dangerous book, Clara.

Your craziness bores me, Trisha. You do this every time. I expect it, but I want a Numero Uno *New York Times* bestseller. I want to turn the world upside down with a novel that will pack houses when we turn it into a film and I want it now. Just a minute...

I leaned back against the headboard and read the words, thick, strong words—

> One night in a brothel in Istanbul the women stopped working. They were beaten and they were raped. They were cut and they bled but they stopped working and said 'no more'.

Trisha, I'm with someone. Call me later.
Curtis?
It doesn't matter who it is.
I can't finish this job.
Why can't you finish the job?
If I finish, it will come true and the world will end.
It's a fucking novel, Trisha. A book. Hollywood thrives on end-of-the-world blockbusters. There have been other books that predicted the end...
Not predicted Clara—this book will cause the end.
Every time you go to the desert it's like you bring the apocalypse with you. This makes me wonder if you haven't gone nuts. You called me just an hour ago.
I did?
You sent me Erica Blackbridge's info.
Erica Blackbridge?
Trisha, you need to talk to Rose. Take a break.
If I take a break, I won't meet your deadline.
Oh for chrissake Trisha. Do your job and get me that manuscript—do you hear me? Caleb is working his little heart out. We want it all to come together at the same time. I want—this is the fifteenth, you have fifteen days. We launch in New York two months from now on the eleventh so you deliver.
What if he kills you, Clara?
Just finish the job, Trisha.

They cannibalize women, Clara.

Trisha, when you lay that bestseller on my desk, you can ask about who shares my bed, but till then don't drag me into your neurotic world. Just finish the edit.

Before I disconnected I saw Curtis yank Clara to her feet. He was thick in the shoulders and heavy chested. Naked. His hands on Clara's shoulders were big, the fingers matted with patches of hair. The screen went yellow. I was exhausted.

Later the scent of words returned, and I tried to re-enter *Citadel,* approaching it after a long journey but something was wrong. I enlarged the 12 point font to 14, but it still felt odd. I marked the scene and grew the font to 18 point, but the walls loomed only when I approached 24 point. At 30 point, the text flooded over me as I circled the walls—two links in circumference. I felt the balance and the beauty of the enclosure—I wanted to be in there, safe, pure. Self-sufficient and impenetrable. The Citadel was me, an independent woman living in the Niche—it required nothing from outside—and as I roamed deeper into the words, I thought of Rose and Daiva. I imagined Bett and Kali lost in their love for one another. But the scars.

I looked at the scars and scabs on the walls and I saw the residue of chaos. I circled the Citadel. Midway around I found the entrance behind a veil of greenery. At the portal, a hunting band exited. I followed them....

## Citadel                                   **Daiva Izokaitis**

Hesta held up her hand and Jana froze. Hesta sniffed the air and turned into the wind rippling the heads of the blades of grass and then, rising into a crouch, she saw him—a Gland in the wild. He was tall and lithe, sunburnt and naked. His hair was golden and long to his waist. He walked straight, parting the grass as he came. Hesta, signaling with hand motions, brought the second team of Hunters to the alert.

I sensed their urgency. Tension showed in the flexed muscles, the panting, the beads of sweat. Jana, raising her hand, pointed ahead. Hesta unfurled her net and she ran.

I followed Hesta through the tall grass.

Jana circled to the right. Hesta saw the grass parting as the second team, Leta and Gae, followed the Gland who came to the alert.

A few units from Jana the Gland broke into a gallop, long strides cutting ahead, but Jana headed him off. He veered to his left straight into a wall of skin and nets. Gae's team blocking him. He squealed.

Not a human squeal of fear and desperation but the mad wild squeal of trapped animals. I felt the thrill, smelled the sweat and an odor I did not recognize as Hesta, on the fly, hurled her net, snagging the Gland's shoulder and arm. He spun, dipping. The net flew free just as Jana closing on his right shot her net up and out and over him. He still ran, dragging the net. The second team attacked. Two more nets flying, tangled him up, and still he squealed and thrashed and then the four Hunters were on him.

I listened to the harsh breathing of the Hunters, heard the gasping of the captured Gland.

Hesta yanked the slip string of the net. The Gland rolled deeper into his trap. Hesta straddled him, her bloody legs smearing him. The nets cross-hatched his skin. Jana, streaked with her own blood, knelt.

Hesta smelled the sweat, the fear, the danger—pure Gland, powerful, smooth, raw, untamed. I wanted to kneel on him, touch him, feel his skin so slick it looked oiled. I wanted to know how many times he had been milked. How many times taken down, netted, bloody and crude.

Hesta looked into his eyes. They were blue. His brows blond. His skin the color of chestnuts. His muscled legs were strong and powerful. He

260

kicked, driving at Hesta, his pelvis thrusting against her. The nets held him tight.

Gae and Leta, still panting, gathered around the prize. Hesta, reaching through the webbing of the net touched the Gland's belly, just a sampling of him. She jerked back as the Gland snarled and pitched against the restraints. Jana whispered,

"Don't torment him."

The Gland lay quiet. His breathing settled into a rasp. He coughed. The wildness in his eyes seethed. His sweaty skin glistened. Hesta, still squatting, looked at her hand that had touched the prey.

The second team stood. Leta, a tall Hunter with amber skin, held the carrying pole like a spear. She laid it on the ground. Together the four Hunters rolled the Gland onto his stomach. The scent of his cooling body changed. The sweat still strong swept up into Hesta's nostrils. She reached through the webbing to grasp the Gland's left arm.

Jana wrapped the Gland's wrists with cord.

Gae laced his ankles together.

Leta slid the carrying pole through the ankle and wrist ties.

"Do you think he bleeds," Jana said.

"He bleeds, just not in the right places," Leta said. Jana laughed. Even the daughters made menstrual jokes. I was part of the hunt now kneeling over the captive. I understood the laugh—it was the sound of puzzlement—the monthly residue of millions of years of selection for blood and this moment when time stopped.

Breathing now quiet, the coolness of the late afternoon soothing away the rush of the chase, Hesta measured the angle of the sun and she grasped the carrying pole, Jana beside her. Gae and Leta hefted their end and they set off at a trot.

They were strong and powerful and

261

well-conditioned but the Gland was heavy. He was solid. He squealed with each bounce and jostle and after two units Hesta pulled up. She said, "Can't keep this pace. Have to slow down."

Leta said, "Can't slow up too long either, have to keep on the run. We took him too late in the day."

"I smell them," Gae said.

"Who do you smell?" I asked.

"The Exos," Gae said. "They follow the Gland. They scavenge his leavings."

"You can smell them?" I said.

"We're still two hours from the walls."

"We can't stay out beyond first moon," Leta said.

"Lift. Go," Hesta said.

And they swung back to the task.

The Gland bounced with each jostling step. In the sway and rhythm of the trot his squeal slowed to a throaty whine. I fell into step with Hesta matching her strides. As we ran, I swelled with pride. Side by side with the Hunters, feeling the give and take, letting the weight of the captive push the whole team forward. I was joyous but tired. It was wearing, the hunt, the days of searching, the vigilance and fear of discovery. But I was also happy except for the blood on my legs from the saw grass.

I had questions. How many milkings before they released him? How strong would his seed be? When in the past did the Y chromosome begin to decay?

Just ahead, as the team cleared the tall grass, I saw lights. Fire. The team held up.

"Exos," Hesta whispered.

I smelled her own sudden fear oozing from under my arms.

The Gland, on the ground screeched. I gagged him with a maxi-pad. He muttered a cry.

"Let him breathe," Jana said.

I eased up on the maxi-pad in his mouth. For a second I was sure the Gland understood. Jana

said,
"Can't let them see us."
"Take it out, he'll smother."
"He'll shout."
"We can't kill him," Hesta said.
"What then?" I asked.
"We wait," Hesta said.
I squatted at the edge of the grass. The Gland beside me rolled his head. His eyes locked on mine. There was a terror in those eyes I had never before seen. In the grass they were safe, but in the open, on the savannah, they were prey and the daughters were the predators.

The smell of menses thick with the residue of decaying gametes brought me out of the words.

My period was a week early. Maybe I was coming into synch with the daughters. I was just like them, like the Hunters. A machine built for one thing. I hated it. Month after month, I bled just as every woman ever born bleeds. That's what binds us together as we diverge from the killing. The blood of men is the blood of death. Our blood was not.

I peeled and inserted a tampon and then went to bed in the motel in the desert. Blood on the sheets. Blood, the one true thing. With it came the strong, sweet smell of all women through all time. It was the scent of pain and agony.

For a moment, I was not myself, alone in the desert, but I was every woman who had ever been banned or stoned or berated. Blood and breasts. Breasts that the shamers told us should not be bared in public. Breasts that defined who and what we are. Breasts and blood. We are mammals.

I sent an email to Daiva asking her to get in touch with Clara—

*You've seen her abrasions, but you don't know the full story. Please check on her as soon as you get this. Love you, Dee, and I love your novel. It's making me see into myself in ways I could not have imagined.*

§§§

It was late, I didn't want to open the door. I didn't care who was there. If it was Rita, I didn't want to see her. If it was Jimbo, he could go back to his horse.

Clara and Daiva.

Clara still wore the black babydoll under a gray overcoat. She was barefoot. Her hair was tangled. Her mouth bruised. Her eyes red and sullen and puffy. Daiva helped her to sit upright on the bed. Clara said she needed water. As she drank, I saw the open cut on her throat. The abrasions on her wrists were fresh. The ripeness of sex wafting up from her had the thick semi-sweet smell of abuse and lust and submission. Clara said,

"I should have listened to you, Trisha."

"What did he do to you?"

Daiva sat on the floor and propped the laptop on her knees. She started in on the section of *Citadel* I had left running while Clara confessed. And it was a confession. She told me that last night was the sixth time she had been with him. She told me a story that should have been a section in *Citadel.* She told me that he gagged her and strapped her to the bed posts with leather thongs and took her rough, hard. Finished, he then stood over her, toying with her sex as if he had gone crazy.

"Show Tee your legs, Clara," Daiva, still reading on the laptop, didn't look up.

Clara uncovered her legs. Her inner thighs had the look of sandpapered skin. I went to the bathroom for a wet a towel and a bottle of lotion. I dabbed at Clara's abrasions and as I worked the lotion into her skin I smelled the odor of man that I had scrubbed from myself so many times. As I cleaned her up, Clara continued to pour her soul out to me. She told me that she was ashamed of herself and that her shame came from the books I had brought to her at Pinnacle.

Daiva said, "She means she's obsessed. She means she gets so deep into them she can't get out."

Clara told me it was true, that she couldn't get them out her head and the first time she was with Curtis he was kind, even gentle, but the longer she was with him the more demeaning he became. She said that the first time she took him home, she was living a fantasy exactly like the stories Pinnacle published with the heaving chests and bared breasts, but after that it wasn't enough to have sex with him, he wanted to use her the way Dr. Coxman uses Sabrina in the stable scene in *Red Red.*

"So much for erotic fantasy," Daiva said.

*Red, Red.* One of the Pinnacle Erotica series. I had lived in that book with its characters. I recalled the scene, smelled the horse barn, the straw, the dust. Clara said that in the stable, Curtis tied her to the horse rail and whipped her with a quirt. My head spun as Clara kept rolling out her experience. I had been there just as I was now living in *Citadel* —with the woman – Sabrina was her name. A pitiful name for an erotic woman. Clara said that the last time in the stable, when Curtis finished with her, he left her tied up blindfolded, her bottom bare. She said she was afraid he was going to leave her trussed up but he returned to cut her loose. Clara paused as if reliving the moment, and then she told me about the night before Daiva had rescued he. Curtis had been brutal. She was ashamed of herself because she realized that Curtis didn't love her, he didn't even like her, but wanted only to humiliate her and he had raped her anally. Clara took a deep breath before she told me about the knife. When he used the knife, she said, she thought of that poor woman in *Citadel.* She said she knew Curtis was going to kill her.

"She means Karen," Daiva said. "From *Women in Captivity.*"

I smelled something new in Clara's sweat, not just fear and danger, but excitement. I knew the images were running in her mind again. She would be tied to the bed, he would use her like an animal. She paused again and then she said that as he pressed the blade against her throat, he said he should gut her because she was just a fucking cunt.

"He cut her loose," Daiva said. "I didn't know what I'd find when I pressed that latch button."

"I have to sleep," Clara said. She didn't wait. She curled up on the bed.

"You're making some progress, Tee," Daiva said.

"And it's driving me crazy," I said. "What did she tell you?"

"Everything. I think that deep down, she sees her interlude with Curtis as one of the motivations for taking Pinnacle out of erotica. I think the word she used was *poison.* Did she ever tell you she'd been raped? Seems we have a sisterhood working here, Trish. When she was fifteen. Look, Tee, can I get a room? I need some sleep, but I want to finish reading what you've done."

Jack Remick

# PALEOLITHIC RESIDUE

## Trisha

Sunlight slotting through the blind woke me. Clara, on her side, lay quiet, her breathing calm. The red lips of the cut to her throat glistened.

Knocking at the door. It was Daiva holding the computer like Salomé offering a head on a platter. There was a calmness in her that surprised me.

"Is she awake?"

"Out all night," I said.

Daiva looked tired. Her eyes were bright but darkened with bags. She sat lotus on the floor with the computer propped on her knees. She said,

"I read everything you finished."

"Including the notes?"

"Everything. I was wrong, Tee. I don't know what to say. I guess I've kind of treated you like shit." The black look in her eyes gave way to shades of shame and she glanced off. "When you started on *Citadel*, I knew you would screw it up. But now I see."

"You wrote it like a science paper, Dee. And fiction isn't science."

"I get that. You opened me up to what I was actually thinking and doing."

"That's my job to find the story and to cut what gets in the way."

"But how do you know? How did you know? I read the scenes you fixed. I see me in there but you found something else. I wrote the novel and didn't shed one tear. But I read what you've done and I cried.. I didn't cry when I wrote the Exos raping the

267

daughter in the Village. I didn't cry when I wrote the brother stoning his sister on the beach. I didn't cry when he slit her throat, but in the Disrupter scene when they disintegrate the captive, I cried. It was all happening so fast. It was so horrible that I felt what I had done and I've never felt that before. And that cannibal scene? Did I write that? When I read it last night the smell of the Exos eating the daughter ruined me. You've changed me into a crazy woman. Maybe I had to step away from it to see it."

I pressed my finger to Daiva's mouth. A rush of shame, a river of glee, a sea of madness swept over me. "You read the notes. That makes me happy."

"Why did you put them in the text?"

"I'll take them out before Clara gets the manuscript."

"You really feel that way? What you wrote in your Kel scene?"

"What are you two plotting now?" Clara said.

Clara sat against the headboard.

"Daiva's been reading *Citadel* – the edited version," I said.

"Is she ready to kill you yet?" Clara swung off the bed and went to the bathroom. She came back drying her face. She said, "I need a change of costume, hon. You got something I can slip into?"

"You need a shower," Daiva said.

Clara peeled off the black and red babydoll. She stood naked without a hint of shame. I tossed her a pair of cutoffs, a shirt, and underpants. She disappeared into the shower.

"Well, she's back," Daiva said.

"No more stable boy for auntie Clara."

Daiva set the computer on the bed and stood and shook her hair. She was changing by the minute. I liked what I saw now—the confidence, the way she held herself. Daiva came to me, kissed me, whispered.

"Forgive me. I was stupid."

We crossed a Rubicon with that kiss. I didn't want it to end, but I pulled away at the sudden rapping on the door.

"You up yet, Trisha?"

"It's Kali." I opened the door.

"Morning, love," Kali said. "Breakfast."

"Kali, you know Daiva."

"Yeah," Kali said. "You sleep okay? You look like you've been drug face first through a fresh cow pie. But a cup of coffee, a couple of eggs and half a dozen of Kali's fresh-baked biscuits will fix you right up. Chow in ten."

Clara stepped out of the bathroom wearing my cutoffs and T-shirt, her hair wet.

"Jesus," Kali said. "There's three of you." She smiled. "I guess the girl wants what the girl wants."

"This is Clara," I said. "She's the publisher."

"I'll be damned," Kali said. "The whole works right here at the Desert Rose."

Kali smiling and with a little girl peekaboo wave closed the door.

Clara ran her fingers through her hair.

Daiva sat on the bed.

I closed the computer.

Clara tied her hair up in a twist. She said,

"I got a book to publish, Trisha. When do I get copy?"

"When I finish."

"The launch in New York City is going hot, so I need it yesterday."

"Where is Caleb with the screenplay?"

"He's getting there," Daiva said. The way she said it, I knew there was more to it than she'd ever admit. But it didn't make any difference. Now.

## §§§

We left Clara in the bar with Bett and Kali while Rita told stories about the strong arm of the law, arresting drunks, and shootouts with drug dealers.

"Long way from the beach at Santa Monica," Daiva said.

"It's not what you think."

"That one's got a taste for you, Tee," Daiva said. "She eyes you like a hungry cat."

Daiva shoved open the door to room 11. It smelled of sweat and the tears of confession. She picked up my discards that lay scattered like drying flowers on the floor. She said,

"You have to do laundry, Tee."

"I don't have time for laundry. You heard Clara. She wants this done, but I can't finish until you give me some answers."

"The answers are all in the text."

Daiva stacked the dirty laundry on a chair. She said,

"I answer questions when you clean up. When did you last shower?"

"I don't know—I was working on the *Expedition*—what's that? Page 182?"

"Shower. Now," Daiva said.

She followed me to the bathroom and stood in the doorway watching. When I got out, she handed me a towel then followed me back to the bed.

"Okay now ask your questions."

"The Exos, Mutants, Glands. I can't get to the core of that—why do you leave three expressions of the same phenotype in the novel?"

"Phenotype. My, my, you've been reading your biology. What's next? A Ph. D.?"

"I still have a lot more to do."

"All right." Daiva sat on the floor, legs stretched out in front of her. "The Exos are like neutered dogs. We keep them to see which traits are riding along on that 13$^{th}$ gene."

"So they can't breed?"

"They're sterile," Daiva said. "The 13$^{th}$ gene is testosterone dependent, so when we silence it, the fertility drops to zero along with the collective aggression."

"But in that Disrupter scene, the Exos use the Disrupter on the captive. That's aggression. But they kill her."

"I know," Daiva said. "Look Tee, it's a novel, in a novel you do novel stuff."

"So you made it up?"

"I didn't make up anything."

"This book will get us all killed."

"How will it get us killed?"

"It's like you're laying out a plan for the extermination of women because it plays right into what's happening in politics, in science, in medicine, in religion. Everyday it's some new absurdity about controlling women's lives."

I opened the computer and scrolled the screen and read—'and the teeth, teeth that could last three million years, dissolved…' They reduce her to dust, Dee. That's not ol' boys playing with their toys."

"One last gasp of throbbing manhood," Daiva said. "I don't want to get metaphysical on you, but sometimes I wonder if maybe men aren't getting terminate signals from the Y."

"Terminate signals?"

"Signals saying 'we're doomed, so let's take everything and everyone down with us'."

"The nucleotides somehow communicate intent back to the brain?"

"Maybe the Y has its own wisdom and part of that wisdom is self-loathing that comes from knowing it's on the way to extinction. The thrust of the Y is to breed humans into oblivion. There are now eight billion of us and no end in sight. *Citadel* just puts a stop to the fascist craziness that's peaking around the globe today."

"What do you want?"

"Complete control."

I closed the screen and sat on the edge of the bed.

"I like what you've done to your hair."

"I cut it when we passed sixty days," Daiva said.

"Is Jahil really pregnant?"

"Oh yeah and it will stick. We're making history by pushing extinction closer to a reality." Daiva's eyes were bright and burning as she said, "I think we're speeding up evolution by publishing this book…"

"It's actually going to happen," I said, "and that brings me back to the three males—the Glands, what's the future of the Glands in your New Society?"

"My New Society? It's not mine. It's the future of the daughters. It's what will be."

"Are there Glands in our time?" I asked her.

"The Glands are designer product. We keep them around in case we decide to reintegrate."

"So you think they're out there?"

"I don't know."

"They're pure?"

"We put a cork in that 13<sup>th</sup> gene," Daiva said, "and we tweak the middle temporal gyrus to produce doses of testosterone so the sperm are viable—unlike Caleb's pathetic little boatloads of sailors."

"Is he sterile?"

"You saw the graphic. A textbook example of the future of the dying Y."

"The Mutant?"

"The Mutants are limited edition androids. We use them as a caveat in the Morality Tale."

"The *Women in Captivity* chapter?" I said.

"I wrote a lab scene in *Extinction* where the geneticists modified specimens by snipping the nucleotide for testosterone and increasing estrogen. The Mutant became feminized, grew breasts, the penis shrank, while the testes resorbed and in the extreme, the Mutant lactated as though it were a primiparous female."

"You can turn the male into a fertile female?" I said.

"Embryonically, males are females. I can do what I want now."

"So it is happening. You have complete control? "

"In the novel, not in the lab, not yet. We can't control the genetic switches long enough to make it permanent."

"So he reverts?"

"Yes." Daiva said, "like dropping hormones for a trans. Which leaves us stuck with the question—what is a human?"

"When I'm in the book, Dee, I see all the pain there and all the death, and I don't want…"

"When we have full control," Daiva said, "nature will be back in balance."

"You want to clean up all the mistakes just so we can start over?"

"In the vision," Daiva said, "when I first saw you, I didn't know who you were."

"You saw me in the future?"

"From the start you were there. A shadow character called Tressa." Daiva climbed up on the bed. "That day on the beach you were wearing just a tiny bit more than you have on now and I knew…The whole book is a vision…and I just wrote what I saw. I don't want to be your lover, Trisha. Remember the *Well of Loneliness.* Desire doesn't mean that because we love one another we have to be genital."

"Who dictated this to you? It's not yours, is that what you're saying?"

"Maybe you're right. If we publish *Citadel*, we all die."

"I spoke to Kirsis in the Heptuant chapter."

"They'll stone us."

"She didn't act like a Planner."

"When you go to New York, they'll stone us."

"Why didn't Kirsis tell me this when I talked to her?"

"In New York, they won't see it as a Morality Tale, they'll see fact."

"I'm going to talk to her again."

"You'll die in New York. I'll die there, too."

"The Citadels become reality."

"When we start over, we'll call the planet Gyna."

"Parthenogenesis. That's not supposed to happen for another hundred years."

"We've been cloning since Dolly. First we renucleated frogs. Then we chemically transferred genes. Ants with butterfly wings. Cats with bioluminescent skin. It was inevitable once we got through the cell wall, once we saw the code for deoxyribonucleic acid and the nucleotides. But parthenogenesis is something else. It gets to that question again—what is a human? Jahil is pregnant. The ICNI process works. Will that make her child human or not?"

"ICNI?"

"Intracytoplasmic Nuclear Injection."

"You've actually done it?"

"We've done it but we're on the edge trying to keep it in the lab as the ethicists want, but how can we keep it in the lab knowing what we can do?"

"So you're a criminal?" I said.

"I'm the future and Jahil is the first Mother."

"Divergent evolution."

"Yes," Daiva said. She sat facing me, hands folded. She looked like a very serious, very matronly schoolmarm with a treacherous gleam in her eyes. I laughed.

273

"What?"

"You look innocent but I know the secret you, and right now you look mischievous."

"Maybe I'm wrong about divergent evolution."

"That and a couple more things I still can't get into my head."

"Where are you and what do you need?"

"I've been through the novel a dozen times, Dee. I've made changes, but I'm still not sure about divergent evolution, the residual evolutionary response, and the idea of Paleolithic residue. Go."

"Okay. In which order?"

I flipped open the computer and got ready to type.

"No," Daiva said. "Just listen. When biologists select for a trait, they find that there is an entire train of behavior and characteristics that ride along on that trait. Rarely is one trait controlled by a single gene which means, of course, that a single gene doesn't drive a specific behavior but it's an interaction."

"I got that," I said. "The Russian fox experiment."

"You're reading again," Daiva said. "I like that. What I did in *Citadel* was extrapolate. Exos in the Old Society were selected for three traits—aggression, speed, and size. If you look at those three traits, you see that the killing is the ride-along and spins out of them."

"And the daughters?" I said.

"Females were selected for quality, stability, and pelvic size."

"You don't exactly pin that down in *Citadel*," I said.

"It's all Paleolithic residue, Tee. Female beauty. Wide hips are co-adaptive with the big brain but there's a limit. The aggression in males is left over with nothing to use it on. Your beach boys were playing the same deadly game the Exos do. They killed off all the beasts but they couldn't burn out the residue of the behavior and that got them to football and then to the Wars of Savagery and the Wars of Religion and their last target—women."

I loved watching Daiva's mouth as she talked. The words had substance, like stones falling from her lips. She continued,

"The question I work in the book is this—when did the residual evolutionary responses become instinct?"

"That's not clear either."

"I don't use the word instinct," Daiva said, "but in *Citadel* trait selection left an instinct for killing. The 13$^{th}$ gene is that killer instinct."

"That's not a happy thought," I said.

"That's the root of divergent evolution. The three work together—paleolithic residue, divergent evolution, and residual evolutionary response. Trait selection over a long span might give you instinct. Instinct is an environmental response that's built in even though we don't like to talk about humans having instincts. In the late Old Society, after the Unification of Religions, the stimuli weren't there while the ride-along had to be expressed."

"An example. I need an example."

"Pronghorn antelope."

"Pronghorn?"

"They're fast. Nothing can catch them. Why are they fast? Some time, in the past, they had a fast predator. But the predator is gone. Leaving just that speed. That's a residual evolutionary response. The environment changed—the predator vanished—but the behavior didn't extinguish. Think of the Exos and their violent reaction to women. Nothing left to kill but that trait is still there and so they kill women. Do you get it now? Divergent evolution—the Exos kill, the daughters had to do something and so they built the citadels."

"Daiva," I said, "you're treating this like it's fact."

"It is fact. The Y chromosome shows us that males are diverging from females. I quoted Irven DeVore to you—'males are a breeding experiment run by females.' But the flow has changed and there's no going back. You can't knock the genes back on the chromosome."

"Parthenogenesis," I said.

"You do get it," Daiva replied. She stretched like a wild animal awakening. Watching her, I got excited and wanted more. "The daughters have to decide the fate of the human race. The question that I ask in the novel is, will we still be human if procreation is entirely stripped away from male to female sex? That leaves the bigger question—what is desire?"

"The way you say it…"

"Desire is a residual evolutionary response, Tee, specific now to females. What's the ride-along? Desire without the object of evolutionary desire is what?"

"Women? Sexual selection?"

"Not exactly."

"Do the Exos have it? Desire?"

"It's residual but separated from the object. When the Planners use the *CRISPR* technique to edit genes, they snip the nucleotides that drive desire in the males."

"CRISPR?"

"It's geek talk, Tee—clustered regularly interspaced short palindromic repeats. It's just the most important discovery in the history of science."

"So the Exos aren't human?"

"In *Citadel* they are almost human—but the parthenogynes might not be. I don't know."

"You wrote the book, Daiva. If you don't know, how am I supposed to work it?"

"I didn't create the genome. That's the Paleolithic residue—what's left when the predator has no prey."

"It's not a beautiful world," I said.

"No, it's not and it doesn't get better. Are you okay now?"

"Yeah. I didn't see the despair before."

"Despair?"

"The death of desire."

"Not death," Daiva said, "just an RER without the right stimulus. Had to take that out of the Exos…"

"The daughters love," I said. "So deeply. The *Crossover*…."

"And it's love without fear. Take men out of the equation and desire is pure—you want to hold your lover. You miss her when she's gone."

"Of course."

"You cry when you think about her."

"Sometimes."

"And there's no fear. Men are afraid women will snigger

when they see them naked, and women know that men will gut them if they get the chance."

"That's the despair I see," I said. "My whole life up to now is just RER, isn't it?"

"Yes, but now you have a handle on it," Daiva said.

She touched my cheek. Fire ran up to my face. Daiva let her hand fall to my arm.

"That," Daiva said, "is desire, pure and simple stripped of fear."

"An instinct?"

"An RER. Paleolithic residue."

"I don't want you to go." I said.

"While the Exos were out killing meat, the daughters were making culture. What?"

"Nothing," I said. "It can wait."

"What did you just say?"

"Culture. What is culture."

"It's what women do while they wait for men to stop killing. I work it out in *Extinction.* Caleb is already telling me he wants to write the screenplay."

"What else is he telling you?"

"He's attentive."

"What does he say about Jahil?"

"I haven't told him."

"So, you have secrets?"

"Don't we all?"

"Is that why you leave Exos in the novel, Dee?"

"Until we solve the riddle."

"Are you talking about the novel or are you talking about reality?"

"Is there a difference?"

"That's how powerful you are?"

"Jahil is carrying two Xs. Our baby will be normal and fertile because she has two parents and forty-six chromosomes. That's how powerful we are now."


§§§


With Daiva gone and Clara back on track and pushing

the limits, I dove back into *Citadel.* The novel gave me that ineffable feeling of floating in another world I couldn't quite pin down. After Daiva's visit, I had changed. I no longer felt estranged from my emotional life after I had discovered my truth in the scene with Kel. The long sections on the *Wars of Religion* clawed at me as if tearing scabs loose from wounds both mine and not mine. Earlier, I thought the spine was captivity/freedom but now, as I read, I was sure the spine of the novel was residue. Left-overs. Bones. Women as waste and excess. Bones of women scattered because there had been no one left to bury them. I grew the font from 12 point to 24 and as the words raged at me in a sea of scents and odors, I entered the world of *The Crossover.*

## Citadel                               Daiva Izokaitis

The corridor was quiet. Carpeted. Soft. Isolated.

Through the mirrored glass, I watched the trees sway. It was an idyllic moment - high up in the Citadel, the twenty-fifth around, high enough to feel apart from all the terror and chaos of Daiva's writing.

How had Daiva gotten here?

Glancing at the text, I shuddered—fused to the words. Every word seemed richer now. I seemed to feel Daiva's presence. I was elated that I had somehow slid inside so easily this time as if I was waiting for a lover at the corner.

I scrolled to page 211 and then the elevator stopped. I heard voices. At last. This moment was the why, the when, the where. I slid into the language of the page and there were two daughters approaching me.

They held hands as they approached. They were tall. They were both muscled and sure.

One of them had golden skin like burnished bronze. The other was dark and mysterious, slow,

careful and nimble. The golden-skinned one had
green eyes and amber hair. Her muscles rippled
as she walked. The dark-skinned one with black
curled hair giggled as they passed me in the
corridor on the twenty-fifth round of the
Citadel overlooking the lake and the trees. I
followed them.

Halfway down the corridor the bronze-skinned
one turned and smiled. Her teeth were the color
of bleached ivory, the mouth meaty and full, so
sensuous.

"Who are you?" She said.

Taken aback but pleased to have been included
so quickly into the flow of the narrative, I
said,

"I am the one who follows. And I am the one
who makes the changes."

The dark and mysterious one said,

"You're Trisha. We hope you will treat us
right."

She opened the door and entered and the one
with the golden skin and the white teeth ushered
me into the room with a palm to the small of my
back.

Note to Dee: Why do these two daughters not have
names? I can't think about you without gushing,
Dee...The day on the beach, when you told the beach meat
we were having our periods. I think I fell in love with you
at that moment.

At a desk of black metal, a daughter, with
ink black hair and vibrant skin sat head bowed,
hands in front of her. Behind her and through
the mirror glass, I saw the reflection of her
thick coiled hair. The detail exquisite.

The daughter with the golden skin sat.

The daughter at the desk glanced up and
smiled. She said,

"The three o'clocks. You're on time."

"Yes," the dark-skinned one said. She grasped her friend's hand and she giggled. I saw her youth—eighteen, nineteen. Young, trained, athletic. The golden-skinned daughter said,

"We want to cross."

The daughter with the wrinkled skin frowned. She said,

"Are you sure?"

"We're in love," the giggly one said.

"Is love enough?" The daughter at the desk asked.

"We have to, we want to," said the daughter with the burnished skin.

"Have you studied the ICNI process?" The wrinkled daughter asked. "It is remarkably complex, and there is no guarantee it will work out the way you want it to."

The two young and glistening daughters looked at one another, startled the way the entitled ones were startled when they found a blockage on a request they deemed was their right.

"But," the dark one said, "others have told us it is a snap."

"There is nothing easy about procreation," the wrinkled daughter said. "If you decide to go ahead with the crossover, you must accept the pain that every woman in the Old Society felt every time she had a child. If pain didn't decay from our brains, the whole earth would scream."

"There are stories about laughing babies," the one with golden skin said.

"So you have no idea," the official daughter said.

She stood. She was one of the perfects—heavy-breasted, narrow of waist, black wiry hair, body lithe, athletic as though aging she did not grow old. She drew up a chair to face the couple. I wandered around the room, standing at a distance, as the perfect daughter said,

280

"This process takes you beyond the species, do you know that? It takes you to the edge of human. In the past, human was the result of sex and sex meant chance..no one knew what the outcome would be. Before the crossover there was one way and it was dangerous and that is what brought us here to the Citadels."

"We don't want an Exo," the bronze-skinned one said, "we want two daughters. We want to be parents. We know that if we cross we can have daughters."

"But you have no idea what this involves." The older daughter was serious, cool, calm.

"The technicians extract an ovum from each of you," the perfect daughter said, "and the crossing involves injecting DNA from each of you to the other. If you cloned, as it was done before, there would be but one parent. This way, the child is born with two. But before you say yes or no remember this. You have a choice. In the Old Society, women did not always have a choice either in the selecting of the offspring they chose to birth or even to birth. The Y was essential, but now, it is not."

The two young daughters glanced at one another and, grasping hands, giggled.

"We want to," the dark one said.

"Are you committed?"

"We are."

"How old are you?"

"Nineteen, both of us."

"Have you considered implantation? Have you read about ovular parthenogenesis? Have you thought about insemination?"

"No!" The daughter with bronze skin said. "We want daughters."

The older daughter opened the device on her desk. She scrolled to a page with diagrams on it. She said,

"This is the procedure you will undergo. It is risky and can cause changes in you that you

281

cannot predict. Have you seen what pregnancy does to the body of a daughter who carries to term? Here." She scrolled through the procedure to the hologram of a daughter's belly where there were stretch marks and a hematoma. The stretch marks were deep and wide. The hematoma a rude purple.

"We have seen this," the dark one said.

"You will not be beautiful. For months you will not sleep at night. For months even years you will not feel like having sex with one another no matter how much you are in love."

"We don't care," the bronze-skinned one said, "we want to cross."

I scrolled ahead, looking for the page where Daiva had written the outcome. The bronze-skinned one had a BMI that was dangerous to her health. Her knees turned out. The skin of her belly sagged but she held a beautiful child with smooth skin the color of a dusky sunrise and hair the color of snow. A designer child?

Note to Daiva: Can they do this? Select the physical traits like selecting bathroom tile or cookery for a kitchen? Did you and Jahil select hair color and eye shades for your child? Is this possible now?

"All right," the older daughter said. "Make an appointment with the technicians in the lab and with your counsel. It will take a few months to prep you. Are you sure?"

The two young daughters still holding hands and unfazed by the cautionary tale leaned together and kissed. The meaty lips of the bronze-skinned one merged perfectly with the soft and tender pinkish lips of her dark-skinned companion.

"We are sure," the bronze-skinned one said, "We're in love. We want our daughters to be immortal."

"Your vanity will not make it easy," the perfect daughter said. She stood and opened the door and passed the couple into the corridor. I stayed.

Alone with the older daughter, I opened the manuscript to the page. I said,

"Do you know the outcome?"

"Of course," she said, "The science is exact. The mixing of nuclear cytoplasm creates a biparental baby immune to ovular partheno-genetic viral infections. So it's not the science we worry about but the psyche and the physical well-being in these privileged crossover cases."

"Because of the speed of the change?"

"You have the text."

"But it will work," I said.

I scrolled to the plot point but the daughter held up a hand.

"You make the decision. They are so beautiful now, so young, so soft, so pliant, so much in love."

"You really want me to change the story line?" I said. "You heard them, they are in love."

"We have taken procreation out of desire, leaving it pure and without the RER that drove us to near extinction."

"I'll make a note in the text," I said. "But I know how Daiva will take it."

Note to Dee—I am so happy that you read my notes. It makes me feel that I am part of you. You say that desire doesn't mean we have to be genital. Are you sure? I learned so much about myself and you, in the Kel-Lang scene and rewrite. In the Crossover scene, I saw...well, you know. There is so much good in this novel, but you take some liberties that lead to inconsistency. For example, some of the Citadels don't have trees. In the Kaavi scenes, she sees that the forests have grown back. Are you making some kind of statement in this world building process? Is there a political reason for it? I am also confused by your inconsistent use of quotation marks. Some scenes have them in the dialogue, others don't. I'll fix that, but I haven't decided yet on the solution. I'm babbling here, don't know what I'm saying because your visit to the Desert Rose completely flustered me. I'm having trouble concentrating. In the Crossover scene I wonder if you want to leave the story line the way it is with the two young daughters changing so much after their deliveries? Also, why don't these daughters have names? You call them the dark-skinned one and the golden-skinned one and the older wiry-haired one. Do you want to leave it that way? I can fix it, but need your okay. If I don't hear back from you, I will make the changes. Am I changing the novel too much? I don't know. I don't know anything right now except that you make me very happy, even when you are going to be a parent in an "obscenely overpopulated world...."

§§§

Working the *Wars of Religion* I had found Kaavi, an archaeohistorian whom I had grown to love. I rejoined her on her Excursion. Kaavi picked up where she had left off—

"The wars started as gangish little fra-cases—a few hyped believers of some sect tangling with another clutch of believers of a different sect—and some died."

"And this is before Hagah released Gynerium?"

I said.

"Before the unification of the revealed religions, yes. That was the paradox that defined the unification. Each of the believers had absolute faith in that belief. At that point, we saw that religion was a disease for which there was no cure."

"But men had been killing women forever..."

"In the beginning, just a few—the breeders, the confused ones, the male-identified ones, the ones who stayed, the ones with soft bones, suffered, but as the numbers grew and the conflicts increased in intensity there were more bodies and the Separation began as the blood flowed."

"Why?" I liked the way Kaavi held herself—dignified but curious. Not afraid to be moral. "Why all this killing?"

"Thought," Kaavi said. "Did they kill a man for what he thought? To take his land, they killed him. To take his woman, they killed him. To steal his gold, they killed him. But what madness made them kill him for what was in his head?"

"That's what happened, isn't it?"

"That's the way Daiva has written it," Kaavi said.

"And the women? Why do they kill the women?"

"For being women. That's the reasoning of the revealed religions."

That night, as we camped in a glen at the edge of a forest, Kaavi handed me a document. She said,

"Read this and tell me what you think."

Her narrative was thick with goddess voice that bothered and excited me. Should I change the voice? Did I have time? I was running out of time.

"In the year 110 After Foundation, the Wars of Religion became bloody battles leaving bodies

285

without heads, hands without fingers, legs
without feet as if, by butchering the corpus,
the belief, the dogma would bleed out and the
dead would be pure and cleansed."

I had three questions—

"Who made the decision to kill?"

"Whose god carried the biggest ax?"

"Which god wielded the heaviest hammer?"

There were, of course, no answers.

"In the wars, women, caught in the Niche
between life and death, had no control over
themselves. In the last years of the Wars of
Religion, men killed the women and then started
on their daughters until the few remaining, to
survive the rape and the murder, migrated to the
Citadels, leaving the killing fields polluted
with slaughter, high with stacks of bones.

"The killing, in 125 After Foundation, came
to an end and the end was an inquisition unlike
any inquisition ever before. The faith, as it
was called, rested only then in the minds of
men, for the women had abandoned belief in favor
of their bodies and in favor of fact, and in
abandoning belief, saw the better way—no more
dogma, no more inquisitions, no more slaughter.

"The killers, demanding blood and armed with
their Disrupters, howled outside the walls of
the new Citadels. But the women did not open the
portals. Where they had obeyed before, they
denied the call to surrender. Before they
acquiesced, now they resisted. The Howlers,
tortured by denial became fierce. They turned on
one another because there was no way except the
bald declaration of faith to satisfy the blood
lust, to cut loose the bloodletting.

"In 190 After Foundation, the first Citadels
shuttered their portals and turned inward,
looking away from the howling of death. Then
came the peace—do good to one another, be kind
to one another, do no harm, hold no grudges,
think what you think without the insane need to

force your belief on those who do not agree with you."

"After the Wars of Religion, after the fire and the rape and the killing, the forests had regenerated, the plains had reseeded their grasses, and on the plains bison grazed and there were no men to hunt them. The killing stopped."

"On my journey through the woods and prairies, across the sand and the rocky detritus of Earth upheavals, I came across the remains of battles and in their skeletal remains the warriors were all alike—their skulls the same, their broken bones the same, their fingers identical and their skeletons, cleaned of meat, all gleamed alike in the sun."

"I made my notes and I took measurements although touching the remains of the dead filled me with sorrow. I kept the record and located on the map the sites where the killing was most intense. I tallied the remains of the disarticulated victims and among them I found the bones of women still in chains as they had been dragged behind the hordes marching in search of infidels. In the skeletons of the fallen women, I found remains of the unborn and though hardened by what I knew and inured by what I had seen, I wept for them—in the Old Society, I would have wailed—and I stayed for days at the battle sites mourning the women and their unborn. I did not feel the need to mourn the killers."

"And on the seventy-fifth day I stood on a hill overlooking a destroyed city of the plain burning in the high hot afternoon sun. I saw the glinting of bones, the white shining of bones and I was overcome with a deep sadness because I knew this was the First Citadel. On my map, I tagged it, C-1.

"I marched off the hill, a day's walk to the glinting and I came to rest at the edge of a huge killing field and there in the sun I saw the metal that had not decayed and the chariots that had not yet rotted and as far as I could see there were bones. There in that field all terror, all fear of all time still smothered the land. A choking cloud of poison. Buried in the backs of the bodies were blades. Blades buried in the backs of bodies fleeing. So many.

"I worked the killing field for two days and I recalled that in the plains where the bloodshed was greatest, the soil turned so fertile the grasses grew tall and thick.

"In the chaos of bones and metal, I found the skeletons of men and horses. Here and there the tattered residue of a wooden cross or a gold crescent, a double cross, a simple cross or a six-pointed star and though far in time from the killing, I could still hear the thunder and the groans and still feel the quaking of annihilation.

"In that field, as I stood over chaos, I recalled the sage's saying, 'There will be no freedom until the last priest strangles the last politician with the entrails of the last lawyer and then slits his own throat.'

"And I cried at the loss of paradise because in the killing all dreams had died."

Note to Daiva: A deep and ugly dread fills each page of Kaavi's story. When did you see all this? In what vision did the future reveal itself so clearly? Kaavi feels like an oracle here. What is the purpose of all the counting and the measurements? How can the Congress look at this horrific history and not vote for Extinction?

"In my report, I wrote that the facts support my findings about the vestiges of the Wars of Religion. It is my opinion that we were right to separate. We were right to preserve our dignity and our truths because now we see the depth of men's hatred and the rewards of their wrath. There can be no forgiveness, no going back. Extinction.

"In my report, I wrote that we are unique, so far as we know, because we are the only species aware of its death and able to imagine its nonexistence. We are the first and perhaps only species capable of making a rational commitment to our own extinction. There were too many of us and perhaps that is what drove the wars. The only way to keep the species alive is to limit our numbers. But men don't do that willingly, and that leaves species suicide in the form of war and killing. To give the species a chance at redemption, the Citadels must set limits. It is only through education of the daughters that the truth of existence can be revealed.

"The decision we make should not be the result of this awful Paleolithic and ancient urge that drives men to kill.

"As I waited for comments and reactions, I wrote this history. I sent pictures of the bones and the spears and photos of the swords notched from the cutting of necks shattered. In 215 After Foundation, I wrote of the hatred that had brought the bloodlust to the hand and the fear that had brought the distrust to the eye.

"When the first reactions came they were muted and soft. I catalogued them and tallied them. As each Citadel reported, it was clear that not even the Virgin Citadels wanted to reintegrate. That finding astounded me. No one held up a standard of correctness, no one compared the tenets of one Citadel to another. In the end, facts were enough. There is some cruelty that can never be forgiven. While it was, however, the consensus of the responders that reintegration without genetic modification of the residual Y would result in a repeat of the apocalypse, many felt that human beings did not merit further existence on Gaea.

"In 290 AF, one year after my report, the citadels voted to wait another hundred years to reassess. Until then the Exos would continue to be expelled, the Glands would continue to be milked, the Mutants would continue to be limited in numbers.

"The Planners all agreed that the race should continue, but at some point in the future, a decision had to be made—either complete extinction of all the race, or extinction of the Y chromosome with its killer 13th gene.

"In the end, until the decision can be made—parthenogenetic births are to continue in the Virgin Citadels.

"The upshot of all my work was a deep and lasting sorrow because I had seen the planet as it should have been. I had seen the sweeping fields of grasses. I had seen forests and rivers. I had seen the birds and their fledglings. I had seen animals drinking the coppery waters.

"All that had been good in the Old Society was eradicated by the religious dogma of go forth and multiply. Any opinion that ran against the revealed religious dogma was heretical, and the punishment for heresy was stoning. I conclude with this—

"All religion shall be abolished for all time in all the Citadels."


Daiva was so cruel. Only a cruel writer would create a character like Kaavi who, in her rejection of religion, had an innocence both saintly and pure.

As the images of bones and bodies, as walls and flowers flowed over me, I was writing a note to Daiva, when Kali came to the door. Kali was so sweet in her sapphism and promiscuity. Sapphism. What did that mean? Post-lesbian love? Each time I read to her and Bett, I watched the changes in her. Her desire to be with Bett was so deep it marked her, it changed her. *Citadel* could not change her the way it was changing me because she and Bett had diverged the day they formed their bond. In divergence she had found a freedom she had not known possible. She asked if I was hungry. She said I hadn't eaten since last night. What time is it? I asked her. Dinner time, she said. She and Bett wanted to hear more of the story. I had already decided to read them Pin's *History* in the *Wars of Savagery*.

I was running out of time. I was a wreck. *Citadel* was killing me. But I was going to finish.

## Citadel                           Daiva Izokaitis

*The wars were so intense that few written records survived. This compilation, from the archaeohistorian Pin in 114 AF, is an overview brought together from bits and pieces of the rare records. It should be noted that the basis for this account is from a battle at one of the first armed Citadels before its destruction. In this summation, Pin uses two composite characters Kae and Fix. There is no record of the true names of the daughters although we do know many were young, often between fourteen and nineteen years.*

*Daughters who have attended the Heptuants will find the military terminology in the composite self-explanatory.*

### Insects in Body Armor

By 65 AF, following the first episode of the Gynerium Plague, the XYs learned to swarm only at night. They often came out of the moonlight in waves and they were silent. The early fighting had shown them that the daughters would not submit, but had vowed to die rather than surrender, so there was none of the roar of war, none of the screaming and adrenaline madness of war, just the slow deliberate pace of killers driving down on to the plain armed and ready to kill with no thought of their own dying.

Kae rammed the magazine into the Mac 10. A flare arced up into the sky and she saw them—clusters of five, ten, wearing segmented body armor blazoned with white crosses and red crescents that made them look like giant black insects.

Kae watched a file of trucks enter the battle on her left flank. She heard the chatter of a machine gun ripe with cries and cursing. An explosion. An RPG. A mortar. Bodies in black armor fell.

Even in the now failing light of the flare, there was blood.

And there was silence.

Then, coming from the silence, the clatter of boots. The grunts and groans of bodies careening. Kae, now seasoned and battle-hardened, did not think as a wraith sprang up in front of her. She fired the Mac 10. There was no movement, no kick, just a rapid firing of the machine gun and then it stopped.

Kae reloaded. Her finger curled around the trigger again as now, out of the right flank, a truck bore down. In the bed, two daughters with two machine guns strafed the clusters of advancing black shadows. Under the weight of the .50 caliber hail, their armor shattered and they fell.

Kae breathed easier then. She squeezed the trigger. Her hand did not tremble, her legs did not shake, her heart did not run wild.

She smelled the welcome odor of fresh blood, not the blood from a cut on the hand, not the smell of her menstrual blood, but the hard odor of blood spilling from a body. A red flare lit the sky. Kae saw the XYs on the ground, on their knees. She saw a phalanx of daughters massing on the killing field. As they swept in, she heard the thut thut thut thut of single shots. The head shot. No survivors.

Kae charged deeper into the field, to the tangle of weapons and blood. She heard the cries of wounded daughters falling. Her heart beat hard, her throat hurt, but she went to work chopping her way across the littered field, cutting XYs down with the Mac 10, single shots. The deeper she ran into the field the more the smell of death covered her—the smell of bowels emptying, the smell of urine leaking through slits of body armor.

She spun, her left leg stinging. Shot. Wounded. She looked at the attacker on his knees.

He aimed a pistol at her. She did not think, she did not stop, her training conditioned her not to hesitate. She fired into the face of the attacker. She knew she had to die. She knew that if they took her, she would be punished, she would be destroyed. As she fired, for one second, she felt remorse. She collapsed. Dizzy and bleeding, she turned her weapon on herself, but just before she fired, she saw Fix blast her way through the swarm.

Fix crouched beside Kae.

"Don't do it," Fix said. A flare arced against the black sky and fell in a rainbow of sparkles. "You just caught shrapnel. You'll be okay."

Fix unfolded a swab from her pack, pressed it against Kae's wound, and plucked out a fragment of steel. She said, "Can you walk?"

Firing from the right flank followed by intense explosions froze the two daughters. A swarm of XYs advanced, firing as they came. Kae fired the Mac again, hammering the attackers who walked over their dead. From the left flank a rush of daughters, machetes in hand, clashed with the shattered column.

Fix unsheathed her kukri and she and Kae swept into the swarm. Fix took the first attacker. In his left hand he held a pistol. Fix slashed at him, caught him in the neck with the tip of the kukri. The XY groaned as he rolled onto his side saying fucking cunt before he died.

Kae followed Fix into the fight and there was blood. She tore at XYs whose faces were streaked with war paint, whose teeth had been filed to points, whose heads had been shaved. She admired Fix's fury as she hacked and stabbed but then Kae took the blunt end of a rifle to the head. She dropped to her knees. As she fell, she gut-slashed the insect holding the rifle. Blood spewed over her. The XY grunted and toppled and there was hatred in his eyes and cruelty on his lips. Fix ripped his throat. Kae stayed calm, her wound still hurting as she sprayed a storm of hellfire at the attackers.

The XYs withdrew. Another flare burned high up. In the light, Kae saw the backs of the retreating swarm.

Kae then saw Fix, on her back, bleeding from the mouth.

§§§

# BIOLOGY OF DESIRE

### Clara

I called Erica Blackbridge to set up a lunch date at Casa Del Rey in the Marina. It was a sunny Saturday. The Marina was crowded. I tipped Carlos big to give me a table on the water.

"Do you want anything to start, Clara?" Carlos asked me.

The pushy devil, using my first name. "Not yet, but bring a couple glasses of Corbière when my guest arrives."

"Sure thing, Clara."

Erica was right on time.

Erica Blackridge was a legend in the business. She grew up on Wertmuller and Coppola. Her mother, Sabela Negroponte, had been a big name in Italy and France where Erica worked crews, acted, wrote a couple of films for bilingual production, then made her debut directing B horror films in Spain before graduating to LA, where she worked in the shadow of Tarantino and Von Trier until she had a breakthrough art-house film and from there to Blackbridge Productions which she had turned into a first-class outfit. She was a striking woman, close to six feet tall. She could have modeled, but she really looked at the world through a viewfinder with a light meter in her hand. She was fit. Tanned. Designer shades. Stylish gray-flecked hair. She wore blue slacks, a white Guayabera shirt with blue buttons, and short-heeled sandals. When Carlos led her to the table, I thanked her meeting with me.

"The pleasure is all mine," Blackbridge said. Her voice was tinged with velvet. The words slid out of her mouth.

Carlos—all muscled charm with the infinite finesse of a

295

hitter spiking a volleyball—waltzed up with the Corbière.

Erica Blackbridge let me order—crab salad, wine, breadsticks. No butter.

"How is Trisha?" Blackbridge said. She tugged down her shades. There was a silver sheen in her eyes—blue eyes, the kind of eyes that either frosted your brain or made your heart pound. My heart skipped a beat.

"She's finishing up."

"I talked to Harry Conklin," Blackbridge said, "over at Blue Wave."

"You know Harry?"

"In the business, you know everybody or nobody knows you."

"He turned down *Citadel.*"

"He told me," Blackbridge said. "Didn't think the post-lesbian angle was a good hook."

"But you're here."

"That's what makes it good," Blackbridge said. She talked as much with her hands as she did with her voice. I watched the sliding gestures you didn't need a dictionary to decode. God, she was smooth. And that silky voice.

"*Citadel,*" I said, "is exactly what Harry Conklin is afraid of."

"Um huh, women in control."

"Given his proclivities, you'd think Harry would lap that up."

"You know what scares the hell out of men like Harry?"

"I have an idea."

"A woman who doesn't need a man," Blackbridge said. "It's not the post-lesbian story that scared him away." She sipped her wine, savored it, caressed it with her tongue, slid it around in her mouth. I looked at her through the lens of the wineglass. Watched her morph into an angel then back. "And that's what this novel, *Citadel*, is all about."

"Harry didn't see that."

"Harry saw it, he didn't know what to do with it. Why did you go to him?"

"I know Patrice."

"Ah, Patrice. She's his eyes and ears."

"And Caleb wrote a treatment."

"Your brother."

"Yes."

"He has some credits."

"You checked?"

"The deal's in the details."

"Just not the right kind of credits."

"He'll write the screenplay?"

"He has a first draft."

Blackbridge said, "Ahead of publication?"

I told her that we were going to New York on the twenty-fifth for the pre-pub party and then to TownTalk with Gloria Cousins before kicking off a six-city book-signing tour.

"TownTalk."

"Gloria and I were classmates."

"Of course you were."

Erica leaned back in her chair—every move spontaneous and smooth just begging for eyes. She was so natural, you wanted to look at her. Why had she quit acting? I felt a tingle charge up and down my back that I tried to push away, but the sheer animal nature of the woman brought out desire so strong that I shook and had trouble drinking my wine. I was thinking of the scenes in *Citadel* that had made me cringe, the scenes that made me want to burn the novel because of what they did to me. I had to fight to control the rush that now had spread from my belly to my neck and face. I touched the scar on my neck. I shakily poured more wine. Wine was good. Erica said,

"I have to be honest with you, Clara—I went to the Desert Rose Motel by design. I heard you got hold of a blockbuster."

"How did you hear that?"

"Estelle. I know Trisha's work through her."

"Estelle from the focus group?"

"She's consulted on a couple of films for me."

"You've been in LA too long."

"What do you mean by that?"

"You're not as direct or as decent as you seem."

"I'm here, Clara, because I know Pinnacle Books. I know what you've done with it. I know you can do more and I know that you wanted this blockbuster so bad you went all in to get it. So, I went to see for myself."

"You could have come right to me."

"Trisha found *Citadel*," Erica said, "and now she's afraid of it."

Blackbridge pulled down her shades again. The eyes were armed. Ready. The blue had changed to steel.

"Erica," I said. I reached across the table and pressed her hand. She didn't draw back, she didn't question why. "But what got you interested in this novel?"

She looked at her hand and then at me and I felt the charge. Desire. Blackbridge didn't slide her hand away when Carlos returned with the crab salads, the breadsticks, the wine. She continued as though Carlos didn't exist in our world.

"Deep in that book, there's something I've been after for a long time but never found."

"Science," I said.

"Law that's not about lawyers and courtrooms."

"Law?" The word felt like grit in my teeth.

"The one thing men hate is a woman telling them what to do. Put a woman in a cop uniform and you've got trouble. Give a woman a gun, and men go nuts. In *Citadel,* I see women controlling not just their own lives, but also saying no to the pissant demands of petty men with pattern baldness and hooked on Viagra. I see women refusing to get on their knees. This book is a revolution in the making and I want to film it. I know craft when I see it, Clara. Depth when I see it. Look at the big themes in that novel— what is a human? What is love? What is desire? Divergent evolution—I've wondered about that all my life—and the parthenogenetic future. There's this passion just burning its way to film. Without victims, there are no strongmen. Women have been victims across time but in this novel, they're saying no more. This writer, Daiva Izokaitis, has written scenes that make you cry but it's not the soapy, sappy, sentimental crying. It's deeper than that. It's kind of a universal sadness for the true condition and fate of women. The connection between violence and sex drives film right now Rape neutralizes woman's natural rule of choice. Every woman who's ever been raped will get her revenge wherever this film shows. I see that in this novel and I want to film it. I can film it."

Listening to her made me realize why I had wanted *Citadel*. And the thing is, Erica knew exactly what she was doing to me. She went on,

"Imagine a society where all the law officers are women. In this novel, the women aren't just the law, they are natural law—choice made us, choice will keep making us—and that is what this novel does."

"Erica."

"In this novel, Daiva shows us how women, by having sons, are complicit in their own oppression. Every man is some woman's son and every son is a soldier in the war on women. In this novel, we see the deep hurt women have suffered for millennia and we see the cure for it."

"Erica." I pressed her hand again. "Leave your motorcycle and come with me."

"I didn't ride my bike down."

"You do take a lot for granted."

"Yes. I do."

## Trisha

Tuesday night, the Desert Rose Motel was quiet. Kali had put on a roast with grilled potatoes, carrots, and Zucchini. We ate at the bar. I wondered if I'd done something to make them hate me. They were silent through dinner. Several times I hinted that I had finished *Citadel* and would be leaving.

Kali brought out a chocolate amaretto mousse.

"I know you like mousse," Kali said, "but this one is going to cost you."

"We want more story," Bett said.

"You've heard most of it," I said.

"We decided to hold you hostage till we hear the rest."

"Okay, but this section comes with a trigger warning."

"Trigger warning?" Kali said. "We're not thin-skins. What we haven't done, we've seen."

"Now you're bragging, Kali," Bett said.

299

"You want more," I said, "I'll give you *Women in Captivity.*"

"Didn't we hear that before?" Kali said.

"No, I didn't read it to you because it's...kind of special."

"I like special," Bett said.

"You like the bearded tulip," Kali said.

**Citadel**                    **Daiva Izokaitis**

**Women in Captivity**
By
Orione C. 194

Part One: Karen

*Note: In the Old Society, this text came with a trigger warning. Trigger warnings were caveats to the reader that the text contained shocking sexual, violent, or pornographic details. The technique is amateurish, so the text is here without emendations or editing as it is in the interest of all daughters to know the truth about a woman's place in the Old Society.*

Blackout came at 9:30. Karen lay on her cot, heart beating so loudly that she knew everyone in the dorm heard it. She tried to stay calm but she was at the same time excited and terrified. Excited to tell Bart, terrified that the sisters would find out. She didn't know what Bart would say to her now, but she had proved to him that she was a woman, she had let him make love to her unprotected.

The other sisters were asleep; it never took them more than a few minutes after their exhausting days, and Karen listened to the staggered rhythmic breathing of her companions

300

and thought that in a short while she would be away from them; she and Bart would go back to the City to raise their child.

She sneaked out of the dorm, just as she had done every night for months; her practice had made her expert in deception; not a sound as she slid into the night. Then she ran, her bare feet padding along the dirt path.

Once outside the commune, she put on her sneakers and walked the three miles to the edge of town. Bart lived in a small house, that Karen had come to look upon as a castle, their castle, merely a beginning, a suggestion of what would come. He had promised her the world. Her heart quickened as she came to the door. She stood outside listening. Bart was with some friends, and they would all be high. She hesitated a few minutes, then she knocked. The voices grew silent, and a heavy tread came to the door.

"Don't want any unless you're giving it away."

Embarrassed, a flutter in her throat, Karen waited until Bart flung the door open, his silhouette looming over her. Without speaking, he grabbed her and ran his hands under her skirt. "Hi baby" he whispered as his fingers invaded her. She did not struggle.

Bart let her go, then led her into the cabin where three men sat at a table. Karen smelled cannabis. Lines of coke were laid out on the table. Bottles of whiskey.

"Boys," Bart said, "this is the little dyke I been banging."

Karen flushed at the reference to lesbianism; Bart knew it wasn't true, but most men believed that all women who lived on the communes were lesbians. They leered at her, unblinking.

Karen knew she should have waited, but it was too late.

"You want a hit," one of the men said. He giggled as he handed her a joint.

301

"No," Bart said. "The doll face don't do doobie, Eddie Ray.

"I need to talk to you about something important," Karen said.

"Sure, baby," Bart said, "okay, you assholes, get the hell out of here. I'm going to parley with my bitch."

"Not here, please?" Karen muttered.

"Okay, what the fuck. Let's go outside."

Alone, Bart turned to Karen and said,

"What's going on?"

"I missed my period twice. We're going to have a baby."

In the sudden stillness Bart's breathing was ragged. Then, his voice raspy, he laughed.

"You stupid cunt," he said, "you puttin' me on? You better not be 'cause you ain't no use to me."

Karen tugged at her skirt. She shouldn't have told him. Bart glared at her.

"Bart, I want you, and I want to have our child, but I can't stay at the commune now. I can't face them. You and I can go away. . . ."

"You think I'm gonna put up with this shit? You shoulda took care of yourself so now you take care of it and leave me out of it."

He walked towards the house. Karen, stunned, felt helpless. Then from deep inside her voice gathered volume, and she shouted,

"Bart! I can't leave you out of it."

Bart stopped. Karen chased after him. Her voice stern, condemning, now controlled, she said. "It's your child! You wanted me, and you wanted me to prove I wanted you. It's your child, it's your responsibility."

Before she could continue, his fist crashed into her temple. She sprawled to the ground. He stood over her, hands hanging at his sides, his voice seething hatred.

"You whore! Don't you tell me what I can and can't do! For all I know, you've fucked everybody

302

between here and that lesbian hole out there. And now you want to lay it on me. Fuck no! I don't owe you nothin'."

The tears came. Karen was shocked. 'I love you baby,' he had said the first time he took her. She had gone willingly. Now as she listened to him tell her what an idiot she was, she couldn't stop crying.

"You were an easy fuck, baby, but you weren't a good fuck. So trot your cute little ass back to those bitches and let them watch your belly swell. How will your sisters take that? How will your sisters handle it when that little bastard pops out? Whatdya think they'll say knowing that they've been doing it by hand and you've been in town getting your fill of cock? I gave you what you wanted, so get the fuck out of here and don't come crying to me."

He left her. He would not come back. She had betrayed her sisters; she couldn't go back to them; she was lost because she couldn't go with him. She was alone.

Without thinking she picked up a rock and ran at Bart and smashed the back of his head. He fell. He turned, his face ridden with disbelief, and as he stood she struck him again. Then he laughed. It was a bitter laugh full of anger, ripe with hatred.

He ripped the rock out of her hand and smashed her with his fist. She scraped and clawed at him, tearing his face. He grabbed her hands and yanked her into the cabin and flung her on the floor.

The three men, still sitting at the table, stared glassy-eyed at Karen.

Bart stood breathing heavily, and then with a dismissive flick of his hand, he gave her to them. She waited. If they had beaten her, she would not have said a word. But they did nothing. They just looked at her.

Then one of them grasped her hair and yanked her to the floor. It was happening. She became limp, passive. Her passivity infuriated the man who had grabbed her and he slapped her, but she only became more passive.

Silent. He hit her again. The others watched him bat her around. Then Bart stopped him. He said,

"Hold on. You can beat this bitch to death, and she ain't gonna fight. That's because she don't hate you. You've got to make her hate you."

He picked Karen up and threw her on the table. He turned her on her stomach and entered her from behind. Her face banged against the table. She tasted blood. Bart slammed into her. Still she said nothing.

And then he pulled out of her and forced her to her knees. "Help me, man," he said to his friends. One of them yanked a handful of hair and forced her mouth open. Bart rammed into her mouth, gagging her and still jammed deeper. He muttered each time he slammed into her, "You like it? You want to make me eat shit because you fucked up, huh? How's that taste now, eating your own shit?"

Karen bit him so hard her teeth cracked. Blood.

Bart yelped. He beat her. She held on. The stoned men attacked her. She worked her teeth deeper into the flesh of the screaming Bart. The men pounded her, ripped at her, tore her lips, her eyes, but she did not give up until Bart pulled away, blood spurting from his wounded manhood.

Karen, still conscious, spat Bart's blood mingled with hers.

Then one of the men grabbed a skillet and smashed her head with it. They beat her. Bart sagged to his knees mumbling. "You've killed me, you've killed me." The men kept beating her until she lay in a widening pool of blood. Finally

304

they stopped. The skillet had destroyed her
head. Her arms were distorted to strange angles.
Bart slumped down on the floor, and his friends
stood around the girl as if she were prey and
they were hunters but unaware of what they were
doing or had done or would ever do.


Part Two: Marta

*Note: The author has researched the language
of the Pre-Foundation Exo culture in order to
write in the dialect of the time. Just after the
Wars of Savagery the populations of the Exo
culture were falling under the control of the
Citadels. Females were either forced out of the
Exo culture, slaughtered by the Mutants, or held
as sex slaves. Marta has been in captivity for
three years. She is common property, their
slave, a public woman. The Exos are worried about
the decreasing size of their population. In the
three years that Marta has been captive, she has
been pregnant four times, and each time she
aborted all but the last, a female child which,
because she was under surveillance she brought
to term. But as soon as the child was born, Marta
smothered it. She was beaten and starved and
then she was bred again.*

Exos clustered in groups of four or five in the
square. Marta came out of the hut. She had been
afraid the first time she underwent the ritual, but
she learned that the grunts and cries the Exos
shouted were words that were losing their meaning
and were relics from the Wars of Savagery. She knew
now they did not intend to kill her.

Her hands tied together, she was led into the
open square. After the time of darkness, she did
not focus well in the bright sun. She staggered.
She stumbled, each misstep met with more derision.
She wore the same dress she had worn in her time of

darkness. In the sunlight, she fingered the ragged neckline, the rips in the cloth that revealed her breasts. But she did not cover. She no longer had the will to cover.

An old Exo came out of the crowd leading a group of young ones. Marta was clean; she had no diseases unlike the Martyrs who had infected themselves and then surrendered to the Exos. Because she was not diseased, she was used to initiate the young ones in the rites. Until they had ejaculated into a woman to prove they weren't afraid a woman would laugh at them, they couldn't become adults in the Band.

The old Exo sat on the ground cross-legged; the younger ones formed a line and passed before him, each exposing his genitals for inspection. He examined them, and when he had finished, he rose.

He went to Marta and lifted her dress to examine her. He bent her from the waist down, hanging her head and exposing her buttocks.

Then he motioned the first boy to approach. He advanced. Beads of sweat broke out on his forehead. He was afraid. He had been filled with tales of horror about women.

He had heard about the infected ones. He heard that a woman sometimes hid pieces of cut glass in her vagina to dismember men. He had heard that women sometimes clamped onto a man and held him in her vagina until his penis fell off. He was afraid that he would be contaminated with evil and sin if he touched her.

He preferred his friends. They weren't diseased or built so strangely. They weren't ugly down there.

The old Exo guided the boy, coaxing him, giving him words of encouragement—

"It's all right, she can't hurt ya. Jist stick yer thang in her thang."

One by one, the boys entered Marta. She felt nothing.

When they had finished, the elder Exos congratulated the initiates. The old Exo forced Marta to her back and tied her legs together with thongs.

He strapped her to a pole. Two Exos carried her
to her hut. She lay in the darkness while in the
square the boisterous ritual continued. The Exos
became drunker and drunker celebrating the young
Exos change into adults.

Marta's mind wasn't in her body; she was not her
body; she remembered not being there. For a moment,
she wondered how she would kill the child if she
were pregnant again. She thought about the Citadel
and what her friends were doing, and then, with a
sigh, she closed her eyes and went to sleep.


Part Three: Zeb


*Note: The time is 265 AF. Zeb is 24, a Hunter.
She had to have an ovariectomy, as all Hunters
then did. It has now been fourteen generations
since a daughter gave birth outside a Citadel.*

*Zeb is taken captive after she broke her leg
in a fall when she separated from her team. She
is discovered by a Band of Exos and taken to a
Village. Zeb knows what is going to happen; the
author enters into her mind as she goes with the
Exos to the village, trying to find the strength
to face what will inevitably happen. The
prolonged narrative gives the reader an
opportunity to come very close to the savagery
of the Exos as the story flashes through Zeb's
mind.*


The Village was silent. A clutch of Exos
followed the retinue through the streets.

Zeb dragged her splinted leg. The pain was
intense. Each step came with a shiver. She had
to close her eyes. She had known that it might
happen to her, and she had always been careful,
but it had happened. The splint, the fractured
bone made her a prisoner without chains.

The complete silence of the Exos was odd. She
expected at least to be insulted, cursed, even

spat upon; she could see hostility in their eyes, but not a word was spoken. When she slowed her pace, they slowed too, waiting for her, so that she was the master of the speed with which she marched to her death.

She knew she was doomed. She knew they would kill her just as their ancestors had killed other daughters, and it would happen in a matter-of-fact way, because no thought could be given to keeping her alive. The Exos could not refrain from killing. Killing was instinctive with them.

The machine was a black box with six knobs resting on a low metal stand. Four tentacle-like tubes projected from it.

Zeb recognized the machine. She had read about it. It was a Disrupter, a remnant of the Wars of Savagery. It was the pinnacle of war technology from the Old Society. It had been designed just for the purpose of destroying women. It was an oscillator tuned to the vibrations of mitochondrial DNA.

The mass cruelty of war, which had always been a distant cruelty, became focused on women following the plague and infection. During the Wars of Savagery, the purpose had not been, as it was in other wars, to conquer or to secure resources but to destroy bodies, to annihilate them. The machine was efficient. Zeb knew how it worked. Every daughter in every citadel knew how it worked.

After so many years, the machine was still intact. That was a credit, if it could be said in those words, to the technical expertise of the Old Society. A war machine that was indestructible.

Zeb watched an Exo put on gloves. He approached her. She realized that the gloves were not to protect him while he used the machine. The gloves prevented his flesh from contacting hers. She had not been touched during the entire time of her captivity except with

308

sticks or prods.

She understood their silence.

They were awed by her. She was the poisonous female, the curse of the race, the epitome of everything they hated and despised. No Exo could touch her, so repugnant had the female become in their mythology.

The Exo reached out to her. After several attempts, he grasped her wrist. The gloves were soft. His grip was only enough to guide her arm. He took one of the tubes and wound it around her head. Another wrapped around her body, binding her arms to her sides. The splint was removed from her leg, and another tube was wrapped around her legs.

The pain made her feel faint. The Exo maneuvered the fourth tube around her ankles. The tubing gripped her. As she flexed, it grew tighter. Exos passed by the doorway stopping to watch the spectacle.

The last tube was placed, the door was closed, and the four Exos who had brought her to the Village remained with her.

The Exo with the gloves activated the machine.

A sharp sensation shot through her body. Pain vanished. She felt exhilarated. Her skin tingled.

The Exos looked on with no expression.

Then the machine was deactivated and the tubes released. Zeb stood hobbling on one leg as the Exo secured the tubes.

Then he lifted a small switch on the machine.

Her body spasmed, the flesh vibrated off the bone and that made the Exos laugh. Their joy intensified as the bones quivered into a mush of cytoplasm on the floor of the cave. Strands of hair spotted the mass of jelly but that too dissolved in the humming and shimmered in the pale light. In the center of the pool that had once been a daughter, a small metal name plaque on a silver chain glistened. Her body was gone.

The Exo turned off the Disrupter. The laughter
stopped as the Exos, one by one, scooped up the
liquid and massaged their inflated DNA injection
tubes until they ejaculated.

After I finished reading *Women in Captivity,* the words
hung in the air like wounded butterflies. Neither Bett nor
Kali spoke. Bett leaned on the bar, Kali's arm draped over
her shoulders. They were both crying. Not sobbing, but
weeping in that deep silence of the voiceless wounded. I
saw, in their eyes, that Kali and Bett understood the
unfathomable anguish of the perpetual victim. I snapped
the laptop shut.

Bett sniffled as if coming out of a bad dream.

Kali blinked like a waking child. She whispered,

"Jesus, sweet Jesus, Trish. That is just so sad. Who'd of
thought what's her name—Daiva—could get that deep?"

"Let me see that," Bett said.

She spun the laptop around, opened it, and read from
*Zeb* in a monotone as if by chewing each word she ate the
pain of the woman roped to the tree, as if she was the
woman seared by the Disrupter until her arms, her legs, her
torso disappeared.

"Stop," Kali said. "I can't hear it again."

"I don't know if anybody can read this, Trisha," Bett
said.

"It's too real," Kali said. "That Disrupter? Too real, you
know?"

"She read us a different scene a while back," Bett said.

"I don't want it to be real," Kali said. "Who built that
piece of shit?"

"Before Foundation," Bett said. "It was designed just to
annihilate women."

As Bett spoke, the words sprang up like corpses buried
in some time vault and I too felt all the pain of the women
who had been hurt, humiliated, demeaned, or raped.

"Hey, hey," Bett said. "It's just a novel, right?"

She came around the bar and took my hand and she
patted it.

"Yeah but a novel that really pisses me off," Kali said.
"Really. Men."

"No, no." Bett shook her head. "Don't go there, baby."
Bett lifted my chin. She said,

"You gonna be okay, kid?"

"The weight of it just came down on me," I said.
"Sorry."

"Sorry? That's one powerful story she put out there. Is
she like that? Like, you know, brutal?"

"Sometimes I wonder just what she really is," I said. "I
have to settle up."

"Settle up?"

"I'm done. I leave in the morning. I sent the manuscript
to Clara. We're going to New York."

"New York." Kali said.

"Before you go," Bett said, "that Karen piece? I've
heard that story before. Your buddy, Daiva, she got it right,
you know. But this book is something you can't like. You
know that? You can't like it, but once it gets in you, you
gotta go with it."

"I hate to see you split," Kali said. "I really like listening
to you read."

"Thanks, Kali."

"When you coming back?"

"Don't know," I said. "The world's coming to an end."

"Well, if it don't come to an end right away, you send
me a copy…"

"You buy a copy, hon," Bett said. "And you get Daiva to
sign it."

§§§

I returned to room 11. I was tired. Ready to change. I
looked at the machine that glowed in the light of the
bedside lamp. Over. Always before when it was over I was
happy, elated even, but this time it was not the same. I still
had so many questions. I had a nostalgia for the abandoned
pages. I had cut so many words. I had changed so much.

Would Daiva even recognize her novel?

I was afraid of finishing.

What if I hadn't done it right?

311

What if there was more to do?
What if I had been blind to the real story in the novel?
Had I finished too soon?

In thinking I was finished, I realized that I could never lead, I could only follow the words. An editor can never bring words into being. What if I was a fake who had given nothing to the novel but had drained its blood? Had I ripped out too much? What if I had gutted the meaning of the novel for the sake of one clear sentence? I had finished, but I had no idea of who or what I was.

This was a new feeling. Dread. Horror. Despair. The room vibrated. My thoughts seemed to echo. I was alone and then the words burst out in a cascade washing over me and I was back in *Citadel,* and *Citadel* was in me. I saw all the mistakes I had made. I saw it all again—the daughters, the bones, the dead, the outraged, the mutilated, the butchered. I saw the daughters vowing never to forgive men for the brutal things they had done to women. I saw every woman who had ever gone out alone with hope in her heart looking for her prince.

No.

It was not over. It would not be over, as Kaavi had written, until the last lawyer strangled the last priest with the entrails of the last politician and then slit his own throat.

The words stopped rushing through me. A strange and silent moment without words. I could not remember a time when they had left me. Memory opened up. I recalled reading Sappho's words at the instant she realized the goddesses had gone silent—"Why have you abandoned me?" Lost in my silence in the light of the desert, I was no longer swimming in words but I was walking in a sea of images. I saw a shining woman in the distance—clean, new, clear, delicate, but very, very real—turning as if on a revolving stage.

And out of the nimbus surrounding the spinning woman there came men.

Men wearing black body armor like the carapaces of large black insects. On the breast of each carapace there was the white cross and on the white cross a blazing red crescent and over the cross and crescent, shone a six pointed gold star. The men carried stones and clubs and they fell on the spinning clear, clean, new, delicate woman with their clubs and stones and I vomited as if everything festering inside me spewed its way out.

I shrank back, hands out to shield myself from the vision, and in the vision, there stood a thick, heavy muscled man, much like the men from the beach I had lain with. He leered at me. He raised a stone, but I did not yield, did not surrender. I snatched the stone and heaved it back at the man wearing the black carapace and he fell.

I had seen the future.

I had seen the future and the future was death.

But who was I now? I had to go back to the city, back to all the rainbow silk of my past, and I had to throw it all away because none of what I had been was now me. I would go to the beach once more before I stripped away the last skin of the woman I had been before *Citadel*.

I was going into the future that now was not just Daiva's but mine as well.

§§§

# DIVERGENT EVOLUTION

### Trisha

My exile in the desert ruined my tan. On the beach, I sat watching the muscles flex and shimmer with sweat, listening to the grunts and growls. I felt a pang of nostalgia—today would be my last day ever on the beach before the end of the world. It was hot. I was sweating. Beads of sweat on my skin made me think of the scales of a reptile. Somewhere in me, there was a reptile. Ancient. Deadly. I did feel serpentine as if my reptile brain had turned on as I watched the sweaty bodies clash but I did not feel lust boiling up in me. Desire. I remembered the residue of my past—the silk, the bikinis, miniskirts and cheongsams with their slits that bared skin.

I remembered the times I had lain in the sand eyeing the beach meat at their games—volleyball, missile ball, Frisbee. Could I count how many times I had left the beach with one of them? I fell back into an ancient time—just weeks ago—and I remembered telling Rose that I did not want to be automatic. I hated being automatic, hated being physical, unthinking, reacting, being led to the bed by the beast in my belly that screamed *make me come.*

I jerked myself out of that time. That was then. I was not the same woman I had been in those days.

Awake now, thinking, I tugged at the bikini top. The redness of my skin flared against the margin of white. I glanced down. The bikini bottom stretched tight across my hip bones—I had lost weight. Every woman in the Niche thinks she is too fat. Looking at my legs, at my belly, I saw not desirable thinness, but a loss. Part of me was gone. Alone in room 11 in the desert, *Citadel* had taken part of

315

me but what it left was the real me. Just then the volleyball skittered to a stop in a tsunami of sand.

I did not screech a little-girl-help-me screech as the dark-skinned, mouth-breathing Exo hauled up, chest heaving, eyes locked on my feet before traveling up my legs to my crotch. He measured me, eyes settling on my breasts and the thin strip of cloth.

He was a specimen—smooth—rippled—hard—sweating. I measured the crotch bulge as I had done so many times, but there was no desire in the measuring. He knew to the pubic hair just how much of himself to show. Before *Citadel,* I would have asked if he shaved everywhere as he posed—the discus thrower, the javelin hurler, the dying Gaul—instead I picked up the volleyball and held it.

"I'll take it," he said.

Before *Citadel* I would have given him the wine test as I smelled the body, the sweat, the cologne masked by pheromones—the residual evolutionary response to a naked woman in the sand. Not now. I pitched the volleyball to him. The lust faded from his lips, the flowering of desire died in his eyes.

I leaned back and crossed my ankles. He rose, scattering sweat and sand like apple seeds. I smelled him as he left. *Citadel* had changed me—I no longer saw beach meat. I saw Glands and Exos and Mutants. I saw the killer in the muscles, in the mouth, in the eyes. And for a moment, I fled to Ket in the Virgin Citadel stacking bones of the dead daughters, feeling once again what I had felt in those days living inside the novel—it's what a good editor does, I told Daiva. But now, in the killing fields, the residue of murder in my nostrils, I hated what I made men do. They were as automatic as I had been.

I watched two of them, two specimens—teeth bared, ripping at one another—blood blooming from the sun-dark skin, flesh tearing under teeth. They rolled in the sand snarling barking and howling. Even at a distance I smelled their blood and in the blood was the terror that women in the Old Society lived under, a terror so complete that, in the end, it drove us to live in Citadels.

I tried to measure it—how much did it take to turn a woman away from the automatic call hidden in the body, away from the call grown out of three million years of sexual selection? How early and in which eon had desire first blossomed?

There was no measure other than self-preservation. As the killer gene mutated we had no choice—live with men and die or go to the Citadels and live free. Free of fear. Desire did not die. Desire did not need the Y.

I sat staring into the sunset. I was in the Niche and I knew how precious it was to be there. It could have been me bleeding, throat slashed, bones broken, teeth smashed. It came down to blood and the killer gene. Desire masked it all. I did not need the Y to live with desire because desire was blind, its only measure the pleasure of touch. The kiss.

I rolled up the beach towel. The warriors did not glance at me, half-naked. I draped the beach towel over my shoulders. For me, the Old Society was finished.

I crossed the sand—the grit between my toes felt good, felt real, freeing. At the Z-Ray I looked back to see the victor standing over his beaten foe. Pounding his chest. Desire steeped in blood.

It was over now and one of them was dead or unconscious. I started the Z-Ray and drove back home.

§§§

Coming home to Santa Monica after I finished *Citadel* was like entering a foreign country. Usually it's good to get back home, but this time things had changed. My condo felt hollow and dark. It even smelled different than I remembered. It wasn't a good homecoming, that warm sense of relief when you walk in the door and you plop down on the sofa. That day, I looked at what should have been comfortable and safe but it was alien and dangerous. Who lives here? Who do these ancient artifacts belong to? At first I thought it was just the travel-halo. Maybe it was from living in room 11, closed up in two rooms with a bed, a desk, a chair, and a shower, but I had the feeling that I didn't belong there anymore.

The books on the shelves? Weird titles. I opened one.
Was it even in English?

The bedroom—curtains open, the eucalyptus mystically
suspended in midair.

I retreated from the bedroom but looking back I
imagined a woman naked on the bed, a woman named
Trisha. A Gland hovering over her. Wars of Savagery.
Women in Captivity. Technicians mapping the Gland's
genome then snipping out the codons that made him
dangerous. What made men hate us? Was it our odors? Our
sweat? The slickness of our arousal? Our blood? Even now,
after *Citadel,* it was a mystery. I knew that if I walked
downtown, a guy in a car would tell me what a great ass I
had. That he wanted to suck my tits.

I yanked open a bureau drawer – underwear, blouses,
bras, bikinis—those colorful bikinis the old Trisha wore to
hunt. A rainbow of panties and blouses, a sea of shorts and
tank tops—the bikini of shame.

Blushing.

Guilt.

Doubt.

Shame. All blooming out of me violent and virulent as
some tropical disease.

I opened the closet. It was like a throwback to a time
when there were no houses or beds, no clothes or even fire,
just the howling and gnashing and panting and huffing of
us emerging from the mist with clubs in our hands and a
kid on our hip. Standing there, I was chilled as I measured
each dress on each hanger for its shame index. I had worn
these short dresses, with tight bodices. *"Nice tits, babe."*
The black dress slit up the side, the leg, bait on a hook.
*"Suck my dick, babe."* On every dress, the hormonal
residue of desire.

Before *Citadel*? No pubic hair. No bare crotch in a
naked bikini or a sheer white dress. But in six weeks in
Room 11 in the desert in the heat, I had not shaved my
pubic hair. Never again. Never.

I glanced at myself in the mirror. The woman I had last
seen in that glass no longer existed. Six weeks in the desert
and I no longer recognized myself. What was I back then?

318

*Clara strapped to a horse rail, Clara naked, whipped.*
*Karen beaten to death.*
*The woman in the sand stoned to death.*
*Zeb evaporated by the Disrupter.*
*The scent of roasting meat.*
*Piles of bones.*
Daiva writing *Extinction.*
*Citadel* was now a screenplay.

"Erica wants you to be an advisor on the film, Trisha," Clara had said. No. No. No. No.

I tossed reject after reject onto the pile of erotic dreams until the closet was empty and I stood again in the words and rush of the novel living in me. It was part of me now. I could not see myself dressing for the role I had once played because I was no longer the woman who had auditioned for it. What had I been thinking?

What was it Daiva said? "When you went hunting for beach meat, what did you do?"

I watched the shade of myself move across the mirror. I ran my hands over the flat belly, down to the delta of Venus where all the primordial urges lived, urges that wore me down, made me walk out of the house wearing two thin strips of cloth that hid nothing. Homecoming to a country where I didn't speak the language.

I had been close to death on that bed after hunting. Where was the protective shell I imagined every time I spread my legs on that bed? It didn't exist. It had never existed. Every time with a man, I had been inches from death. Never again.

I bundled the Old Society clothing into a ball and squeezed the life out of it, as if by squeezing I could pour out the residue of desire and with it my shame.

After a reading at the Desert Rose Motel, Bett had said to me, "That's all they see. All they want is the treasure between your legs and you wanna give it to them 'cause you're a breeder, Trish…a breeder." She knew me before I knew myself.

My past lay in a pile on the bed. A bleak past.

Bleakness and doom and blood and death and carnage and pain. So much pain.

I remembered asking Daiva, before I read Kel and Lang—"Do the daughters in the future orgasm? Do the daughters know what love is? Do the daughters need to be loved? Do they have sex?"

And Daiva had said, "Of course—the only thing that changes is their need for men. Desire is eternal. This is a post-lesbian novel, about a post-lesbian, post-coital, post-family, post-Y chromosome world, and in it, you are you. You are not the one defined by your orifices but you as you are, as you can be."

I dove into the mound of soft fabrics and my past skimmed by. I caressed the tender silks and the filmy chiffons and smooth satins. And then I heard the buzzer.

The woman, Charlene was her name, was a chunky hungry-looking blonde who exuded sweetness.

"Oh, what a darling place," she said.

She handed me a card with the price list for her time.

"Oh, my," Charlene said, "you have a ton of stuff. What goes? What stays?"

I led Charlene through the condo to the bedroom.

On the bed—the stacks of bikinis—one a day for thirty days, a rainbow of bikinis.

A stack of sarongs—floral, plain, a chromatic display. Each one full of memories.

A stack of skirts, a stack of blouses, slacks, bras, and thongs.

"Can't do the undies, hon," Charlene said. "Have to donate the undies."

"All right."

"Furniture?"

"Yes. Everything."

"Okay," Charlene said. "When do you want the open house?"

"You tell me."

"Oh my, oh my, oh my," Charlene said as she wound her way through the apartment running her fingers over every object, every piece of furniture, every plate as if by touching she calculated not only the value but the history of each piece and then she glanced at me, her eyes wide and very green.

"Oh my," she said, "are you sure? All of this is just such excellent stuff."

"All of it goes."

"All of it? Oh, my. Gosh, to tell the truth, there's some of this I'd take for myself in a pinch."

"In lieu of?"

"Will you be here?"

Charlene made a second run through inventorying the goods and when she returned, she said,

"You can't be sure."

"What do you mean?"

"Oh. Well. Are you leaving LA?"

"Does it matter?"

"Oh. Well. No."

Charlene took a second run at the silverware and the China, and she raised her eyebrows. "I'd say, round figure, 15 K."

"Okay."

"Oh, well that's just my estimate. Right? Okay? You mean okay? I have to price everything and all the sets have to go as sets—can't break up those sets, you've got some really cool stuff, Trisha. And of course I take thirty percent of everything that moves, and I have a—on the card, you see, my minimum. Oh, my, but…" Charlene grimaced—"but why? Some of this… I mean…You want a weekend? Weekends, you get a different class of buyer you see. Weekdays you get breeders."

"Breeders?"

"Sorry. Oh. Well, I figured…you…know…you alone… Really, breeders look for kid stuff, you know, baby clothes, baby furniture, baby everything. And I have an assistant…"

"Weekend is fine. But soon."

Charlene circled the dining room checking the crystal, wine buckets, wineglasses and the set of bird clocks. She wrote out a contract. I was about to sign it when Charlene said, "Seller's remorse."

"What?"

"Oh, well I mean, not everybody, but stuff like this— you sell it and then you think maybe you shouldn't have, and you go out and buy some of the same stuff back so instead, just make up your mind right now what you want, like one time when I sold an entire estate back to the woman for thirty percent on top of my thirty percent fee. All profit."

I signed the contract.

I showed Charlene to the door.

"Thursday," Charlene said, "my pricer will be here."

"Fine."

I watched Charlene walk down the corridor, watched her climb into a green Carrera and wave as she drove off. Breeders. Charlene was living *Citadel* and she didn't know it.

I wandered through the condo, knowing this was the last time I'd see it. I remembered days on the beach in those bikinis. I had never in eight years, gone into the water, not once.

I sat on the bed and fingered the blue sarong with a yellow hibiscus. I remembered wearing it. Seller's remorse?

Never.

In the kitchen, I opened a bottle of Château Vieux, picked a flute from the array of crystal on the table and went out to the patio.

Sipping wine, I leaned on the rail and thought maybe I was being rash. Maybe it would be okay. Maybe it was a mistake to get rid of everything. I polished off the wine, dropped the bottle in the trash, and returned to the bedroom.

The black bikini was strung across the bed. It embarrassed me now to think that I had ever worn it. Hope. I had hope then, on the sand. But *Citadel* had changed all that. Now I knew I didn't need to go to the beach. The need that had driven me was dead. I threw the black bikini in the pile of spandex and silk.

In the Old Society, Daiva told me, you'd be a courtesan you know, hawking your body for diamonds and rubies. You'd have died from the pox.

But *Citadel* had rescued me.

## Daiva

I rang Trisha in the security door. She looked like she'd been living on oatmeal for six weeks. Before I had a chance to say hello she told me that she had sold it all, everything she owned and she was selling her condo.

"Sit down," I said. "You look beat."

"Dee, I'm really confused. Clara has the manuscript."

"Forget the manuscript. How long since you ate something?" I said.

"I had some wine at home."

She drew pages from her pack and spread them on the lab counter.

"What is this?" I asked.

"I found them hidden in an envelope at the end of your manuscript, Dee. They're written in longhand. A pretty elegant script. Read them."

Okay. I started reading. I knew right away that I hadn't written them, but I had no idea where they came from—

*Questions to the Congress Regarding The Fate of the Y*

*"Pursuant to the unanimous request of the delegates to this Congress, a Council met to formulate questions that the delegates are to consider and vote upon.*

*"In the event there is any objection to the language of the questions, discussion will be open and changes made if needed. The questions are:*

*1.     Knowing what we know now about the nature of the three cultures, do we wish to continue the present system of procreation and separation of cultures without considering that any changes need be made? This is the Status Quo question.*

*2.     Knowing what we now know do we wish to reintegrate the two cultures and to re-introduce physical sexual procreation as a consequence to that integration, giving due* consideration to the possibility that peaceful coexistence might entail further genetic alteration of the males? This is the Integrationist question.

3. *Knowing what we now know, do we wish to eradicate all males from the earth by ceasing henceforth all male births and destroying the extant stores of androsperm, giving due consideration to the possible necessity of future generations to rely upon alternative means of procreation? This is the Eradicationist question.*

4. *Knowing what we now know, do we wish to eradicate the male forever or do we wish to stop all male births for five generations, thereby annihilating all presently existing males, without destroying the sperm banks, thereby allowing future generations the option, with all due consideration to the questions of social and physical evolution, of reintroducing the male of the species as they so choose? This is the amended Eradicationist question.*

5. *Knowing what we now know, do we wish to take the extreme view of declaring that no further human births will take place within the Citadels, thereby bringing about the stabilization and eventual decline of the human race? This is the Extinctionist question.*

6. *Knowing what we now know, do we wish to introduce another variable in the present rate of male births and lower the rate from its present 1 male to 100 daughters, to a rate of 1 in 200, recognizing that such a ratio would allow for the occasional emergence of a Gland hence the continued genetic combination of natural biology? This is the amended Status Quo question.*

*"These are the questions we have formulated and which we must now decide before this Congress. We recognize the difficulty which they pose. We recommend that each delegate give them due consideration and in tranquility bear in mind the seriousness of her decision before casting her vote in the name of her sisters and for the benefit of humanity.*

### Decision of the Congress

*Let it be recorded that today, Vente/19/490 AF, the Congress of Citadels rejected its option to reintegrate the Citadel cultures and the Exo cultures. We recognize the profound implications of this decision, but we also recognize in light of conditions discovered by scientific, objective, and intuitive data, that this is the problem we must solve for ourselves at this time.*

*We separated from the Old Society to protect the planet and to contain the greed that was destroying it.*

*We could not to participate in a disexual society wherein we were instrumental in breeding humanity into oblivion. We recognize that future daughters might not share our temporal provincialism but should have a say in their own destiny. For our part, however, we cannot and will not take the risk of committing countless daughters to slavery for the personal gain of another person or persons as was the course of events in the Old Society. We cannot and will not take the risk of subjecting any daughter to capricious and irrational control by another human being, person or persons of any sex. This Congress, knowing the archaeohistory, cannot allow* the Citadels to be degraded back to the status quo ante Foundation.

We recognize that we are human beings who cannot stop and start evolution without drastically altering our recognizable humanness.

We therefore reject our options to further genetically manipulate males and to eradicate all males. We are locked into an evolving system of chance that cannot be reversed or changed at any level which might alter that chance itself. To erase for perpetuity one aspect of the species would disrupt our phase with the rhythm of evolution, with the dynamics of evolution, and we would devolve into masses of protoplasm alien to a world whose continuity, for better or for worse, is, despite its limitations, necessary and natural. We refuse our option to stop all male births for five generations, because we cannot allow ourselves to assume the power to put to death and then to resurrect out of time beings whose absence would make them alien to the system that generated them. To kill the beast entirely would be to destroy the race, and to the extent that daughters and males evolved from the same root, we acknowledge the right of that aspect of the species to live, albeit in limited numbers, which we will ascertain and maintain in balance with nature and our desire.

We choose therefore not to eradicate the human race as a species of life on the earth, bound into an ever-changing, nonsimultaneous chain of events, and in so choosing, we assert the concept that life with its vicissitudes should and can take its evolved course.

We further assert that to live is a choice we make in full

*consciousness of the possibility of death, but we henceforth commit ourselves to the investigation of the possibilities of eternal life within a single body.*

*Citadel Cuernavaca*
*Vente/19/490*


"Where did you get this?"

"I told you I found them in that envelope tucked in the back of *Citadel*. Did you write them?"

"No," I said. "I don't write in cursive."

"They look old and the script is like nothing I've ever seen before. If you didn't write them, who did? How do they wind up at the end of your book?"

"Are you testing me?"

"If they were supposed to be in the book you should have given them to me sooner. Did you stick them in the manuscript when you came out with Clara?"

"I did not."

"What do I do with them?"

"No idea. I read all your edits. I saw how you were changing things. I hated some of your fixes at first, but then I saw your logic. Do I thank you for pulling out the story that was hidden under all of my bad writing?"

"Sometimes," Trisha said, "when I was going deep, something happened to me, and it's like I was in the story, living it. That's when I noticed the odor of the words."

"You said each word in the novel has a scent, right?"

"Um huh."

"Do these words in these longhand pages have a scent?"

"Only one," Trisha said. She picked up the first page and pointed to the word *future*. "This one has a peculiar odor of wet iron. Maybe the odor of fresh blood. You lost control of your characters, didn't you? I talked to most of them because that's the only way an editor can get to their core."

"And they talked to you?"

"Yes, they talked to me about the way the book should be. There are things they didn't tell you, Daiva. Things they didn't like. They didn't tell you everything they know. You want to know what I think? I think these pages come from one of your characters. I think she wanted to see this ending. She wanted to tell you and to take some credit instead of leaving all the glory for you."

"When are you coming back?" I said.

"What?"

"To reality, Trisha. You're in the city, you can leave the novel. It's gone."

"This is reality, Dee. I know that like all literary characters, they hate the author and so they always hold something back."

"Are you trying to say I didn't write *Citadel*, Trisha?"

"No, love, I know you wrote it, but I also know you took dictation from them, from Kirsis, from Lang, from Ell, and from Filina. I know you wrote it, but it's their story too and you just got the privilege of writing it down. Everything they told me made the story better. The whole story is there just as they dictated it to you. You did it and they are jealous because they could not do it themselves. Without you their story dies. The metaphysics of fiction are stranger than dark energy and gravity waves. Without the author the characters stay mute and stupid. You save them with your words and that's why I had so much to do. They are all scientists. Every daughter in every Citadel you write about is a scientist and they all speak the truth, but they are lousy writers. You did what you could. No one has to know about any of this. This is the secret of the author and the editor and every novel ever written has the same secret romance. Every one. Without them there is no you, Daiva Izokaitis, author. Without you there is no them. Without you I am nothing but a crazy woman editing words for Pinnacle Books. I saved *Citadel* for them and for you and you all saved me. Art is salvation, Dee, and without it we die in darkness. It was my duty, my job, my obligation to art to save this novel. Believe me there were sometimes, like *Women in Captivity*, when I really thought about abandoning you. But what kind of editor would I have been then? You brought it back, Dee, this monumental mess of words that somehow sticks together, and yes I smell the words—sometimes I was so enraptured with the smell I couldn't move but always—even in despair I saw the story, and without story there is nothing. We are story. Clara is publishing this novel and we are going to New York to launch it and we will die there. In writing this novel, you brought the world to an end."

"You make me laugh when you talk like an idiot. Why did I ever turn it over to you? If I'd known you were such an idiot…"

"And Erica Blackbridge is going to film it, Dee. Using Caleb's script. I don't see how anyone can ever film the images you wrote…"

"Did you sleep with her?"

"Not physically," Trisha said.

"You dreamed about her?"

"Yes, but she and Clara have gotten close."

"What about Curtis?"

"Clara has finished with the fantasies. She and Blackbridge… Well you know. Your novel changed her, Dee. You brought it back and it changed her just as it changed me. And that changed Blackbridge too. And that changed Caleb. It changed Bett and Kali at the Desert Rose. You see just what you did?"

"But we're going to die in New York."

"We will die in New York, Dee, but Bru and Syn and all the others will live because you didn't settle for realism. You believed in them and the art."

I picked up the pages. I said, "These Questions to the Congress Regarding the Fate of the Y don't sound like any of the characters."

"No they don't," Trisha said.

"So, nothing is really mine?"

"Ummm," Trisha said. "That's a hard question to answer because every author has to own her criminality."

"You once asked why I left men in. Choice. Selection. The daughters have a choice and the Glands are the objects of choice. For once in the history of the world all women have a choice whether they want to bear offspring. For the XYs, the Glands are the choice. Jahil has passed twelve weeks."

"Did Jahil have a choice?"

"She did. At every step, just the way it happens in the novel."

"In the novel, you let the fictional Jahil terminate."

"Say it, Trisha, say it."

"All right, you let her abort."

"That's her choice. That's the way it should be in the Niche. In the East, there was no choice. In the East, no citadels ever formed. But in *Citadel*, she decides what she wants to do and when she wants to do it and no man is going to tell her when, where, or how she's going to do it, and no Exo has a claim to our offspring."

"You created the Howlers. You created the future and now it's coming true."

§§§

# FOUNDATION

### Clara

The bar at the Trianon Hotel is an elegant Art Deco remnant. The staff is attentive and beautiful. The Margaritas are perfect. I sipped the Margarita—tangy, lemony, the tequila smooth, that bite of salt kind to my tongue. I was waiting for Caleb. He was always late, but waiting in the Trianon left me feeling that I'd dived back to another time. There aren't any Lempickas on the walls but "The Bugatti" would have found a home there.

I was living in the Niche, all right. The Trianon was my showplace. You came there for expensive Margaritas instead of buying a glass of wine in a corner bar with sawdust floors and oyster shells where some madman sits on a barstool quoting bad poetry. I looked at the copy of *Citadel* on the table and I thought about a page I had read the night before. I went to the text and found the passage—

> Before the unification of the revealed religions, yes. That was the paradox that defined the unification. Each of the believers had absolute faith in that belief. At that point, we saw that religion was a disease for which there was no cure."
>
> "In the wars, women, caught between life and death, had no control over themselves. In the last years of the Wars of Religion, men killed the women then started on their daughters until the remaining few, to survive the rape and the murder, migrated to the Citadels, leaving the

killing fields polluted with slaughter, high
with stacks of bones.

*Unification.* I had made up my mind to tell Caleb
everything. Just as I checked my watch, Caleb blew in with
Erica Blackbridge. I licked the salt from the rim of the
glass. My face heated up and it wasn't from the tequila.

"Clara," Erica said. That voice. How did a woman get a
voice like that? In the amber lighting her skin looked
bronzed. She was a walking Tamara Lempicka portrait. I
was still surprised at what was happening to me. I felt safe,
for the first time in ages, I felt safe and I knew it was the
safety of same sex relationships. I liked everything about
this woman. Her hair, her blue eyes, the shape of her face.
She sat facing me and for a moment I had a thought that if
Lempicka walked through the door, she'd be so taken she'd
die to paint Erica. With the finesse of a practiced
boulevardier, Erica nodded at my Margarita and held up a
finger to the waitress approaching the table and Caleb said
two, and I giggled.

I do not often giggle but I had no secrets anymore. Once
you've tasted a lover's mouth, smelled her breath after sex,
you can never hide anything. A man who sees you naked,
sees only the residue of his ego. A woman who sees you
naked, understands your soul. I touched Erica's hand.

"Enough niceties," Caleb said, "let's get down to
business."

"The script?" I said.

"Finished," Caleb said. "It's really the first thing I've
finished that works."

"It's a fine piece of work," Erica said.

"Yeah," Caleb said, "and it's all because of Erica. It's
taken me thirty-six years to see how women build
relationships."

"I have no idea how a collaboration works with these
things," I said.

"It's a simple method," Erica said. "I sit at the computer
while Caleb reads his script to me as I type it. You need to
hear the dialogue coming from a mouth."

"Do you change it?" I asked.

"You have to. With Caleb it was easy. He had already cleaned it up, but this story has a lot in it so the question was how much to leave out."

"And what did you leave out?" I said.

"*Only the parts people tend to skip,* and that gives you this tight visual storyline and a limited set of characters."

I recalled the images of *Citadel* that had slammed into me the first time reading the manuscript. I remembered the first time Erica touched me—hands smooth and supple—and I remembered the scenes in *Citadel* ragged with blood and bones. I said,

"Erica, I don't see how you can film it."

Erica reached for my Margarita. She licked the salt from rim of the glass. I remembered the slickness of that tongue and just then I didn't care what she filmed.

"She means," Caleb said, "that we cut out the duplicate scenes, trimmed the longer scenes, tightened the dialogue—Daiva has a lot to learn about dialogue."

"And we ended up with a good script," Erica said. She slid the Margarita back to me. I sipped the Margarita, lips settling over the very spot Erica's lips had touched.

"Caleb told me Trisha and Daiva are driving to the East Coast."

"They called this morning," Caleb said. "Stayed in Gettysburg last night."

Erica glanced at her watch as the waitress returned with the Margaritas. Raising her glass, Erica said,

"To blood and bones, to Gynerium, to Daiva who thought all this stuff up, and to Clara for having the vision to take it on."

I sipped the rest of my Margarita. Erica stood. She said,

"Sorry to leave you but I have to go."

"Trouble?" I said.

"Nothing to worry about. Dinner? Tonight? Eight o'clock?"

I blushed. I'm too old to blush, but there it was. Erica held her gaze just long enough. I had told her about Curtis and the way he treated me. "You're through with the Curtises of this world," Erica had said. I was grateful. I had never opened up to anyone the way I opened up to her and the reward was freedom. She left us in a moment of silence before Caleb said,

"Did you know her name is Erica Negroponte? Her mother was a big star in Italian film. She worked with Bruno and Ferugio." I had to strain to focus on my brother. The residue of Erica's smile, the wound of her departure lay on me far longer than it should have.

"I know. She told me."

"Did she tell you she started as an extra when she was just a kid? She worked on crews all over Europe picking up six languages and the details of the business. She wrote a screenplay called *La Protectora* when she was eighteen. Her mother had the lead in it. Then she got into acting and from there to directing and now you see her—a woman born and bred in the film industry and something sure as hell is going on between you two."

"I know," I said. "We had a good chat about our past."

"Clara, how long?"

"Three weeks."

"Three weeks."

"She's the first person I've ever really been able to talk to."

"It won't get in the way, will it?" Caleb said.

"It hasn't so far."

"You know she's never been married."

"Neither have I."

"Why do we do this, Sis?" Caleb said. "You know if this novel doesn't have legs, the film will die just like *Justine* in an excruciating death spiral."

"Erica will make it fly, Caleb," I said.

"She's really got hold of you, hasn't she, Sis?"

I took Caleb's hand. "I have a confession, Caleb. Okay? When I read this novel, I admit that I saw just money. It had what I needed—just a touch of salaciousness, but that's on the surface. When I got into it, I actually got lost because I became a character. I identified with Kirsis, the Planner, and well, not just with her mind, Caleb. It was a painful read and in some places it made me sick. I had to put it down, but then I had to finish it. But..."

"What's going on, Sis?" Caleb said. "Something has

changed. You've changed."

"Jackie Best."

"What about him?"

"He raped me when I was sixteen."

Caleb tensed. His face went flat and white and his hand shook.

"That prick. I'll…"

"Don't," I said. "You can't do anything and I can't hide behind my shame anymore."

"When?"

"One evening, mom was out and you were I don't know where. He came over and he wouldn't leave."

"Why didn't you tell me?"

"I wasn't without blame, Caleb. I…"

"You think you led him on?"

"In a way."

"But you were sixteen. I'll kill the son of a bitch."

"No, you won't. I had to tell you. I told Erica. I have told her everything about me. I told her about every man I ever slept with, and believe me that was hard because anyone else would have judged me but not Erica. She told me that most of the books we had published were about me. She told me that Curtis was the problem and *Citadel* is the solution. She's so clear, Caleb. She told me I had to read this novel in a different way because it wouldn't make any sense until I saw myself in it. She has some history, too, you know. Every woman does. I told her how my shame that kept me on my knees because I've been living with what Jackie did to me and I couldn't have a normal relationship with a man. To tell the truth, I really didn't know what that meant—to have a normal relationship, so instead I had these self-destructive affairs. The only thing I knew I needed for sure was to hurt myself. But I'm not a cutter. I just couldn't do that so I let them humiliate me. Erica is helping me get past that."

"What can I do, Clara?"

"This novel makes me want to clear out all the darkness from my life. I need to start over. This is a good place to do it and Erica is a good woman to start it with."

Caleb sat back. There was a puzzlement in his eyes, the

helpless look of a man who has seen his sister raped and not been able to do a thing about it. He got up and came around the table and pulled me from my chair and hugged me. He held me until I was short of breath. He said,

"Well, I guess this is a confessional day."

"What?"

"You know I went out with Daiva? At the beginning? She took me to her lab and she did run the sperm count. I'm a dead end."

"It doesn't matter."

"It's the end of the line for the Kreisler Y chromosome. This book is changing a lot of us."

"If I hadn't read this novel, I'd have gone on buried under my guilt until some man killed me. This book set me free, Caleb."

Caleb grinned then. He said,

"Yeah, it kind of does that. Before I got into it, I saw only this crazy fucking lunatic scientist ranting about a City of Dykes getting it on all over the place. Erica doesn't see it that way."

"And you're happy now?" I said.

"It still can be a disaster for us."

"This is going to pay off. It already has. We've gotten more ink because of this book than we got for everything we've ever published. This is the blockbuster. Daiva wrote it, Trisha delivered it. I should have told you about Jackie years ago, but it took this book to bring it into the light, Caleb. There's a little bit of Karen in me and there's a whole lot of Marta and there are others I didn't tell you."

"What else aren't you telling me? Did that shithead knock you up?"

I opened my purse and laid out a set of photos of Daiva holding a hard copy of *Citadel.* In them she looked like a heathen angel in black leather and nasal studs.

"Sis?" Caleb said, "did he?"

"Look at this woman, Caleb."

"Sis?"

"Oh, and I ordered a different floral spray for each table."

"Tell me," Caleb said.

"And I have Trisha's Château Vieux Chardonnay by the case. What you think? And I have five hundred books coming."

"He did, didn't he, Clara?"

I held Caleb's hand. "Yes, but we took care of it."

"You and mom?"

"Yes. Mom and I."

"When? How?"

"We went to New Orleans. You don't remember that but a woman never forgets. It's why you cross the street when you see a man coming at you. Any dark street is enough to bring it right back up. If you're with another woman, you remember. If you have a business, you remember. At first you hide the pain but it gets so enormous you can't keep it inside you and then you start to talk to other women and you find out the truth. If you're in a room with five women, one of them will be a victim. In the focus group, the night we decided on *Citadel,* we talked about the book, but we talked just as much about women and rape and fear. You find out just how many of us have been forced. And you never forget the fear. And you know something, Caleb? You get the benefit of that fear. All men, rapists or not, benefit from the fear all women live with. And this book made it absolutely impossible for me to forget. It opens up so many wounds."

"Is that why?"

"Why what?"

"Why you never had kids?"

"I never had kids, Caleb. Because I can't have kids. He ruined me. The *doctor* if he was a *doctor* ruined me. Remember? Mom told you I had a serious case of the flu and had to stay in bed for a week."

"So it is the end of the Kreisler line."

"We're going out with a roar, Caleb. My revenge will be a gaudy, splashy, expensive event we'll always remember if the world doesn't end."

§§§

## Trisha

There was wine. A lot of wine. But I no longer drank Château Vieux. I didn't need it now.

The reception hall was huge and full of light, full of people and balloons and wine. I tried to scuttle the sense of doom that had lived in my brain since I finished the job with *Citadel.* The world was going to end. There were signs everywhere if you knew how to read them.

A balloon exploded.

I jumped.

The end.

People laughed and the laughter spread like a disease and the faces scabbed with time and lined with age melded into a mass of flesh—that's the way worlds end—in masses of bodies and balloons and wine. In the past, I would have downed six or eight glasses of Château Vieux and gotten sick.

Mine is an existential sickness that overwhelms me unless I'm on a manic high and then nothing matters until I dive into the desperation of hope. I threaded my way through the bloat of faces and balloons and wine to the restroom where I vomited from the knot in my stomach. But a good vomit can never smother the sense of doom that lasts from dark day to neon night. All of us, the bipolar genies, know the ups and darks as well as we know despair. I looked at my face in the mirror. It was a large mirror, the frame was floral ormolu. The faucets of the sinks were gold and the counter was black marble with yellow flecks in it. Black. The color of doom. What had I done? I had warned Clara. I wanted to stop it, but it could not now be stopped. I should have let the novel die. I was the bringer of death. I pulled my eyelids up, looked at my naked eyes. Nothing there but the infinite well of doom. Red streaks in my eyes—another sign. Blood.

And then I heard the chant –

"Daiva! Daiva! Daiva!"

I left the toilet, left the mirror with its ormolu floral frame and entered the hall where Daiva stood at a podium—pictures of her like posters for a political candidate alternated with blowups of the cover of *Citadel* with its gray stone walls, its Solerian, drawn as if the artist and Daiva shared the same vision of the future. I knew it so well now. I had been inside the walls. I had seen the bones and the death. I had seen the little girls pillaged. I had seen the death throes of the Old Society. I was sick and I needed to vomit again, but I did not return to the gold restroom with its gold faucet fixtures and the black marble counter.

On her night of nights, Daiva was not the blonde innocent wearing her white skirts, white blouses, and white Mary Janes. She was the Daiva of Leather and Latex, a black-booted Daiva of shorn hair and silver ear studs. I did not want to smile, but her metamorphosis from lab-bound nerd to black Madonna gave me a break from the gloom. Maybe this wasn't the end. Maybe it was just nerves. Maybe this monumental seven-day celebration was a new beginning for all of us.

Balloons. Wine. Faces. People. Daiva. *Citadel*.

"Tonight," Daiva said, leaning into the microphone, her leather pants shiny as if oiled, "I want to thank my publisher, Clara Kreisler, and my editor, Trisha de Tours, because without them there is no *Citadel*."

Scattered, polite applause followed by cheers and calls of Daiva Daiva Daiva. A frisson of dread crept up my back as if an insect had crawled under my skin. *Citadel*. The end.

"And," Daiva went on, "I want to talk about the Genesis of *Citadel*." Again, the shock of reality froze me—It was finished. It was here, in front of me, the end. "A novel, as my editor says, isn't a book until it has an ISBN. This novel started out as a vision and the deeper I got into the vision, the more it morphed into a story that I call the Post-Lesbian Experience."

Cheering. More shouting. Daiva Daiva Daiva. No one chanted Trisha Trisha Trisha.

This was what had to happen. I knew it would happen. I had brought the beast to the world and now the world was going to tear the beast apart.

"It wasn't easy," Daiva said. "All the pain and fear were there and this burning urge to be loved was there and there came a point where I couldn't tell what was real from what was not. But in the end, Trisha, my darling beautiful Trisha, saved me. She gave the vision clarity. It is a vision of a time when women are not on their knees, a time when no man would dare kill a woman."

The faces were all laughing and voices shouting and the hands clapping and Daiva gloried in the adulation. It was a kind of author-worship, worship that the editor never enjoyed. The Editor. Like god in the universe, as Flaubert had written—everywhere evident, nowhere visible.

She milked the adoration. Gazing out at her acolytes, she seemed to shine in the spotlight, a goddess ascending to heaven. She started softly when she spoke again, and her crowd went quiet. As she spoke she held up a huge mounted photograph. A life-size color photograph of Daiva in her white skirt and frilly blouse, her hair in curls down to her shoulders, exactly as she had looked the first time I saw her. Daiva said,

"This was me before *Citadel*. This was me before the change. How did I change?"

She halted. I cringed. I had no idea where she was going with this.

Daiva said, "I stopped being an object of desire."

The audience again exploded with cheers and bravos and Clara approached Daiva holding a copy of *Citadel*. Again I held my breath. Was this when the bombs exploded? Was this the moment when the world ended? She was going to read. What would she read? Wine. I needed wine, no, I didn't need wine. Daiva read from her typescript,

"In the beginning, they started as gangish little fracases—a few hyped believers, tangled with another clutch of believers—and some died.

"In the beginning, just a few—the bleeders, the ones with soft bones—suffered, but as the numbers grew and the conflicts increased in intensity there were bodies. And there was blood. And there were killers with weapons and hatred in their eyes. The killing started slowly, in faraway places, and like a severe infection it spread and the targets were women."

Daiva held up there. The faces turned grim as if some

primordial memory had surfaced in each of the women in the room. The laughter changed to a strangled silence.

"Women had a choice—to stand and be killed or to fight back. To fight back meant to betray everything they had ever been taught."

Daiva paused again. The quiet that settled in the huge ballroom belied the size of the crowd and I felt it, the secret bond—the women in the room knew the exact pages Daiva read from. They even mouthed the words along with her. The scenes in the pages rose up in their minds reminding them of the truth behind the words. Maybe it would be all right, I thought. Maybe it was the beginning and not the end. Maybe the apocalypse came in another century.

"The choice was simple—to stand as they had always stood and be beaten and raped and killed, or to take up arms and be free. The 13<sup>th</sup> gene had mutated and with its mutations the Exos became killers and the geneticists knew that they had to turn back evolution, but they also knew that men and women were on divergent evolutionary paths. The choice had to be made—separation or reintegration. Separation meant women had to find sanctuary. Without sanctuary, the race would go extinct."

The tingling at the base of my spine turned hot and ran up into my scalp. Separation. I searched the ballroom for Clara. Where was Clara? This was what she wanted. I felt the separation in me. What I once had been, I no longer was. I no longer needed what I had once needed. In separation, I ceased to be who I had been just as Daiva had changed from the innocent in white to the dragon in black. It was true. If you read *Citadel*, if you let *Citadel* inside you, you changed—you understood the biology of desire.

"That," Daiva read, "was the task of the Congress—to determine the fate of the human race. Could the human race be rescued from itself?"

The silence in the big room held. They were waiting. They knew what came next, but now they were hearing it from the oracle herself as if she were spreading the vision that the universe had given her when she wrote the first word. I scanned the faces and I knew the women understood. I also knew the men never would.

"The answer," Daiva said, no longer reading, but speaking as if already quoting from the sequel— "The answer is no. No matter how much we massage the genome, no matter how much we manipulate nature, the end is clear—the Y chromosome is dying, the future of the race is in the hands of women.

"As we stand here now, we are all human. We were conceived in sex, we matured in a womb, we were born, we grew, but in the end, everything after that, all of our actions are residual evolutionary responses—we are automatic and we can no longer be automatic. As the Y dies, the X becomes Savior. In the end, we will have to choose."

My throat was dry. My mouth and tongue were raw. I watched the women in the room turn on the men who could not see the coming horror because it was buried in every cell, in every body, and there was no hope.

I wanted to cry as I looked at the women—trim, kempt, in control, while the men hovered ragged as derelict castaways unshaven, overweight. Exos.

Here it would begin—the separation, the beginning of Extinction.

Daiva closed the book. Out of the crowd a single male voice, anger-tinged and hoarse called out, "What do you mean by post-lesbian, you cunt?"

"I'll answer that tomorrow night on TownTalk with Gloria Cousins, you shithead."

And she left the podium.


## Daiva

It was cold and noisy. I did not expect it to be cold and I did not like the noise. The book had already made my world noisier and noise made me uneasy and when I was uneasy I couldn't think. I needed to think because thinking grounded me.

Gloria Cousins. TownTalk host. Famous. Would her questions be hard? Easy? Was Gloria Cousins an Extinctionist, a Separatist, a Reintegrationist? Would she ask the personal questions other interviewers already

342

asked—have you been molested? How do you know so much about rape? Are you in a relationship with another woman?

A knock at the door. The assistant.

"Two minutes, Doctor Izokaitis."

Doctor Izokaitis. No one ever called me Doctor Izokaitis. The name made me uneasy. The cold made me uneasy. Sudden quiet made me uneasy. What if I froze at the first question?

The green room, which was not green but light blue with pink trim, had a huge mirror at a huge dressing table. I touched my lips, tingly. Maybe I shouldn't wear black leather pants. Maybe the red blouse is too tight. No. Okay. But no skin. I leaned close to the glass to check my eyes. "You are so special," Trisha had told me. Was I special? All of this because I had written a novel. It's just a novel, why all the fuss?

The assistant said, "You look great, Doctor Izokaitis. Gloria really likes your book, you know."

"Have you read it?"

"I love it and if you'd sign it, that would be so great. We should go now."

I followed her—a very young woman with a pleasant voice—to the edge of the set. Trisha was already seated. She looked dazed. She wore emerald slacks, a red, high-neck blouse, and red heels. Clara, at ease, as if she had come into her own, sat legs crossed, black heels, a gorgeous red dress and a diamond choker.

The crowd buzzed. The studio was jammed. I stepped into the light. Gloria Cousins stood like a cheerleader, and clapped. Really clapped. Her clapping embarrassed me. I aimed for her—careful, don't trip, don't make a spectacle—and as I stepped up on the dais, Gloria whispered,

"Relax, they love their writing gods."

§§§

When the red light came on Gloria said,

"Welcome to TownTalk. Our guests tonight are Doctor

343

Daiva Izokaitis, author of that mind-bending, gender-twisting *Citadel*, Trisha de Tours, who edited the novel, and Clara Kreisler, publisher of Pinnacle Books."

Six interviews in two days, a round of radio talk shows, the six-city book tour on tap, and now TownTalk televised not just in New York City but around the country.

"Let's get right to it, Daiva," Gloria said. "The critics are split. I'm sure you've kept up with the trades—so let's hear what you have to say—is *Citadel* an anti-male tract?"

"Gloria, *Citadel* is not anti-male, but it is a post-lesbian novel."

"The pundits are taking you task for that. Is post-lesbian a new genre?"

"Okay," I said, "let me answer by asking you a question."

"I love this," Gloria said, "without a little give and take, it's not a show."

"Can you, can anyone in this audience give me a word about males that means the same thing as lesbian?"

Without hesitating Gloria said, "Gays."

"No. Men use lesbian to marginalize women who love other women. It means just one thing and one thing only. Let me say it clearly—post-lesbian means *Citadel* is a novel about women, told from a woman's point of view, involving women living without men and in complete control of their lives."

Gloria, said, "I'm sure you've read the reviews—some scribes say it's a revolutionary novel, others say it's not a novel at all but just a plain old male-bashing political tract. So, is *Citadel* a political tract?"

"*Citadel* is the kind of novel that makes you think not just about who you are but where you're going."

"And that brings us to divergent evolution. Can you give me your take on that, Doctor?"

"How candid do you want me to be?"

"As candid as you need to be."

"Simply put—men and women are on different evolutionary tracks."

"How is that possible?" Gloria said.

"It's a question of Quality, with a capital Q, Gloria, and Quantity. Men and women want different things. The common ground is eroding and has been eroding since…"

"Eroding?"

"When the first woman wrapped her first baby in a sling so she could use both hands to dig roots, she set us off in a different direction."

"So you're saying…"

"Science is saying, Gloria. Right now, under the current administration, you would think that we're living in a post-science world where facts don't matter. But they do matter."

"Let's take a break," Gloria said. "We'll be back after these words."

The red light went off.

I grasped Trisha's hand. She was hot. Excitement flushed her face. She flared her nostrils. It made me happy to see her in battle mode.

Clara said, "Well done, Daiva. I published it and it made me antsy until right now."

I noticed Trisha searching the audience. It was an audience of women. More women than men. Women of all sizes and shapes. Women with short hair, women in long hair. Women in tennies, women in Blahniks, women wearing boots, women high on Choos. But in the back, in the dark recesses of the studio, I saw them. The men from the launch wearing black T-shirts with white crosses and red crescents on them.

Gloria raised a finger. The red light came back on. She welcomed the audience back and then said,

"As I read *Citadel*, Daiva, I sense something deeper than fiction. This is clearly science fiction, but it reads in some ways like a documentary of the future. Is that how you intended it?"

"Can I answer that?" Trisha said. "Women already control the future, Gloria. In *Citadel*, Daiva wrote that science had become an exclusive club with women in control. She just extends that control to all aspects of life."

Clara broke in and said,

345

"Gloria, what Trisha means is that in *Citadel* the daughters make decisions about the future without deferring to men."

"So," Gloria said, "do we see a future without men?"

"That's a possibility," I said. "The Y chromosome is in decline."

"That's another point that critics are after you for. Will you clarify what you mean by that and what you mean by the daughters?"

"Do you want the genetic explanation?" I said.

"Or the novelistic one," Trisha said. That got a laugh from Gloria and a few giggles from the audience. Gloria said,

"I'll take the novelistic one because we're talking about a novel."

"Every cell in genetics is a daughter cell, Gloria. In *Citadel* there are three kinds of males—the Exo, the Gland, and the Mutant."

"Now I'm confused," Gloria said. "I don't see men in this novel except as...."

"Oh, but remember that glorious hunting scene," Trisha said. "The daughters hunt, capture, and take Glands back to the Citadel for milking."

"And that's why it's not anti-male," Clara said. "There are males in the future."

"And most of them are pitiable creatures," Gloria said.

"That's because of the 13th gene," I said. "The 13th gene on the Y chromosome is the killer gene. The only way there can be any peace is to silence it. Or as the technicians say *switch it off.*"

The women in the audience applauded and from somewhere a chant burst out "switch it off, switch it off, switch it off." Gloria fell silent until the chanting slowed. Then she said,

"I'm still confused—you talk about this as if it were true."

"It is true," I said.

"But isn't this just the novel?"

"Is it?"

346

Gloria rocked back in her chair, she nodded, and she said,

"With that, let's take a break."

Trisha was watching the black shirts who had moved into the aisle on both sides of the studio. The red light flared up. Gloria, smiling and back on camera, said,

"Welcome back. Tell us more about that 13th gene, Daiva. As a scientist, what evidence do you have for saying the 13th gene is the killer gene?"

"*Citadel* is a novel, Gloria, and, as my editor told me for weeks, what's in the novel is fiction and so is the link between divergent evolution and the 13th gene, which the daughters tag as the killer gene but, of course, in the world of genetics, it's more complex so I use a metaphor that sparks some discussion."

I got to my feet and went to the edge of the stage. I needed to talk directly to the women in the audience. I saw copies of *Citadel* out there so I knew they already had an idea of what I was saying.

"The Y chromosome, the male component in the sexual process once had over five hundred genes. Over time, the Y has given up all but those twenty-seven genes to the X which is the female sexual component that controls not only the sexual process but also the future. Many of my colleagues think that the Y chromosome is in rapid decay and there will come a time when it will not be necessary for reproduction. We have evidence, for example, from the biologists, that the males of some species have no Y chromosome which means that nature found a way to create viable, reproductive males without Y chromosomes. They are called XOs. The future isn't male-less, but it is devoid of the Y chromosome."

I sat back down. Maybe I had broken protocol, but I found it easy to speak to the faces in the crowd instead of to the camera. The audience murmured and whispered among themselves and Gloria glanced into the wings. She said,

"So this is a novel, but it's based in science."

"Yes," Trisha said. "And Daiva is a first rate scientist."

"Is it true, Daiva, that you have created a human being in your lab?"

The producer at the edge of the dais held up a sign on which she had written *keep her talking the ratings have just gone ballistic.* Gloria said,

"A scientist who has her critics and some of her critics are saying she has violated ethics by creating a human being in her lab. So Daiva, will you tell us? Is it true?"

"Gloria," Trisha said, "that question pushes a lot of buttons, but the deeper question is what is a human?"

"Don't we already know what a human is?"

"Is being born without the Y chromosome human?" Trisha said.

"I don't understand," Gloria said.

"What is sex, Gloria?" I said.

The audience roared.

"You don't know what sex is?" Gloria said.

"Sex is the exchange of genes, Gloria. Bacteria exchange genes daily, hourly. Humans exchange genes just once every nine months. If a being is born without the natural exchange of genes, that is to say without copulative sex or its mechanical equivalent is that being human?"

"Are we getting a little bit off course here?" Gloria said.

"Not at all, Gloria," I said.

"So is this a roundabout way of saying what you wrote in this novel is based on what you have created in your lab?"

"Let me avoid a direct answer to that question, Gloria. *Citadel* is just a novel. In the novel, the daughters have a choice. They can choose to be fertilized by a haploid gamete with twenty-three chromosomes, they can choose to crossover which means taking nuclear material from each parent, or they can choose to be inseminated by the Y with the 13$^{th}$ gene switched off. They can choose—and a choice it is—not to be inseminated at all, of course, because the crossover results in a parthenogenetic offspring with forty-six chromosomes, two parents but no Y at all."

"Wait, wait, wait," Gloria said. "A simple yes or no, Doctor—have you created a human being in your lab?"

"In the novel, if a daughter is inseminated with the Y intact, she will possibly produce a Mutant. Unless the 13$^{th}$ gene is silenced or switched off the fetus has a chance of being an XY. If the gene is switched off, then the offspring has a chance of being an Exo. If the gene is unmodified and left intact as it was before the gene mutated, then the offspring has a chance of being a Gland."

"But in the novel, the daughters," Gloria said, "I mean the women…"

"The daughters," Trisha said. "The daughters control everything."

"Men have no say?"

"The daughters have to take control because of that deadly 13th gene, Gloria. In the Mutants, the gene is virulent. Mutants kill anything and everything. They have slaughtered most living things on the planet, they've destroyed the environment, and they are on their way to annihilating all XXs. The only way to control that is to control their numbers while leaving the genome intact."

"But it's a novel," Gloria said, "and you both are talking like this is a living document."

"*Citadel* will become a living document in the very near future."

In the audience, two clean shaven men stood and stripped off their shirts revealing black body armor segmented like the thorax of an insect. On the body armor the white cross, overlaid with the red crescent, blazed in the stage light.

"What the hell?" The producer shouted.


## Trisha

The violence came the way I knew it would come—fast and with blood and in one second the world changed. It came as a stone, a rock with jagged edges arcing out of the audience. And there was the shocked silence before another stone smacked Daiva in the head. She fell on the arm of Gloria's chair. I faced the man who had thrown the rock. Behind him a cluster of about six men wearing crosses and crescents around their necks on silver chains. They charged the stage. One of them hurled copies of *Citadel,* another threw stones. In the rain of rocks and books I took two hits.

Clara ran to the wings shouting. Gloria Cousins stood frozen yelling what's happening? What's happening? And then a torn cover of *Citadel,* sailing like a missile, slashed her face splitting her nose. Another rock landed on my arm.

Daiva, defiant, as if this was what she had expected, what she had counted on, fended off a flurry of torn book covers and stones. She did not go down but picked up the stones and books and used them like clubs. A vision of women in the Old Society popped into my mind as Daiva fought her way off the dais. I heard the sound of bone cracking. I glanced back to see a group of women tearing into the attackers using copies of *Citadel* as weapons.

§§§

Outside the studio, I flagged a taxi and told the cabby to take us to the Hotel Governor Wilson. I felt calm. Strange. In the chaos my voice stayed calm and focused. Daiva slid into the backseat just as a stone hammered the door of the taxi.

The driver yelled, pulled a pistol, and hit the gas. The cab swayed around a corner. I glanced out the rear window. A dozen Howlers hurling rocks at the taxi.

"What the hell was that?" the driver said.

"It's coming true, isn't it, Trisha? *Citadel* has cut them loose."

Yes, it was all coming true. *Citadel* wasn't just a novel, it was a prophecy and Daiva was the visionary. The driver stopped at the curb of the hotel. I stepped out of the cab. A stone cracked the cab window. A trio of Howlers carrying stones. Hands on me. The smell of sweat. A Howler, eyes a Mutant wildness, chanting "God hates dykes God hates dykes die all dykes die Jesus hates commie libtard fags and dykes."

I knew I was going to die. I didn't want to die because I didn't know the end. I didn't know if the entire prophecy was coming true. I looked at a Howler. He was just a boy, blond and blue-eyed and pale of skin but he was armed with a stone. I remembered the moment in the Desert Rose Motel where I saw the spinning woman and I remembered how she handled herself—she did not surrender. She stood her ground and took the stone and used it in a way women through the eons had not dared. I punched the beautiful adolescent Howler. Startled, he dropped the stone. He started to cry. I picked up the stone. I cracked the beautiful boy who, in another world, in *Citadel,* could have been a Gland, in the forehead.

And I then saw Clara and Caleb pushing toward me.


## Daiva

"We're on the front page of the *New York Times*, Daiva."

Clara unfolded the newspaper. I saw a photo of the TownTalk set. The chair. Gloria. Trisha. Clara. Me.


### POST-LESBIAN AUTHOR ATTACKED

> A bloody melee on the TownTalk set left three dead and a hundred hospitalized. Investigators say the battle started when a hate group stoned the host and guests, Ms. Daiva Isokaitis, Ms. Clara Kreisler, and Ms. Trisha deTours.

Clara said, "That photograph, Daiva, is good for at least two hundred thousand copies. My god, I never believed it could happen, but you've pushed Pinnacle Books into the limelight.

"I owe you and Trisha an apology. When I read it, I saw the core but you found the language and that's what they're writing about now. I really love you Trisha and I owe you so much. If this were my birthday it would be the best birthday present I ever could have gotten. And you gave it to me."

I said, "We're at war."

"We are women," Trisha said. "We've always been at war."

## Trisha

The ballroom was jammed. Exuberance flowed with the wine. I watched Clara steer Daiva through the crowd, stopping to shake hands—who were these people? After twenty years in the business, Clara knew them all—the culture lords, the culture makers, the trend setters. The noise just fed into my sense of doom. Last night had been the first round. I knew what was coming. Me, the Cassandra of Pinnacle, had shouted the truth about the future but no one was listening.

The air heated up as the crowd got bigger and the voices grew louder until they hammered at me. I hid in an archway festooned with a flight of balloons, each one printed with two pictures—Daiva on one side, the cover of *Citadel* on the other. As the balloons twisted in the heating air, the photos spun in a hypnotic fury.

I relaxed as Daiva performed in the center of a fleurette of women—tall women, short women, dark and light women, thick and thin and heavy women, and it was clear that she had ascended.

The warm bodies churned around her. Daiva moved, chatting with reporters, with the Lords and Ladies of the Written Word, the people who wrote words about her words—"This novel clamps a wrench on the lug nuts of the Old Society…"

"…about TownTalk…"

"The Crosses and Crescents tried to kill us…."

"They just want us to shut up."

"That's not going to happen now."

New faces came close, old ones faded away and each of Daiva's followers carried a copy of *Citadel*—the image repeating itself around the hall—gripping the book like a long-lost sister. I bumped into Clara who guided me back into the storm of perfume and lipstick, into the maelstrom of persuasion, and as we approached, I heard Daiva talking about how *Citadel* came to be—

"I had no idea in the beginning, just a feeling," Daiva said. "I knew I wanted to write a novel but I didn't know how to go about it."

I remembered the day the manuscript landed on my doorstep. The paper cracked and crumbling as if it had been lost for a thousand years in a cave in the desert to be revealed by a priestess then hidden until she came out of the dark elevating it like a sacrament—"and then," Daiva said, "I had the vision. It all came in a flood, as if it were writing itself. I typed faster than I thought I ever could..."

"Is it true that you write on an antique IBM Selectric typewriter?"

"Yes, that is true."

"You don't use a computer?"

"No. It took me weeks of frantic and furious work to get it and then I knew it had to rest. I didn't read it for three years."

"Three years?" A maven in jade-colored leather pants said, "Unbelievable. It reads like you wrote it just yesterday."

"*Citadel* rested until I met Trisha de Tours—and here she is, the daughter with that unique mind."

Daiva reached for me, pulled me loose from Clara, wrapped me up, and kissed me.

"I wrote a novel, but without Trisha it would still be a pile of paper."

And as a wave breaks, the circle opened. I was smothered in love and sweetness, covered with accolades, and swamped in awe. Breaking the magic spell, Clara said,

"Doctor Izokaitis, we have waited long enough. It's time."

She embraced Daiva with that public embrace that had been in every newspaper ever printed. I felt a touch of jealousy, but I swallowed it and followed Clara and Daiva to the podium into the circles of light, into the one place where there was room for only one person. The one.

The one who made it possible.

Without the words there was nothing to edit.

Without the words there was nothing to publish.

The words brought story and story wormed its way into memory and what had been an idea, what had been sentences, what had been chapters lived in the mind of a reader and once there its chemistry changed the brain the way soda changes vinegar.

The room exploded in applause as Daiva entered the light. Behind her on a screen, a photo array played—where had Clara gotten all those pictures? Daiva was there in her lab coat, and her graduation gown holding a plaque that said Summa cum laude on it. Daiva in the spotlight did not look innocent. Black leather, tight black leather pants, tight leather vest, no bra, her hair with its mohawked strip, and the makeup—lips outlined and outrageous, eyes darkened and dangerous, nails long and black painted—who was she now? I wasn't sure.

Daiva held up two copies of *Citadel*. She looked like an oracle breathing enlightenment from the fumes in the crack in the world. The room answered with silence.

"This," Daiva said. She shook the novels so they flashed in the light. "When I wrote *Citadel* I was a scientist, but as I read what I had written I changed. I found that I had written the most personal story possible and every character in it is me."

I glanced around at the hands in front of faces—that mask of disbelief.

Daiva said, "The daughters who are raped in *Citadel* are me. The daughters in Origin of Plague are me. The parthenogenetic mothers are me. The crossovers are me."

I felt swords being raised. I waited for the smashing of stone on flesh. But Daiva went on, "I am Hagah, the bringer of death. I am Ell the seer who tells the future. I am Zil the daughter who discovers the bones of the dead girls in the Virgin Citadel. Before I wrote this novel, I was a scientist, now I am not."

I wanted to rush into the light to stop her, but Daiva had risen so she loomed like a rising goddess ten feet tall. She held the room so tight there was no jostling, no shrugging, no shuffling of feet.

Daiva said, "How do you change? You stop being an object in the biology of desire. You stop being a victim in the cruel history of woman being woman. You stop obeying. You stand apart. That's the future—separation— and the time has come to take the first step into it."

I felt the sledge of doom being raised. I expected the walls to cave in and the ceiling to collapse—Daiva was calling for Revolution.

Daiva said, "All we have to do is to get off our knees, say No, and take our freedom."

From her copy of *Citadel,* Daiva read the final, printed version of Kaavi's *History* in a confident, clear, full voice—

After the Wars of Religion, after the fire and the killing, the forests had regenerated and the plains had reseeded their grasses, and on the plains bison grazed. There were no men to hunt them. The killing stopped.

On my journey through the woods and prairies, across the sand and the rocky detritus of Earth upheavals, I came across the remains of battles and in their skeletal remains the warriors were all alike—their skulls the same, their broken backs the same, their fingers identical, their skeletons, cleaned of meat, were the same.

I made my notes. I took measurements although touching the remains of the dead filled me with sorrow. In the record I located on the map the sites where the killing was most intense. I tallied the remains of the disarticulated victims and among them I found the bones of women still in chains as they had been dragged behind the hordes marching in search of infidels. In the skeletons of the fallen women I found remains of the unborn and though hardened by what I knew and inured by what I had seen, I wept for them. In the Old Society, I would have wailed.

I stayed for days at the battle sites to mourn the women and their unborn. I did not feel the need to mourn the killers.

And on the seventy-fifth day of my journey, I stood on a hill overlooking a destroyed city of the plain burning in a hot afternoon sun. I saw the glinting of bones, the white shining of bones. A deep sadness overcame me. I knew this was the First Citadel. On my map, I tagged it, C-1.

I marched off the hill, a day's walk to the glinting until I came to rest at the edge of a huge killing field. I saw metal that had not decayed and chariots that had not yet rotted and sown in the ground were bones. In that field all terror, all fear of all time smothered the land like a choking cloud of desperation. Buried in the skull of the bodies were blades. Blades buried in the backs of fleeing bodies. So many.

I worked the killing field for two days. I recalled the writings of the archaeohistorians who said that in the plains where the bloodshed was greatest, the soil turned fertile, the grasses grew tall and thick.

In the chaos of bones and metal, I found the skeletons of men and horses. Here and there the residue of a wooden cross, the relic of a gold crescent, a double cross, a simple cross, a gold six-pointed star. Evidence that the Unification of the Dogmas was not a fiction. Though far in time from the killing, I imagined the thunder of war, the groans and the quaking of annihilation.

In that field, as I stood over chaos, I recalled the sage's saying, "There will be no freedom until the last priest strangles the last politician with the entrails of the last lawyer and then slits his own throat."

I cried at the loss of paradise because in the killing our dreams had died.

Daiva closed the book and stood in the lights in the silence in hall of the hotel and then there was clapping and stomping of feet and from the collective there came a chant, first slow and rhythmic and then louder and louder and faster and faster—

**"No More Victims, No More Killing
No More Victims, No More Killing
No More Victims, No More Killing. "**

The sound of glass shattering sent me diving to the floor.

§§§

## Rose Katz

I don't have time to read a lot of novels, and *Citadel* isn't the kind of novel I read when I do, but Trisha had shamed me into getting a copy. I felt sorry for Trisha after I heard about the stoning in New York. That was the problem with *Citadel*—it seemed to open a lot of wounds. As I got deeper into the novel, I saw Trisha's hand in the way a phrase turned, the beat of the lines, even the words the characters spoke. I knew it was impossible to sort out what was Trisha, what was Daiva, and what was the union of them.

I admit that the book echoed my own life as if Daiva had listened to my sessions with Camille. I read for three hours, sometimes going back to look at a passage again, sometimes to ask why it was making me uneasy or sad.

At 3:30 AM, I closed the book, showered and tried to get to sleep, but I wasn't tired. Maybe the book was changing me too because I saw a lot of myself in the writing. Fear? Yes, fear, the fear that had lived in me for years was there. With therapy or without it, I lived covered with the residue of rape. It never really washed off. At first, I had showered three times a day, but it didn't make any difference. No smile can ever mask the brutality. No perfume can block out the memory. Now, every time I looked in the mirror, I saw not the woman I wanted to be, but the woman he turned me into.

Around 3:45 as I brushed my hair, I smelled the vestiges of vanity—the scent of perfume, the odor of shampoo, the residual smell of body lotion. I thought about Trisha selling everything she owned right down to her bikinis. No more adornments, no more charades, no more hiding behind the silken costumes or the cascades of coiffed hair—no more.

I went back to bed but I was too raw to sleep, so I picked up the novel again. The cover. That image of the *Citadel*—it was out of another time. It was from the future but very much of the now—how does a vision like that come to be?

"I specialize in creative people," I had told Trisha on her first visit. "And they always ask if I can cure their nightmares."

I never said yes.

357

The *Citadel* vision lived beyond nightmares. It was beyond the words on the page, beyond anything I had ever let into my mind and it now felt like a repeating nightmare that didn't have a cure. I remember asking Trisha what she feared most and she told me she had nightmares about being tied to a bed and gutted and butchered like a sow in a slaughter house.

Daiva had written two sections in *Citadel* that frightened and shocked me. Trisha had told me that when she read the novel, she felt Daiva was in her head talking to her. As I read *Citadel* I knew that somehow, Daiva had written me into the novel but I had never met her so how was that possible?

I turned to the section titled *Women in Captivity* and re-read *Karen* and my own fear was born again—

Then one of the men grabbed a skillet and smashed her head with it. They beat her. Bart sagged to his knees mumbling. "You've killed me, you've killed me." The men kept beating her until she lay in a widening pool of blood. Finally they stopped. The skillet had destroyed her head. Her arms were distorted to strange angles. Bart slumped down on the floor, and his friends stood around the girl as if she were prey and they were hunters but unaware of what they were doing or had done or would ever do.

*The things we do to please them, the things we do to make them love us, the things they do to us once we have submitted to them. No More.*

*Women in Captivity* was fiction but I sensed the darker truth hiding in it. When I put it together with *Syn in Sacrifice,* I was ashamed and curious and guilty. I went back to re-read the passage—

And the rain of punishment falls harder upon her but she remains erect, she remains aware as if reveling in her own destruction can atone for the lies she has wreaked upon her innocents. The canon says, "Women are sick, it is not the culture that is sick." The canon says, "Women are out of synch, it is not the culture that is out of synch." The canon says, "Women are the chattel, the possessions, the wards and lovers. They belong to men and if men kill them, that is the will of God. This is the revealed word of God—'It is always woman under man, always man superior to woman."

And she grieves for those who died before her, for those who cut themselves, for those who said No.


In therapy, in rare moments of clarity, you achieve an epiphany as if a curtain drawn back in a dark room reveals a light that sings through the large once dark panes, and truth shreds all the lies you have been masquerading behind all your life. You cannot ignore them. You cannot keep doing what you were doing. Reading Syn's story was like looking in a mirror. Once light comes into you, you must change. Daiva's novel was the light and I was Syn and Syn was me. I knew then that Daiva had seen into my mind. Without knowing me, she had dug deep into me as I had dug into the pliant and pitiable women I had betrayed. In *Citadel,* there was the personal salvation that had eluded me.

I knew what I had to do.

I hauled the suitcase from the top shelf of the closet.

I pulled clothes from the closet and underwear from the bureau but then I stopped.

A new life demanded simplicity. Two pairs of slacks, one pair of Levis, eight T-shirts, eight underpants. I rummaged a pair of hiking boots from the closet and a pair of running shoes–pink with orange laces. No. No pink. I set them aside. I packed the red revolver. I was not leaving without it.

I zipped the suitcase, took one long look at my bedroom. My house. On a nice street in Santa Monica. I picked up *Citadel*—felt its heft and thickness—thicker than

Jung's *The Archetypes and the Collective Unconscious*, thicker than Freud's *Interpretation* of *Dreams*.

Jung, Freud, Menninger, Rogers, Kant, Marx, Hegel, Washington, Madison, Lincoln, Nietzsche, Roosevelt—white men shaping women, controlling women, telling women what to do and when to do it. I knew that religion coupled with politics for one single purpose—to control women. *Citadel.* One of only a few books by a woman about women daring women to revolt against the oligarchs who saw women as chattel, possessions, objects to be had and used and beaten then discarded. Born of a rib, indeed.

*Karen.*

*Somethin' to stick your thing in....*

Suitcase in one hand, *Citadel* in the other, I shut off the lights in the house. *"When you finish this novel, you won't be the woman who started it."*

My eyes opened.

I was awake. Not just awake but conscious of everything that had ever been as if I was all women living a single moment in time.

I had to find Trisha. I had to apologize to her for sending her away when she most needed direction. I had done it so many times—sent the women back, women with their cut lips and bruised bodies. "It's what I do," I had told Camille. "I give women back to the men who kill them."

My shame. My guilt. I had been asleep. *There are millions of us still dreaming of a golden prince to kiss us and make us whole.* No more. No more.

I would contact a realtor on Monday. I would cancel all my appointments, maybe refer my clients to Camille. Camille. My last session with her hadn't gone well. Camille had dropped a bomb when she asked if I loved Trisha. How could I answer that? Did I love her? Camille asked if Trisha loved me. I had to say I didn't know but I knew I was turning my clients into slaves. I told her my entire training wasn't to free them, but to hand them over to their men who killed them. That ended my life with Camille. I no longer needed her.

I closed and locked the door. I did not look back because I was never coming back

### §§§

The night was cool. The Z Ray silent, the highway buzzing with the long-haul semis. I left the city, winding up to the San Gabriel Mountains headed for Barstow and into the desert, the Desert Rose Motel.

I checked the gauges, the lights a soft blue restful on the eyes.

On the plateau, the sky cleared. Starlight undimmed by the city haze tattooed the darkness. A yellow gash cut the horizon as a Perseid slid its ancient time into the now.

No sense of what was coming. I knew nothing would be the same now.

Ahead of me, highway lights disappeared then flickered back until I hit the flat where the road opened up and I saw the charging station.

*I stop there, Trisha had told me, on my way to the desert. It's about halfway. I know the clerk. Her name is Syl.*

### §§§

The TV was on mute. The station smelled of strong air cleaner mingling with the faint odor of diesel and gas. The residue of Pine-Sol crept from the restrooms.

Bulls, it said on one door.

Belles, it said on the other.

I checked the counter—no Syl.

In the Belles, a splash of water on my face.

The scent of soap—coconut.

The clerk was at the counter. I handed her my credit card. She said,

"Rose Katz."

"Do I know you?"

"You don't remember me?"

She had graying hair and sallow cheeks that reminded me of Camille. She had the same aquiline nose. The same narrow and very black eyes, the same thin, claw-like hands but she was smiling. Camille never smiled.

"Sylvia. Redondo Beach? I was a patient of yours."

Syl. Sylvia. A client. From early in my practice in
Redondo Beach. Embarrassed. Sad. Guilty. One I had sent
away. She was a Texas belle who got married right after
her debutante ball. She followed her man from Austin to
LA. She had a degree from UT Austin but found herself
isolated on the Coast. No friends, no family. She came to
me after a referral from Manchester Urgent Care where she
reported that the bruises were from a fall. I worked with her
for a year. I loved the way she talked in an evasive, indirect
way about her situation. But she masked her pain behind
her shame and her favorite words were—"I know I brought
this on myself." After each session, she cried as she recited
her mantra, "I just know things will work out and he won't
do it again and I love him so much..."

"I've been waiting for you," she said.

That confused me. I hadn't seen or talked to her in ten
years.

"I don't understand," I said.

"Daiva knew you'd be here, but Trisha said you
wouldn't."

"You knew I was coming?"

"Yes. You have a signed copy of *Citadel,* don't you?"
she said.

"I still don't understand," I said.

"They came through here a couple of weeks ago on their
way to the Desert Rose. Trisha was sure you're never leave
the city, but here you are."

"Sylvia, I am sorry."

"No, no, Rose. Don't be sorry. That's so Old Society."

"The last time I saw you...I want to apologize. I can't
make it up to you."

"Oh, honey," she said. "I'm glad you did. I went back to
Buzz. He knocked me around a little, broke my arm. Of
course, you know that was followed by the loving respite
which lasted about a week before he lit into me again. So, I
left him, changed my name, started a new life. I don't know
where he is now, and I don't care."

"You forgive me?" I said.

"There is absolutely nothing to forgive, sugar. I
should've left the jerk the first time he smacked me, but

I'm a slow learner. Look, Rose, I love that name. I must have known a dozen Roses in Austin. Rose. You're just a sweet little flower but the thorns, right? We have to go."

"Where are we going?" I said.

I glanced up at the silent TV screen. A reporter, mike in hand, talking to a policeman.

Syl said, "Daiva and Trisha were on that book tour, you know. Six cities. That was at a reading up in Minneapolis. They keep running the tape because after the signing in New York, the crosses and crescents popped up there but that time the Daughters of Daiva got them by the short hair. Now everything is moving to the Desert Rose. It's exciting."

The skin on my back tingled. I recalled the images of men in black shirts with crosses and crescents on them hurling stones and torn books at Trisha and Daiva.

"Do you believe what Daiva has written?" I asked.

"If it's happening, you just can't not believe it. The killings have started and it's getting worse. The Howlers won't let up till women are back in the kitchen praying to the Great Bearded One in The Sky who thinks we sprouted from the bone of some creep who was afraid of snakes."

"This is all very weird, Sylvia."

"Call me Syl. Short name, just like in the novel. Last time Rita came through she said they're starting the first Citadel out in the desert."

"Who is Rita?"

"She has the beat between here and the Desert Rose. Are you ready?"

"What are you doing?" I said.

"We're going to the Desert Rose. I don't belong here anymore. When your eyes are closed, you just swallow whatever they feed you, but once you wake up, you can't give in. We're daughters of the Citadel now."

"You mean that?"

"Are Trisha and Daiva warrior goddesses of the new society?"

I reached across the counter and pressed Syl's hand.

"You are just incredible," I said.

363

"Your Z-Ray is charged, Rose. We're going to join the revolution."

§§§

The road to the Desert Rose Motel was jammed with a convoy of supply trucks—food trucks, semis loaded with steel bars and jersey barriers, a gasoline tanker—all driven by women. Cars carrying women. Armed women on motorcycles.

Closing on the Desert Rose Motel, I saw the litter of burned out SUVs skewed into an obstacle course. I threaded the Z-Ray around the obstacles feeling that Syl and I were coming to a place we might not like. The world was changing by the minute.

In the cloudless morning sky, an unnatural red tinge stained the horizon. Rising into the blue-pink was a snake of smoke. We were driving into hell. I tried the phone. No service. Cut off. I checked the gauges. Battery at three quarters.

I thought about turning back—back to what?

Syl pointed to a cruiser blocking the highway, lights flashing, where a tall cop stood, weapon drawn. She wore body armor. We stopped. She leaned down, peered in. Her eyes were yellow and heavy and she looked hard. Her name tag read Rita. She said,

"Syl, you made it."

"This is Rose," Syl said.

"You're Rose? Ditch your Ray here. I'll take you in."

She headed back to her squad car. I hauled my sack with the red pistol from the back seat then opened the trunk and dragged out the suitcase.

Rita squared around and headed down the road. Every 50 meters Jersey barriers blocked the way and ran off into the desert on either side. Rita zig-zagged through the course until we came to a ruined half-track, a stack of body armor alongside it. All emblazoned with the cross and crescent exactly the way Daiva had written about it in *Citadel*. There was a pile of face masks riddled with bullet holes. A half dozen male bodies sprawled in the sun. Black boots.

Black shirts. Black cargo pants. It was the outfit they wore on TV. Dead and stripped of their armor, they no longer looked like insects.

At the half-track Rita sorted through the stack of body armor. Holding up a unit, she told me this one looked like it would fit me. I had to admit that I didn't know how to strap it on. Rita asked me if I had ever worn a corset or a bustier. I said I had. She replied that in the bedroom or battle field, you go to war, you wear armor.

Rita dug out a shell for Syl. Two tugs at the Velcro and she was ready for anything but then she said, in that Texas belle drawl that made me laugh,

"Honey-bunch, does this make my ass look fat?"

"You look pretty fine to me," Rita said.

"Why thank you, darlin', but it doesn't do a thing for my tatas."

"In that gear," Rita said, "you two could be daughters from the *Wars of Religion.*"

"I guess I'm ready for my close-up, sugar…"

Syl pirouetted, hands on her hips.

Rita opened the door of the half-track and chose two automatic weapons. She said they were Mac 10s she pulled off the dead goons from the night before when she had shot them in the head. Always go for the head shot, she said, as she handed me a heavy bag that had the ammo for the Mac. Holding the Mac and the bag made me realize that my pistol was cute but it was light weight while the Macs were battle heavy. We had come to the right place.

"Where do these bad boys come from?" Syl said. In her armored shell, she didn't sound like she'd ever been to a debutante ball. Rita said,

"These Exo clowns came over the hill on the far side of the Citadel. There's an abandoned base they're staging their attacks from. You'll see tonight."

Rita got us back in the squad car and pulled around the half-track. I felt awkward in body armor. I tapped on the shell. There was a thud. Syl laughed then pounded on her chest and said,

"Is this what my mama meant when she said you have to hit a man between the eyes with a two by four to get his attention?"

"A two by four won't stop these idiots," Rita said. "Last night we fought off maybe a thousand Mutants."

"Exos, Mutants, you use the words from *Citadel*," I said.

In the distance, I saw a high circular wall.

"Oh, my goodness," Syl said, "this makes me think of that opening in *Citadel*.

As we approached the wall I noticed a boom truck and a film crew.

"They're filming this?" I said.

"Erica Blackbridge. She's the director. They're doing the Foundation Story. Later they'll shoot *Citadel* starting with the *Wars of Savagery* 'cause that's where we are now."

Rita pulled up to a staggered line of semis, pickups, SUVs. Another truck loaded with cameras and lights. A crew on a camera dolly rolled up the track that approached the wall.

The Director, Erica Blackbridge, followed the camera that was tracking two actors. They had long hair. They were broad shouldered and muscled. They carried futuristic looking instruments but no weapons. They passed rusted, rotting vehicles. In the vehicles, there were bones in ragged, sun-bleached cloth. Cracked leather boots. Black body armor.

They stopped at a gate made of welded lattice steel. One of the actors squatted beside a corpse and flipped up the face mask. The teeth were filed to points. Embedded in the teeth there were diamonds. The other actor picked up a boot. There was a leg bone protruding from the boot. The actor looked into the camera.

"Cut!" The Director said. She walked into the scene. "Nice work, everybody."

"I'm beat, chief," the actor said. "This outfit weighs more than I do and I'm thirsty."

"Jan! Will you please bring water for Kate and Ellen?"

An assistant trotted up carrying bottles of water that she handed to the actors.

"Do we get hazard pay for dressing up like men," Ellen said.

"I know it's hot, Ellen, but we'll shoot your interiors tomorrow," the Director said.

Rita drove past the film crew toward a barricade in front of the wall. The barricade was a tangle of burned-out cars and machinery, trucks and their trailers tipped over, refrigerators and washing machines. Behind the wall there was a high tower and in the tower two sentries positioned at machine guns. Actors? Women dressed as violent looking men?

"Is this all a movie set?" I asked Rita.

"Nooope. This is the real thing."

"This is a Citadel?" I said.

"Yeeep," Rita said, "C-1. Foundation, Year 1, Floral 26. Ground Zero. This is where it all came down after New York and the book tour."

"Just like the novel," I said.

On a steel pole driven into the ground, a black and battered skillet dangled from a wire. From the skillet, there hung a sign. Hand-lettered. The sign read—

FRY YOUR OWN FUCKING PORK CHOPS, BART

"Bart," Syl said. "He's a character in *Citadel,* and that's the skillet from *Women in Captivity.*"

Jack Remick

*§§§*

# 459 AF

## BRU

From the crest of the fossilized sand dune, Bru looked out on the wide desert plain. Wind whispered a gritty rattle as it shushed in her hair. She scanned the desert through binoculars— a tower, a wall circling the tower, vehicles, dozens of them. She stowed the binoculars, set the recorder, opened the scanner then worked her way down the dune. The slope was steep, the rock hot and gritty. Several times, she slid, but righted herself. The only sound the scraping of her boots.

Heading across the plain, she stopped to scan the rusting, rotting vehicles, not surprised to find bones in them, bones in ragged black or sun-bleached uniforms, cracked sun-eaten boots.

As she walked, the scanner chimed as it catalogued the bones, dated the age and size of the remains, and counted the equipment.

Pushing on into the sun, she came to a stack of skulls. She knelt. She found a hole in the forehead of each skull. Legend said that at C-1, there was a daughter who had six hundred kills, all of them shots to the head. But Bru saw no horse bones. Kaavi had written that there were bones of horses at Foundation, but she saw none. Perhaps Kaavi had made a mistake.

Bru closed on the wall that loomed up like a rusted red shield. A structure of welded metal. Leading up to the wall there were killing channels, machines of all kinds strapped together with rusting steel bands. The channels narrowed into kill boxes as they approached the wall where firing slots ranged. And in the kill boxes, the carnage had been catastrophic.

She remembered the text written four hundred years before – *The Solerian stands in the center of the Citadel like a spindle in the nucleus of a cell.* The Founder had written it down and from the writing came the structure of all Citadels.

The walk was slow and hot as she circled the walls. She counted as she paced—one hundred, two hundred, three hundred units. To her left, the sun now behind her, she saw the gate and at the gate thick piles of machines rusting. Entering the kill box, she threaded her way through matériel and skeletons to the gate where she stopped.

The gate, a massive barrier of steel plating, still pocked with the black residue of explosions, was shielded by sharp-pointed spiles driven into the ground and anchored in concrete to create a hedgehog.

She entered the gate. Inside she saw the tower tilting to one side. The steel latticework had not yet decayed. Around the footings of the tower there were stacks of bones and weapons. She examined the skulls. From the angle of the holes in the skulls, she judged that gunfire had slanted down on the attackers. She left the tower and approached the buildings—thick concrete blocks—no doors, all blown open, hinges ripped like paper, and she held up. A half-destroyed sign over the entrance, in faded black lettering, read Dese  R se Mote . Her heart beat faster. Was she the first daughter to see the mythical C-1. Was this the beginning of time?

Her hands were clammy, sweat soaked her jerkin and rolled down her sides. And she then entered the ruin.

It was primitive—wood chairs, a long wide bar, a broken mirror. In the mirror, she saw herself in her transformed body—heavy shoulders, thin waist, long hair the color of rusted steel. Her arms were thick and muscular. Her beard trained down her chest. She was shocked. The transformation had taken two months. The genetic knock-ins had made her sick, the facial hair turned her into an animal. She had not looked at herself in a year and a half.

She turned away from the mirror.

Her scanner chimed. Body count—ten thousand Exos.

She scrolled through the inventory—a thousand daughters.

At Foundation, in C-1, one thousand daughters stood off ten thousand Exos for a year. This was C-1.

She squatted and ran her fingers through the dust on the floor. If the Founders died there, there would be DNA. She reset the scanner.

She drew the device from her pocket and clicked talk. The first words she had spoken since she left the team in the extinct lake bed came as a rough croak in a dry throat.

"It's here."

## JACK REMICK

I am the author of seventeen books—novels, poetry, short stories, screenplays. I co-authored *The Weekend Novelist Writes a Mystery* with Robert J. Ray. (Dell) My novel *Gabriela and The Widow* (Coffeetown Press) was a finalist for the Montaigne Medal as well as a finalist in Foreword Magazine's Book of the Year Award.

IS Version 2018